KILL ORDER

THE GUILD #3

TATE JAMES

For the partners of bookworms.
Grab some lube, hydrate, and remember to thank Tate later.

SHADOW GROVE WORLD

Interconnected series

While each series in the Shadow Grove world can be read independent of the others, this is the *recommended* reading order for a chronological timeline. You do not *need* to read in this order, but it may help with overall background and cameo character appearances.

MADISON KATE

#1 Hate

#2 Liar

#3 Fake

#4 Kate

HADES

#1 7th Circle

#2 Anarchy

#3 Club 22

#4 Timber

MADISON KATE NOVELLA

#4.5 Vault

THE GUILD

#1 Honey Trap

#2 Dead Drop

#3 Kill Order

WANT TO CHAT ABOUT BOOKS WITH TATE?

Facebook: shorturl.at/qstN6

Readers Group: shorturl.at/npv01

Twitter: shorturl.at/prvO3

Pinterest: shorturl.at/qI135

Instagram: shorturl.at/exzN6

Stay up to date with Tate James by signing up for her mailing list:

http://eepurl.com/dfFR5v

Website: https://www.tatejamesauthor.com

KILL ORDER

THE GUILD #3

TATE JAMES

- Tate

CONTENT WARNING

The Guild series is a part of the Shadow Grove world which contains several interconnected series. The tone and content tends to lean toward the dark, and reader discretion is advised.

Please be mindful of your own content triggers and limits.

The characters within The Guild series are not heroes or heroines, please kindly don't hold them to a heroic standard as they will fall short of expectations. They do bad things, and they own their actions.

If you're here, then you've already read both Honey Trap and Dead Drop, so you are already well acquainted with these characters. This installment touches on dark themes for some supporting characters also.

Should you have concerns around specific triggers, please reach out for content clarity before reading.

1
KAI

The sound of my gun firing in Danny's hand made me flinch. She should have just shot me, it probably would have hurt less than watching her drive away. Far less than hearing those cutting words come out of her mouth. We're done.

Goddamn, that hurt. So much more than I had prepared myself for. Accept it. Move on.

As if that was even possible. I would never accept her absence. Not like this, when she so clearly still loved me. No, no way. And I sure as fuck wouldn't move on, even if she chose him.

Part of me was relieved that she hadn't chosen him. The selfish part that constantly debated about killing Leon in his sleep... If I thought I could get away with it, I might have done it by now. I was relieved she hadn't picked him over me, but I was totally fucking destroyed at the pain on her face as she walked away from both of us.

She showed us that of the three of us, *Danny* had the biggest balls. She chose to hurt *herself* to save both of us. Because surely she knew that we wouldn't kill one another until one of us had won, fair and square. It'd be cheating.

Leon snapped out of the shock so much faster than I did, running over to his car even as Danny's van paused at the front gates, waiting for them to open.

"What are you doing?" I shouted after him as he threw open the driver's door. "She shot out your tire, you idiot. You can't chase her down on rims."

He just leaned inside and popped the trunk. "Fuck me, you really are all muscle, no brains, aren't you?" he muttered, circling to the trunk and lifting out a gun case. Setting it on the ground, he went back and opened the false bottom to reveal the spare tire.

Shit. Of course, he could replace the tire. Maybe I *was* an idiot.

Not willing to be left behind, I reached in and hauled out the spare tire while Leon went to work on the flat, cranking it up with the jack to remove it. Even working together, though, it took a solid ten minutes until we were operational. It was too damn long; she could be *anywhere* by now.

"Can't you drive faster?" I growled before we even turned out of the driveway. "This is painful."

"You know what'd be painful?" Leon shot back from the driver's seat. "Me kicking your ass out of this moving car. Shut the fuck up, dickhead. This is entirely your fault."

"*My fault*?" I exclaimed in outrage. "Are you for fucking real right now? This is—" I broke off my accusation, dread and disgust flowing through me. "This is *our* fault, Leon. Both of ours. *We* fucked up, and now *we* need to fix it before she decides neither one of us is worth the trouble."

He didn't disagree, just grunted a noise and drove faster.

"If she hasn't already decided that," I muttered under my breath, replaying how she'd walked away from both of us in my mind. She'd rather choose no one than be forced to pick between us. That knowledge was confronting, to say the least. It told me that all the certainty I felt with her, all that love that I *knew* she reciprocated... she also felt for *him*.

Fuck.

"She hasn't," Leon snapped, his knuckles turning white as he gripped the steering wheel.

I scowled. "How can you be so fucking sure? She seemed pretty determined to get the fuck away from us *both*."

He flashed me an arrogant smirk. "Because she ran. Danny DeLuna doesn't *run* from anything or anyone. She wants to be chased. She wants us to put her above our grievances with one another."

He gave a dramatic pause, and I soaked his opinion in. Was he right?

Leon gave a frustrated sigh and swept a hand over his face, not even braking slightly as he took the tight corners. "Work it out, man, she just wants *us* to choose *her*. It's really not that hard to figure out."

And yet, he'd seen it where I couldn't. I'd taken her actions and her words at face value. She said things were over and... I believed her. It gutted me, made me feel like my heart had been ripped from my chest, but I'd *believed* her.

Not Leon, though. He read between the lines and saw what she truly wanted. Fuck, what she *needed*. The signs were all there, how she'd accused us both of using her as a replacement for Charlotte. Layla. Whatever the fuck her name was. She was basically *screaming* at us to prove that it was her—and *only* her—that we wanted. That she was more important than our vendettas and revenge plots.

And she was. One hundred percent, she was.

"So that's it, then?" I asked after a long silence. "You just wanna be buddies now?" I couldn't hide the disgust in my voice. The idea of voluntarily *sharing* the woman I loved with anyone— let alone a Guild Circle member—made me feel sick. It was bad enough while I waited for her to kick him to the curb, but... were we talking about long term? No fucking way.

Leon shot me a glare of pure venom. "You killed Layla."

I winced. "You killed Mauricio."

He grunted. "Who the fuck is Mauricio?"

Of course, this motherfucker didn't even *know* who he'd killed. I bet he couldn't even count how many lives he'd taken. I almost launched into more insults, but... he also had a point. I did kill Layla. Charlotte. Whatever. I'd *loved* her and still killed her. Didn't that make me worse than him?

Christ. I never thought I'd see the day when my actions were more reprehensible than that of a *Circle* member.

Swallowing hard, I changed the subject. "How do you know where you're going? She could have gone that way." I pointed to the cross street we'd just blown past. Leon wasn't even hesitating with each turn, like he already knew where she was.

He gave me an unimpressed glance, then unclipped his phone from the holder on the far side of the steering wheel where I couldn't see it. "You didn't think I was just *looking* at that van earlier, did you?"

On the screen, a red tracking dot blinked its way across a map, and my brows shot up. "You put a tracker on the van?"

Leon clicked his tongue. "Wrong. I put a tracker on *Stanley*... the fucking *plant*. She loves that damn thing. She won't leave it behind no matter where she goes. Not now, while she's feeling vulnerable."

I huffed, because that was actually really smart. I wished I'd thought of it. He may not have known Stanley was a plant until today, but he recognized how attached Danny was to the leafy bastard.

"The tracker's stopped moving," I told him, frowning at the screen. "GPS says we're twelve minutes away."

"Fuck that," Leon growled. "Just give me directions, we'll catch up."

As much as I hated the guy, I wasn't going to argue. We wanted the same thing, so we needed to work together. For now, at least. So I barked out directions as we drove, rapidly gaining on the blinking red dot.

As we approached, as the van came into view, I could swear my whole fucking world stopped turning. Leon skidded to a halt beside the wreckage of the rusty van, and we both leapt out in panic. He had a gun in his hand already, ever the professional, and I was unarmed. Danny had my gun.

Fuck. *Where is she?!*

"Danny!" I shouted, frantic. "Siren! Where are you?" I dropped to my knees beside the wrecked van, peering through the broken window. It was empty.

"Got a body over here!" Leon shouted, and my stomach dropped to the pits of hell. I scrambled to my feet, staggering over to where he was standing.

The relief that rushed through me when I saw the unfamiliar body on the gravel was enough to knock me to my knees. "Thank fuck," I exhaled. "Thank fuck."

Leon made a disgusted noise. "Have a little faith, Malachi. It'd take more than a car crash to kill DeLuna. She's one of the best, even at her worst."

It made me sick that he knew her so well. So much better than I did. But it also made me all the more determined to get her back and *learn* these things. So I swiped a hand over my face and pushed back to my feet.

"Now what? I don't suppose you put a tracker on *her* as well?" It was wishful thinking, which Leon confirmed with a tight grimace and jerk of his head. Shit. But then suddenly I remembered—

"Stanley!" I rushed around to the back of the van, where one of the buckled doors lay open.

He was still in there, still held by one of the safety straps, but his dirt was scattered all over the inside of the van, and several stalks were snapped and hanging limp. His stupid fucking Christmas bow was still attached to one of those broken fronds, and I almost sobbed at the pathetic sight of it.

Acting on instinct, I climbed into the van and unhitched the one remaining strap to free the injured euphorbia. Stanley was no lightweight plant, though, even missing as much dirt as he was, so I called for Leon to help.

Together, we manhandled the plant out of the wrecked van, even as a fire lit up in the engine. We dragged the damaged Devil's Backbone back to the Aston Martin, then watched the fire spread through the van with morbid fascination. We'd gotten there just in time.

"What the fuck do we do now?" I asked again, at a loss for ideas myself. I hated that Leon was taking the lead, but I was flailing. This wasn't my area of expertise, it was his. So for Danny's sake, I'd let him call the shots.

Leon didn't respond for a minute, pacing around the crash scene with an impassive expression. Then, finally, he returned to where I waited helplessly beside Stanley.

"We need to go back to the house," he announced. "We need to grab the data drives and then go our separate ways."

My jaw dropped. "Fucking excuse me? You're *giving up*?" I roared the accusation, grabbing his shirt in my fist and *shaking* the weak-ass motherfucker. "How dare you claim to love her when you're so ready to walk away when—"

He struck me in the trachea, making me choke and stagger backwards. My hands clutched my throat, but I knew the feeling of suffocation would be short-lived, no matter how startling it was in the moment.

"Simmer down, sweetheart," he mocked me with a sneer. "I'm not walking away from *shit*. Best you accept that fact now. Are you getting in? Or am I leaving you here with the plant?"

I dragged a long breath in, reinflating my lungs and glaring daggers at the psychotic bastard who was fighting for my woman. "Fine," I croaked. "Load Stanley into the trunk. If he dies, so do we."

Leon shrugged and popped the Aston Martin's trunk. No way

was Stanley actually going to fit, but with his heavy pot secured, it was as good as we could manage. I just crossed my fingers and hoped none of his other stalks would snap on the drive back to our rented house.

"Why are we retreating?" I growled when we were on the road once more.

Leon just shot me a flat glare. "Do *you* know where to find her now? Without a tracking device? No? I didn't think so." He paused a moment, his nostrils flaring as he stared at the road ahead. "She was ambushed. The van was rammed off the road by a stronger vehicle. Hummer is my guess. There were at least four other vehicles here, too, and probably ten to fifteen operatives. Whoever took her, this was well planned. They'll have covered their tracks."

I drew a deep breath, my throat aching and not just from Leon's strike. "Why? She didn't have the data sticks on her. Why take her?" *Why not just kill her, if that was the objective?*

Leon didn't answer for the longest time. Then he gave me a dark, murderous look. "That's what I intend to find out. Someone made a huge mistake, taking her from me, and they're about to pay for it."

I swallowed instinctively. I'd killed my fair share of people in the past, mostly mercenaries, but this motherfucker terrified me. For the first time since he'd turned up in my life, I was glad to be on the same side as him... because a whole lot of people were

about to die. Painfully.

2
DANNY

The pain in my chest when I woke was so sharp it stole my breath away. As consciousness returned to my head, drip by drip, the sharp ache behind my ribs only got worse. It wasn't from any physical injuries—though I was sure I had plenty of those—this was purely emotional pain. An injury of the heart and soul... like an unwanted amputation that left a weeping, infected void where two pig-headed alpha male assholes once resided.

In spite of all my training, all my composure in the face of capture and torture in the past, my strength faltered. I no longer had it in me to deny the pain anymore, and I wept.

"Ew, you're getting snot everywhere," someone said, and my puffy eyes popped open as I gasped.

Fuck. Where was I? I was in a bed. A normal queen-sized bed with good quality linen. Strangest prison cell I'd ever been in, that was for sure. And on the foot of my bed, a child sat staring at me in horrified fascination.

"Do you want a tissue or something? Gross." The child was a boy, maybe eleven or twelve years old, by my guess, wearing an oversized T-shirt and a backwards hat. He wrinkled his nose in extreme distaste, and I felt the wetness under my nose that was causing such drama.

"Sure," I replied, my voice thick and croaky.

The young boy gave a small nod and hopped off my bed. He crossed over to an attached bathroom, then returned to me with a handful of thick tissues. "Here."

I took them from his outstretched hand, and he casually sat back down on the side of my bed, studying me with curiosity.

"Thanks," I murmured, blowing my nose and drying my eyes. "Um, where am I? And who are you?"

The boy offered me a lopsided smile. "You're in my house, dude."

My brows shot up. "*Dude?*"

He rolled his eyes, full of sass. "Okay, dudette. Whatever. And isn't it obvious who I am?" He indicated to his face, like I should have recognized him already. Now that I studied him closer, there was something strangely familiar about this kid.

Not that I interacted with children often, but there was something about this one that I couldn't put my finger on. He was skinny, gangly, like he was on the brink of a growth spurt that hadn't quite hit yet. His features were pretty, almost too delicate to be masculine, and his button nose scattered with faint freckles.

Apparently, I took too long to say anything, and he threw up his hands. "Maybe you do have brain damage or something. How many people have you *ever* met with hair this color?" He whipped his hat off, revealing silver-white hair identical to my own. "I'm your little brother, dumbass."

My jaw dropped, and he beamed a wide smile.

What the shit...

But then the crash came back to me. The army of mercenaries who'd taken me. The white, blonde woman who'd shot the guy who hit me. My *mother*.

"I think I might be sick," I whispered, throwing back the bed covers and racing to the bathroom this kid just showed me. My knees hit the tiled floor hard, and I heaved into the toilet. Fucking sedatives always messed me up.

"Gross. I thought girls were supposed to be like... I dunno. Less disgusting." The kid had followed me into the bathroom and boosted himself onto the vanity to watch me vomit. Little weirdo.

I snatched a hand towel and wiped my mouth, then flushed. "You clearly don't interact with girls much."

He flashed me a smile. "Uh, actually I—we—have two other sisters, and if you ask them, they don't even fart. Ever."

"You have two other sisters?" I repeated, shock rolling through me and making me tremble.

He arched a dark brow—apparently another genetic trait we shared. "*We* do. Yeah. But between us? I'm pretty sure they're adopted. Oh, and we have a brother too, but he's old like you."

Surprising myself, I laughed. "I'm old? Rude. What's your name, brat?"

"Koen. What's yours?"

"You don't already know? How do you know I'm your sister?" I stood up off the tiled floor and pushed him off the vanity so I could splash some water on my face. Fucking hell, I looked a mess. A huge bruise darkened the side of my face, and a gash on my hairline had fresh stitches.

Koen shrugged in the mirror, stuffing his hands in his pockets. "Uh, I might have accidentally overheard Mom in her office when they brought you in. So I came to investigate." He flashed me a toothy grin full of mischief.

"I'm Danny," I told him, patting my face dry and wincing at the bruise pain. "So, you're not supposed to be in here?"

He shook his head. "Nope. If Mom found out, I bet she would—"

"Koen Alexander Atwood," a sharp female voice cracked through the bedroom behind me, and the boy flinched. "I should have *known* you'd have found your way in here."

Koen winced, then offered a sheepish smile at the woman standing in the doorway with her hands planted on her hips. "Mom, we were just talking about you."

The woman who'd pulled me from a crashed vehicle, then shot a man for hitting me just gave her child a soft smile and shook her head. "You're going to land in trouble one of these days, Ko. Go annoy Carolina in the kitchen; I need to speak with Danny alone."

The boy gave her a mock salute, shifting out of the bathroom with a teasing *yes ma'am*. Then he paused and turned back to us. "Oh, Danny just vomited, by the way. She could be pregnant or something."

I scowled, and his mother rolled her eyes, exasperated. "Koen, *leave.*"

His laughter faded out of the room, and the door clicked shut behind him, leaving me alone with the woman who claimed to be my mother. It'd be laughable if not for the fact that she looked just like me, with a few more lines around her eyes.

"You're not," she told me with a cooler voice. "My staff ran a blood panel while you were sedated."

I scoffed, rolling my eyes. "Of course I'm not, I have no uterine lining, and my tubes were tied sixteen years ago. But thanks for checking." My sarcasm on that *thanks* was *thick*.

To her credit, she didn't seem bothered by my attitude.

Instead, she indicated I return to the bed while she sat herself down in the armchair beside it. When I didn't immediately follow her direction, she just shrugged and folded her hands in her lap.

"Danny, I'm sure you're confused. Koen won't have helped on that front." She gave a soft smile, and I got the distinct impression that she genuinely loved her son. It was jarring. Love was not something the Guild ever encouraged or fostered. Love was a weakness, a tool for exploitation, and leverage for blackmail.

Wetting my lips, I moved closer to her but didn't sit back on the bed. I wasn't anywhere near comfortable or safe enough to lower my guard like that. Shit, what was I wearing? Pale purple satin sleep shorts and lace camisole were not my style.

"Let's see," I said carefully. "You orchestrated that crash when I was leaving Shadow Grove."

She inclined her head, accepting that responsibility.

"And you brought enough backup that even had I not smacked my head so hard in the crash, I couldn't have escaped." I ran a hand through my hair, wincing at the way it pulled my hairline stitches. It was tangled, and my fingers caught way too many knots. I needed to brush it before dreads started forming, which made me question how long I'd been asleep.

The woman said nothing, just waited. She was patient and calm, the only sign of tension showing in the stiff set of her fingers in her lap.

I took a deep breath, exhaling heavily. "You're Guild." She

nodded, and my eyes widened. "You're *Circle*." Another nod. *Fuck*. I pushed the instinctual wave of panic down and focused on the present. "Were you responsible for that attack the day after Christmas?"

Her lips tightened. "Absolutely not. I couldn't care less about Layla's blackmail."

There was familiarity in the way she said Layla's name. "You knew her."

"I met her," she corrected. "She didn't heed my warning about sticking her nose in Circle business."

I processed that, casting my eyes around the room. There were no bars on the windows, no locks either. The door seemed like a typical door, with no reinforcements that I could see or advanced locks. Why go to so much trouble to abduct me, then make it so easy to escape?

"You called me your daughter," I said in a flat voice, bringing my gaze back to hers. I wasn't emotional, because I was an adult. I hadn't had a mother for twenty-eight years and certainly didn't need one now. This wouldn't be some tear-filled reunion, it was merely strategic. She wanted me *now* for a reason. "Do I even get your name?"

The woman's perfect brows rose slightly, like she was shocked that I didn't already know. Or maybe at herself for having forgotten to introduce herself?

"Carol," she said softly. "Carol Atwood."

The name meant absolutely nothing to me. "What do you want with me, Carol?"

Stanley. What had happened to Stanley? He was in the crash, his dirt all scattered and his stalks broken... Would someone save him? Would Kai and Leon find him and nurse him back to health? Or was he dead?

Goddamn, that idea hurt. He was all I had left of Jude.

"Whatever you're thinking, Danny, you're wrong." Carol stood up from her armchair and smoothed down her pristine pants. "You've already assessed the room; you know you can leave at any stage. But I'd like it if you would *choose* to stay. At least for a few days. We have so much to discuss... if you're interested."

Once again, I was being asked to choose.

"What do we have to discuss, Carol?" I tilted my head to the side, studying her expression.

Her smile was small but sincere. "Well, you can find out if you choose to stay." She checked the time on her delicate gold watch. "It's ten in the morning right now, but we have an event this evening. Take the day to recover from those sedatives, sleep, shower, and explore the house if you wish. My daughter Carolina is baking pastries right now. I'll have Koen bring some up when they're ready. Help yourself to anything in this room, it's all yours no matter what you decide."

Stunned, I said nothing as she crossed over to the door. Then she paused with her fingers wrapped around the handle, glancing back at me with raw vulnerability on her beautiful face.

"I hope you will stay, Danny. I'd like to know you."

She didn't wait for my response before leaving the room, and I was glad. Because I had *no fucking clue* what my response should be. All I knew was that my heart was hurting, and those brief moments with Koen making fun of me had eased the pain ever so slightly.

I'd lost Jude and Carlos. Stanley was probably dead. Kai and Leon… I wasn't convinced either of them ever truly loved me as they claimed to. I was just Layla with another face, an opportunity for them both to right their wrongs against her. It hurt so much more than I ever prepared myself for. And I couldn't even call my best friend to cry it out. She was dead, because of me.

The only glimmer of hope I had to cling to was that Sabine had gotten herself to safety.

Maybe Carol held the missing keys to this whole mess. Maybe she didn't. But at this stage, what did I have to lose in hearing her out?

3
DANNY

Carol hadn't been lying when she said I was free to leave. The door was left unlocked, and my room was on the ground floor with easy escape routes from the windows. When I was reasonably sure it wasn't a trap, I took myself for a shower. Even if I did intend on running for the hills, I could do it clean.

The bathroom was fully stocked with products, none of that three-in-one crap here. High-end shampoo, conditioner and treatments were lined up in the niche, along with a face cleanser, body wash, and razor. All of them were brand new, still sealed.

That made me pause, but Carol was Guild. She knew—probably better than me—all the many, many ways to drug or poison a person. She was going out of her way to reassure me that she *wasn't* doing that. Not now, anyway. I could probably excuse the abduction and sedation earlier, because no way in hell would I have *willingly* gone if she'd turned up and asked nicely.

Come to think of it, her extreme measure to bring me here actually gave her more credibility and supported the idea of her being Circle. It was the type of dramatic, violent, unrestrained shit that all Guild mercenaries quietly loved. Including me.

The walk-in wardrobe was full of clothes in my size, all with tags attached, which meant that either Carol had been planning this for a while or I'd been sedated longer than I realized. Or both.

Still, I had no qualms about accepting the clothing, and dressed myself in a pair of jeans, with a scoop-neck, tight-fitting black sweater. Even the underwear was my size, which I was grateful for. Nothing worse than feeling vulnerable and in danger *without* panties or a bra on.

Okay, there were plenty of worse things. But that ranked fairly high up there.

Sleeping off the sedatives never really worked for me, so I dismissed the idea of going back to bed. I needed to work them out of my system by being active, so I decided to take Carol up on her suggestion to explore the house. I needed to map the floor plan and assess exits anyway.

"Hey, big sister!" Koen called out as I wandered down the corridor outside my room. "Where ya going?"

I spun around to face him, eyeing the plate of still steaming pastries in his hand. "Nowhere now. Are those for me?"

He gave me a wide smile. "Yup, fresh out of the oven. Want to eat them outside? Just promise not to vomit on me again, okay?"

I rolled my eyes, unable to resist his goofy little kid humor as I followed him back the way he'd come. He led me through what seemed like a totally normal—albeit rich as fuck—living room, complete with family photos on the walls and tasteful furniture. Before we reached the glass French doors that would take us outside, Carol appeared from the kitchen, drying her hands with a tea towel.

"Sorry, Danny, can I just steal a quick word?" She gave her son a pointed look, and he shrugged, carrying the plate of pastries outside with him.

My stomach rumbled in protest, and I couldn't stop the frown creasing my brow when I looked over at Carol.

"This is quick," she assured me. "My children don't know about my… extracurricular activities, if you will. I'd really appreciate it if you could save your questions until we speak privately?"

My eyes widened. "They don't know about—" Her gaze flashed with warning. "About your politics?" I finished with a small, mocking smile. "That seems risky, but what would I know? I don't have a family."

Her brow dipped. "My eldest son, Bram, is the only one who knows. I told him when he turned twenty-one, like I will the rest of my children. Until then, I'd prefer they live normal lives outside of my *politics*."

As much as I wanted to make a sharp quip about that, a sour taste coated my tongue. "How nice for them," I murmured. "Don't worry, Carol. I'm well trained in secret-keeping."

Her eyes flickered with sympathy, or pity, then she gave a slight nod and indicated for me to head outside where Koen was waiting. "I need to prepare for this evening's party, but Ko will show you around. We can speak later, if you'll be patient?"

She wasn't commanding me or barking orders, which threw me off. I just jerked a nod, at a loss for words. Really, though, I had nowhere else to go. My friends were gone, and my lovers… well. *I'd* left *them*. No doubt they'd come looking for me; neither one of them was likely to roll over and take my decision to break it off lightly. But maybe staying here with Carol for a few days might give me some perspective. If nothing else, she must surely be able to offer me valuable intel to clear my name.

What did I have to lose?

So I just gave her a tight smile and let myself out onto the huge veranda where Koen was seated at the table, his mouth full of pastry.

"I thought they were for me," I said, propping my hands on my hips and glaring daggers that I didn't feel.

Little shit didn't even flinch. He just shrugged and adjusted his backwards cap. He tried to say something in reply, but there was too much food in his mouth to understand the words.

"Gross," I teased, sitting down opposite him and reaching for a pastry from the plate. But I hesitated before picking one up, my own experience with drugging food far too thorough to trust *anything* at face value.

Koen—observant little brat—finished his mouthful, then swiped the pastry I'd been about to select. Arching a brow at me, he took a deliberate bite out of the side of it, then offered me the rest.

I took it, shocked, and gave him a curious look.

"See? Totally fine," he verified, licking his lips. "Carolina is an uptight bitch, but she's a really good cook. Don't tell her I said that, though."

I took a bite of the pastry—because I was starving—and instantly understood what he meant. It was *delicious*, perfect Danish pastry glazed with sticky sweetness. "Yum," I mumbled. "Don't tell her you called her an uptight bitch?"

Koen snorted. "Nah, she knows that. Don't tell her she's a good cook, or she will stop trying to perfect these recipes and I won't get to taste test everything."

I grinned around another huge bite of pastry. Koen was a smart kid. "So, your mom is hosting a party tonight?"

He grimaced. "Yup. I promise, it'll totally suck. Her friends are *so* boring, and all they talk about is the state of the stock market and making plans to play golf." He gave a gagging sound. "Carolina and I have to make an appearance, but then they usually don't mind if we bail out to our rooms. Tonight might be different, though."

He took another small bite of a pastry before handing it over to me.

"Thanks," I murmured. Fucking kid was poison-checking my food, and his mom thinks he doesn't know about the Guild? "How old are you, Koen?"

He gave me a wide smile, puffing out his scrawny chest. "How old do I look?"

I shrugged, keeping my expression serious. "I dunno, like eight or nine?"

The stricken look on his face made me crack a smile, and he scowled back, realizing I was teasing. "Not cool, Danny. I'm nearly eleven. How old are *you*, huh?"

"It's not polite to ask a lady her age, kid." I gave him a pointed look, then stuffed the pastry in my mouth.

He smirked. "I know. But I've seen you vomit, so no way you're calling yourself a lady."

Little shit. I turned my attention to the view, taking in the white sand and rolling waves of the ocean. "Where are we, anyway?"

"Hamptons," he replied without hesitation. He didn't even question why I didn't know where we were. Yeah, Carol needed to keep a closer eye on her son. "If you wanna run, I'll totally show you where all the car keys are stored."

I narrowed my eyes. "But?"

He blinked those sapphire blue eyes at me. Eyes that we both shared with Carol. "*But* I kinda hope you'll stick around for a bit. I know you're like… super old, like basically decaying, but you're my sister."

He was so sure of that, and I couldn't deny the physical resemblance. But that led to a whole raft of questions that Carol was going to need to answer for me.

"You have other sisters, Koen. Younger, less crusty ones." Ones without twenty years of contract killings staining their hands. I pointed to a different style of pastry, and he handed it over with a bite out of the side.

He adjusted his hat again, a sadness crossing his face. "You'll see what I mean when you meet Carolina."

I barely knew this kid, and technically his mother had kidnapped and drugged me. But goddamn, if I never wanted him to look sad like that again. So I pointed to a couple more pastries and changed the subject.

"Give me those two, then show me around this house. If I'm going to hang out for a few days, I need to know where the gym is at least."

His expression brightened instantly, and he handed over the food happily. "I can do that! Mom said we can do whatever so long as we're cleaned up and ready by six for the party." He pushed back from his chair and indicated for me to follow him as he headed back into the house. "Uh, well, that was the beach—obviously—but you don't really look like a beach chick."

I wanted to laugh, but as I glanced back at the water, all I could picture was the view from Kai's window. The deep blue of the sea surrounding his island paradise and how desperately I'd wanted to stay with him there.

But if I had… I never would have fallen for Leon as deeply as I had. And despite the pain it now caused, I didn't regret *feeling* that for even a second. Even if I never saw him again, or Kai, then at least my memories could keep me warm at night.

So I turned my face away from the ocean, away from my bitter thoughts and regrets, focusing instead on the confident kid taking me on a tour of his Hamptons mansion.

"Damn," I murmured when we *finally* reached the gym. Thank fuck there was one. "After the music room, library, formal dining, and ballroom, I was starting to think your architect skipped the gym."

Koen smirked. "I know, you were getting all twitchy and shit." He strode across the gym floor, heading for the half-court on the far side. "You any good at basketball?"

I shook my head. "Hopeless. I never really had time for games in my life." Not those kinds of games anyway. The games we played as children usually ended up with someone bleeding out on the cold concrete floor.

Koen wasn't deterred by my answer, grabbing a ball from the

rack and dribbling it a couple of times. "Want me to teach you? I won't laugh if you suck. Promise." He deadpanned me for a moment, then cracked and let out a laugh. "Okay, I won't laugh *much*."

He bounced the ball over to me, and I caught it, arching a brow at him. "I thought you were giving me a tour of the house?"

Koen's response was to pretend to snore before flashing me another grin. "Come on, big sister, show me how bad your skills are."

I scoffed, then bounced the ball a couple of times, and shot it without even moving further into the court. It sailed through the net, hitting the floor with an echoing bounce, and Koen's jaw dropped.

"I thought you said—"

"I said I'm crap at *playing* basketball, brat, but my aim and marksmanship are impeccable no matter what the projectile is." My smile turned brittle, remembering Carol's request not to mention the Guild to her children. "What else can you show me? We still have five hours to kill before this party."

Koen squinted at me, thinking. Then he gave a quick nod. "Alright, I have an idea. How are you with video games?"

I shrugged, enjoying his competitive little spirit. "One way to find out."

The kid threw up his hands like he already sensed an ass-whooping on the horizon, but credit to him, he was willing to rise to the challenge. He'd have made a great mercenary, if Carol was inclined to train him. Of course, then he wouldn't be Koen anymore. He'd be a hollow, broken, cynical shell that just looked like Koen. Like me.

4
DANNY

Spending the afternoon playing video games in Koen's room was a million times better than wallowing in grief and despair alone. I was actually grateful that Carol abducted me, because she'd saved me from the gut-wrenching pain I'd been drowning in when I broke up with both my lovers.

I forced myself not to think about them. Or the loss of my friends. But more than anything, I tried not to think about Stanley. I held onto the hope that maybe Kai found him, rescued him, and was nursing him back to health. Kai knew how much I loved that fucking plant; he would do it... if he found the wreck. Surely he would. One of them would.

The mysterious Carolina made an appearance in the late afternoon, and it wasn't hard to see why Koen wasn't a huge fan. Aside from having raven black hair and zero features in common with the kid, she was also a stuck-up bitch. Barely even gave me a cursory glance as she reminded Koen to get dressed for the party.

"What's her problem?" I asked when she stalked out of Koen's room again.

He tossed his Xbox controller down and screwed up his nose. "I wish she had a good excuse, but she doesn't. She's always been like that, but hey, she makes great pastries, so I put up with it."

"Good point," I murmured. Her attitude didn't bother me; I had no need to make friends with an eighteen-year-old who had no clue her mother was one of the seven leaders of the Mercenary Guild.

With a sigh, I left Koen and headed back to my own room to figure out what I was supposed to wear. Carol had beat me to it, though, and I found a dress laid out on the bed already, along with a pair of shoes and a velvet jewelry box.

By the looks of the outfit she'd chosen, this party was more formal than I'd anticipated. Still, I was curious enough to play along, so I made my way into the bathroom to sort out my hair and makeup to match the dress.

A soft knock on the door surprised me as I was zipping up the dress, and I went to see who was there. So far, no one had hurt me or forced me to do anything against my will—with the exception of how they'd brought me here—and I was waiting for the other shoe to drop.

To my surprise, though, no one was coming to attack me. It was just Carol, with a tightly guarded expression and a long velvet box gripped in her hand.

"Danny," she commented, running her gaze over my outfit. "You look…"

I arched a brow. "Considerably better with my bruised face concealed with makeup?"

Carol's eyes flicked back to my face, inspecting the cheek that I'd spent a whole lot of time layering makeup over. "I was going to say, you look like me. But that, too. Can I come in a moment?"

Shrugging, I moved out of the way. "It's your house."

A frown pulled at Carol's brow, but she entered "my" bedroom cautiously and glanced around. "I hope you found everything you needed in here, and the clothes all fit?"

Indicating to the dress I was wearing, I gave her a confused look. "Obviously. Do I want to know why you have my exact sizes and even know which shade of foundation I use?"

Her smile was tight as she perched awkwardly on the armchair near the window. "Most of your information is in my file," she admitted. "As for makeup, I took a guess that we would wear the same shade. Looks like I was right."

I had nothing to say to that. This was all *beyond* weird, but I was in no hurry to make her start talking. Surely I couldn't be any safer than in the home of a Circle member? While I was here, as her guest, I suspected no one would try to kill me.

Was I curious about why I suddenly had an entire family? Absolutely. Was I distraught over why Carol had abandoned me and left me to grow up as a child assassin? Not really. I was an adult and had plenty of time to come to terms with my situation. I no longer *needed* all those explanations, because what good would they serve me? We couldn't turn back time, and I doubt I would even if we could.

Our experiences shaped us... and I liked me just the way I was.

"Can you sit?" she prompted, nodding to the bed. I did as she asked, perching my butt on the edge of the mattress and waiting for her to speak. Awkward silences didn't bother me in the least.

Apparently, they didn't bother Carol much either, because, for a long time, she just sat there staring at me. Eventually, though, she must have remembered why she had come to see me right before her party was due to begin.

"Danny, I apologize I haven't given you a whole explanation today. The timing of all of this was less than desirable, to say the least, and I want to give you my undivided attention when we talk properly. Without my assistant interrupting every five minutes or my youngest son eavesdropping at the door."

I flashed a quick smile at the mention of Koen. It was

impossible not to like that kid.

"I didn't feel comfortable just ignoring the whole situation, though," she continued. "So, I wanted to pop by and very quickly address the biggest issue. Or it's the biggest issue in my mind. I can't speak for you."

Crossing my legs, I gave her a curious look. "Go on."

She pursed her lips, glancing down at the box in her hands. Her fingers were gripping it tightly, the strongest indication of how uncomfortable she was. Distressed. Otherwise, she was calm and composed. Graceful.

"Until two weeks ago, I never knew you existed." She dropped that truth bomb like a B-52.

I tipped my head to the side, thoughtful. "You forgot birthing a child when you were, what? Eighteen?" I was guessing her age, but the moment I said those words, realization washed over me. "You never gave birth to me."

Carol shook her head. "I did not. And I was sixteen in the year you were born, thank you."

I blew out a breath, connecting the dots. "Project Remus strikes again."

Shock flickered across her features. "You know about Remus?" Then she sighed. "Of course you do. Leon told you. Well, nonetheless. We can speculate on the how and why tomorrow. I just wanted to be perfectly clear that I *did not know* I had a daughter out there. That it was *not* my choice to have you raised the way you were. You've met Koen and Carolina. You can see for yourself that the upbringing you experienced is not how I treat my children."

It was nice for her to say but really made no difference to me. The days of lying on the cold concrete floor, sobbing over why my mommy hadn't loved me... they were so far in my past I could barely remember them. By the time I made my first kill, I'd accepted my position and never looked back.

Her admission did raise another question, though. "How *did* you discover me so recently?" I asked, studying her features carefully. "What suddenly brought me to your attention when I've lived within the Guild my entire life?"

She winced ever so slightly. "Leon Marx," she replied with a sigh.

That made my brows rise. "He knows you?" And he never told me? I'd fucking kill him.

Carol smiled. "No, but I know him. Contrary to what he might think, he's not *actually* the smartest kid in the playground. He recently made a move that garnered a lot of Circle attention, which then led to one of my team seeing your file. And your photo."

I scowled. "What the fuck did he do?"

"He issued a protective order on you. Something that... I can't even remember when it was last done. Basically, it prevents any of the Guild executioners from harming you for a period of ninety days. Which makes me ask, why were executioners coming after you? There are no official contracts on you, nor has a Kill Order been issued. So why did Leon take such a drastic measure to keep you safe?"

An amused smile curled my lips. "I'm really good in bed."

Her curious gaze flattened. "I'm sure you are."

"I thought we didn't have time to talk now," I replied, not totally sure I wanted to share my whole story until I heard *hers*. For all I knew, she was in bed with Blanchet.

Carol sighed, then nodded. "You're right, we don't." She put the box in her hands on the chair behind her, then leaned forward with her elbows on her knees. "Here are the details you may need to know this evening. This party is not Guild business, it's for my public life in investment banking. My son Bram is working abroad, and Carolina's twin sister, Suzette, is on vacation with friends in Aspen."

I nodded, understanding these might be things that I'd be expected to know. "Got it. Your husband?" I had to assume she was married, thanks to the enormous diamond on her ring finger.

"Dead," she replied without emotion. "Several years since."

"Understood. And who am I in all of this?"

Carol inhaled a deep breath, pushing to her feet and crossing back over to the door. "You're my daughter, Danny. There's no denying that fact. Even if the DNA test hadn't been leaked to the media already, there could be no denying our resemblance."

I shot up off the bed. "What?"

She gave a frustrated sigh. "I had my team run tests while you were unconscious, obviously. Unfortunately, one of the lab techs decided the confirmation of my secret daughter was too juicy not to sell to the tabloids. The story will run in a couple of days."

Panic rippled through me. "Is there a picture? Of me?"

Carol knew full fucking well why I was distressed and didn't offer me any apology for it. Instead, she just gave a short nod.

I breathed a curse, swiping my hand over my face in horror. Even if it wasn't a national tabloid, it was out there now. She'd fucked me. Hard. And now I wasn't so sure her lab tech *leaked* the information.

"It's probably for the best, Danny," she told me with a small frown. "Sometimes, you need to stand in the spotlight to stay safe from the shadows."

She left my room then, and I crashed back onto my mattress like my strings had been cut. She fucking *knew* what this meant for my career. I could never work a honey trap again… not with my face and name in tabloid newspapers. If I was right in suspecting Carol just downplayed her public face, I'd bet it wouldn't be long until her *secret daughter* was splashed across the internet for any fool to see.

Carol had just slit the throat of my career, all in the name of protection.

Now what the fuck was I fighting for? Other than my life, of course. My now meaningless, empty life.

My gaze snagged on the box Carol had left on the armchair, and I frowned. No way had she just left it by accident, so I reached over and picked it up. It was long, probably the length of my forearm, but shallow. I doubted it was jewelry; she'd already left that with my dress, so I pried it open to see.

"Huh, I didn't expect that," I murmured aloud, taking out one of the delicate blades. There were three of them, small and well-balanced for throwing, and a lace garter belt to hold them underneath.

If she was arming me, did that mean she was on my side? Or was this an elaborate ruse to make me trust her? Ugh, to what end, though? If she wanted me dead, I'd be dead.

Regardless of her motives, there was no denying I felt better being armed.

5
LEON

It was harder than I'd have liked to ditch Kai. But the moment I shook the determined fuck from my tail, I was gone from Shadow Grove. The logical part of me knew I needed to go home and get Layla's data cache decoding asap. Whatever she had uncovered was worth killing for, and it had put my woman in the firing line.

But whoever took Danny, took her alive. That gave me an element of hope. It meant Blanchet wasn't responsible... but who the fuck was? I needed to get to my office. My travel computer just didn't have the same capability to hack the databases I needed.

First, though, I needed to do something for Danny. Something I knew she would want taken care of *before* rescuing her. Because it was highly unlikely she really needed rescuing; she was too resourceful to be held captive for long.

"Wake up, Kenneth," I said aloud, rousing the man sleeping soundly in the bed I sat beside.

He startled, jerking against the bonds holding him to the bed. No doubt his instinct had been to reach for the gun on his bedside table, but I was already holding it.

"Wh-what? How?" he demanded, blinking at me in bewilderment. "Who the feck are you?"

Kenneth was a big man, strong, with a bright red beard, receding hairline, and Scottish accent. I'd recognized him on the security footage while Danny had desperately searched for any sign of her best friend, Judith, leaving her building before it went up in flames.

He didn't know me, but I knew him. I also knew he had a fondness for lighting fires.

"I don't think it really matters, do you?" I replied, tipping my head to the side. I'd given him a small dose of sedative to keep him asleep while I trussed him up, but now I wanted him awake. It was no fun killing a man who didn't know he was being killed.

He grunted. "I dinna suppose it does." Giving me a weary look, he heaved a sigh. "Looks like all me bad deeds have caught up, eh? Go on then, have at it."

His lack of panic didn't surprise me in the least. All

executioners knew that at some stage, we'd find ourselves on the other end of a contract. It was inevitable, and as professionals, we all understood how futile begging and bargaining were.

"The arson job in Edinburgh a few days ago," I said casually, tapping his gun on my bent knee thoughtfully. "Was it an official contract?"

Kenneth curled his lip in disgust. "Aye, it was. I'd not take an unofficial with that many casualties."

Well, he had that in his favor. I gave a small nod. "Any thoughts on who paid the contract?"

The man frowned his confusion. "Ye make a habit of sniffin' the hand that feeds ye? No, I dinna ask questions. Never do."

I nodded again, because I could understand his attitude. Still, I had to kill him anyway.

"The target in that building was someone who mattered a great deal to a woman I love," I murmured, explaining why I was holding him responsible despite him just having carried out someone else's orders. I already knew it would have been Blanchet, and I'd also deal with that bastard when I found him. Slippery son of a bitch.

Kenneth winced. "Fair enough, then. Can I ask ye make it quick?"

I gave a sigh, pushing to my feet. I'd intended to make it painful and slow, really punish him for the pain Danny was experiencing at the loss of her best friend. But it was Blanchet who deserved that treatment, not Kenneth. This man was just doing his job, same as the rest of us.

So I did as he asked. Two bullets to the heart and one between the eyes. Done.

It gave me very little satisfaction to eliminate another Guild executioner—there were hardly any of us left these days—but Danny would want it done. She would want *everyone* involved in Jude's death to pay in kind, so it was the least I could do to comfort her.

Still, I felt like shit as I let myself back out of Kenneth's apartment and stripped off my gloves. We needed to quit wasting time taking out the foot soldiers and go after the general instead. Maybe we could strike it lucky, and Layla's encrypted drive would tell me the exact location where Blanchet could be found. I wouldn't know until I decrypted them all, and the fastest way to do that was to go home.

Running a hand over my tired eyes, I made my way back out to my car. A quick check for explosives later, and I was on my way to the private airfield, where I had a plane waiting for me.

Usually, I liked to maintain my anonymity by flying commercial, but I was past caring whose attention I drew. By the time this whole mess was over, I had no doubt there would be some replacements within the Circle. Fuck it. I could erase my footprints later.

International travel never used to bother me. I spent my time working or catching up on sleep and generally accepted it as an unfortunate side effect of the Guild growing so multinational. But now, with Danny's disappearance weighing on my mind and Layla's thumb drives burning a hole in my pockets… I was on edge. Big time.

It was probably a good thing there was no one on the plane except me—ignoring the crew—because I likely would have stabbed someone if they annoyed me with snoring or loud voices. Yeah, I'd best stick to private until I got my woman safely back in my arms. And my bed.

Out of sheer frustration, I spent a good majority of the flight digging up dirt on that muscle-bound meathead, Kai. There was plenty to be found, he clearly didn't pay enough when he "erased" his records, but grudgingly even I had to admit there was nothing that Danny would condemn him for.

After all, both Danny and I had committed crimes a hundred times worse than anything Kai, or his criminal pseudonym of Ares, had ever done. The only atrocity I had to hold against him was the bombing of those Guild orphanages, killing dozens of kids.

But… evidence to prove that was elusive. Which gave me an uncomfortable feeling.

If that slick motherfucker was actually a decent human being, I was going to vomit.

Eventually, I admitted my own limitations and closed my eyes to catch a nap. My dreams were sporadic on the best of days, probably because I never relaxed enough to really enter REM, but this time they were vivid.

Vivid and full of Danny DeLuna. Weirdly, it was a non-sexual dream. I was just walking through dark city streets with her, our fingers twisted together in a Gordian knot. She tossed her starlight hair and shot me a sly grin as we stopped at an unmarked door.

Curious but utterly trusting, I followed as she pulled me into the building.

Inside, blood covered every inch of the walls, the floor, and even some dripped from the ceiling. Confusion rippled through me, and I turned my gaze to Danny, the question falling silent from my lips. Like I was inside a sound vacuum. But she heard me, her smile arching wider and her teeth... sharp.

"Are you happy, Bunny?" she asked in an innocent, girly voice. "I killed him for you."

One of my brows arched. Him?

Still smiling, Danny nudged a chunk of flesh on the floor. A chunk of flesh with dark skin and a Royal Marines tattoo. Oh. *Ohhh*. Him.

"It's what you wanted, isn't it?" she prompted, fluttering her dark lashes. "Now I'm just like you."

It was what I wanted... wasn't it? For her to toss that loser to the curb and be *all mine*? But I couldn't extinguish the guilt and disappointment unfurling within me. Yes, I wanted her all to myself... but not like this. I didn't want her to become *me*. I never wanted *anyone* to become me.

She liked that Kiwi son-of-a-whore. Fuck it, she might even love him. And she'd stopped me every damn time I wanted to kill him… I liked that she stopped me. I liked that she stood up to me, wasn't afraid of disagreeing with me.

So I shook my head and stepped away from the Danny-puppet. "Not like this," I murmured, my lips twisting with disgust. "You're not *you.*"

She tilted her head, giving a tinkling laugh that was *not* her own. "What do you mean, silly Bunny? I'm *you.* Because you know no one else will ever love you. Certainly not a strong independent woman… that's why the real Danny has *him.*" She nudged the chunk of tattooed flesh again. "Because *he* is deserving of her love. *He* isn't a mentally unstable murderer. *He* didn't kill his mommy. Not like you, Bunny. Not like *us.* We're fucked up. Damaged. Broken. That's why no one else can ever love us."

This was a dream. I was attuned enough to my own subconscious that I was well aware of the fact this was a dream. And yet… I couldn't deny anything this fake Danny was saying. She spoke the truth, and it made me sick.

"The last person who called me unlovable got her throat slit," I muttered, closing my eyes to avoid looking at her. My DeLuna wouldn't spew such venom, even when I deserved it. For all the blood on her hands, she was still a good person. She cared.

That laugh bubbled out of her again, and with my eyes closed,

I recognized it. That wasn't Danny, as if there was any doubt.

"Yes, you slit mommy's throat… and yet here you are. Still unlovable. Face it, Bunny. Danny will never love you like she loves *him*. They're perfect together, and you? You're just going to drag her down and get her killed. I bet she isn't being targeted for Project Remus at all… Didn't all this start happening after *you* started showing an interest? Maybe someone is seeking revenge against *you*… by taking away the only person you've ever really cared for."

I snapped. My lids flicked open, and I grabbed her by the throat. Her eyes bugged out, her perfect lips parting as I slammed her into a wall with my fingers tightening. "Fuck you, Mom," I snarled. "You were a shitty mother and an even shittier therapist. You made me into the monster I am. You."

Danny's sapphire eyes pleaded with me, her moonlight hair soft over my tight grip on her throat, but I wasn't fooled. This wasn't Danny. It was the whore who raised me as a killer. The manipulative bitch who turned me into an executioner and used her education to break my mind.

"Please," she squeaked, her face turning purple. Her hands beat weakly on my chest, and I swallowed deeply as I screwed my eyes shut. I'd already killed her once. This was just a figment of my imagination, and she couldn't manipulate me into killing her twice.

So I released her with a heavy exhalation, blinking my eyes

open as she spluttered and gasped for air.

Only then did my surroundings flicker and fade from the blood-soaked room, transforming back into the interior of my private plane. On the carpet in front of me, a woman I didn't recognize was doubled over, panting and crying as she clutched her neck with both hands.

Oh shit. I just strangled the cabin crew.

"Sorry," I muttered, sitting my embarrassed ass back down in my seat and clearing my throat.

The woman gave a pained nod, climbing back to her feet. "Can I get you a drink before we land, sir?" Her voice was husky and weak, but professional. Made me wonder just how much she got paid, to pretend that hadn't just happened.

I shook my head, turning my attention out the window to see we were indeed close to our destination. Good. I was itching to get into my office, and that dream only made me more uneasy.

Fucking childhood trauma picked a hell of a time to rear its ugly head, that was for sure.

Stupid Kai and his stupid heart-on-his-sleeve feelings for *my* woman. I hated him so much, but I couldn't deny the sincerity of his feelings for DeLuna. Or hers for him. It made me sick inside and my palms sweaty with fear.

He was the logical choice. The safe choice. But I refused to bow out like a gentleman… because I wasn't one. Far fucking from it. If he wanted her all to himself, it'd be over my cold dead corpse.

6
DANNY

Carol was a mystery to me. The woman I observed when I stepped into the party was every bit the wealthy, accomplished, respected woman of society. She was poised and feminine, proudly introducing Koen and Carolina to her friends—or associates—and holding her weight in conversation with stiffly suited businessmen.

Maybe the drugs and trauma of the car crash played a part, but it was extremely difficult to line *this* Carol up with the woman who'd abducted me from Shadow Grove. The one who'd ordered someone to literally run me off the road, then shot a man in the face for punching me. That woman, she was

Guild. She was *Circle*.

But this one? Like an identical twin. It was impressive and a little bit inspiring to see how flawlessly she slipped into her alternate identity. I couldn't shake the desire to know which Carol was real, though. Call it professional curiosity.

Her flippant revelation to me upstairs, the casual way she ended my career as a honey trap, still had me pissed off, so I made no effort to join her. Even when she met my eyes across the room and tried to beckon me closer, I just gave a tight smile and walked away. Biological parent or not, she had no right to make that choice for me.

Accepting a glass of champagne from a passing waiter, I wandered through the house with no real destination in mind. I observed the guests, committing faces to memory but recognizing none. To be expected, though. I had no reason for my world to have ever overlapped with this one. Ever.

I paused in the music room, a painting behind the baby grand piano catching my eye. It was a Manet, and I took a guess that it was an original, not a print. Which then made me shift my attention to the handsome, well-dressed man admiring it while he sipped a tumbler of scotch.

Smiling, I moved closer.

"Fancy meeting you here," I said softly, tilting my head

slightly to watch the man from the corner of my eye. "Are you browsing? Or acquiring?"

My tall companion gave a soft smile, sipping his drink. "Merely admiring. You look rather alive for someone with a Guild target on her back. Though I suspect your mother has played a hand in that."

I jerked in surprise, turning to face him. "You knew about—"

Hermes shrugged. "The resemblance *is* rather uncanny."

My brow drew tight. "You could have mentioned it."

He tilted his head, giving me a curious look. "Why would I? We aren't friends, and Guild business is none of mine. Unless you asked, why would I offer?"

He had a point. Just because we'd conducted business in the past didn't mean he owed me anything.

"Oh, there you are!" Carol called out, striding toward us with a smile on her beautiful face. "John, I see you've already met my daughter."

Hermes—or *John*—gave a gracious smile. "I have. Danny provided me with a most interesting job recently. How is your plant doing, by the way?" He turned his attention back to me, totally unfazed that we were discussing his work openly with Carol.

I scowled, remembering how broken Stanley had looked in the crash. "I don't know," I murmured, shooting a glare at Carol. "I've been *here* for… how long has it been?"

"Six days," Hermes told me with a confident nod. "A friend of yours reached out to me a couple of days ago." This seemed to be an explanation to Carol for why he had that knowledge. Probably Leon, since he would know Hermes.

Carol just gave an understanding smile in response, like this information didn't shock her. "Well, you are the best at locating and returning stolen items, John. It's only logical that someone might call you."

I blinked in disbelief as she sipped her champagne.

Hermes gave a lopsided grin, like he could see how baffled I was with the whole situation. "Quite so, Carol."

I seethed with a flash of anger. "I'm not a stolen diamond, and I resent being discussed as such. More to the point, if I had wanted to leave, I would be gone already."

A flash of relief crossed Carol's face, and Hermes chuckled.

"I don't deal in human transportation, anyway," he told me with a wink. "But this Manet, Carol, is lovely. How long have you had it?"

Carol's eyes narrowed. "If that goes missing, John, I'll know who to blame." She gave him a hard look before shifting her gaze back to me. "Koen is looking for you, Danny. He's taken a real liking to you… I hope you will take the time to tell him if you decide to leave."

"Ah yes, the youngest Atwood," Hermes murmured thoughtfully. "Talented kid."

Carol shot him another glare but quickly returned her attention to me. "I do suggest meeting with some of my guests, Danny. I'd say at least a few of these men and women have been on the paying end of your contracts over the years." She offered another smile to Hermes, then gracefully sashayed away from us once more.

"Weird woman," I muttered, not caring that Hermes could hear me.

He cast a curious glance at me, then sipped his drink. "If you'll excuse me, I have some work to take care of while I'm here." His wink was pure mischief, and the ease with which he disappeared into the party crowd was enviable. Who knew such a big man could blend so easily?

At a loss for what the fuck I was meant to do, I tracked down another waiter and exchanged my empty glass for a full one. Despite Carol's suggestion, I actually had no desire to meet the people who paid me to do the shit I did. The fact they were willing to go to such lengths for revenge, power, or leverage told me everything I needed to know about them.

So I decided to go looking for Koen instead. I only met the brat this morning, but I couldn't deny the soft spot he'd already carved out in my frosty chest.

I found him out near the pool, sitting on one of the sun loungers as he chatted with a little girl around his own age. Cute.

"That better be soda," I commented, coming to sit beside him and tapping the drink in his hand with my own glass.

He sent me a wide grin. "As if I'd touch that alcohol crap you old people drink. I've seen how sick Carolina gets after she sneaks into Mom's wine cellar." He pulled a disgusted face. "No, thanks."

I smiled back at him, unable *not* to. Goddamn kid would be a heartbreaker with that confidence and charisma. He just needed to get through puberty first.

"Oh, this is my friend, Stell," he told me, gesturing to the little girl. "She also finds our mom's parties lame."

"Shocking," I remarked in a dry voice, then extended my hand to the other kid. "Nice to meet you, I'm Danny."

"You too," she replied in a small voice. "My name's not actually Stell, it's Estelle Blanchet."

I froze, staring at the little girl. She was ten *at most*. Was this why Carol had pushed me to stay for her party? Did Carol even know about what was happening with Emmanuel Blanchet? She had to. She was Circle, after all. But weren't they all meant to be anonymous?

"That's an old lady name," Koen informed us. "Stell is way cooler."

I wet my lips, studying the little girl. "Who are you here with, Estelle?"

She gave a small shrug. "My aunt. She and Koen's mom are friends."

I bit the inside of my cheek to keep from peppering this little girl with my questions. She had sad eyes, there was no mistaking that. Poor kid.

"Where are your parents?" I asked, taking a guess.

Estelle shrugged. "They died. It's okay, though. I don't really remember them, and Aunt Liza is nice enough."

Koen gave me a less than subtle elbow to the ribs, and I forced myself to bite back the questions I was burning to ask. Mainly, was her father Emmanuel Blanchet by any chance? Because if so, he wasn't dead. Just a shitty human being, apparently, if he let his daughter think she was an orphan.

"You seem kinda old to be Koen's sister," Estelle commented, wrinkling her nose at me. "How old *are* you?"

I choked on the sip of champagne I'd just taken.

"Stell, dude," Koen hissed, "that's like... rude or something. Mom always says you don't ask a lady her age."

Estelle frowned. "Why?"

Koen was at a loss, shrugging then running a hand through his white-blond hair. "Beats me."

"I'm twenty-eight," I told Estelle, not caring about the

antiquated etiquette around that question. Who gave a crap how old a woman was? That idea of secrecy around a woman's age was a carryover from far less progressive times, when a woman's age directly correlated—in a man's eyes—to how beautiful, desirable, and chiefly how *fertile* she might be.

I liked to think our modern world was smart enough not to relate any of those attributes to age. After all, science and cosmetics could wind the clock either way, depending what procedure was undertaken.

Still, to a ten-year-old, I was practically a dinosaur. So I laughed when Estelle gaped and made a hushed comment about how I was the same age as her Aunt Liza.

For a while, I was content to sit there by the pool with Koen and Estelle, listening to them complaining about their fancy boarding schools that they attended and lamenting that their vacations weren't long enough.

Soon, though, Carol tracked us down with a young woman at her side. Based on the authority in her voice when she spoke to Estelle, I could guess this was Aunt Liza.

Estelle gave me a friendly farewell, then hugged Koen before leaving with her guardian. Koen gave no complaints about being sent to bed, either, and I ruffled his hair when he asked if he'd see me in the morning.

Alone, Carol gave me a pointed look.

"So, Estelle *Blanchet*, huh?" I said softly, not wanting to be overheard if Koen was lurking and listening again. "Daughter?"

Carol's brow creased. "Granddaughter. Emmanuel is one of the older Circle members currently. He grew paranoid some years ago that his identity had been uncovered and that someone might target his heir. So he faked his son's death and hid him away under a new identity. Apparently, that identity had no room for a child, so Estelle was given to her maternal aunt." Her lips twisted in disgust, her feelings on the subject clear.

I filed that information away but was failing to see the point.

"Why am I here, Carol?" I asked after a long, heavy pause. "Why did you bring me here? Why did you ask me to stay?"

She didn't answer immediately, instead, she took a couple of steps away, peering up at the stars like she was considering her words carefully.

"Would you believe me if I said I just wanted to know my daughter?" she asked eventually, giving a heavy sigh as she turned her gaze back to me.

I bit the inside of my cheek to hold back the sarcastic sneer that wanted to escape. "No, I wouldn't."

Carol gave a half-smile. "Good. You're too smart for

that. Too… experienced. So I'll level with you, Danny, because whether you buy it or not, we *are* on the same team."

I gave a grudging nod. "For now."

Her answering smile was sad. "For now," she agreed. "But someone needs to pay. *Someone* is responsible for harvesting my genetic material and creating *you*. Someone then went to great lengths to hide you from me but also raise you right under my nose. Why? There had to be some sort of gain for whoever was responsible, and I intend to find out who, what, and why. Then make them pay."

It was a reasonable desire. "Okay. So, why bring me here?" It was the same question, because her need for revenge didn't necessarily *require* my cooperation. She could have done all that without ever meeting me. She certainly didn't need to bring me into her home and introduce me to her children.

Carol gave me an intense look, then tipped her head back to the party behind her. "I should get back to my guests. If you're still here in the morning, let's chat about how we track down old man Blanchet. That fucker has been begging to catch a bullet for *years*, and I'm more than ready to provide it."

With a smirk, she headed back into the house, leaving me alone under the stars with my head swirling.

What the fuck was I meant to make of this whole weird

situation? Now that I'd met little Estelle Blanchet, though, I was curious to see who else had been invited to Carol's party. Maybe I would mingle a bit, after all.

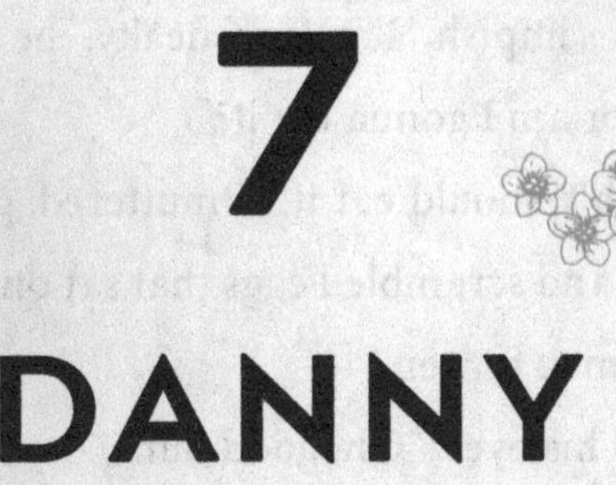

7
DANNY

The smell of bacon and fresh coffee woke me, and I rubbed my eyes in confusion. I'd stayed… because I saw no reason to leave. But the fact that I'd *slept* was what had me all disoriented and shit.

"Carolina says bacon helps a hangover," Koen informed me, and I squinted up at him standing over my bed. "And that you look like a coffee drinker."

"How the shit did you get in here without waking me up, squirt?" I mumbled, sitting up with a yawn. The door stood open, but I could have sworn I had locked it *and* barricaded it with a chair before crawling into the big comfy bed. It certainly wasn't impenetrable, but it should have woken me up if anyone tried to get in.

Yet there was the chair, innocently sitting clear of the door. I frowned at it, then at Koen once more.

His smile was impish. "I'm very sneaky," he informed me. "So? You want this, or am I gonna eat it?"

"You probably should eat it," I muttered, grabbing the plate of crispy bacon and scrambled eggs that sat on my bedside table. "You're kinda small for ten."

Koen rolled his eyes. "Oh, good burn," he replied with heavy sarcasm. "I've never heard that one." He flopped down on the end of my bed, and I held onto my food to avoid tipping it everywhere.

"Besides," he continued, getting comfy, "you're no giant yourself. I guess it's genetic."

I didn't have anything to say to that, so I just hummed a thoughtful sound and filled my mouth. I'd pretty much accepted the fact that Carol wasn't going to drug me by this point, and I didn't want Koen's slobber all through my breakfast just to check.

"Shouldn't you be at school or something?" I asked after a huge sip of coffee, arching a brow at the kid on my bed.

He wrinkled his nose in disgust. "That's such an old person thing to ask, Danny. I thought you were cooler than that."

I couldn't help my smirk. "But I *am* old, Ko."

Koen shrugged. "Age is just a number, Danny. You're as old as you feel. But no, I'm not supposed to be at school, dingbat.

It's winter break for another two days. But even if it weren't, I wouldn't be going back to school."

"Why's that? I'm guessing not just because you want to lurk around here listening to your mom's private conversations. That's *got* to be dull ninety-five percent of the time." Or maybe it wasn't. Koen probably knew all kinds of interesting things that Carol didn't realize.

He sighed dramatically. "You're not wrong. Before all this drama when she found out about *you*, all she ever talked about was some *game*. It sounded lame and involved paintings in some crusty old person museum or something. Anyway, I can't go back to school, 'cause I got suspended on the last day before break."

I grinned. "For how long?"

"Three weeks," Koen pouted. "They majorly overreacted."

"What'd you do?" I knew there was a reason I liked this kid.

He sat up, giving me a very serious, very stern look. "I did what the stupid school board was too scared to do, so they should be *thanking* me. One of our teachers had been spying on the girls' locker rooms." His face screwed up in disgust. "So, I felt like it was my responsibility to air a video of him drunkenly serenading his broom while dancing naked around his kitchen."

I snorted a laugh. "How'd you get that clip?"

Koen shrugged. "CGI mostly. But it played during an assembly for the whole school, and he got fired for it."

Impressive for a ten-year-old with no *official* Guild training.

"So how come you got suspended? Didn't you cover your tracks?"

Koen looked positively offended. "Of course I did. I even sent the video file from *his* laptop so nothing traced back to me. Unfortunately, some Goody-Two-shoes saw me keying the teacher's car while he was being berated by our principal, and *that's* what the suspension is for."

I snickered. "Rookie."

A soft knock on the open door announced Carol before she stepped into the room. Her gaze was soft on Koen, then sharpened slightly as she turned to me. Not that it was hard, just more apprehensive.

"Danny, I'm sorry to rush you, but I've had something come up and will need to head into Manhattan later today. I thought you'd want to have our chat sooner rather than later?"

Ah yes, our little chat about how I came to be me and what we were going to do to whoever was responsible. No way was I putting that off indefinitely, even if Koen was great company.

"Absolutely," I agreed, putting my half-eaten breakfast aside.

Carol gave a relieved smile. "Good. I'll be in my office, just come in when you're ready."

She left, and I shooed Koen out so that I could shower and dress in peace. The amount of clothing, underwear, and shoes in the closet implied Carol wanted me to stay a whole lot longer than just a few days. Or maybe she just liked to provide options. Either way, I appreciated having fresh clothing to put on after my shower.

I'd just finished putting my hair in a braid when awareness skittered over my skin. I wasn't alone. The lack of sound, such as a door opening or a window sliding, was as much of a clue as if there had been one.

Still…

I closed my palm around one of the newly acquired blades I'd been about to strap on and kept it hidden in my hand as I turned. The door to the bathroom was open, so all I had to do was take two steps…

My visitor sat in one of the chairs by the window, one long leg crossed over the other, a bemused expression on his face.

"Hello, *John*," I greeted him. While Hermes didn't have a reason to kill me, and it really wasn't his deal anyway, I didn't relax my guard. The man had let himself in, and while we'd been professional acquaintances on and off over the years, we were not *buddies*. "Twice in two days, I'm honored."

He chuckled. "You can put the blade up, DeLuna, I have no interest in harming you, and even if I did, I'd prefer my balls to stay attached."

A grin kicked up the corner of my mouth before I could quite stop it. Tsking, I tucked the blade into a sheath hidden by the belt I'd chosen. Carol really did provide some great accessories. "It wouldn't be your balls I hit."

Spreading his hands, he gave me a droll look. "You say

potahto, I say potato…"

"I say French fries usually." Tossing my braid over my shoulder, I folded my arms. "Is this business or…"

It wasn't a pleasure. That was for damn sure.

"A little of this, a little of that," he admitted in a cryptic tone that would usually irritate the fuck out of me. Course, after a few days here in the Hamptons palace, apparently I'd evolved.

Or maybe I was numb.

Probably both.

"You didn't ask me," he commented. Vaguely, I might add.

"You're going to have to give me a few more details there, *John*," I said. Damn, that name was just—weird. He was a lot of things, but John seemed almost too *normal* for him. "I ask you for very little."

For a damn good reason. Business was business, after all.

"I mentioned a friend of yours called me," he repeated his comment from the night before.

"I heard you." Raising my brows, I stared at him, waiting.

Interest seemed to kindle in his eyes as he studied me. The silence didn't stretch too long. I'd always found Hermes to be a pragmatic man. "I find myself in a bit of a quandary."

"Pretty sure I didn't do it." Keeping it light, I gave a shrug. "We don't always run in the same circles."

"True. But I like you, DeLuna. I don't like many people."

Well, of all the things the giant of a man could have said, *that* would not have even made my top twenty-five. "Thank you?"

The barest hint of a smirk twisted his mouth. "You're welcome."

"You liking me is your quandary?" I asked after he went into another protracted silence.

"Yes."

"Right, well, spit it out then. I have things to do." Fully-packed schedule over here. "I know you do." The Game was coming.

"Very true." Without further hesitation, he rose. I stayed where I was. At this distance, I didn't have to crane my head to look at him. "I prefer discretion in all things."

I gave him a little shrug. This wasn't new information.

"But as I said, I like you. Ask."

"Ask what?"

"Ask what friend reached out to me."

I stared at him for a long moment. "I ask, you tell?"

One nod.

"That sounds an awful lot like a favor."

It was his turn to shrug, and it looked a lot fiercer on a guy with his build. "Ask. Or don't."

Considering Leon knew I'd hired Hermes to get Stanley back—the little twist of pain in my chest was definitely for my plant—he was probably the "friend" that reached out.

"I'm good." I nodded once and dropped my folded arms. "Maintain your discretion."

Surprise flickered through his eyes. Or maybe it was something else. The emotion was there and gone again. "As you wish." He headed for the door. "Take care of yourself, DeLuna."

"You too."

But I was talking to the air.

As promised, Carol was in her office. She sat at her desk, with a pair of glasses perched on her nose as she took notes on a tablet while studying a computer screen. She held up a finger as if to ask for a moment.

Rather than sit, I paced away from her and her desk as the sound of the electronic pen on the screen filled the hushed silence. I looked out the window at the near serene landscape, the sharp angle of the land where it sloped toward what was probably a private beach.

"Very well," Carol said after a moment in a brusque tone that indicated she was *not* talking to me. However, I'd heard that tone before—about three seconds before she shot the guy who hit me. "He failed to comprehend the parameters of the mission. Burn the threads. Eliminate him. Clean it up. Move on."

Guild business.

Letting my eyes drift half-closed, I continued to study the bluish skies with the little puffs of fluffy clouds. Idyllic. Peaceful. Alien.

"Did I stutter?" Carol asked. Yeah, the person on the other end of that line was about to find themselves erased if they chose the wrong answer. My lips twitched. Carol Atwood was a bit of a badass.

Not that I expected anything less from a member of the Circle.

"Good. Don't waste my time again." The moment punctured when she sighed. "Sorry, I didn't expect that to take so long. Though you were delayed."

The shift in tone was enough to give a person whiplash. Pivoting, I faced her. Her voice warmed by several degrees, and a wry smile softened her mouth. I knew that expression. I'd given Jude and Sabine similar looks when I knew damn well they'd made me wait.

"A friend dropped in," I said, choosing Hermes's words.

"I noticed. Is John going to be a problem?"

"Not that I'm aware of."

"Good." Rising, she moved over to the sideboard where I'd just been eyeing a pot of coffee and poured a cup. "Would you like some?"

I hadn't until the scent of it hit me. Sweet, rich, and nutty. Course, I'd have made do with sludge. The luxuries were nice, but everything here was almost too soft, and it was starting to mess with my head.

"That'd be great." I could have made it a power play and

forced her to bring it to me. But I was all diplomatic and shit. I met her halfway.

Now I took a seat in front of her desk. We stared at each other, and I had to wonder if the same thoughts went through her head that went through mine. Someone stole her egg, fertilized it, then—what? Parked me in a surrogate womb for nine months.

Sounded like something out of a science fiction novel. I took a long drink of my coffee. She pressed something on her desk, and there was a click from the doors behind me.

"Privacy," she said with a faint smile.

Ah. "Koen." It wasn't a guess.

Her expression turned into one of exasperated affection. "That boy is too smart and far too talented for my peace of mind."

"He's a brat," I commented. "I like him." Not that I'd intended to admit it aloud.

"He is." She shook her head, not jumping on that comment, but then she didn't need to say anything, did she? "You have questions."

"So I do."

"Yes," Carol said, and something cold flashed in her eyes. The warm, giving mother with the patient amusement at her children's antics was a far cry from the woman who gazed out of her eyes right now.

This woman I got.

"I have some answers," she said slowly. "Not enough. But

some."

"Well, I guess we should start at the top." What the actual fuck was I going to do with the rest of my life? Yeah, I'd figure that one out on my own. "Or maybe we start a little lower."

"Project Remus."

"Seems like as good a place as any." The question was whether she'd discuss it.

For too long a moment, she simply stared at me with an unreadable expression. A flash of fresh emotion sparked her cool eyes, and I knew the answer before she nodded.

"That does seem like the right place to start." Settling back in her chair, she pressed her fingers together and kept her gaze on me. "Project Remus…"

8
KAI

eon's house was a fucking mess. Worse than just regular untidy—not that I believed Leon was anything but anal when it came to his house cleanliness—but like someone had ransacked the place. Or had an extremely physical fight all through the luxury cabin.

"Fucking hell," Jae muttered as his boots crunched over broken glass. "You'd think he could afford a cleaner or something."

"I doubt *affording* one is really his problem," Moana snarked, brushing past us both with her bag slung over her shoulder. "I'm going to find a bedroom, I'm wrecked. Wake me up when the fireworks start, would you?"

Jae smirked. "You bet, Mo."

I just glowered. They really had no idea how badly we were tempting our own fate by coming here. Leon wasn't home—and hadn't been in a while, by my guess. But sooner or later, he'd come back to his base. After all, he was the one who said he needed to decode Charlotte's files here.

Layla's.

Her name was Layla.

I needed to remember that.

"I'll set up our own surveillance, boss," Eli murmured, shrugging off his heavy snow jacket. None of us liked the snow or cold. We were all tropical climate people. The frosty, isolated location totally suited Leon Marx, though. Cold bastard that he was.

"What do you want us doing?" Cyryl asked, taking a few more steps into the vaulted living room and peering around. "Should we... clean up or something? Not that I'm interested in helping this Guild piece of shit, but I don't really want glass in my foot."

I sighed. "Good point. Yes, do that. You too, Jae."

Jae groaned but tossed his bag onto the couch and went in search of supplies. Or I assumed that was what he was doing. He might just be heading to the bathroom for a shit to avoid cleaning.

I took the opportunity to do some snooping around, but there were very few personal touches in Leon's home, not that it surprised me. He didn't strike me as the kind of guy who had personal attachments to fucking *anything*. Upstairs, I found his office—the computer securely passworded and biometric-locked—and several bedrooms. Most were clean and tidy, one contained an already snoring Moana, and one, the largest, was just as trashed as the rest of the house. Splatters of blood decorated the carpet and rumpled white bedding, and fury burned hot through my veins.

He'd hurt her. I just knew it.

All my pent-up frustration and rage snapped, and I put my fist through the wall.

Fuck. Now my knuckles were bleeding. Another thing to blame that dickhead Leon for.

Furious at myself for losing my shit, I stalked through to the bathroom to wash the drywall powder out of my cuts. I ran my hand under the water, then froze when I glanced up at the mirror.

Yeah, he'd hurt her... and she'd taunted him to chase her. Shit. Did she write that note in *blood*? And were those lip prints? Sick bitch. And yet my dick was getting hard just picturing her scrawling that message.

"Dammit, Danny," I muttered, staring at the dried blood of her lip prints. "Where the hell are you?"

"Did you punch a hole in my fucking wall?" an outraged voice jerked me out of my trance.

I scowled, eyeing Leon standing casually inside his bedroom

beside where I'd put my fist through his wall. "How the fuck did you get in here without my team seeing you?"

Leon just gave me a disgusted look. "It's my house. Fuck, you really are as stupid as you look, aren't you?"

Scathing comebacks burned on my tongue, but I'd come here with a plan, and killing Leon—no matter how satisfying that would be—wasn't part of it. So I gritted my teeth and drew a calming breath before responding.

"We need to work together," I told him with a thick undercurrent of frustration. "It's been six days, and we have *no* clue where she is or who took her."

Leon scoffed. "Speak for yourself. Get out of there, I need a shower. That was a long fucking flight."

I shifted out of the bathroom, just enough to let him in. But I didn't give him privacy... fuck that. I'd already seen his pierced dick—with Danny's lips wrapped around it—so he had nothing to shock me with now.

"From where?" I demanded. "What was so important that you needed to take care of *before* coming here?"

He gave me a considering look, then shrugged and stripped out of his clothes. He clearly had no issues being naked, so I refused to be the insecure one by looking away.

"I had to go take care of the prick who killed Judith. It's what Danny would want me to do, and I didn't want to give him a chance to disappear before I caught him." He stepped into the shower, closing the glass door that obscured nothing. Fucking hell, Leon must have a gym somewhere in this secluded cabin. And spend a whole lot of time in it.

Wait, what did he just say? "You killed the guy who set the fires?"

Leon shot me a dry look. "That's what I just said. Maybe if you weren't checking out my ass, you'd have heard me."

My eyes bugged and I nearly choked on my outrage. "I wasn't—"

"Sure you weren't," Leon sneered. "No offense, or whatever, but you're not my type. Besides, I'm taken."

Anger and frustration burned through me. "Listen, you sarcastic fuck, I wasn't checking out your ass. In case you forgot, I'm *also* taken by someone a whole lot sexier than your psychotic ass. Can we just focus on getting Danny back?"

"Okay, tell me your plan, genius," he taunted. "How are you getting my woman back for me?"

My fists tightened at my sides. "She's *not* your—" I broke myself off, taking a few deep breaths and reminding myself that he was deliberately baiting me.

"Look," Leon drawled, turning off the shower and stepping out. This time, I averted my eyes, so he didn't have any more snarky remarks about me looking at his dick. "Danny doesn't need saving. She proved that when you *abducted* her."

I frowned, but he was right. She could have left my island

at any time. She stayed, initially, to do her job. Then... well, shit. Then I liked to think she stayed because she was falling for me. But at no point in time had she ever really been my captive.

"That doesn't mean she doesn't need our help now," I argued, folding my arms over my chest. "She had to have been hurt when they took her. No way would she have left Stanley like that. She loves that plant like it's a human."

Leon grunted, toweling his hair dry with another wrapped around his hips. "How is the sad little tree, anyway? This weather isn't good for his variety."

My lip curled. "Obviously. I'm not stupid enough to bring him here. I dropped him off with a friend, a botanist. He'll take good care of him."

I didn't miss Leon's eye roll, but I wasn't fooled. He knew how much Danny loved Stanley, and Leon loved Danny, so ergo...

"Well, good for you," he remarked, shouldering past me to leave the bathroom.

I gritted my teeth, reminding myself over and over that I couldn't kill him. Besides the fact I needed him to help me find my siren... she was in love with him. Whoever killed him would *not* get a happily ever after, so for now, I was stuck with the sorry shit stain.

The need to save Danny made my skin itch, and Leon's casual attitude was rubbing me the wrong way. It was so at odds with how he'd reacted when *I'd* taken her... Something wasn't adding up.

"I hope you brought food with you," Leon commented, changing the subject so fast it made my head spin. "I didn't have time to call in a grocery order, and there's not enough dry stores to feed your whole fucking team. Why'd you even have to bring them with you, anyway? Were you seriously feeling so inadequate that you needed backup?"

Don't kill him. You can't kill him, Kai. Remember the biometric locks on the computers? You need this asshole.

In response, I just grunted and left the room. I needed to go fill my team in and give Eli a hard word about Leon slipping into the house undetected. Even if it was *his* house.

He followed me, of course, because god forbid I ruined his dramatic entrance. And it was dramatic indeed, though not from infuriating Leon's actions. He just calmly followed me downstairs in a pair of sweatpants and a black T-shirt, but my guys nearly tripped over each other, reaching for weapons when they saw him.

"Simmer the fuck down," I grouched, glaring at them. "If he wanted to kill you, you'd already be dead."

"True story," Leon agreed, padding over to the kitchen in bare feet, seemingly unaware that it had been scattered with glass not long ago. Or maybe he was just a freak that got off on pain like that. Either way, he made it to the fridge and pulled out a beer.

Wait. That wasn't beer.

"Soda water?" I asked aloud, confused as fuck.

Leon just stared back at me and took a gulp of his non-alcoholic, non-caffeinated beverage. If I wasn't convinced he was a psychopath before, that'd do it.

Footsteps coming down the stairs told me we'd woken my sister, and a moment later, she spotted our host standing in the kitchen.

"What the *fuck?*" she exclaimed. "That's the bastard who fired a grenade launcher at us!"

I rubbed the bridge of my nose. There was definitely a headache building. I tried to leave her and the rest of the team behind, but they weren't having it. And after Sam... I held enough guilt that I let them win that argument.

"I'm sure you're mistaken," Leon drawled.

Mo glared daggers, parking her hands on her hips. "I'm sure I'm not."

Leon huffed an irritated sigh. "Listen... whoever you are, if I'd fired a bazooka *at* you, then you wouldn't be standing in my house throwing around wild accusations. Now, if you're saying I fired a bazooka *near* you, well, then take a fucking number. You weren't the first, and you won't be the last. It really drives home whatever point I'm making, you know?"

Mo's jaw dropped, like she had no clue what to even do

with that response. Yeah, Leon was nuts, but I was getting used to it.

"Who even *are* you?" Leon asked, taking a step closer to my sister and raking his gaze over her from head to toe. "You look vaguely familiar…"

"She's my sister," I snarled, giving him a hard warning glare.

Leon just tipped his head to the side, considering Mo. "Mmm, yes, that. But that's not what I meant. Why are you *here*, Kai's sister? Why do you care about helping a Guild agent who pulled the wool over all your eyes so very effectively? Hmm?"

I was itching to intervene, but Moana was a big girl. She could handle herself.

Her chin tipped up and her eyes blazed with stubborn defiance. "I'm her *friend*, that's who. You're just a—"

"No, you're not," Leon cut her off. "She's got two friends, and one just got murdered. No offense, gorgeous, but you're not a honey-blonde stripper named Sabine either."

Before that argument could deteriorate into bitch slaps and hair pulling, a loud ringtone peeled through the room. I arched a brow in question, scanning my team, but it was Leon who pulled a phone from his pocket and answered it.

The prick had the audacity to hold up a finger to me, telling me to be quiet while he listened to what the caller had to say, then a sly smile twisted his lips. Suspicion rippled through me.

"What?" I demanded, even though he was still on the phone. "What do you know?"

Leon gave a sigh and rolled his eyes. "Do you mind? This is private and nothing to do with you." He started stalking away from us all, heading for the stairs, but was deliberately loud and clear when he replied to the caller on his phone. "You found her? Fantastic. Send me the location immediately."

"What the *fuck*?" I roared, storming after him. "You said she didn't need rescuing!"

"I lied," he called back, flipping me off over his shoulder and continuing up to the second level.

I stormed up after him, hearing a door slam, but I was too slow. The fucker had shut himself in his office and locked the door.

"Leon, I swear to god, if you don't open this door, I will kick it the fuck down!" I bellowed, rage making me see red.

From the other side of the door, the clicking sound of rapid keystrokes reached my ears. "Oh no, I'm so worried," Leon called back, sounding positively *bored*. "Be sure to kick it really hard, I wouldn't want you failing. How embarrassing, and in front of your sister too."

Enraged, I gave a roar of anger and slammed my foot against the door… then gave a yelp of pain. Motherfucker had a steel-core door on his office.

Fuck, I hated him.

9
DANNY

Carol left for her meeting that afternoon, seemingly without hesitation. She made it clear that I wasn't a prisoner, nor would she force me to stay against my will. If I wanted to go, I had my pick of cars within her garage... but the subtext was loud and clear.

She *wanted* me to stay.

But why? I was a grown-ass woman now, not a child who needed her mommy to hug her and chase away the monsters at night. What was the point of asking me to hang around? Carol had an ulterior motive; I was sure of it. And I was curious enough to let it play out... because it was better than facing my own reality.

Deep down, though, I knew my time in the Hamptons was limited.

The way things had ended with Leon and Kai... I didn't believe for a second that would be the last I saw of them both. They were too stubborn, too *proud*, too fucking fixated to just accept defeat and move on. Truthfully, that was part of what I liked about them both. They would *fight* for me... and I wouldn't want it any other way.

I just needed them to choose *me* this time. I needed them to reorganize their list of priorities and put *me* at the top of the list, above their bad blood and resentment of one another. Yeah, it was arrogant of me and egotistical. But who the fuck cared? If I couldn't want that for my own happiness, no one else would.

Maybe some time and space would see them work through their issues, but I knew where my head was at. Either I kept them both, or I left them both. There would be *no* choosing for me, and they could go sit on a fucking pineapple if they thought they could force my decision anymore.

Carolina—who Koen still insisted wasn't related to us— barely gave me the time of day when I ran into her in the hallway that afternoon. It didn't bother me. She clearly felt threatened, and I'd be gone before she needed to really confront her issues.

There were a few staff working in Carol's house but not as many as I'd expected from someone with her obvious status and wealth. Few enough that they were rarely seen, but when I wandered into the expansive kitchen after a workout, there was a full roast dinner laid out on plates under the warming lamps.

Koen joined me to eat, then asked me to play more video games with him before bed. I agreed because he was just enjoyable to be around. He was a *kid*... something I'd never been. I was envious and fascinated and just couldn't get enough of his energy.

I kept his age in mind, though, turning the console off at a reasonable hour and telling him to go to bed. He snarked at me for being old but did as he was told. Fucking cutie.

Sleep was somewhat more elusive for me, though. The article about Carol Atwood's long-lost daughter had been printed that afternoon, and I could practically feel the minutes ticking past as I waited for *someone* to show up. But who would be first? Part of me wanted Blanchet to take the bait... even though I knew he wouldn't.

Somewhere past midnight, I threw the covers back and got up. I'd seen some good spirits in Carol's bar; maybe that'd help relax my mind.

I made it only a few steps down the hall when I heard the low murmur of voices, and I paused a moment. It was a man's voice... a *familiar* man's voice. And... Carol's?

Frowning, I continued somewhat more cautiously. Was that *Leon*?

Ready for anything, I followed the voices all the way to Carol's office, where I found her seated at her desk, with my freshly dumped lover sitting casually opposite her. He had an ankle hooked over his knee, looking totally relaxed as I paused in the doorway.

"Seven days, Marx," I commented, propping my hands on my hips. "You're losing your edge."

His lips tugged up in a grin, and his intense gaze raked over me from head to toe. I was wearing those tiny satin pajama shorts and lace camisole, and his perusal was like a physical touch.

"Oh, don't be too hard on him," Carol commented with a smirk. "I had him chasing his tail a bit with some false leads and dummy servers."

Leon's expression turned sharp and angry. "And here I was thinking Carol Atwood had the worst security in the history of the Circle." He stood up from his seat and crossed the space between us in three quick strides. "Fuck, I missed you."

His lips were on mine before I could process what was going on, and I melted into his kiss. Yes, I was the one who walked away, but it didn't mean I suddenly stopped loving him. So I kissed him back, moaning when his tongue met mine, and his teeth scraped my lip. Damn it, Leon was *addictive*, and I hadn't fully processed how bad my withdrawal was until now.

"Should I give you two a minute?" Carol offered in a dry voice, and I had to force myself to stop kissing Leon.

"Yes," he replied without hesitation, leaning back in to kiss me again, but this time I dodged.

"No. Sorry," I corrected him. "Dare I ask where Kai is?" *Had he given up?*

"Is that this one?" Carol asked, pointing at the floor beside her desk.

I separated myself from Leon—albeit reluctantly—and moved closer to Carol's desk, spotting a pair of legs first before seeing a whole-ass man unconscious on the carpet.

My lips parted in shock, and I turned my questioning gaze at Carol, who shrugged.

"He was a touch too aggressive for my liking," she told me, unapologetic, "so I Tasered him."

Unable to ignore the worry running through me, I crouched beside Kai's unconscious form and checked his pulse. "How strong is your Taser, Carol?" I murmured in shock.

Leon just snickered. Of course he did, fucking troublemaker. "He's fine, DeLuna. A big boy like him can handle a few volts."

"And maybe he will learn a few lessons in manners for the trouble," Carol added, smiling sweetly. "Now, as for you two breaking into my house in the middle of the night to *rescue* Danny…"

I quirked a brow at Leon. "Do I look like I need rescuing?"

"I tried to tell him," Carol said, and Leon gave an exasperated sigh.

"For the record, beautiful, I never thought you *needed* saving. Just that you might *like* it. It was the meathead who decided that you were being held captive here." He gave Kai a pointed look, then refocused on me. "Since you quite literally ran out in the middle of a conversation a week ago, I thought it was only polite to track you down to set the record straight."

Amusement pricked at my chest, and I had to bite back a grin. But goddamn, it made me happy to see his crazy ass.

"Perhaps we can speak in private?" Leon suggested. It probably wasn't a bad idea, considering the way he was looking at me… like he was barely restraining the need to strip me naked and bend me over Carol's desk.

A shiver ran through me, and I nodded. "We can talk in my room," I offered. "Can you carry Kai? I'm strong, but not *that* strong." The unconscious man groaned on the floor, and Leon snickered another laugh. Shithead.

Still, Leon did as I asked and hauled Kai up off the ground, slinging him over his shoulder in a fireman's grip.

Carol slid open her desk drawer and handed me a Glock 19 and two pairs of handcuffs. "Just in case you need them, sweetheart," she murmured. "I'll let my security know to stand down. You can handle yourself."

I frowned at her casual use of endearment—*we were nowhere near that stage, Carol*—but happily took the gun and handcuffs. There were plenty of things they might be useful for, even if the boys were behaving themselves.

Cautious not to wake the whole house up, I gave Leon a nod and led the way back to my bedroom, holding the door open for him to carry Kai inside. I closed it softly as Leon dumped Kai none too gently onto my messy bed.

"How hard did Carol Taser him?" I asked with concern,

nudging Leon out of the way to place a hand on Kai's cheek. His skin was warm but not clammy, and he sighed in his sleep as I stroked his face. Maybe he was just snoozing, as highly unlikely as that was.

Leon smirked, grabbing one pair of handcuffs out of my waistband where I'd tucked them. "She zapped him a couple of times. He wasn't getting the message, but that's nothing new." He deftly cuffed Kai's limp wrist to the bedframe and gave me an innocent look when I frowned. "What?"

I stifled an eye roll. "Bunny, why are you cuffing him? He's unconscious."

He shrugged. "Yeah, for now. But he'll wake up soon and might be aggressive, so I'd rather not take chances that he accidentally punches you." He took the second pair of cuffs, securing Kai's other wrist. "Besides, it'll be funny."

I shouldn't have expected anything less. Actually, no, that comment seemed streaked with *amusement* rather than malice. Or had I imagined that? Shit, maybe I was just overtired and reading too much into things.

Running a hand through my hair, I gave a sigh. "So, you found me."

Leon straightened up, Kai seemingly forgotten as he looped an arm around my waist. I hadn't moved away after checking Kai, so it was all too easy for Leon to reel me in. Not that I was complaining.

"Of course, I found you, *ma moitié,*" he said in a low, husky voice. His eyes burned through me, like he was peering into my soul, and his free hand cupped my cheek. Shit, that new endearment sent electric eels into a frenzy within me... *ma moitié,* my other half.

Words failed me, and I just gave a small gasp before his lips met mine once more. His kiss started gentle, *loving,* but when I sighed and parted my lips, letting him in, it turned intense. Hot. Scorching hot.

His hand shifted from my cheek to my hair, his fingers tangling with my locks and his teeth scraping my lower lip. I moaned when he sucked my tongue into his mouth, and he pulled me closer so our whole bodies were touching. I'd never hated clothing as much as I did right then.

"Leon," I groaned as his other hand slipped between my shorts and camisole, his long fingers teasing the skin of my waist. "We shouldn't—"

"Yes, we should," he cut me off, his voice rough and firm. His arm banded around my waist, and my feet left the floor. Damn, he was tall when I wasn't in heels. Okay, fine, he was also tall when I was in heels, but it was a shit load more noticeable in bare feet.

A small squeak of surprise escaped my throat as Leon tossed me onto the bed—throwing me *over* Kai—then pounced on top of me. I allowed myself a moment of indulgence, eagerly kissing him back and wrapping my leg around his body. Because I *missed* him. The fact that he'd come for me, that they'd both come to "rescue" me... it meant a lot. So much that I couldn't quite find the words.

So for a moment—or ten—I just took my time making out with him, remembering how fucking *good* we were together. But when Kai let out a pained groan, I reluctantly pushed Leon away and flipped us over, pinning *him* to the mattress instead.

"Marx," I groaned, licking my lips. He gazed up at me with raw hunger, and my pussy throbbed in response. Traitor. "We should talk."

He dragged his lower lip through his teeth, his gaze devouring me as his hips rolled beneath me. God damn it all to hell, he was *so* hard. "So talk," he taunted, "I can multitask."

My resolve weakened, and he sensed it. Leon was never one to pass up an opportunity, so a breath later, he'd reversed our positions, pinning me down. Kai gave another pained groan, waking up, and I bucked against Leon's grip.

"Bunny, for fuck's sake," I growled, but it morphed into a moan when he rolled his hips and ground his cock against my throbbing cunt.

His sly smirk dripped in satisfaction. "DeLuna, my heart, we're talking, remember?"

"What the shit?" Kai mumbled, frowning and blinking at us right beside him on the bed. Confused, he tugged his wrists and found them cuffed. "Hey—"

Smack. Leon knocked him out again.

I gasped, and Leon just sat back on his heels. "What?" he asked innocently. "I didn't want interruptions while we sorted our shit out."

10
DANNY

It was unnecessary how hard he punched Kai. And right after he'd been Tasered with fuck knew how many volts to knock him out for that long, too. Maybe a few months ago, I'd find that kind of aggressive, competitive shit sexy. But the rivalry between Kai and Leon was exactly why I'd left.

Irritation washed through me instead of arousal. Okay, fine. *As well as.* But it was enough to make me give Leon a hard shove and clamber off the bed away from him.

"You didn't need to do that," I snapped, scowling my anger and ignoring my desire. "Don't even try and pretend you knocked him out so we can talk privately. That was purely selfish. You two clearly haven't sorted anything out in the last week."

Leon stood up, his brows raised like he was offended by my accusation. "DeLuna, we're here *together*, aren't we? And he's still breathing, with all his fingers and toes still attached to his body. Surely you can see the progress we've made?"

I mean... I guess he had a point there. Still frowning, I ran my gaze over him from head to toe, instinctively checking for injuries. Then I checked Kai over. Other than the swelling coming up on his face, he seemed unscathed. And they'd had a week without me playing referee...

"You still didn't need to punch him," I huffed, biting the inside of my cheek to keep from softening. Leon's unique brand of logic and reason was so hard to resist. "I'm going to grab him an ice pack. Don't... just don't do anything. Sit there, don't move." I pointed to the chair. "Understood?"

Leon gave me a mock salute and sat down where he'd been told. "Yes, ma'am."

He sat down, the picture of innocence, and I narrowed my eyes. He was up to something. But I was too twitchy and annoyed to examine it further, so I gave him a warning glare before leaving the room.

The rest of the house was still dead silent and dark, but in the kitchen, I found Carol sitting at the island and reading some papers. She had a bowl of cereal in front of her and a coffee in hand.

"Everything okay?" she asked, seemingly unconcerned by the

break-in.

I nodded, opening the freezer in search of an ice pack. I found them easily in a drawer on the top shelf and pulled one out before replying, "Everyone's alive, if that's what you mean."

Carol flicked me a grin. "Which one of them are you involved with?"

I wet my lips. "Both of them, of course. You've seen them; could *you* choose?"

She barked a sharp laugh. "Good point. I'm surprised *those two* are willing to share, that's all. From all accounts, neither one of them has a history of healthy, stable relationships. Lots of childhood trauma that will have shaped their personalities, particularly for Leon. His mother deserves a special corner of hell for her brand of evil."

I paused. "You knew her?"

Carol inclined her head. "Professionally, yes. She was…" She trailed off with a wince. "She got what she deserved, in the end."

I dragged my teeth over my lower lip. "Does that mean it's true, then? Leon is on the Circle?"

Her answering look was totally unreadable. Then she sipped her coffee and shifted her gaze back to her paperwork. "If he is, I hope he would tell the woman he loves. Maybe he can spare himself the mistake of so many other Circle members… *if* he is one."

Oh, because that was so helpful. It only left me curious about what mistakes Carol herself regretted. Maybe about Koen's dad? But I had my own shit to iron out before asking about hers, so I gave her a tight smile and headed back to my room.

"Seriously?" I hissed when I closed the door behind me.

Leon was sitting in the chair where I'd told him to wait, his eyes wide in question. "What? I'm still here."

My eyes narrowed, and I shook my head as I moved over to Kai on the bed. "Uh-huh, and Kai drew a fake mustache on his own face with eyeliner? Fucking hell, Marx, what are you, ten?" Because I could totally see Koen doing some childish shit like that.

Leon chuckled. "Babe, I'm still sitting here where you left me." Technically true, but it didn't mean he hadn't gotten up. "Besides, don't you think I'd have drawn a penis on his face?"

I couldn't even argue with him like this. He was too fucking funny when I was trying to be mad. When I *was* mad at him. Unless there was a house-elf hiding out under the bed with an eyeliner pencil.

Letting out a long sigh, I gently held the ice pack to Kai's swollen cheek and eye, and he gave a low groan.

"Why are you here, anyway?" I asked Leon over my shoulder. "I thought I made myself pretty clear when I dumped you both in Shadow Grove."

He hooked his ankle up on his knee, tipping his head to the side thoughtfully. "*Mon cœur,* you ran away without waiting for us to come to a compromise. Then we found the wreckage of a crash and your precious Stanley left behind. You really think we would just shrug our shoulders and say, 'Oh well, she left us, not our problem'? I'm sure I've told you before, but maybe you didn't really *hear* me. I *love* you, Danny DeLuna. You're my reason for breathing… of *course* I tracked you down."

Oof, my heart. It thumped so hard inside my chest that it actually hurt. Also… *Stanley*.

At a loss for words, I bit my lip and shifted my attention back to Kai. Shit, it wasn't just a mustache, it was a little goatee too. Fucking Leon, trying to make me laugh when I was angry.

"That doesn't change the reason why I left," I eventually said, keeping the ice pack on Kai's cheek even as I turned my face to Leon. "I won't be forced into making a decision I don't want to make."

Leon spread his hands wide. "And you made that point very clear by running away with your anthropomorphized plant."

Guilt reverberated through me, and I shifted to sit on the bed so I could see Leon better. "How is he?" I asked in a pained whisper. "Did he…"

Leon stared back at me, and I half expected him to make fun of my attachment to a potted plant. But he didn't. "Stanley is recovering with a friend of Kai's. A botanist, he said. He's getting the best help a plant can get." He winced as he said that. "And they call *me* crazy."

I flipped him my middle finger and glared. "Fuck you. I'm not crazy. I'm *lonely*. There's a difference."

His gaze flared hot. "Not anymore, you're not. You've got me, *always*. And *him* too, I guess." He curled a sneer at Kai, who was *still* unconscious. Or maybe he was just faking it to listen in… it was something I would do.

It wasn't lost on me that Leon had just included Kai as

something more than a passing inconvenience, though. I tilted my head, studying Leon closely. "And you're okay with that? With Kai being in my life?"

Leon's jaw tensed. "Our life."

I blinked in shock. "Sorry?"

He let out a frustrated sigh. "He's not in *your* life, he's in *our* life. And no, hell no, I'm not okay with it. But you know what I'm less okay with? Losing you."

Christ, he knew *just* what to say to win me over. I was all lightheaded and tingly already but couldn't just let him off the hook so easily. Could I? After all, he'd just punched Kai in the face for *no* good reason.

An evil idea popped into my brain, and the corner of my lips tipped up with a smile.

"What are you thinking right now, beautiful?" he asked with intensity.

It wasn't lost on me that he hadn't moved from the chair I'd told him to sit in. Aside from his little mischief with the eyeliner while I was gone, he was proving he could follow directions by not getting up from his seat. So far.

Glancing down at Kai, I placed the ice pack aside and touched my cold fingers to his throat. His pulse was quick, and if I watched carefully, his breathing was a touch too shallow for actual sleep.

"I'm thinking...," I said slowly, trailing my finger down the front of Kai's top, "that you need to learn a lesson for bad behavior, Marx."

A grin pulled Leon's lips. "You gonna spank me, DeLuna?"

I scoffed. He looked way too into that idea. "Somehow, I don't know if that'd be the punishment it was intended as." My finger hooked under Kai's belt, tugging it free of the buckle. His body gave a tiny jerk when I unzipped his jeans, but it was enough to make me grin. Asleep or not, he was getting hard.

"DeLuna…" Leon growled. "Don't…"

I turned to look at him again, even as my fingers circled Kai's rapidly hardening dick, freeing it to continue rising. "Don't what, Leon? Don't test the pretty words you're throwing my way? Don't deliver some consequences for throwing a punch at an already unconscious man? Hmm?" My grip on Kai's cock shifted, and I stroked him, reveling in the way he thickened under my touch.

Leon's expression burned with anger, jealousy, frustration, and *desire*. His hands gripped the arms of the chair like he wanted to rip them off. I held his gaze as I moved to straddle Kai's legs, my intentions pretty fucking clear by now.

"Dammit, DeLuna," Leon muttered.

"Don't," I snapped as he started to stand up. "I told you to sit the fuck down, so *sit the fuck down*. Consider this a warning to play nicer if you want me back."

Leon's butt hit the chair, and I ran my tongue up Kai's length.

"I think I'd prefer it if you spanked me," Leon admitted, the frustration dripping from his words. But he did as he was told and stayed in the chair. Good boy.

I smiled, then swirled my tongue around the head of Kai's cock. "I know you would," I replied. "But this is more fun." My lips closed over Kai's tip, and his eyes shot open, locking with mine.

"Holy fuck," he murmured, his voice thick with sleep.

I held his gaze as I sucked, my tongue flicking the tight line of skin on the underside. He jerked against the handcuffs, then looked up in bewilderment. "What the hell? Why am I handcuffed? *Fuck*, why does my face hurt so much?"

"Really? Those are the questions you wanna be asking right now?" Leon snapped back. "You just woke up with your dick in my woman's mouth, but you wanna know why you're handcuffed. Honestly, DeLuna, his priorities are fucked. Just come over here and sit on my face."

"Shut up, Leon," Kai barked.

"Hush, Bunny," I said at the same time, stroking Kai with my fist so I could glare at Leon. "You know why you're there."

Kai laughed, then gasped as I deep throated him. My mouth robbed him of speech, and I took my time in Leon's punishment. I moaned around the thick cock in my mouth and shifted onto my knees to get a better angle as I took him deep, over and over.

"Alright, point taken," Leon snarled some minutes later. "Can I get up now?"

"Hell no," Kai groaned, bucking his hips to try and increase my pace. "Stay the fuck over there."

It was impolite to talk with a full mouth, so I said nothing, waiting to see what they'd do. Leon met my eyes, staring intensely like he was checking if he had my permission. Then he smirked at Kai and stood up.

"I don't take orders from you, *Big Man*." He strode over to us, his hands clamping down on my hips where I'd been waggling my ass in the air. My satin sleep shorts came down in one swift motion, and he didn't even bother getting them past my knees before sinking two fingers into my aching cunt.

I shuddered and groaned, pushing back onto his hand as my pussy fluttered in excitement. Tightening my fingers around Kai's base, I sucked on his tip like a lollipop, tipping my head so I could meet his eyes.

The expression on his face was torn, tortured, and he strained so hard against the handcuffs that a thin line of blood ran down one strong, tattooed forearm. Shit, that shouldn't be such a turn-on.

"*Mon cœur,*" Leon murmured, pumping his fingers into my pussy forcefully as his teeth scraped the flesh of my bum. "You're aching for more, aren't you? I can feel how tight you're gripping my fingers, babe. You want my cock, don't you, beautiful?"

Was it that obvious? Fuck yes, I did.

"I'm not okay with this," Kai protested without any real conviction. His hips were rocking, pushing his dick into my mouth desperately.

Leon scoffed, and the mattress dipped with his weight.

"Tough shit, Malachi, because this arrangement has DeLuna so wet she's practically dripping."

I mean… he wasn't wrong. My eyes fluttered shut as he pulled his fingers from my core, dragging my own slickness over my clit as he lined up his pierced tip.

"Oh fuck," Kai groaned, biting his lip *hard* as he stared down at me.

Leon pushed into me slowly, letting me feel every delicious inch stretching my walls, and I needed to slip Kai free of my mouth so I could drag some deep gasps of air.

"You feel so good, *mon cœur*," Leon purred as he slid deeper. His index finger toyed with my clit, just enough to make me quake with intense arousal but not enough to make me come… yet. He was edging me. "Fuck, I missed this pussy. Sweetest damn pussy."

Kai swallowed heavily as I whimpered and licked my lips. My hand was still stroking his saliva-soaked shaft, and his abs were all tensed up like he was holding off his climax.

"Shit," he whispered. "Is this what you want, *kaikohuru iti?* You want us both?"

I swallowed and nodded firmly. "More than anything."

Rocking my hips against Leon, I closed my lips around Kai once more, spurring them both into motion. I knew Kai meant *in bed*, but I meant *forever*. That strength of certainty, that feeling of vulnerability… it scared the shit out of me. So I distracted them both.

Not that either of them needed much encouragement. Kai was already *so* damn close to finishing that I just toyed with him, dragging it out as Leon fucked me hard and fast from behind. When I felt the pulse and twitch of Kai's cock in my mouth, I let him slip out and parted my lips wide.

He grunted and cursed as he watched himself spurt directly into my mouth, coating my tongue in his seed and not spilling a drop. When he was done, I made a show of swallowing, then just held his gaze as Leon slammed into me, harder and harder.

Within moments, my own orgasm crashed over me. My inner muscles locked up, and I cried out, my eyes closing tight. Leon joined me a second later, his hips jerking against me as he pumped me full of his release.

For a moment, the only sound in the room was our combined heavy breathing. Then Leon pulled out, shifting off the bed even as he grasped my cheeks and spread me open.

"Fuck, that's sexy," he muttered. Then he gave my ass a playful swat. "Did I pass your test, babe?"

I smiled at Kai's confusion, then tipped my head at Leon. "For now."

Leon gave a small nod, accepting my answer. Then he cast a sly look at Kai. "Shouldn't he have to prove he's a *team player* too?"

"The fuck is that supposed to mean?" Kai growled. The side of his face was puffy and red but shouldn't bruise *too* badly.

Post-climax haze made my brain a bit slow, because I wasn't even following Leon's evil train of thought until he spelled it out. "Sit on his face, gorgeous. Make him make you come again before you unlock those cuffs."

11
LEON

My woman was a dirty, dirty girl. As if I hadn't already worked that out from the way she got off on being the meat in a man sandwich or how she'd squirmed and creamed herself on the stage at Meow Lounge. But the way her eyes lit up when I challenged her to sit on Kai's face, to make him eat her out while she was dripping *my* cum? Fucking glorious.

Kai's shocked expression was just icing on that cake, and I smirked in his direction. *Put your money where your mouth is, dickhead.*

To my immense displeasure, though, a knock on the

bedroom door interrupted the tense mood, and Danny quickly pulled her little satin shorts back up, hiding that perfect ass and dripping cunt from view. Damn it.

"Uncuff him," she ordered me in a hard voice, then gave us both a pointed look. "And stay quiet... or there will be trouble."

I couldn't help the sly smile curling my lips, although the way her eyes narrowed said she was more likely to *withhold* sex than get kinky if we disobeyed. So I rolled my eyes and grabbed the handcuff key where I'd left it beside the bed.

Danny went to answer the door, only opening it an inch and blocking the room with her body.

"What do you want, squirt?" she asked someone, her tone friendly and *warm*. Who the fuck was at the door?

The response was muffled and quiet, but I chuckled when I made out what was said, nonetheless. Kai clearly couldn't hear as well as me, because he elbowed me as I uncuffed one wrist.

"Who is it?" he whispered, jerking his head to the door where my woman was replying to her guest in a hushed voice.

I shrugged, unlocking his other wrist. "Dunno, but whoever it was got woken up by Danny's *nightmare*." I snickered, her sweet moans and cries still ringing in my ears. I would never get enough of that, no matter how long I lived.

The grin that flashed across Kai's face was every bit as sly as I was feeling, even as he sat up and fixed his pants. He gave a grimace when he saw the blood on his wrist, then picked up the ice pack that Danny had dropped on the bed.

"You're a cunt, Marx," he muttered. "So we're clear, I hate you."

I scoffed quietly. "Bullshit. You just woke up getting your dick sucked, so I think you meant *thank you*."

He grunted, a stupid smile sitting on his lips. Not that I blamed him, I was feeling pretty jovial myself. A good nut had that effect, and blowing it in Danny's perfect cunt just made it a hundred times better.

She closed the door firmly, spinning around to face us with her cheeks stained pink in embarrassment. "I can't believe that just happened," she whispered in a strangled voice. "You're both *shitty* influences, and you damn well know it."

"Are you blushing, *ātaahua*?" Kai asked, entertained as fuck. He held the ice against his face—pussy—but otherwise seemed just *fine*.

Danny glared daggers at him. "Yes," she hissed, "because my ten-year-old brother just heard me getting spit-roasted."

"Technically," I drawled, "for a spit-roast—"

"Shut up," she snapped. "I'm going to shower. Then you and I are going to have a conversation." That was directed at Kai. *Hah, suck it, asshole. Your turn to face the music.*

He looked slightly worried, then fired a menacing look in my direction. "What about crazy-pants?"

Danny arched a brow and propped her hands on her hips. "We've already talked, but that doesn't let you off the hook." Without explaining that any further, she stalked through to the bathroom and slammed the door shut. Then locked it.

Damn. I guess that wasn't an invitation to join her then?

For a moment, neither Kai nor I spoke. Then the sound of the shower running snapped us both out of the weird trance we'd fallen into with Danny's exit.

"What'd you say to her?" he asked suspiciously, rubbing at his wrists. "And where the fuck are we? I thought she was being held *captive*, but this is…" He trailed off, looking around at the bedroom.

I shook my head, fixing my belt. "Told you she didn't need saving."

Kai gave an outraged sound, rising up from the bed. "What? *You* are the one who tracked her down!"

Damn right I was, and he'd do well to remember it. Useless fuck. "Still doesn't mean she needed saving." I reached for the door handle to leave the bedroom.

"Whoa, bro, where the fuck are you going?"

"To find another bathroom and take a piss, is that alright with you? Or did you wanna help hold my dick? I saw you checking out my magic cross." I sent him a leering wink, amused at the disgusted look on his face. He had no idea how to respond to those taunts, and it entertained the fuck out of me.

When he offered no verbal response, I let myself out of the room and closed the door carefully behind me. Despite the fact that I gave zero shits about anyone else's comfort, this *brother* that Danny mentioned seemed to mean a lot to her. So I stayed quiet as I strolled through the enormous house.

Fucking Carol. She'd been hiding right in plain sight. I couldn't *believe* she'd fooled me with those dummy servers and heavily edited personal files. Having met her now, in the flesh, the resemblance to Danny was *unmistakable*.

In my research into the Circle members, her photo had been ever so subtly Photoshop edited. At a glance, it was still her, but the key features had all been tweaked. Her jaw line, the tilt of her nose, the shape of her eyes... but mostly her hair and eye color. In her file, she had blue/green eyes and a darker shade of blonde hair. In person? Her hair and eyes were *identical* to Danny's.

I was kicking myself that I'd been fooled by her seemingly crappy cyber security. Of *course* a member of the Circle would be better than that. I'd gotten too cocky, thinking no one could fool me. The only saving grace was that Carol seemed to want Danny alive, which was more than could be said for other Circle members.

"Who the hell are you?" a kid asked when I entered the kitchen.

I paused, eyeing the child. White-blond hair, sapphire eyes, dark lashes. "Your sister's boyfriend."

The kid screwed his face up and made a gagging sound. "Gross. I thought she was cooler than that. What are you doing in here without her then?"

Sassy little shit. Must be genetic.

"Making her a coffee," I informed him, contrary to the bullshit I'd just fed Kai about looking for a bathroom. Just because I told Danny I wouldn't kill him didn't mean I wasn't going to one-up him every freaking chance I got. And Danny loved coffee.

The boy gave a sage nod. "Good thinking. I'm Koen, by the way." He stuck his skinny little hand out to shake mine, and I smiled.

"Koen. I'm Leon." I shook his hand. He had a strong grip for such a scrawny fuck.

The kid flashed me a toothy grin. "You hurt Danny, and I'll kill you, got it?"

I swallowed hard to keep myself from laughing and gave him a solemn nod in response. "Got it."

He squinted at me for a moment, like he was trying to figure out if I was making fun of him. Then eventually relaxed. "Good. Then I'll show you where Mom keeps the good coffee, not the crap Carolina drinks."

Amused as all hell, I let the child show me around the kitchen and went to work making breakfast for my love. If her chat with Kai went as smoothly as mine, she would be done soon. But knowing how bullheaded and tactless the big moron was, it was probably going to go badly.

"Here," I said to Koen, who was sitting at the counter watching me cook. He was eating a bowl of brightly colored cereal. So bad for him. "Eat this instead of that crap."

I slid a plate of parmesan and chive scrambled eggs, crispy bacon, and toasted croissant over to him and snatched the plastic cereal away.

"If you insist," the kid muttered, but the grin on his face said he was more than happy with the swap. He filled his mouth, then barely chewed before talking again. "Do you kill people?"

It was muffled around all the food, but I understood.

Quirking a brow, I examined the child harder. Nothing about him said he was getting any kind of Guild training from his mother. He was too relaxed and open, not even remotely guarding his expression. More than that, he had that unfakeable glow of being well-adjusted and *happy*.

There was no reason to lie, though, so I nodded. "Yep."

Koen swallowed his food and hummed a thoughtful sound. "I figured. My mom does, too. She never admits it to me, but I can tell."

Well, he wasn't wrong there. Carol was a ruthless bitch, when she wanted to be. Her besting my hacker skills was still burning at the back of my mind. I hated being humbled, despite the fact I knew I was far from perfect. Sometimes I messed up, sometimes I didn't dig deep enough. Usually, it was when I was distracted... often by obsessive thoughts about Danny DeLuna.

"Do you love her?" Koen asked, shaking me out of my thoughts. I gave him a small frown of confusion, and he elaborated. "Danny, I mean. Do you *love* her? Would you kill *for her?*"

"Unquestionably," I replied without hesitation. "There is nothing and no one I wouldn't destroy to keep her safe and happy."

The child nodded again. "Cool." He ate some more breakfast, and I stared in bewilderment. "Are you taking her away today?"

"Yes," I confirmed. "We've got things to do that can't be done here."

Koen looked sad at that but not shocked. "Will she be able to stay in touch?"

I scratched the bridge of my nose, glancing past him to lock eyes with Danny in the corridor. She'd just been about to walk in when she'd paused to listen.

"I don't see why not," I replied, feeling... *something*. Warm. It was unusual and made my skin all prickly, but it wasn't horrible. "You like her?"

Koen nodded firmly. "She's my sister. What's not to like?"

Danny pressed her hand to her mouth, her eyes huge and round as she stared at the back of Koen's head. Were those *tears* in her eyes? Surely not. Still, I couldn't fault the kid for his instincts. He'd only known my love a few days and was already fiercely protective of her.

Maybe there was more to be said for blood bonds than I ever realized.

12
DANNY

Kai was one *infuriating* son of a bitch when he wanted to be. I took my sweet ass time in the shower and found him waiting for me like a naughty schoolboy when I got out. I foolishly thought he would accept responsibility for being a selfish, chest-beating caveman, like Leon had.

Stupid. Fucking. Me. Kai was *way* too arrogant to roll over and show his belly that easily.

I ended up storming out before I said something hurtful and untrue, following my nose to the kitchen. Maybe the cook had started early?

As I drew closer, I slowed down. That wasn't the cook's voice coming from the kitchen, it was Leon's. And Koen's. Oh crap.

I rounded the corner just as I heard Koen ask Leon if we would be leaving, and stopped dead in my tracks. There was so much vulnerability in my little brother's voice, and my heart ached. We'd only spent a couple of days together, but I already knew I couldn't just walk away and never think of him again. Little shit was part of me now.

When he asked Leon if I would stay in touch, my heart almost broke. I'd never had *family* before… The *only* people I'd ever cared enough to stay in touch with were my friends, Jude and Sabine. Now Jude was dead, and Sabine was in hiding. Then there was Carlos, but he'd made his feelings pretty fucking clear when he sent Stanley back with that slimy fuck Tito.

The fact that Koen *wanted* to stay in touch, that he *wanted* a relationship with me… it shocked me speechless. My eyes heated with looming tears, and I backed away before I could give myself away. Leon had seen me, but he hadn't alerted Koen.

I just needed a minute to pull myself together, so I returned to my bedroom and ran straight into Kai as he was opening the door.

"Danny, we weren't finished—" he started, then paused when he studied my face. "What happened? What's wrong?" His strong hands circled my waist, picking me up off the floor as he kicked the door shut.

I swallowed hard. "Nothing. Nothing's wrong. Kai, I'm fine."

He scowled, sitting down on the bed and placing me in his lap. "Bullshit, you look like you've seen a ghost." Horrified, he brushed a stray tear from my cheek with his thumb, then cupped my face. "Siren, baby, talk to me. Who hurt you? Was it me?"

That made me laugh, and I sniffed away the tears. "Oh trust me, Big Man, this little argument barely even scraped the surface. Not like our last discussion." I sighed, resting my forearms on his shoulders and settling in closer to him. "I'm fine, I promise. No one hurt me *today*. I just overheard Leon talking with Koen in the kitchen, and—"

"Koen?" Kai interrupted me to ask.

I smiled. "My little brother that I never knew about. He's cool, you'll like him."

His brows shot up high. "The kid that knocked on the door before? You said *brother*, but my brain wasn't working super-fast at that point. I was focusing on other things." His gaze turned heated, and it wouldn't take a genius to guess where his head had been so that he missed my revelation.

I clicked my tongue against my teeth. "Kai… if you only want me for sex, then—"

His hand clamped over my mouth, cutting off my bitter accusation. "Let's get something really fucking clear, right here and now. The moment you ran from my island, when you told me on the bridge that you felt nothing for me, then leapt into *his* waiting arms… I thought that was true pain. I didn't fully understand how much I cared for you until *right* then, and a second later you were gone."

He eased his hand off my mouth, trusting that I would hear him out. And I would. I wanted to hear these truths from him without the arrogant posturing and insatiable need to *win*.

"But what I felt then, it was *nothing* compared to the way you ripped my heart from my chest last week." He swallowed visibly, his expression sober and sincere. "I didn't see how selfish I was being until you called me out. Until you left us *both* to prove your point. I was obsessed with beating Leon simply because he is Guild… and I've spent so fucking long hating everything about the Guild. Lines got blurred, Siren. I lost sight of what was truly important. You."

It was what I wanted to hear, but I had my doubts. He wasn't built for sharing, and I wouldn't settle for anything less.

Wetting my lips, I chose my words carefully so as not to be misunderstood. "Why do you want me so badly, Kai? Honestly. Is it just a literal way to fuck the Guild for messing up Moana's life?"

His eyes widened. "Is that what you think?"

I held his gaze, refusing to back away from the hard conversations. "Do you blame me? Everything you've shared of your life, of your past, it paints a decade-long picture of hatred and vengeance. Do you even have a clear goal anymore? Or are you just taking cheap shots at the Guild whenever your mystery source slips you a tip? It's hard not to feel like you're only fucking me because of my position in the Guild."

He seemed stunned speechless, his eyes searching my face in pained disbelief.

Dread and anxiety curled through me, making me want to throw up. But I couldn't back down now. "Because, if that's *not* the reason... why are you here? Why do you want to get me back so bad that you'll actually consider *sharing* with Leon? You hate him, you hate our employer, you hate our lifestyle and careers. So *why*, Kai? *Why* are you here?"

The silence between us after I spoke that question was so tense it was hard to breathe. My ribs locked together, my skin tight, and my throat clogged as I waited to hear his response. I cared *so* much more than I ever wanted to admit. I wanted him to want *me*... but I needed to voice my doubts. The air had been murky for far too long, and if they both wanted me back so badly, it had to be cleared.

Kai took a moment to gather his thoughts, which I appreciated. He'd apparently learned from our little spat just ten minutes earlier, because he was carefully thinking through his response rather than just blurting out the first thing that came to mind.

"You think that I'm just *fucking* you out of spite," he murmured eventually. "That this is some kind of revenge on the Guild for stealing and killing my nephew."

I said nothing, and his dark eyes held my gaze steady.

"I hate that you even need to ask me this, Siren," he admitted in a husky whisper, full of distress. "I hate that my intentions toward you got so tangled up with my competitive bullshit toward Leon. The fact you've ever questioned my feelings for you, for even a second, makes me feel like the biggest fuckup known to man."

A small sigh escaped my lungs, easing a small measure of tension. "And yet," I said softly, "here we are. Leon was right when he said I didn't need rescuing. Regardless of how I got here, I *left you* willingly. So why the fuck should I take you back?"

Even in the height of the bitching and one-upping between Kai and Leon, I'd never doubted how Leon felt toward me. He wanted me for me, bloody hands and all. He had no ulterior motives; when he said he was obsessed and *loved* me... I believed him. But Kai? There was always a question in the back of my mind. He didn't "fit" like Leon and me. That was part of the reason I loved him, even if it did make me feel uneasy and open to being stabbed in the back.

Kai's brow dipped with a frown. "Why? Because I'm completely, irreparably, unconditionally in love with you, Danny. Everything you said is true, I do have a vendetta against the Guild that has soured my mind and ruled my life for years, but that has *nothing* to do with how I feel about you. Would I prefer you actually worked in a bank? Yeah, I probably would. But if you weren't a mercenary, you wouldn't be *you*. And there isn't a single thing about *you* that I don't love. I hate the Guild, and I love you. Can't both statements be true?"

Could they? For my entire life, I'd *lived* and *breathed* Guild. For the bulk of my conscious life, I'd sincerely believed Danny DeLuna and the Mercenary Guild were one and the same. But recent events had me reassessing those beliefs. Could Kai love me as deeply as he claimed and still hate the Guild?

Yes. Because I was starting to feel the same way. At least for some members of the ruling Circle, anyway.

Processing those facts, I gave a small nod. "Okay."

He looked confused. "Okay?"

My lips tilted in a smile. "Okay," I said again. "I believe you. But where does this leave you with Leon? I won't be forced into that corner again, Kai. You either accept this is a three-way thing, or we're done."

His expression darkened. "Is that what you told him, too?"

"Absolutely, it is."

Drawing a deep breath, his nostrils flared. "I refuse to lie to you, *taku aroha*, it'll take a bit longer to work through my shit with that slick fuck. Doesn't help that he keeps punching me, either."

I bit my cheek to hold back a laugh, gently stroking his bruised cheek. "I'm not asking you to date him, Kai. I'm asking you to simply accept that I love him just as much as I love you."

He stared at me for a long moment, then gave a slow nod. "I can accept that."

Relief crashed through me so hard I sagged into his hold, my face burying in his warm neck. "Thank you," I whispered. "That means more than you realize." Because it spoke volumes for the sincerity of his love, so much more than just pretty words. If he and Leon could put their grudges aside... maybe this could be something really special between us. After all, the two of them were more alike than either one of them would ever admit.

"My *kuia* used to use proverbs all the time," Kai told me, wrapping his arms around me firmly, holding me in his strong, safe embrace. "She'd constantly be trying to impart wisdom onto us, not that many of them really stuck. One did, though. It's been echoing around in my head since the moment you told us you were done."

I sat up just far enough that I could meet his gaze once more. "Yeah? What is it?"

He gave me a lopsided smile in return. "*Whāia te iti kahurangi, ki te tūohu koe, me he maunga teitei,*" he rumbled, making my skin shiver and my heart race. "It means, *seek the treasure you value most dearly, if you bow your head, let it be to a lofty mountain.* In other words, when you find the thing you want more than anything on earth, don't let anything stand in your way. That's you, Siren. My *taonga nui.*"

Oh fuck, my panties are drenched.

"That's beautiful," I replied, trying really hard to slow my racing pulse. "I bet she was an amazing woman."

Kai gave a sharp laugh. "She was tough as nails and stricter than a Catholic schoolmistress. But she loved us."

I envied him that, and a streak of sadness tainted the fizzy warmth filling me up inside. "We should probably make sure Leon isn't corrupting my little brother."

Kai shook his head, disagreeing. "No, we're not done here."

My brow quirked. "We're not? I thought…"

A sly smile touched his full lips. "The key part of a 'kiss and make up,' *ātaahua*, is the kissing."

I gave a short laugh, then smacked a quick kiss on his mouth. "Done."

"Nice try," he growled, fisting my hair and crashing his lips back against mine.

I groaned into his kiss, obediently parting my lips when he demanded entrance and melting as his tongue wrestled mine. He kissed like he wanted to consume me, like he wanted to taste my whole damn soul. It was utterly intoxicating and made my pussy flutter like the brazen ho she was.

Unsurprisingly, our kisses quickly got heated, and before I knew it, our shirts were both on the floor and I was flat on my back. Kai kissed his way down my body, toying with my nipples through my bra and making my back arch in delight.

"Kai," I gasped as he unzipped my jeans and started wiggling them down. "We should—"

"Be quick," he finished for me with a wicked grin, kissing my mound as he stripped my jeans down my legs, "and quiet, because that door isn't locked, and I want you all to myself… this time."

Well, shit, how was a girl to argue with that? She didn't, that's how. I reached for his pants, frantically yanking his belt open and shoving the denim down far enough to free his cock. Yeah, we better be quick because I needed to spend some time with Koen, and I *really* didn't need Carol walking in on this.

"Hurry," I urged him as he played with my clit, teasing me. "Kai, come on, *fuck me.*"

He gave a groan, then quickly kicked his pants off the rest of the way before hitching my legs up with his huge hands, spreading me wide for him. "One thing Leon and I can agree on," he murmured, staring down at my cunt, "this pussy is fucking perfect. So sweet and strong, the way your walls grip onto my cock and demand more…"

I was basically writhing in need, and he was just *looking* at it. Arching my back, I reached behind me to unclasp my bra. I wanted my tits jiggling in his face while he fucked me.

"Shit," he breathed. "Alright, keep quiet for me. Can you do that?" He shifted his position, stroking the hot tip of his cock along my seam.

I whimpered—quietly—and nodded.

He grinned. "Good girl." Then he slammed into me, and I screamed. Fuck.

Kai clapped a hand over my mouth, but he was barely containing his laughter. "That's not quiet, *taku aroha*. I'll have to keep my hand here, or we'll get caught."

I moaned, nodding under his palm, and he started to move. Now that he was in, it felt like he didn't want to pull out. He just fucked me deep, in short thrusts so he spent minimal time outside of my pussy. The risk factor, knowing most of Carol's house was now awake, had me all kinds of turned-on. I barely survived two minutes before I came with muffled screams under Kai's hand.

He slowed his movements as I climaxed, slamming deep while my cunt tensed and tightened around him, and his hand gagged me effectively. The second my orgasm started to recede, he shifted to grab one of my legs, pushing it up so my ankle hooked over his shoulder. Then he drove his cock back into me so deeply I basically choked on it.

"Oh yeah," he grunted, his dark eyes locked on mine. "You like that, baby girl? Your nipples are like fucking diamonds right now."

I nodded enthusiastically under his hand, and he went to work, fucking me harder and faster than before. The new angle had him repeatedly striking my G-spot, and in no time at all, I was coming again in a rush of slickness.

"Fuck," he groaned, "you feel so damn good, Siren, I can't—" His words broke off as his hips jerked with his own release. He took his time, thrusting deep as he came inside me, then finally let out a huge breath and released my mouth.

I gasped for air, and he kissed me long and slow, licking along my lips and whispering his love.

Eventually, though, he sat back and released my leg from where he'd bent it up so high my foot had touched the headboard. Luckily, I was flexible.

"Was that quick enough, *taku aroha*?" His grin was pure mischief.

I rolled my eyes. "Uh-huh, was I quiet enough?"

He scoffed a laugh, reaching for my jeans and panties. Giving me a heated look, he threaded them back onto my legs, wiggling them up. Before they reached my ass, he swiped his fingers over my inner thigh where his cum had leaked out, then thrust those fingers back into my pussy.

I groaned, bucking against his hand, then he finished fixing my pants back in place. The message was *dead* clear. He didn't give a fuck if he couldn't get me pregnant, he just wanted to know I'd be going out to Leon with *his* cum still inside me.

Shit, that was hot.

13
DANNY

Logically, I knew that returning to Alaska with Leon—and Kai—was the smart thing to do. Only his equipment there could efficiently decode Layla's drives, and even Carol was curious to know what information was held on them.

My rational brain understood that Blanchet still had a target on my back, that someone was killing off Project Remus mercenaries, and Sabine was at risk of being murdered like Jude. But emotionally... I didn't want to go.

No matter what circumstances saw me arrive in Carol Atwood's Hamptons house, I'd found something there that I never thought I'd have for myself. Family.

Koen made a point of telling me at least six times that he'd put his number into Leon's phone—of course the spoiled brat already had his own phone—and reminded me I had no excuse not to call him. Even if it was just to entertain him during his three-week suspension.

Carol was more reserved, but the warmth was undeniable when she bid us farewell later that afternoon. She apologized for kidnapping and drugging me, and I brushed it off. Shit like that wasn't worth getting bent out of shape about in our line of work.

As we drove away, an uneasy feeling curled through my belly, and I chewed the edge of my lip while staring out the window.

"You okay, Siren?" Kai asked after a few moments of silence. He was driving, and Leon was buried in his phone in the back seat.

I gave a small sigh and shook my head. "I can't help feeling like Carol just put a target on her own back by exposing me as her daughter. What if that bastard goes after Koen next? He's already murdered Jude."

Christ, I was going to cry. I'd been actively trying *not* to think about Jude... It was just easier to push my heart-sister out of my head entirely than constantly face the crushing weight of grief.

The idea that Koen could suffer the same fate? Or even Carol, for that matter, it made me sick.

"Carol can handle it," Leon said from the back seat, and I

tipped my face to meet his eyes. "She knew what she was doing by exposing you, and it was purely for protection."

That reminded me... "I thought I had another two months of your protective order? Why would she feel the need to throw her hat in the ring?"

His brows hitched slightly. "Chatty Carol. You do have two more months. But that only stops Guild executioners from coming for you. As recently proven, it won't stop any two-bit idiot with a gun coming for a juicy paycheck."

"What protection order?" Kai asked, flicking me a confused glance before returning his eyes to the road.

"Irrelevant," Leon replied before I could. Not that I really had much to explain, and it wasn't the time or place to grill Leon about whether he *was* on the Circle. It was a question I had deliberately let drop, probably because I hadn't wanted—or been ready—to hear the truth.

Kai scowled at the dismissal though. "It's not—"

"Carol won't let anything happen to Koen, DeLuna. She's been on the Circle for a long time, she knows how to keep her loved ones safe." Leon's gaze softened when I met his eyes again. "I promise, the little shit will be fine. Besides, I suspect Judith was killed for other reasons. Did you know she was fucking her boss at the library?"

I gasped. "Franklin? No, surely not. She hated him!"

Leon just shrugged. "I saw her sucking his dick in the archives.

But from the little bit of digging I did on this *Franklin*, I think he might have had a motive. Fake identity, probably covering his history within the Guild—"

"Isn't that normal for you guys?" Kai interrupted. "When you get too old for active mercenary work, you get given a new identity and put in a cushy desk job or some shit?"

I gave him a long look. "Interesting that *you* know that, but yes, it's normal. If you survive to that age." My head was spinning, though. Jude and Franklin? Leon had to have been mistaken. But this was Leon, and he didn't make mistakes. Gross. "What was his motive?"

Leon clicked his tongue. "The usual. Wife at home and Judith was threatening to expose their relationship. He was paying her a pretty hefty allowance to keep her mouth shut and legs open, by the looks of things."

My lips twisted in disgust. Not about the age gap; that didn't bother me. But because Franklin was a *dick* and constantly made Jude's work life a living hell. Although now the late nights made a whole lot more sense. *Ew, Jude, what the fuck?*

"If this Franklin prick was ex-Guild," Kai mused aloud, "what if he spilled some secrets that he shouldn't have during pillow talk?"

I swiped a hand over my face. It was a better theory than Jude being murdered for blackmailing an older married man. If Franklin spilled info on high profile Guild clients... *Shit,* he was the head archivist; he could have endless secrets stored away that Jude might have accessed. But surely, she'd have told Sabby or me?

"We need to go and chat with Franklin," I said. "If he had *anything* to do with Jude's death, then he needs to pay."

Kai grunted a sound. "Leon already took care of the merc that set the fires."

I turned in my seat to stare at him. "You did?"

He quirked a brow. "Of course I did. You wouldn't have wanted him to live after killing your best friend, so I took care of things."

It was such a sweet thing for him to do, thinking about what I would want and acting swiftly before the opportunity dried up. The thoughtfulness made me all warm and fuzzy inside.

"Then that's what we'll do," Kai agreed, giving a nod as he kept his eyes on the road. "We'll go to Edinburgh and interrogate this librarian."

I groaned. "We can't. We need to go back to Leon's house to decode Layla's drives."

"Fuck the drives," Kai said without hesitation. "They can wait."

"Can they, though?" Leon asked. His question wasn't pointed, he was genuinely asking. *Could* the drives wait? None of us really knew, and that was the problem. We didn't know what secrets Layla had uncovered, secrets she'd gone to such lengths to hide and eventually been killed for. The fact that it was Kai who killed her was irrelevant. He was just a means to an end for whoever Layla had crossed. Probably Blanchet.

I said nothing, mulling over the question. Could the drives wait? Or could Franklin wait?

"I don't see why it needs to be one or the other," Kai pondered, flicking me a quick, thoughtful look. "Why not both?"

Leon followed that train of thought quicker than me and flipped Kai off behind his back. "Screw you, Big Man. We're not splitting up. Not now."

I frowned. "That's creepy, don't use my nickname for him. Get your own. But I agree, I don't want to split up."

Leon shot me a smoldering look, and his tiny smirk told me he had plenty of names to call Kai. But, *shit*, when I called Kai "Big Man," I wasn't talking about his height or shoulder width. Sure, the same could have been said about Leon, but he was already my bunny.

"What's the problem, Leon? You scared I might win Danny over without you around?" Kai was smirking, glancing in the mirror to taunt Leon, and I punched him in the arm.

"Cut it out," I snapped. "I thought we were past that shit."

Kai gave me a teasing smile, taking the impact out of his jab at Leon. "Sorry, Siren. You're right. We're all friends now. Right, Leon?"

Leon glared daggers at the back of Kai's head, then gave a

brittle smile. "Right."

"So, then we're agreed," Kai said with a nod. "Leon will go home and start decoding the drives while you and I will go to Scotland to interrogate Franklin."

Wait, what?

"Absolutely not," Leon snapped, making me frown.

"Why not?" I retorted, reacting to his instant refusal rather than Kai's suggestion. "Are you under some illusion that I can't handle myself without you around?"

He scowled back at me. "You know perfectly well that I don't think that, DeLuna."

I held his gaze, stubborn as fuck. "So, what's the problem?"

Leon was smart enough to know when he was trapped between a rock and a hard place. Fucked, no matter what he said. So he just narrowed his eyes and gave a slow shake of his head.

"None, I guess," he muttered, but his gaze promised this discussion was far from over. Even if he was just plotting a punishment for later.

Kai was smirking his victory but was wise enough to keep his eyes on the road and his mouth *shut*. As much as I didn't want to split up with Leon, my pride wouldn't let him treat me like a damsel in distress. I was entirely capable of keeping myself alive, and as much as we'd made fun of Kai, he wasn't a liability either. One didn't become a legendary arms dealer without *some* lethal skill.

Blowing out a breath, I ran my hand over my face. It'd been less than twenty-four hours since they'd found me in Carol's house, and already we were diving back into danger. On the one hand, I just wanted a month… or even a *week* to spend time with Kai and Leon. Just to work on our personal connections and explore what the future might look like for the three of us.

On the other hand, this was what I lived for. If I had to give up all the action, adventure, and adrenaline of my mercenary life, I'd likely die of boredom.

So when we reached the private airfield half an hour later, it was with a heady mixture of anxiety and excitement that we organized separate flight plans. Leon was scowling and pouting the whole time, and I had to give credit to Kai for managing not to gloat like a three-year-old with the last piece of candy.

When our plans were finalized, Leon all but dragged me outside and pinned me to the wall of the little terminal. He kissed me with all the frustration of knowing he couldn't argue with me, making sure that when one of the aircrews indicated that my plane was ready—to take Kai and me across the Atlantic—I was weak-kneed with desire.

"Don't fucking forget me, *ma moitié*," he ordered me in a husky, vulnerable voice. "I'll be counting the minutes until you return to my bed."

I kissed him again tenderly. "I couldn't forget you if I tried, Bunny. Keep that hot tub warm for me." Winking, I peeled myself out of his embrace and hurried across the tarmac to where Kai waited. If I gave myself a chance to hesitate, I'd change my mind and demand Leon come with us.

But those drives... Layla had inadvertently died to hide that information. Whatever she'd found *had* to be useful, and we couldn't waste another week without decoding it. It was gut instinct, and I'd learned a long time ago to trust my gut.

14
KAI

Everything I'd said to Danny, I meant. One hundred percent, every word was the truth. Yes, it'd taken her leaving me—leaving *both* of us—to make me pull my head out my ass. But watching her drive away with Stanley, then finding the wreckage of her van and fearing for her well-being? It'd given me the wake-up call I so desperately needed.

It'd put shit in perspective and made me accept the fact that my feelings for her kept me a thousand times warmer than my hatred for the Guild ever had. Being forced to work *with* Leon to find her had made me grudgingly accept that Leon Marx and the Mercenary Guild were not one and the

Danny and the Guild weren't.

But when the opportunity presented itself to get her alone for a few days, you better believe I grabbed it and ran. Just because I *accepted* her relationship with Leon—for the sake of her happiness—didn't mean I needed to start sucking his cock.

My suggestion to split up and go after Judith's boss wasn't entirely selfish, though. If we'd all gone back to Alaska with Leon, we'd have just been sitting around getting irritated and short-tempered. Danny would have hated *wasting time* like that when Leon was the only one who could work on decoding Layla's drives.

It gave me a spark of hope when he agreed—albeit reluctantly. Maybe we could come to some sort of truce, at least as far as Danny was concerned.

She gave a heavy yawn as the private jet we'd hired started to taxi down the runway. Her gaze remained fixed out the window, staring out at Leon like it was killing her to leave him behind. I said nothing, not wanting to insert myself in whatever was going through her head, but she looked so conflicted I couldn't do *nothing*. So I reached out and slipped my hand under hers, linking our fingers together and giving her just a small squeeze of reassurance.

We'd see that prick again. He was indestructible, like a cockroach.

My stomach dropped as the plane started gaining altitude,

and Danny snuggled into my shoulder with a sigh. Her fingers remained twined with mine, and I couldn't think of anywhere I'd rather be.

She fell asleep within moments, probably exhausted after our dumb asses had arrived in the middle of the fucking night. As carefully as I could, I reclined both our seats and slipped a pillow under her head. I needed to release her hand to grab a blanket, but it was worth it to see how her face relaxed when I tucked it around her.

Resisting the urge to curl up beside her, I grabbed my phone and headed to the back of the plane so I wouldn't wake her up. I needed to make some calls to arrange things for when we landed, because I sure as shit wasn't hunting a retired mercenary without a crapload of more weapons. I also needed to check in with my team and break the unwanted news to them.

With a sigh, I called Eli first.

He answered within two rings, as always.

"Eli, how are things there?" I propped my elbow on the windowsill and stared back down the plane at my siren's sleeping form.

"All under control, boss," he replied. "When are you back?"

I cringed internally. "Small change of plans. I'm heading to the UK right now, but Marx is on his way back to you. He's got work to do, so I need for you all to leave him the fuck alone, alright?"

There was a pause of disapproval, then Eli agreed in one

clipped word. "Understood."

"He's also going to want to look into our Guild mole. Please ask Moana to share the dead drop dark web address with him."

Another pause. "You sure that's a good idea, boss?"

Fuck no. "Yes," I muttered. "We need to work together now that we no longer have Sam."

His betrayal was still a fresh wound, and one that most of my team was just carefully avoiding. The fact of the matter was that he'd broken our trust. He hadn't put a hit on Danny because he hated her, he'd done it to hurt *me*. He blamed *me* for Mauricio's death and decided to make an irreversible declaration of war in retaliation. He signed his own death warrant that day.

As much as it'd hurt me to do, I couldn't allow that kind of disrespect to slide… not when he'd gone public with his hit. My business was built up on a shit load of carefully planted lies and exaggerations, bolstered by facts and reality after we'd already gained a foothold. The reason we'd remained in a position of power within the arms trade was that our team was rock solid. No weak links.

Sam left me no choice.

"I trust your judgment, boss," Eli replied, emotionless as ever. "We all do."

That both reassured me and made me feel like a massive asshole. "I promise, I haven't forgotten our objective, Eli." I rubbed the bridge of my nose, feeling the weight of the world crushing me. "This shit with Danny, it's all tangled up with Project Remus. This is a huge step forward, especially now that our mole went dark."

Eli just grunted a sound that was neither agreeing nor disagreeing. I called him for that exact reason—even when he thought I was being reckless, he kept those opinions to himself. Moana, on the other hand, would be yelling my ear off by now. The only reason she hadn't come for Leon with guns blazing was because I impressed upon her how much Danny cared about the smug fuck. And Mo had a huge soft spot for my siren.

That, and I agreed to let her buy an army tank. When I asked why she wanted it, she told me it was none of my damn business, but I suspected she just wanted to squash things with it for fun.

"What takes you to the UK, then?" Eli asked, changing the subject. "Anything I can help with?"

I sighed, running a hand over my close-cropped hair. "Nah, I doubt it. We're going to interrogate a librarian who might have ordered the hit on Danny's best friend. I'll stop by our storage locker on the way."

"Good thinking. If you have time, maybe stop by and have that chat with Sonny while you're in town." Eli was reminding me of Ares business, and it made me wince. I'd been dropping the ball on my own shit because I was so focused on Danny.

"Yeah, good idea," I murmured. "I'll sort him out. When Marx gets back, maybe keep Cyryl away from him. If he finds out that

Cyryl harmed Danny..."

Eli grunted. "Heard. I'll send him back down to Dogwood to sort out things with Vega and the Death Squad."

That was good thinking too. "Tell him to stop by Shadow Grove and drop some boxes of ammo to Hades. We owe them a couple of bullets." And a thank you for saving Danny's ass in that ambush.

"Can do, boss. Call me if you need anything else." Eli ended the call without making further small talk, and I lowered my phone with a yawn. I couldn't sleep just yet, though. Everything needed to be lined up when we landed in order to eliminate any opportunity for danger to Danny.

The rest of my plans didn't need phone calls, just a handful of emails. So I buzzed our flight attendant for a drink and opened up my secure inbox. Something told me I would need some liquor in my belly to sift through my emails after basically dropping off the face of the earth lately.

I was right. Several hours—and several drinks—later, I managed to untangle the mess I'd inadvertently caused for myself with my negligence. Arrangements were in place for when we landed, and my contacts in London knew to expect me at a specific time.

When I powered off my phone and returned to where Danny slept, I was exhausted. But I was also a whole lot calmer than I'd felt in a long time. It wasn't a case of finally getting off the roller coaster that was loving Danny DeLuna, more like I'd just learned to ride it out and lean into the bends.

I'd stopped trying to make her fit the idea in my head, instead just accepting her as she was… Leon and all. Now I needed to get in control of my own business once more. I'd worked too fucking hard building myself up as *Ares*, one of the world's most successful arms dealers, to just walk away from it now.

Regardless of what my reputation might be—carefully crafted as it was—I liked to think our weapons sales were doing good things for the world. Ares didn't always sell to the highest bidder but instead to the most deserving. Our past sales had helped tip the scales in countless gang territory disputes, and while neither party was *good*, there was often a clear *worse* of the two.

Faced with a choice of arming a gang known to trade in human flesh, in underage sex slaves, versus one peddling prescription pills? There was no hesitation. I'd arm those drug rats to the fucking teeth, even if they couldn't pay.

Danny stirred as I lay back down beside her, getting comfy on my own reclined seat to catch a couple of hours of sleep myself. She didn't open her eyes, but her hand reached out to rest on my hip. I loved that she wanted to touch me, even in sleep. I just had to hope she was dreaming about *me*.

That was another thing on my to-do list. Even the score with Leon. Just because we'd agreed to tolerate each other didn't mean I had to let bygones be bygones, and he'd tried to poison me once already. Not to mention his childish stunt of removing my door handle.

When we got back to Alaska, I'd need to make sure he realized who he was messing with. I sure as fuck wasn't going to just keep taking those hits without dishing them right back. So long as it seemed *joking*, then surely Danny wouldn't mind? It was something I needed to think on.

I fell asleep easily, the hum of the plane soothing me and wiping away the million anxious thoughts from my mind. When I woke, I was in a confused daze, with Danny shaking my shoulder.

"What?" I mumbled, foggy with sleep.

She smiled, and it was like the fucking sun rising. "Sit up, Big Man. We're coming in to land, you need your seat in the upright position."

Groaning, I swiped my hand over my face and sleepily did as she said. Further down the aisle, I spotted the flight attendant watching. This company took safety seriously, and I liked that.

"Dammit," I muttered as Danny buckled her safety belt and started twisting her disheveled hair into a braid.

She arched a brow at me. "What?"

"I was hoping we'd have some time to join the Mile High Club before we landed," I admitted quietly so we weren't overheard by the flight crew preparing for landing.

Danny snickered a laugh, giving me a sly look. "You've never joined the club, Big Man?" I shook my head, and she wet her lips. "Well shit. We'll have to fix that on the way home. For now, though, talk me through our plans when we land."

I shifted in my seat and gave her a look that hopefully conveyed how badly I was looking forward to the flight home. But business came first, and I needed to let her know about the Ares errands that I had to sort out while on the British Isles, too.

She listened attentively as I outlined everything, then responded exactly as I should have anticipated.

"That sounds perfect," she commented, "as a decoy. But let me run point when we land. We'll do things the Guild way."

My brows rose. "And how is that?"

Her smile spread wide and her eyes glittered with excitement. "Totally unpredictable and spontaneous. No one can lay a trap if not even you know what you'll be driving or in which direction until you get there."

I hated the unpredictable. But she was the expert, so I gritted my teeth and reluctantly agreed.

15
DANNY

Before we'd left the Hamptons, Carol had packed a carry-on bag for me with clothes and toiletries, which I was super grateful for when we finally arrived at our hotel. Kai had booked us a suite and arranged for fresh clothes to be delivered for him there, but I'd insisted we check into the hotel across the street instead.

Not that I didn't trust his plans, but I'd been burned too many times before. Now, more than ever, we needed to remain as spontaneous as possible to avoid anyone tracking our movements.

Kai didn't *love* my insistence to change everything he'd

planned, but he also didn't argue, which I appreciated. When we were secure in our room, he called the hotel concierge to have his clothing delivered from the other hotel.

"So, we're stopping by one of your weapons caches first?" I asked while combing out my wet, slightly tangled hair.

Kai nodded from his position reclining on the big bed. "One gun between us doesn't feel like enough weaponry to go interrogating an ex-mercenary."

I gave a slight smile. "You're right about that." Most mercenaries who lived long enough to retire were far more dangerous than most people gave them credit for.

He gave me a long look, his arms linked behind his head. "You look excited, Siren."

My smile spread wider. "I am." Because he was going to let me loose in his weapons cache. It was like letting a toddler loose in a toy store and telling them they could have *anything*. My stomach growled in hunger, and I grimaced. "Can we eat on the way there?"

Kai's expression lit up with excitement of his own. "Absolutely we can. I know just the place."

A knock at the door announced Kai's clothing delivery, but I tossed him Carol's gun before he opened the door... just in case. Executioner Bryan had taught me to be suspicious of *all* entry points into a hotel room, including the valet cart. Flexible fucking unit that he was.

This delivery seemed devoid of hidden assassins, but to be safe, Kai tipped the bag out on the bed to make sure no one had slipped an explosive into it somewhere. I knew that level of paranoia probably didn't come naturally to him, so I appreciated that he was doing it for my sake.

"Hurry up and get changed," I urged when we were both satisfied nothing was jumping out to kill us just yet. "I'm starved and horny, which is not a great combination. If I tried to suck your dick right now, I might use too much teeth."

Kai cringed, then laughed. "Fair call, let's get you fed. Then deal with the other part."

Now, if that wasn't my idea of a great date night, I didn't know what was. Add in the promise of new guns, and I was one happy little mercenary.

Kai didn't keep me waiting too long, ripping the tags off his new clothes and getting changed in a matter of minutes. We headed downstairs and hailed a taxi on the street rather than ordering an Uber or taking a car service. Kai gave the driver an address in the West End that I wasn't familiar with, and we settled in for the drive.

Neither one of us spoke for the journey to wherever we were going, but when I reached out to him, he linked our fingers together and gave me a small squeeze. I liked that. We didn't *need* to be chatting all the time to feel connected. Also, taxi drivers had ears, and we weren't dumb enough to discuss our plans for weapons and torture interrogation in front of a stranger.

The taxi dropped us off at a busy eatery, and Kai opened my door for me like a fucking gentleman. I smiled at him, then peered at his choice of food. "Sushi train?"

He smirked and shook his head. "Close, but not quite."

There were enough people around that I didn't get a look at the menu signs, instead just following Kai into the shop where people were all seated around the steadily moving belt loaded with little plastic plates.

A staff member greeted us, then led the way toward the back of the shop, where two stools were vacant. Kai indicated for me to sit, and I wriggled out of the coat I'd been wearing. He took it, hanging it on the little hook under the bench, then sat down himself. The size of him on the little stool was comical, but I was too hungry to make fun of him about it.

Licking my lips, I peered at the little plates gliding past us, then did a double take.

"Cheese?" I said aloud, frowning at Kai in confusion. "Wait, isn't this..."

Kai chuckled and handed me one of the laminated menus from in front of us. I glanced down and read the restaurant name aloud.

"*Cheese The Day.*" The sound that escaped me was embarrassing, to say the least. It was a strangled laugh combined with a snort. "Oh my god, I'm dying. Wait, what if I was lactose-intolerant?"

Kai gave me a long look. "I've seen your coffees, Siren, you have guts of steel."

I mean, true. Grinning, I reached for the first plate I could get on the moving belt and plucked the frosted plastic lid off. On the plate, the name of the dish was printed, and I gave another unattractive chortle as I read it. "*Life Is Gouda.*"

It was actually a little grilled cheese sandwich, presumably made with gouda. The cheesy names had me all giddy, so I chose one for Kai because he was taking too long.

He shot me an indulgent look, then lifted the lid off to see what he had. "*To Brie Or Not To Brie.*"

I chuckled, eyeing his artfully sliced brie and grapes. "I love this place."

His answering smile was pure satisfaction. "I thought you would." He put two slices of Brie in his mouth and indicated for me to pull more plates from the belt. They were each bite-sized, just like sushi, and I loved that. It meant we got to sample so many more.

At the end of it, when I was full, and cheese was probably seeping from my pores, Kai and I had to each pick our favorite plate.

Kai picked *Arch Neme-Swiss*, which I agreed on. For me, it was a hard tie between *Praise Cheeses* and *Fifty Shades of Gruyere*.

The best part about it was that they served wine so we could indulge with all our cheese. Total perfection.

"This was fun," I told Kai with a relaxed smile as we paid the bill and he helped me into my coat. "Kinda like a date or something." I had by *no means* dropped my guard, but my caution was so second nature that I could push it to the background and enjoy the present with Kai.

It was raining when we stepped outside, and Kai placed a hand on my back to guide me around the corner from my new favorite eatery in the whole world. We ducked beneath an awning, and Kai pulled out his phone to check something.

"Do you want to go on a date with me, Siren?" he asked, glancing up from his screen to give me a curious look.

My brow dipped slightly. "I've never been on an actual date, but with you? Yes, I would." He looked confused, so I elaborated. "The only *dates* I've ever gone on were for work. Honey traps mostly. At least nine out of ten resulted in the person I was *dating* winding up in a morgue somewhere, so, you know, not an actual date."

He dipped his head in a nod. "That makes sense. I'll have to think of something incredible, then."

I smiled, the warmth of wine heating my belly and smoothing all the rough edges of my prickly personality. "Good luck finding something better than a cheese train with wine *and* puns. The bar is high, Big Man."

His smile was all mischief and delight, an unfamiliar look on Kai. "Well, the day isn't over yet. Come on, I saved the best until last on this not-date date."

Well, shit, color me intrigued. Kai reached down to take my hand in his, then tugged me back out into the rain to hurry along the street further. He ducked us into an alleyway and approached a door halfway down. A fairly basic seeming combination lock let us in, and Kai flicked on a light as the door closed heavily behind us with a click.

"If you're taking me down here to kill me..." I murmured, eyeing the narrow staircase leading down into a basement.

Kai gave a soft chuckle. "I still can't work out if that would be your idea of a good or bad time. But I guess we'll find out." He took the lead, confidently striding down the stairs and leaving me to follow... Granted, I wasn't a scaredy-cat.

A heady thrill zapped through me, and I took the stairs slowly, making Kai wait for me when he reached the bottom. There was another locked door there, but this one had a much more secure lock requiring a passcode and an electronic key from Kai's phone before it unlocked.

"Just warning you," he said, hesitating before opening the door, "this is only a small stash. Our main storage warehouses are located less conveniently."

Yay, we're going gun shopping! I knew it. Fuck, this is a good day.

"Understood," I replied. "I won't laugh at your pitiful collection."

His eyes narrowed, but he pushed open the door anyway. The

room was dark and musty smelling, but Kai flicked on a light switch, and the halogen globes flickered to life.

Gasping, I gawked. Legit gawked. My eyes widened, and I took in the so-called *small stash* of guns.

"Kai..." I said his name on a groan, and he brushed my hair over my shoulder to kiss my neck.

"Yes, Siren?"

I glanced up at him, amused at all the smug satisfaction on his face. "Big Man... you're a dirty tease, you know that?"

He gave a chuckle, brushing a kiss over my cheek. "You like my cache?"

I let out a small moan as I took in the *enormous* room full of weaponry. It reminded me of the Guild gun stashes dotted around the world, which I no longer had access to. But better, because Kai and his team had more eclectic taste than the Guild weapons buyers.

"Like it? I think I just came."

Instead of laughing, Kai just gave me a smoking hot look as he moved further into the room. "Not yet, but you will. Go shopping, *ātaahua*, take whatever you want."

Excitement had my pulse racing and my breath quick. I took a few steps closer to him *and* the weapons. There were all kinds of things lining the racks on the walls, from the smallest purse pistol right up to long-range sniper rifles. There was even a whole section of explosive devices and boxes on boxes of ammo.

"And then?" I prompted, because it sounded like there was a second part to his offer.

The corner of Kai's lips tilted up as he glanced over at me. He was standing in front of a rack displaying dozens of knives in varying sizes and lengths, some in sheaths. On his other side, was a display of military-grade handguns.

He stared at me for a long moment, holding my gaze as he tucked his hands into his pockets. "And then, Siren, I think we should take a trip down memory lane."

How did he know? That was my favorite lane.

16
DANNY

With the promise of kinky weapon sex hanging in the air, it was hard to concentrate on selecting the weaponry I wanted. Was I just taking enough to interrogate Franklin? Or restocking the supply I'd been forced to walk away from at my house in Iceland?

"Do you have bags, or are we just taking what we can conceal carry?" I tipped my head as I looked over at Kai. He was still leaning against the shelves, watching me with a heated gaze.

With a small smirk, he crossed to a locker near the door and opened it to pull out a large black duffle bag. He placed it down on the stainless steel table—housing drawers beneath—in the middle of the room and arched a brow at me. "Will this work?"

"It'll do," I murmured, selecting a couple of basic, dime-a-dozen Glock 19's from the rack and placing them carefully in the bag. "Is anything off-limits?" I was mostly asking just out of curiosity. I didn't think we had any need for the more dramatic, bulky shit, but I was curious whether he was particularly attached to anything.

Kai shook his head, choosing a few guns for himself and adding them to the bag. "Nope. What's mine is yours, *kaikohuru iti.*"

Oh, be still my heart.

Kai pulled open one of the drawers beneath the tabletop and selected several boxes of ammo to add to our bag for the guns we'd already selected. Then from a lower drawer, he pulled out a .500 Smith & Wesson. It was a Model 500 Revolver, a Cartuccia Magnum, and sported a distinctly *phallic*-looking barrel on it.

I gave him a sidelong glance. "Revolvers aren't very practical, Big Man. Not enough bullets, fiddly to reload… quick way to get yourself killed."

He gave a low chuckle, leaving it sitting out on the table—not in the bag—then circling around to open another drawer. From that one, he pulled out a set of Smith & Wesson tactical handcuffs in a pretty brushed gray-blue metal. Apparently, he had a brand preference.

He wasn't explaining his choices, clearly waiting for me to ask, so I deliberately turned back to my shopping trip. I added two M4s, at least ten knives in varying lengths and weights, some holsters and straps, and then a dozen mini grenades because they were freaking adorable. Especially the way Kai kept them packaged in an egg-crate kind of box.

Kai supplied all the appropriate ammunition and added more choices for himself before zipping the *very* full bag up and placing it near the door.

"Now what?" I asked with a lazy grin, tipping my head to the revolver and handcuffs still on the table.

He arched a brow, then tucked both items into the back of his pants to clear the surface.

"Hand me your phone," he told me in a tone that brooked *no* arguments. "And take your clothes off."

I shivered with excitement, then pulled my phone from my back pocket. I unlocked it with my thumbprint before handing it over, and Kai gave me a small nod. He swiped the screen open as I tugged my top over my head, then unzipped my jeans.

"I'm guessing *six-two-seven-nine* is Leon?" He looked up at me with a questioning glance as I kicked off my boots and jeans.

I swallowed hard, excitement thick in my throat as I stood there surrounded by guns and weapons, wearing nothing but my bra and panties. My suddenly rather damp panties. "Yup. Why?"

As if I needed to ask. Kai raised the phone and snapped a picture of me, then presumably sent it to Leon. He was poking the bear, and I was kinda here for it.

"Lose the underwear, Siren," he ordered, "then get up on the table."

I wet my lips and did as I was told without hesitation. The metal table was cold on my bare skin, and I sucked a sharp breath, but it was quickly forgotten as Kai guided me to lie on my back. My arms were raised above my head, and I gave a small groan of anticipation when the cool metal of Kai's handcuffs kissed my wrists. He'd looped them through one of the drawer handles, holding me locked in place.

"We good, *ātaahua*?" he asked, checking that I was okay being restrained. So cute.

I nodded my approval, and his lush lips curved in a smile. "Good," he murmured, looking back down at my phone. He pressed a button, then held the phone to my ear as it started to ring.

"DeLuna," Leon answered, his voice warming me right through. "Is everything okay?"

My breath hitched as Kai's lips closed around one of my nipples. "Um, yep!" My voice was high and strained, and Leon *instantly* suspected what was going on.

"Are you getting fucked right now, DeLuna?" he asked in a low growl. "Did you just call me while riding *his* dick?"

I moaned as Kai spread my legs with his hand, then teased a finger along my slit. "Not *quite*," I answered Leon. "Not yet, anyway."

He breathed some curses. "Put me on video chat, *mon cœur*, let me see what he's doing to you. He might need pointers."

Kai's fingers pushed into my cunt, making my back arch off the table, and I gasped. Still, he held the phone to my ear with his other hand. Multitasking bastard.

"I can't right now, Bunny," I admitted. "My hands are a little... tied."

Kai grinned at me, smug as fuck, and arched a brow in question.

"Leon wants visuals," I told him. "Can you help him out with video?"

I half expected Kai to just hang up the call and leave Leon hanging, forcing him to use his imagination for what we might be doing next. So I was pleasantly surprised when he withdrew the phone from my ear and swapped it to a video feed.

It must have been selfie-facing, though, because Leon gave a loud curse. "Fuck, Kai, turn the damn camera around, I don't need to see your face. Talk about a boner killer."

Kai laughed but swapped the camera angle and nudged my legs wider to give Leon a better angle.

"I'm going to mute you, Marx," Kai told Leon. "You can watch, but you don't get to talk. Clear?"

If Leon replied to that, I didn't hear it as Kai hit the mute button on my screen, then looked up at me with a wicked smile on his face. From the back of his pants, he pulled out that pretty long-barreled revolver once more.

"You want me to fuck your sweet cunt with this, don't you?" he taunted. Using the tip of the barrel, he teased my clit, and I writhed at the touch of cool steel. "You want to really walk down memory lane and recreate that first night we had together, huh?"

I moaned, my back arching. "You'll ruin your gun," I warned him sensibly. "Pussy juice doesn't mix well with weapons."

His chuckle was low and husky. "That's a matter of opinion, *ātaahua*." He held the phone steady as he pushed the barrel just barely inside me. My breath caught, and I tilted my hips, begging for more, but he pulled it out again. The silver barrel glistened with my slickness, and I wet my lips as I watched him raise it to his own lips. Then suck it.

What in all the holy hotness was that?

"While you were shopping, I found something else to play with," he told me, placing the gun to the side. A promise for later. But Kai wanted to *play* first, apparently. He produced a small handheld device from his pocket, and I arched to try to get a better look.

He just shook his head with a mischievous smile, then glanced around.

"Sorry, Marx," he said, balancing my phone on one of the

empty gun racks I'd just raided. He seemed to adjust the camera angle and zoomed it a bit, then stepped away. "You'll have to hang out there for a minute, I need my hands."

Returning to me, he showed me the device in his hand.

"Taser?" I asked, taking a guess, because it wasn't one I'd seen before.

He gave a small nod. "Of sorts. It's a close range stun device. But the cool thing about *this* one is that you can turn the voltage way down." He depressed a button on the handle a half dozen times, then pressed the stun button. A tiny flicker of visible electricity zapped between the two metal points, and my breathing quickened.

"How strong does that make it?" I asked with dizzying anticipation. Not that I would wuss out, even if it was full strength.

Kai shrugged. "Let's find out, shall we?" He brought the little Taser to my chest, then slowly stroked it down between my breasts, not turning it on… yet. He was just teasing and giving me a chance to stop him. But I didn't, so when he reached the sensitive skin just above my pubic bone, he zapped me.

A sharp cry escaped me, but it was just surprise, not pain.

Kai held my gaze, his eyes intense and questioning as I panted. Then I smiled and licked my lips.

"Do it again," I urged. "Lower." The voltage really was low, nowhere near intense enough to hurt, and I wanted to see how hard it might make me come if it zapped my clit.

Kai grinned at my enthusiasm but didn't do as I asked. Instead—now that I'd given my encouragement—he took his time using it all over my body. Just tiny zaps here and there as his lips moved over my skin. When he used it on my nipples, I screamed loud enough to echo around the room.

Then I begged him to fuck me. Begged. Because I was shaking all over, so wet I could feel the table slick beneath me, but he was still *fully fucking dressed*.

He ignored my plea, taking full advantage of my handcuffed wrists as he tortured me. But eventually, he placed the little Taser down and stripped out of his own clothes.

The table was high enough that he needed to climb up there, and he lifted my ass up so my thighs rested over his, my lower back off the table.

"Please, Kai," I whimpered as he slowly coated his hard dick in my wetness. He was dragging it out, sliding against me but not penetrating. Fucking man was going to be the death of me. "Please, Big Man, fill me up. Fuck my pussy, make me come."

"Yes, ma'am," he replied, notching his dick and thrusting deep with a grunt.

My wrists stung as I tugged on the handcuffs, my hips rocking as I gasped and moaned. Kai's control had snapped though, thank fuck. Once he was in, he was *on*. He fucked me hard, pushing me up the table slightly as he thrust, his hands gripping my hips to hold onto me.

I came hard with his dick still ramming into me, but he didn't slow. He knew—there was no way he could miss it with the way I cried out and thrashed—but he just held me in place with a firm hand between my breasts as he continued.

Then he grabbed the Taser again and zapped my clit.

I *exploded*, my muscles all locking up tight and my toes curling against the edge of the table. This time, he paused to ride it out with me. Probably couldn't have kept going anyway from how tight my inner walls were choking his cock.

Eventually, the overwhelming sensations faded and my muscles relaxed enough that he started moving once more.

"Fuck, that was gorgeous," he grunted, pulling out almost entirely, then slamming back in hard enough to shake the table. "Fucking *beautiful*. Will you come again?"

I moaned, hooking a leg around behind him to pull him closer. "I don't think I can. That was… intense."

Kai smirked, licking his lips. "I reckon you can." That hand he'd been pressing between my breasts snaked up to my throat. He just rested it there for a few moments while he found his rhythm once more. Then his eyes widened, and his breathing sharpened with his own impending climax.

His fingers tightened, the pressure precise and perfect on my throat so that within a handful of harsh breaths, I started to see blackness. I wouldn't pass out fully, I was too practiced at going without oxygen for extended periods, but it was enough to make me dizzy and heightened the intense arousal as Kai pounded my cunt.

Just like he predicted, I came again. Those first hot jets of his release lashing my insides saw me shatter in deep shudders of orgasm.

He released my throat, and I sucked greedy lungfuls of air, dimly watching as he withdrew from my pussy and climbed off the table. Rather than releasing my handcuffs, he tossed me a grin and grabbed my phone from where he'd set it up.

"Oh good, you're still there, Marx." He made no move to get his clothes. Instead, he came back over to the foot of the table with my phone in his hand. He paused for a moment to adjust the zoom, then tapped my knee to tell me to open my legs once more.

Fucking alpha-male men and their cum fascinations. Kai clearly wanted to give Leon a prime view of *his* cum dripping from my cunt. Okay, fine, I kinda found it hot too. So I spread my thighs and tipped my pelvis, feeling the wet slide trickle down to my ass.

"Remember what I said, Siren?" Kai asked with a darkly mischievous grin on his face. "About memory lane?"

Words failed me. I just sucked a deep breath and watched in hunger as he picked up the revolver again. Carefully, slowly, he pushed the thick, long barrel of the gun into my saturated pussy.

"That's my girl," he purred as I moaned and writhed. "One more for me, beautiful, you can do it. Come on my gun, Danny, just like old times. Make Leon see what he's missing."

Christ.

His motions were slow and deliberate, the wet sounds filling the small space in the most hedonistic way as he fucked me with his gun. All the while keeping the camera trained on the action to ensure Leon wasn't missing a thing. The small sight ridge on the tip of the barrel brushed over my G-spot as I rocked my hips, and I felt myself about to shatter.

"Kai," I moaned, repeating the motion to get the barrel of the gun right where I needed it. "Kai, is it loaded?" I was so close. So fucking close.

He wet his lips, his eyes wide. "What do you think?" His thumb flicked the safety off, and he pushed the barrel deeper inside me. That was the final straw, and I detonated, drenching his gun and hand with a small rush of fluid. That was a first, but hardly unexpected considering…

"Fuck," Kai groaned. "That was *so* hot. We need to play with my guns more often." He withdrew the revolver and set it aside. Glancing down at my phone, he licked his lips. "Damn, I kinda wish I'd filmed that instead of showing Leon. Have fun fucking your hand, Marx." He ended the call, and I started laughing.

My boys were deviant as fuck, and I was *here for it.*

They were also learning to share, and that—above everything else—had my heart soaring.

17
LEON

Cum and electronics didn't mix. Full stop. End of story. Especially keyboards. If it got between the keys, then it was fucking impossible to clean out, and then keys started sticking. Nightmare.

Luckily, I had a spare keyboard to swap it out with, so I could get back to work straight away. Not that I was complaining... much. It was a weird feeling, the mixture of post-ejaculation euphoria and acidic, blood-boiling jealousy. The fact that I'd just witnessed that kinky scene from the other side of the world...? I probably could have done without the close-up of his ass while he fucked her, but shit... the payoff was worth it.

The whole call was hot as fuck, and a heady reminder of that Halloween night when I'd listened to her being fucked by Kai's gun for the first time. At least *this* time, he knew I was listening.

I'd jerked myself off then, too. Maybe if I hadn't been so busy fucking my hand that night, I could have rescued her before the big oaf whisked her away to his island. Before he stole half her heart.

"Productive train of thought, idiot," I muttered to myself as I unboxed the new keyboard and plugged it in. The old one, still wet with my cum, went straight in the trash. I needed to book my cleaners to come back out soon... especially now that I had house guests.

Fucking squatters. I needed to get rid of them, but I doubted I would be allowed to just kill them all. Kai seemed weirdly attached to the whole damn group of them, and if he got all butt-hurt, then it'd become my problem, and that'd damage my relationship with Danny. Not worth it.

Maybe I could convince them my house was haunted and just scare them off. The Asian guy looked gullible enough to buy it. The silent one, Eli, he would be the hardest to get rid of. He'd seen me arrive last night, just giving a silent nod as I entered my own home through the trapdoor in the roof. Creep.

Why were they even still here? Their fearless leader was on the other side of the world, fucking my woman with the barrel of a revolver. Fucking hell, getting the visual on that was even better than I'd imagined. I just wished I'd been the one controlling the gun and feeling her fall apart rather than watching it on my computer screen.

Irritated and restless, I checked that Layla's codes were still ticking away in my decoding program and left my office. I needed to hit the gym and work off some excess unease. Logically, I knew the only thing that would *actually* settle my nerves would be to have DeLuna back in my arms. But that wasn't physically possible right now, and I wasn't stupid enough to mistake this for anything but a test.

She knew how possessive and unhinged I was. She wanted me to *prove* I could trust her to come back to me. This sharing thing was about more than just fucking her at the same time, it was about *trust*. Not my finest trait on the best of days, but for her, I wanted to try. I wanted to do better.

Danny DeLuna was more than worth it, even if that did mean suffering Kai's moronic team in my house. But seriously, *why* were they still here? Didn't they have their own house to stay in?

Muttering under my breath about all the painful ways I could kill them and dispose of the bodies, I settled into a workout inside my own gym. As always, I cranked the music up *loud* because I liked to drown out my own intrusive thoughts while I exercised. I couldn't do that with silence, and Danny wasn't here to distract me with her body. Not for sex—not always—but just with the incredible strength and flexibility she possessed. Perving on Danny in the gym was a guilty pleasure.

I made it all of half an hour into my workout when the gym door burst open, and Kai's scowling sister stomped in. Her black hair was disheveled, and she was barefoot, wearing a pair of flannel pajamas. Her glare was pure venom as she curled a disgusted lip at me. She grabbed my stereo's central unit off the shelf and *hurtled* it across the room, smashing it to pieces as the music cut off abruptly.

She started to stalk back out of the gym, but I was pissed now. I got up from the weights bench I'd been working on and threw my drink bottle. It smacked her right in the middle of the back, nothing wrong with my aim, and she stiffened like I'd just bitch slapped her.

"What the *fuck* is your problem?" I snarled, stalking across the gym to get up in her face when she turned around.

"My problem?" she barked back at me, her eyes blazing. "I was *sleeping* until you started blasting that fucking music through the entire goddamn mountain. I knew you were a head case, but enough is enough. This is downright—"

"If you don't like it," I cut her off, my voice even and calm but firm as fuck, "leave. I don't remember ever inviting you to stay, and frankly, *Moana*, you're not fucking welcome. Don't like my music? Fuck. Off. Want me to show you the door? Hell, I'll even pack you some snacks for the journey."

The urge to reach out and strangle her—literally choke the life out of her—was almost overwhelming. My fingers twitched with need at my sides, but I gritted my teeth and restrained myself. This bitch, with her bad attitude and appalling manners, was Kai's sister and Danny's *friend*.

But shit, she had a death wish.

Her chin tilted up, and her eye twitched with fury. "You think I want to be here?" she sneered, looking at me like I was a sloppy dog shit she'd just stepped in. "You think I enjoy sleeping in the snake pit? This is the last place on earth I want to be, so save your *welcome* for someone who actually wants it. I sure as fuck don't, but Kai wants us here, so we have no choice in the matter."

Like I fucking cared what she wanted. "Tough shit, it's not his house, and he doesn't make the rules. I've played nice for long enough; you can all leave today."

I didn't think her expression could get *more* disgusted, but she proved me wrong. "I don't take orders from Guild scum like you," she spat, then shoved me.

For a second, I thought it was a joke. Surely it was a joke. But no... she *actually* just shoved me. Well... she fucking started it.

"Argh!" she screamed as I slammed her into the wall, her arm twisted up behind her in a wrist lock and my knife at her throat. "Let me go, you psychotic *fuck*!"

We'd made enough noise that the rest of Kai's merry band of idiots had come to investigate, and the door burst open again right as I was debating just *how bad* the fallout would be if I slit Moana's throat.

"Oh shit," the Asian dude exclaimed, his eyes wide and... scared. This bitch was *scared* of me. Good, he should be. But fucking hell, Kai needed to take a long hard look at his so-called *team*.

Eli was unfazed. It seemed to be his perpetual state, and it made me want to rattle him a bit.

He just took in the scene and gave a small sigh. "Leon, please release Moana." He was polite, but it wasn't a request.

I tilted my head to the side, like I was thinking. "Nah, I think I've had just about enough company in my house to last me a lifetime. It's time to take out the trash, starting with this bothersome pest." I tightened my grip on Moana's wrist, making her squeak with pain.

Eli just gave me a level stare. "I can understand this situation is less than desirable for you. Mo apologizes for overstepping, don't you?"

The woman just gave a furious sound, and I could imagine she was probably glaring daggers at Eli.

For his part, he stayed calm. "Moana, apologize to Leon. We are being terrible guests, and it looks like you came down here looking for a fight."

That was exactly why she'd come in. Not that I was averse to the idea, but I wouldn't be satisfied unless it was a fight to the death.

"Sorry," she gritted out, sounding anything *but*.

Eli gave her a long look, then shifted his gaze to me. "I'm also sorry, Leon. We will do our best to stay out of your way for the rest of our stay. I understand you have important work to do."

His point was clear as day. Put the knife away and release Kai's sister with her head still attached to her neck. What a fucking shame. I paused a beat longer, then very reluctantly released my captive.

"Break my shit again, tough girl, and I'll break your fingers. We clear?" I was an equal opportunity killer, and she wouldn't get special treatment for having a vagina.

Her furious glare flickered with fear, and it gave me a sense of satisfaction. I left her there to be chewed out by Eli and Jae, stalking out of the gym in search of some fresh water.

I grabbed a bottle of San Pellegrino from my wine fridge and headed upstairs to shower. It was tempting to take a soak in my hot tub, but I found myself reluctant to use it without Danny. Somehow, in the short time she'd stayed with me, it had become *her* hot tub.

When I was clean and dressed, I headed back toward my office. To my intense irritation, Eli was waiting for me in the hallway.

"What?" I snapped, fresh out of fucks to give.

His deep brown eyes studied me, and he gave a small nod. "I

appreciate your restraint with Mo."

I scoffed. "That was for Danny, not her. Trust me, if I started drawing blood, I wouldn't be able to stop. And then I'd have to kill the rest of you and set up a car crash further toward town to make it look like you all died in an accident. You know how much *work* that would be? I don't have the time for that shit."

Brushing past him, I entered my office and firmly closed the door behind me. It locked automatically, and I settled back into my chair. Unlocking my monitors, I checked on the progress of Layla's drives. The first one—the smallest one—was close to finishing, and my skin itched with anticipation.

Fucking Layla, using my own tech against me. She'd *asked* me to write an encryption code for her about a year before her death. Something unhackable, she said. Something not even I would be able to access without the key. I'd done it, because I thought I loved her... I did a *lot* of things simply because she asked. But like I tried to tell her at the time, nothing was *one hundred percent* unhackable. And because I wrote the fucking code, I knew how to untangle it. With time.

While I waited, I turned my efforts back on Blanchet. The slippery fuck was harder to track down than I'd ever anticipated, but now that I had Carol Atwood as an ally—for now—then maybe we could make progress.

Accessing the file I'd compiled on the Circle, I browsed through the members. I'd thought I was so fucking smart, gathering names and data on the "anonymous" Circle members, but Carol had all but laughed at me. Apparently, their identities weren't anywhere near as guarded as the rest of the Guild had been led to believe, which made sense. Of course they would want to know who else they were dealing with. It was only common sense.

After all, it was the first thing I'd dug into when I took my own seat on the Circle.

18
DANNY

Walking into the basement fight club later that night, I felt like Danny DeLuna again. Like the Danny of six months prior, before my own guild turned on me, before I reached out to Leon, before *Kai*.

I was dressed in a black leather dress, tight to the knee with a split up my right thigh, offering easy access to the decorative—and functional—array of knives strapped there. Kai assured me that our outing was a location where visible weapons were acceptable, so I didn't hold back. Strappy leather holsters crisscrossed my chest holding guns *and* making my tits look great, and long daggers sat nestled in my calf-high boots.

Some women liked to show their strength in the absence of weapons. I knew one who struggled with the belief that over-arming herself was a sign of weakness or of feeling threatened. I didn't give a fuck. People could think whatever they wanted about me, because I had nothing to prove. And I liked my new weapons. They were *pretty*.

"Have I told you how fucking sexy you are tonight, *kaikohuru iti*?" Kai murmured as we entered the room via a steep industrial staircase. His hand rested on the small of my back, and it was a comforting warmth.

I shot him a sly grin, remembering how he'd made me come on the drive over. "You might have mentioned it."

His answering smile was pure sex, and I felt it all the way to my still throbbing cunt. "Well, I meant it." He reached out and fixed my lipstick with his thumb, and I couldn't help biting him playfully.

I was wrong. I didn't feel like the old Danny DeLuna. I felt a million times better than that, because I had Kai here with me. I wasn't alone anymore, and I had a life that was independent of the Guild. For the first time, I was starting to feel like a *person* rather than an asset.

"I thought we were here for business," I reminded him as the crowd roared for the bare-knuckled fighters in the shitty cage. The place was like a low-budget version of Anarchy in

Shadow Grove, but judging by the number of people drinking and spectating, no one cared that it was somewhat rough around the edges.

Kai gave a nod, his dark eyes searching the crowd subtly. "We are. But hopefully, it's something I can handle quickly so we can make the most of our night."

The way he looked at me when his gaze shifted back, I'd put money on the fact we weren't making it back to the hotel before fucking at least once. Sounded like my kind of night.

Kai had warned me that he needed to speak with someone about Ares business and made it crystal clear I wasn't to get involved. Not because I couldn't handle myself or because I was a weak woman, but because this was *his* business. Criminal types put a lot of stock in reputation and appearances, so tonight I was merely observing.

"I don't see him yet," Kai murmured, guiding me in the direction of the bar. It was made almost entirely of milk crates, all zip-tied together with an old door laid over them as a bar top.

"Creative," I murmured, eyeing the structure with amusement.

Kai chuckled and ordered us a couple of beers. It was likely the only thing they were selling, anyway. While we waited, I caught a couple of guys leering at me from a few feet away. It was hard *not* to notice, considering they weren't being real subtle. Fair enough, though, I was wearing more weapons than they probably owned.

The bartender handed over our drinks, and Kai passed one to me. We moved away from the milk-crate structure when one of the drunk guys stepped directly into my path.

"Excuse you," I said in a cold tone, making it perfectly clear I wasn't interested.

He wasn't taking the hint, though. "Don't I know you?" he asked, swaying slightly.

I inspected him closely, considering whether he was a previous mark. But nope, nothing about him seemed familiar, so I shook my head dismissively. "No, you don't. Get out of my way."

Brushing past him, I gave Kai a reassuring smile that I had it handled, and he nodded in return. He took my free hand in his and led the way through the edge of the crowd to where a low corridor was marked by a sign announcing it was the way to the gaming lounge. I had no doubt they were using the term *lounge* sarcastically.

We'd only taken a few steps into the corridor when the guy followed us, grabbing onto my arm and splashing some of my beer on my shoes. Motherfucker.

"No, I definitely know you," he insisted. His friend was still with him but looking decidedly less confident. Or maybe just less drunk.

I peered at his hand on my arm, then cocked one brow at him. "Take your hand off me," I advised him. Kai released my other hand, and I sensed he was content to let me put this dick in his place.

"You're that chick from the gossip magazines," the guy continued, oblivious to the danger he was in. "That long-lost heiress to some hot rich old chick. Danny something, right?" He was snapping his fingers, trying to remember my name, and a wave of cold anger settled in my stomach.

"I said, take your hand *off* me," I repeated, giving him one more chance to save his skin.

"Atwood!" he remembered with a broad leer. "That's it, right? Danny Atwood? Poor little orphan girl turned princess, eh?" He licked his lips, and my anger built.

"It's DeLuna, actually," I snapped, yanking my arm out of his grip.

The drunk guy barked a laugh. "Oh, even better! Danny DeLuna." He tossed a sleazy grin at his friend. "Get it? Double dee. Looks about right to me."

Then he committed suicide, grabbing my tits with both hands and burying his face in my cleavage to make motorboat noises. I slammed my elbow down on the back of his neck, dropping him to the floor, then Kai shot him in the head. Blood splattered my boots, and the echo of the shot made my ears ring. Meanwhile, the crowd had gone silent, everyone looking around to find where the gunshot had come from.

I glared up at my man. "I had that handled."

He just stared back at me, eyes blazing as he tucked his gun away. "I know. But I've told you before, *no one* touches what's mine and gets away with it."

Oof, and there went any illusion of dry panties. "Except Leon." I had to point out the obvious.

Kai grunted, waving over some security guards and flashing them some kind of token that saw them dragging the dead man away without a fuss. Dead guy's friend was nowhere to be seen.

"Except the *kohuru rapeti*," he agreed quietly. "Because I'm smart enough to recognize when I'm out of my league."

Tucking a possessive arm around my waist, he escorted me through to the "gaming lounge," and I couldn't help looking up at him with pure lust and adoration. Fuck me, I forgot how hot *Ares* was.

"What does that mean?" I asked out of curiosity, ignoring all the eyes on us from shocked patrons. "What you just called Leon."

Kai smirked, taking a sip of his beer that he'd held onto even when he shot that idiot a moment ago. "*Kohuru rapeti*? Means murder rabbit. Don't tell him, though. It's way too close to a compliment."

I grinned, then looped an arm around his neck, pulling him down for a kiss. Fucking hell, what was it about casual murder that got me so hot and bothered? Whatever it was, Kai wasn't complaining. He kissed me back like he was devouring his favorite snack, and I found myself losing track of time and location. It wasn't until Kai reluctantly peeled me off him that I remembered we were in the middle of a bar with a whole lot of spectators.

Not like that'd stopped me before, in fairness. But this was a slightly different crowd from Meow Lounge, and we were here for a reason.

"Ah, there's my guy," Kai murmured, his eyes locking on someone across the room.

I glanced over where he was looking and spotted the guy instantly. He was the only one sweating and trying to make a speedy exit. Stepping out of Kai's way, I gave him a smile. "Go get him. I can wait."

Kai gave me a fierce look that said I'd better stick with him, then strode across the room to apprehend his target with a heavy hand on the back of the guy's neck. I followed more slowly, not wanting to get in the way, but caught up when a security guard unlocked a door and held it open for us.

The door was closed and locked again the moment I followed Kai through—with his companion—and my eyes adjusted to the lower light of the narrow space we were in. It was a corridor of sorts, containing a bunch of thick pipes running along one wall.

Kai gave me a glance to ensure I was following, then marched the sniveling man along the dark corridor with long strides. I damn near needed to run to keep up, but I wasn't complaining. Hell, I was having fun seeing my big man at work.

Another door led us into an empty room set up with a chair. Oh yeah, this bar was no stranger to these types of interactions, that was for sure. Kai pushed the guy down on the chair as I closed the door behind us and flicked on the overhead lights.

"Daniel Rowdy," Kai said, addressing the pale, sweating man. "You're in deep shit, my friend."

Kai started rolling up his shirt sleeves, displaying his thick, tattooed forearms, and I needed to clench my thighs to stop myself from jumping him.

"Ares, man, look, I don't know what you think you heard, but they're lying. Okay? I'm your guy! Totally loyal. This is all just, you know, like a big misunderstanding." The sweaty man, Daniel, was glancing from Kai to me and back again, like he was trying to decide if I would help him.

Silly. Not all women were tenderhearted. This one sure as fuck wasn't.

"If they're lying, why are you so nervous?" Kai asked. Valid question, in my opinion.

I leaned my shoulder against the wall, casually crossing

my ankles as I observed. He had good intimidation technique, utilizing his impressive size over his prisoner. If he'd had the balls to torture me himself back on the island, maybe he'd have cracked me. Tempting fucking thought, that one. Or maybe we could have skipped to the good part sooner.

"Why am I nervous?" Daniel repeated in a squeaky voice. "You just shot a guy for touching your girlfriend! Of course, I'm nervous. That shit is fucking crazy!"

"Matter of opinion," I commented quietly, thinking of Leon. Really, Kai was the sane one of the three of us. By a long shot. Judging by the grin Kai sent my way, he agreed.

Just when I thought the night couldn't get more exciting, Kai pulled a pair of brass knuckles from his pocket and slipped them on. Fuck me dead. Was he trying to make me embarrass myself?

Apparently, Daniel Rowdy was a mid-level salesman who delivered Ares's weapons to lower-level customers. Ones who didn't warrant a personal meeting with the big dogs themselves. But Daniel had been placing his own markups on the price, and if the customer wouldn't or couldn't pay, he'd sell to someone else.

From what I gathered, Kai was *very* particular about who he sold to, so aside from the theft involved in Daniel's additional fees, the core issue was Daniel selling to unvetted buyers. These indiscretions couldn't go unpunished, that was understandable. You go easy on one mouthy little asshole, then the next one takes a dump on your bed.

I had no objections when Kai made an example out of Daniel Rowdy. Such was the nature of the game, and Daniel knew that. He took a gamble and lost.

Kai was barely even winded when he was done, which was impressive. Beating a man to death was no walk in the park. He glanced over at me, silent, with a question in his eyes. It reminded me so much of the night I'd tortured a hitman in front of him. Made him watch me cut the guy's nipples off and tear strips of skin from his balls. So he'd get zero judgment from me.

Just to make that perfectly clear, I crossed the room to where he stood and gently slid the bloodied brass knuckles from his slightly swollen fingers. I slipped them into his pocket, then gently pushed him until his back hit the door. Then I sank to my knees.

"What are you doing, *ātaahua*?" he asked, his voice husky as I unbuckled his belt.

I looked up with a lopsided smile. "I think that'd be pretty obvious, Big Man." I freed him from his pants, palming his huge cock and holding eye contact as I licked the tip. "Are you just going to stare at me? Or are you going to fuck my mouth so hard I choke on your cum?"

He whispered a curse, then gathered my hair up into a

ponytail with his fist.

Good boy. Just like that.

19
DANNY

Despite how badly I wanted to go to Edinburgh and interrogate Franklin over Jude's death, to find out whether he had anything to do with it, I found myself reluctant to actually get there. When Kai suggested we drive from London, rather than fly, I happily agreed. I claimed it was because I didn't want to check all my new toys into baggage and risk losing them, but really I just wanted to drag my heels a bit longer.

Kai saw straight through me, giving me gentle reassurances that I didn't *have* to do it. I didn't *have* to face my best friend's death so soon when it was all so raw. He even offered to work with Leon's contacts to have Franklin interrogated by a third party.

As tempting as it was, I had to see it through myself. I *needed* closure, and if Franklin *wasn't* responsible, then I *would* track down whoever was.

So I chose a blood-crimson lipstick and went thick on the eyeliner, my version of pulling on my big girl panties. I owed it to Jude not to be a coward.

The seven-hour drive seemed to evaporate in an instant, but Kai spent the entire time showing me why I was an idiot to think I could break things off with him. He didn't force me to talk about the stresses on my mind, instead regaling me with stories of his childhood with Moana and maintaining physical contact at every spare moment.

Although I didn't give much in return, I loved every second of his distraction technique. And it made me feel closer to Mo too. Throughout the drive, I exchanged multiple text messages with Leon. He assured me that he hadn't killed Kai's team despite their best efforts to piss him off. I told him I was proud of his restraint.

It was probably a good thing I'd picked up a new phone while we were in London, because that saved Kai from seeing the explicit video Leon sent after I told him that I missed him. I had no doubts Leon wouldn't have thought twice before sending it to Kai's phone if I were still borrowing it.

The sun had long since dropped below the horizon when we

arrived in Jude's old neighborhood, but I still needed to swallow a ball of dread.

"The library is closed already," I told Kai as we approached that block. He was relying on me to direct him, though, so he arched a questioning brow. "Continue on, and take the second left."

It wasn't what I'd planned to do, but now that we were here, it just felt right. I continued directing Kai until we pulled up in front of a charred shell of an apartment building. Police tape covered the doors and windows. The buildings on either side wore a heavy dose of soot and scorch marks too.

I waited for Kai to ask something dumb, like "are you okay?" but he didn't. He just got out of the car, then came around to open my door for me. He grabbed a gun from the glove compartment, tucking it under his coat before handing me the second one.

Wetting my lips, I accepted it. Better safe than sorry when we were literally in the Guild's front yard right now. The leather jacket I wore had a black fleece hood, so I pulled it up to hide my white-blonde hair as I approached the destroyed building.

"I've got your back," Kai murmured as I ducked under the caution tape covering the front door. "Just be careful where you step, okay?"

I nodded, not trusting my voice. Inside the building was pitch black, and the stink of smoke was still thick. I turned the flashlight on my phone to light my way, taking Kai's warning seriously. The last thing we needed was to fall through a patch of weakened floor and impale ourselves on jagged, broken wood.

Jude's apartment was on the first floor, but the building had solid construction. The main staircase was made of concrete, and each floor seemed to be well reinforced. Not enough to stop the fire, but enough that there were still *floors* rather than a shell.

Sadness and despair welled up inside me with every fucking step closer to Jude's apartment. By the time I passed through her broken door, I was choking on the overwhelming sense of loss. My friendship with Jude had been stronger than *any* other relationship in my life. Jude and I were always closer than Sabine and I had ever been. I loved Sabby, but Jude was my soul sister. The idea that I would never see her again, never hear her laugh or ask her advice… It was gut-wrenching.

My knees gave way in the middle of the room, and I collapsed to the sooty floor. The couch on which we'd spent so many nights hanging out was nothing more than a frame and floppy springs. The table that had held our martini glasses was gone entirely, having been made of wood.

"Holy shit," I exclaimed on a harsh exhale, running a shaking hand through my hair. My whole body ached with the pain of Jude's absence, but I wasn't crying. I was just… *sick*. "She must have been so scared."

Kai moved closer, sitting down on the floor beside me with his face to the door—keeping watch. "I know it's little consolation, but smoke inhalation would have probably seen her die before the fire ever would have touched her."

Was that little consolation? Which would I prefer, in her shoes? Dying quickly from smoke inhalation—essentially suffocating as the oxygen was consumed by the flames—or burning alive? Yeah. Easy choice.

Swallowing hard, I looked around the remains of Jude's home. Everything had been destroyed. Everything. Even her favorite painting of a naked lady riding an elephant that she'd paid half a year's wages on at auction. She loved that fucking painting *so* much.

"This can't be real," I whispered, feeling light tremors running through my limbs. "I can't believe she's really gone. She *must* have gotten out somehow. Secret basement corridor or... something. Right?"

I looked over at Kai, pleading with him to agree with me. Begging for some other explanation, something other than *Jude's dead*. Because that was just too hard to wrap my head around and fucking unfair.

Kai didn't tell me I was wrong, but the sadness in his eyes didn't offer hope. Pity. Not even the shadows could hide his pity. He thought I was grasping at straws; he just didn't want to say it. He was probably right, too. I wish I could have seen her body, seen with my own eyes that it was, in fact, *Judith Mackenzie* that they'd declared dead and not her neighbor or someone else.

"Kai... she can't be gone." This time my voice hitched, and a sob escaped.

He reached out an arm, pulling me closer to him. I buried my face in his neck, and he scooped me into his lap right there on the floor, his strong fingers stroking my hair as I shuddered.

"Tell me how you met her," he suggested after a few minutes like that. "The best way to honor our loved ones who've passed on is to remember them fondly. I never met Jude, but you clearly loved her. I bet she loved you too."

I drew a shaking breath, turning my face to rest my cheek on his shoulder, my gaze returning to the burned-out room. "She did. She was always worrying about Sabine and me when we were on assignments. We could never share the details of contracts, but she made us check in with her regularly. Like a big sister, even though she was the youngest of us by a few months."

Kai gave a low hum, his fingers still stroking my hair in a soothing way. "I like that you had someone like her. Everything you've told me about your life before we met, sounded so lonely."

"It was," I agreed with a sigh. "But it would have been so much worse without Jude and Sab. We didn't see each other every day, but when we did get together—at least for Sabby and me—it was a reminder that we were still capable of genuine emotion. That we did hold the capacity for true affection and love for another human. Not everything about us was fake."

And now I had Kai and Leon to remind me of this. My feelings for them were nothing but sincere and for no personal gain. I wanted nothing from them, except all of them.

"We met at boarding school in Vermont," I said quietly, answering Kai's question about how I'd met Jude. "She and Sab were already enrolled when I turned up mid-semester. Her parents are Guild legacies with generations worth of ill-gotten gains to their name. They wanted the *best* education for their little princess."

"And Sabine? I thought she was an orphan like you?"

I nodded against his shoulder. "She is. But she got placed into a foster family situation when she was ten. They paid for her to go to school, knowing it was a school with heavy Guild influence and affiliations."

He made a sound of irritation. "It never fails to shock me how far the Guild's reach extends and what lengths they go to in order to recruit mercenaries."

I gave a hollow laugh at that. "It's one of the oldest secret organizations in the world, Big Man. Of course their reach is global. And unfortunately, mercenaries have a tendency to wind up dead before they hit thirty-five. If they weren't constantly recruiting and training, the ranks would dwindle quickly."

"I'm not used to hearing logic applied to the Guild, *ātaahua*, that will take me a minute to get used to. Anyway, tell me how *you* ended up at this fancy school. Didn't you grow up in France?" His hand moved from my hair to my back, his arms holding me tight against him.

I loved how firmly he held me. Like he was physically sharing his strength and never wanted to let go. "I was there on a contract. Honey trapping one of the students, the son of some influential politicians. Back then, I relied on the information that my handlers provided to me for my targets. I trusted that the background info was complete and accurate. Nothing in this kid's file mentioned he was a rapist, though."

Kai stiffened like a board, and I pressed a kiss to his shoulder in reassurance.

"I was somewhat less jaded back then and had a whole lot more self-respect. Instead of doing my job—"

"Letting him *rape* you?" Kai translated, sounding horrified.

"—I freaked out and killed him. Then I panicked that I would be in trouble with the Guild for fucking up the contract. Luckily, Jude was the one who walked in on me with this douchebag's body at my feet." I smiled at the memory. I'd been standing there, practically hyperventilating after having just snapped a teenage boy's neck, and Jude just looked annoyed. "She helped me get his body into the principal's car without anyone seeing us, and then we crashed it into a tree a few miles away from the school. Everyone assumed he'd been killed in an *accident*. He already had a reputation for doing shit like stealing the principal's car, so no one questioned it."

Kai's laughter was soft and warm. "So, you bonded over

covering up a murder together? That's oddly fitting for you, *kaikohuru iti*."

I smiled wider. That night had bonded Jude and me so tightly that we had never looked back. Sabine had joined us when she was the only person to suspect I had something to do with Gregory's "accident" but just *thanked* me for whatever I'd done.

"How old were you?" Kai asked, still hugging me tightly.

I gave a small sigh, the smoke smell starting to hurt my nose. "Twelve," I replied softly. "Nearly thirteen, I think."

"Jesus Christ," Kai exclaimed on a heavy exhale. "You were just a kid."

My nose itched, and I released my grip on his shirt to rub it. "I was never just a kid, Kai. My first kill was on my eighth birthday, and every day leading up to that had been preparing me for it. Do you think less of me for it?"

He shifted away then, pulling back far enough to cup my face and peer into my eyes. "Danny DeLuna, at this stage, I'm so head over heels in love I don't think there's anything you could tell me to change that. I hate that you were robbed of your childhood. I wish more than anything that I could wind back the clock and *fix* it. But then you wouldn't be *you*. And I love *you*."

My eyes burned and I drew a shaky breath. I wasn't used to this level of openness or the acceptance. It was making me uncomfortable and awkward, but at the same time, it filled me with a warmth that I never wanted to lose.

"You're going to make me cry again if you keep talking like that, Big Man." I gave a weak laugh and raked my fingers through my hair again. "Thank you for coming here with me. I needed this."

My heart still ached like it'd been beaten with a meat tenderizer, and my skin hurt with the weight of grief and loss. I still couldn't comprehend what my life looked like without Jude in it... but that pain was tempered with the lightness of my memories.

"Are you ready to go?" Kai asked, his hands shifting back to my waist. "We can get some sleep and tackle the librarian tomorrow."

I nodded my agreement and climbed out of his lap, waiting as he picked himself up off the floor. He left the apartment first, but I lingered a moment longer.

The silence in the blackened space was suffocating, and hot tears slid silently down my cheeks as I took one final look around.

"Goodbye, Mackenzie," I whispered aloud, my voice choked. "I love you, girl. I'll never forget you."

Nothing but silence returned my sentiment, and I forced myself to leave.

As I stepped back out into the street, my phone lit up with an incoming call. I glanced at the caller ID and gave a short, tearful laugh before answering.

"You must be psychic," I said by way of greeting. "I've just been thinking about you."

"Uh, and me about you," Sabine replied. "I just went into this postage stamp town near my hideout and found a tabloid magazine with your face in it! What the what? You have a *mom?*"

Oh shit, she was *really* out of the loop. Kai held open the car door for me, and I slid inside, taking some of the sooty stench still lingering on my clothes with me before responding to Sabine. "Yeah. But I need to tell you something else before we get into all of that, babe. You're safe there, right? No one knows where you are?"

Sabine paused for a moment. "Yeah, of course. I'm bored as shit, but I'm safe. What's going on, Dan? You sound like you've been crying."

That only made me sob a laugh. But shit, I should have made more of an effort to get in touch with her sooner. I was an asshole, and she deserved to know what was going on, if only for the sake of her own safety. Even if saying the words out loud felt like I was stabbing myself with a hot poker, I owed her that much.

"Jude's dead."

20

KAI

Danny's conversation with Sabine was rough, and by the time she ended the call, her eye makeup sat in black streaks down her face, and her shoulders were slumped in exhaustion. Fuck, I wished it was a weight I could take off her shoulders. I wanted to scoop her up and carry her back to my secluded island... just shut the whole world out and pretend it was just her and me again.

However, those days were long gone, and she wouldn't appreciate being coddled. I understood that now and was man enough to admit that it was something I'd only truly accepted after she chose herself and walked the fuck away.

Until that moment, I had been under some kind of misguided delusion that I could make her fit the fabricated version of Danny DeLuna living in my head. The one that was a combination of the real her and the fake one who I'd *started* falling for.

It took losing her to make me wake the fuck up to my own shitty behavior, and now I was *determined* to prove I was worth the second chance. I needed her to see that I could handle everything she was—bloody hands and all—because my own were far from clean.

Fuck, it was a difficult balance, though. My desire to *protect* her was so intense it nearly choked me sometimes, but she needed for me to show I trusted her. Or more than that, I needed to show that I *respected* her as a badass in her own right. She'd been killing since she was eight, she didn't *need* my protection. But maybe one day, she'd want it, and I'd be right there.

When that drunk fuck had motorboated her tits, though, I'd snapped. He put his hands on her, and I saw red.

Glancing over at her now in the passenger seat, I ached to just take her away from the Guild, to kiss away her tears and remind her how loved she was. Not just by me, but by Leon—that crazy fuck—too.

"Where are we?" she asked in a dull voice, frowning out the window. She'd been in a daze since speaking to Sabine, so I'd taken us to a hotel that I knew had good security. "The Dorchester Inn?"

I hopped out, passing the keys to the valet, then opened Danny's door for her. A bellboy loaded our bags onto a cart, and I just linked my fingers with Danny's to take her inside the hotel with me. She remained silent and lost in her own head while I checked us in, then yawned heavily while we rode the elevator up to our floor.

As soon as we got into the room, I did a quick sweep for security's sake, then debated running her a bath. One look at her, though, decided it for me. She was so tired and drained that she was swaying slightly, so I gently coaxed her into bed instead, peeling her clothes off without any sexual intent. Big steps for me, right there.

When she was tucked in and I'd cleaned her face with a washcloth, she grabbed my hand and pulled me back to her before I could leave.

"What's up, Siren?" I asked in a low whisper, studying her face. She was processing, and revisiting Jude's home had been a huge step toward closure.

"Sorry," she mumbled, blinking slowly. "I'll be me again in the morning."

That made my chest ache. "You're you now, beautiful. Just a sad version of you." I brushed her hair out of her face and kissed her lips softly. "Sweet dreams, *ātaahua*."

She went to sleep in no time at all. I waited for our bags to be delivered just a few minutes later, then showered the cloying smell of smoke off my skin. When I slipped into bed, she rolled toward me and snuggled into my arms without ever waking up.

Somehow, I slept longer than she did. When I woke up the next morning, she was already exiting the bathroom, wrapped in a hotel towel with a billow of steam following her, like special effects on a goddess appearing or some shit.

"Hey, Sleeping Beauty," she greeted me with a smile, her eyes sharp and alert. All the shadows and sadness from the night before seemed totally gone. "I wondered when you'd wake up. Shall we get breakfast before we grill old man Franklin?"

I studied her a little closer, but her posture was relaxed and calm. She was more like Moana than I'd realized. My sister had moments when grief and loss built up so heavy she just needed to break. Then a day or a week later, she buried it all back down inside, and it was like it had never happened.

I suspected it wasn't the *healthiest* coping mechanism, but at least it was one. If that was what worked for Danny, then I wouldn't go poking holes where they weren't needed.

"Absolutely," I agreed, stretching and yawning. "Give me five minutes."

She moved out of my way, letting me have the bathroom while she hunted out some clothes to wear. I didn't close the door, preferring to watch her while I showered. I liked to think of it as a caution, but obsession might be closer to the mark.

I washed quickly, using the cool water to wake myself up,

then threw on some clothes.

Leon called her as we walked down the street to breakfast, and I tried to pretend I wasn't listening in. The soft smile that always touched her lips when she spoke to him tested me, though. The only thing that I held onto was the blind trust that she looked the same when it was me on the other end of the phone. For now, though, I was happy to be the one holding her hand, even if she was flirting with another guy on the phone.

"Does he always call you so often?" I couldn't help myself asking when she ended the call.

We'd just sat down for breakfast, and she gave me a lopsided smile, her gaze assessing. "No, not always. I would almost say he's feeling threatened right now and trying to make sure I don't forget about him."

I grinned before I could stop it. She rolled her eyes but refocused on the menu. When our server came over, I ordered a full Scottish breakfast. Danny wrinkled her nose at my choice and ordered Eggs Benedict for herself.

"What?" I asked when our server left.

"Black pudding," she commented, giving an ick face. "You know what that's made of?"

I chuckled, nodding. "I do. But when you grow up hungry, you learn all food is good food." Ah crap, there I go dousing the mood. "Mo used to tease me about how I'd eat literally anything. In addition to being short for Malachi, *Kai* means food in te reo."

Her expression softened, and I suspected she was feeling sorry for scrawny little neglected Malachi. So I smoothly shifted the conversation to our plans for the librarian. Despite how Danny described him as a stiff-necked old man, he was still a former mercenary. And only the best lived long enough to retire into a boring archive job.

He wouldn't be the kind of guy we could snatch and beat the shit out of, so much to Danny's annoyance, we both decided that this was a fly better caught with honey than shit.

Which was how, an hour later, I was forced to sit back and watch the woman I loved *flirt* with a man in his seventies.

Okay, maybe flirting was an exaggeration. But it was a far cry from the torture techniques I'd been imagining when Danny first said she wanted to interrogate Fake-Name-Franklin. He was working on the library floor, and there were enough people around that violence wasn't going to go over well. Especially since it was a Guild-owned property and at least half of the people within the enormous building were lethally armed.

Franklin didn't seem charmed by Danny despite not even trying to disguise the way he eyed her up. After only a few minutes, his patience seemed to snap, and he slammed a book down on the cart he was pushing.

"Miss DeLuna," he snapped, peevish as fuck, "if you would like to accuse me of something, perhaps you'd like to do it in my office? Your friend can come too, if you need the protection."

The way he looked down his nose at her had my blood boiling, but she seemed unbothered, just calm and serene as she accepted his offer. Franklin huffed again, then led the way to the big glass-walled office behind the main desk of the library.

I followed, because fuck waiting outside like a puppy, and closed the door behind myself once I was inside.

"Now then, am I understanding you're here with accusations that I was somehow involved in Judith's recent passing?" He seemed irritated as he sat behind his meticulous desk, his glasses perched low on his nose. But there were lines of tension across his weathered face, and his eyes were red and glassy.

Danny sat in the chair opposite, folding her elegant legs and drawing a slow breath. "Yes. It's been confirmed to me that she was targeted by a Guild executioner on contract."

Franklin barely flinched. "Oh? That's news to me. How do you know?"

Danny's answering smile was cool. "We also know you and Jude were… involved." She didn't even try to hide the revulsion on her face at that.

Franklin just sat there, staring at her for the longest time with *zero* facial expression whatsoever. Then he drew a deep breath and exhaled slowly, folding his hands in front of him.

"I see," he murmured. "Then I also assume you've uncovered the payments I was making to her to stop her talking to my wife?"

Danny just stared back, meeting him with a blank expression

of her own. It was like watching the most intense game of tennis imaginable. Or chess. Maybe more like chess.

"Then I don't blame you for looking at me. I would be my first suspect too." His gaze flicked to me with curiosity, then back to Danny. "Fortunately for you, Miss DeLuna, I know why Judith was really killed, and I promise it wasn't because of her affair with me."

I couldn't keep my mouth shut. "You know who killed her? Why haven't you—"

"I said I know *why* she was killed," Franklin cut me off with a scathing glare. "Not *who* was responsible."

"Why?" Danny asked, keeping the conversation on track with total calm.

Franklin refocused on her, pursing his lips. "I'm sure you're aware, as archivists, we have access here to a lot of sensitive information. I trust this won't go any further?"

Danny's eyes narrowed, but she said nothing. She just waited for him to continue speaking.

After a moment's deliberation, he sighed. "One of the Circle has been missing for a number of years. Inactive, rather. He isn't dead. Several other Circle have confirmed contact with him at regular intervals, so his seat cannot be replaced. But a Circle seat can only remain inactive for a limited period of time before that member is declared 'dead' for the sake of succession."

I could see that information ticking over in Danny's mind.

This wasn't news to me. My mole had told us this years ago. But what purpose did it serve in relation to Judith's death?

"Does that Circle member have heirs?" Danny was following a lot faster than I was.

Franklin's old eyes lit up with appreciation that she was on the right path. "He does not."

Surprise flickered over Danny's face. "So what happens when he is declared 'dead' for inactivity?"

Franklin's smile said she had asked the right question. "The seat gets passed to the next family line in the document of hierarchy. Essentially a list that was drawn up by the founding members of our Guild, naming the hundreds of families who assisted them in those early days and ranking them in order of importance. When a seat becomes vacant, it passes to the next in line."

"Let me guess," I muttered, "Jude had the list?"

Franklin looked irritated. Again. "Of course not. Are you stupid? I am the *only* person within the Guild who can even access it. I don't care how pretty Judith was, I don't break the archive rules for *anyone*. You two included, so if you think I'll be showing you the list, you can forget it."

Danny was frowning in thought, though. "So, if Jude was killed because of this line of succession... the Mackenzie family was next in line for the seat, weren't they?"

Franklin didn't *confirm* it, but he also didn't deny it. He just stared.

"Wait, what about her parents?" she asked, shaking her head.

"She wasn't the last of her line. Her parents are still alive, as are her uncle and cousins."

Franklin grimaced, looking genuinely distressed. "Were. The entire family was found dead in the Mackenzie estate a few days earlier. I crossed their name off the list this morning. Before you ask, I can't tell you anything about the remaining names. Only the deceased lines."

Danny's careful, calm mask slipped, and distraught pain flashed through. "Blanchet," she hissed under her breath. Her hand curled into a fist in her lap, and I understood just how murderous she was feeling. Franklin seemed confused, though.

"Emmanuel Blanchet?" he asked, adjusting his glasses. "What does he have to do with this?"

Danny gave a scoff. "He's the bastard who's been trying to kill me for months. This has his sticky fingerprints all over it." She seemed to realize she was letting too much slip, though, because she quickly pulled her mask back into place and offered Franklin a cool smile. "Thank you for your time, Franklin. You've been helpful."

The old librarian frowned with concern as Danny stood up, and he gave a slight shake of his head. "Miss DeLuna, I'm not one to go offering personal opinions over facts, but... I think you're being misled about Emmanuel." He stood up himself, offering her a tight smile in return. At her cool look, he shook his head again. "Then again, what would I know? I could swear some days, I'm already sliding into dementia."

I opened the door for Danny, then followed her out of the office with Franklin trailing after us.

"Miss DeLuna," he called out before we got too far away. Really, just announce to everyone she was here. I scanned our surroundings as she glanced back. "I have her things…from her desk. If you'd like those."

"They weren't taken by the Guild?" Suspicion sharpened each word.

"No." The older man actually seemed… *older* all of a sudden. "They were personal items, and the end of a line means…"

She studied him with a dangerous intensity. "Means absolutely nothing because they are dead and gone, so who cares?"

He just sighed. "For what it's worth, I loved her. I'm just as upset by her passing as you are. I hope you find whoever did it and make them pay."

"Count on it," Danny replied, her gaze hard. "And yes, I guess I'll take her things."

The strong set to her shoulders helped me to understand her better. She wasn't pushing all the pain and grief aside or pretending it'd never happened. Instead, she was using it to sharpen her focus and harden her resolve to do whatever needed to be done.

There was no doubt in my mind that she'd avenge Judith's death.

21
DANNY

As disappointing as it was to walk away from the archives without any concrete answers, I wasn't shocked. The idea that Franklin had killed Jude over their affair was just too... predictable? Far too mundane, at any rate. Despite how badly I wanted to bring her murderer to justice, I was kind of relieved to find it was twisted up in a Guild power play.

Jude would have been *so* offended to be killed by a lovers' tiff. This was a much more fitting scenario to justify the use of an arson executioner and multiple casualties.

There was no way in hell Franklin was going to part with

prime suspect. And he was too experienced to just have it lying around somewhere we could steal it, so I wasn't going to waste my energy there.

Instead, I called Carol. After all, if she really was on my side and wanted to help, surely she could use her Circle power to pull some strings?

Shit. That reminded me, I still needed to have an honest conversation with Leon... but it was a chat best done face-to-face, not over the phone from opposite sides of the globe.

"You trust her?" Kai asked after I ended my call with Carol. I'd given her a brief overview of the whole Jude situation, and she'd promised to send over a copy of the Guild's investigation file. Of course they'd handled the entire crime scene, sealing off the records and sweeping the casualties under the rug away from government bodies.

Because of that, I couldn't access the files. Even if I was ballsy—or stupid—enough to log into my Guild account, I wouldn't have the necessary level of clearance to download those documents. Carol did, though. She wasn't optimistic that it'd give us any solid leads, but she—like me—was of the opinion that it couldn't hurt to read over the notes anyway.

I nodded slowly. "I do... as much as I trust anyone, I guess." I paused at that, shaking my head. "That's not true. I *trust* you. And I trust Leon. How I feel about Carol... probably as equal as I trust Sabby, which is as good as it gets outside of you two. Do you think I'm wrong?"

He glanced over at me, considering my question for a moment before returning his eyes to the road. We were heading to the private airfield where Kai's plane was waiting for us after he placed a call to Jae last night.

"My instincts," he said carefully, "or rather my experiences and preconceptions, tell me that none of the Circle can be trusted. Not a single one of them. Because as far as I was concerned, and from everything I'd been led to believe, they were *all* complicit in the atrocities the Guild commits."

He paused, thinking, and I didn't rush to contradict those statements. He had spent ten years believing he knew everything there was to know about the Guild, never really questioning the validity of those beliefs.

"Since getting to know you," he continued in a pensive tone, "and *kohuru rapeti*... I find myself needing to reassess everything I *knew*. Or everything I *thought* I knew. It's becoming painfully apparent that I really knew very little about the organization I've been waging war on for years. So when it comes to Carol Atwood, I honestly don't know what to think. She's Circle, but she's also your biological mother."

He drummed his fingers on the steering wheel, processing. I just watched him, quietly enjoying the fact that he was taking the time to reflect on his own mistakes.

"I think you have impeccable instincts, Siren. I personally don't know that I could trust Carol—or any Circle member—but I trust your judgment." He gave a short sigh. "But if she double-crosses you, I won't hesitate to kill her."

Aw, I loved when he was all growly and protective. "Maybe I'd let you help," I teased.

He sent me an amused glance, a smile playing over his lips. "Seeing as we're speaking honestly right now, can I tell you something that's playing on my mind?" He took the off-ramp toward the private airfield, and in the distance, a small aircraft was coming in to land. It wouldn't be long until we were back in the air and on our way back to Alaska. Back to my bunny.

"Of course," I replied with a frown. "Don't we always speak honestly?"

He quirked a brow at me, and I grinned. Okay, so maybe we never outright *lied*, but all three of us were well versed in dancing around the truth and making carefully worded, misleading statements. Not that I thought any of us *intended* to lie, but it was just second nature.

"Point taken," I murmured to his unspoken challenge. "So tell me."

He wet his lips. "I don't want to go back to Alaska. Could I convince you to come to my island instead?"

That wasn't what I'd been expecting. "That depends. Is it the cold that you want to avoid? Or Leon?" He gave me a long look, and I sighed. "Then no."

He nodded. "I figured but had to ask."

"I thought you were okay with him," I said, feeling a pit of anxiety open up within me. "Haven't we put this whole competitive shit to bed already? Kai, I can't go back to—"

"No, we have," he assured me, cutting me off before I could spiral. "I have *accepted* that you need—or want—him in your life. I've made peace with that. But it will take some time before I stop *wanting* you all to myself."

Oh. Well, shit. When he put it like that...

"That's understandable," I said softly. But I missed my bunny... phone calls weren't cutting it, even though it'd only been a couple of days. "You're okay to share, but not *all* the time?"

He nodded again, giving me a smile. "As much as I hate putting myself in *his* shoes, I bet Leon feels the same way."

It was a fair point. And something I would need to seriously think about, to take *their* feelings into consideration. Each of my guys was dating me, not each other. So to expect them to constantly be around one another, knowing how close they were to literally killing each other so recently, was an unrealistic expectation. And a selfish one, now that I really thought about it. Shit, why'd I have to make this all so freaking complicated for myself?

I was spared the need to delve deeper into that subject as we pulled into the parking lot of the private airport. Kai seemed content to let it drop, too, hopping out of the car to grab our bags.

"Boss man!" Jae called out as we exited the tiny terminal building a few minutes later. He was bouncing down the narrow stairs of their jet, a huge grin on his face. "It's good to see your face."

He grabbed Kai in one of those manly bro-hugs, then turned his smile to me.

"Hi, Jae," I said, not matching his energy. Not even close. I was carrying the archive box full of Jude's personal belongings, though, so it was easy to avoid a hug.

"Danny-cat, you're a sight for sore eyes." His eyes were just a *touch* too interested, and my own smile chilled somewhat.

Kai kept a hand on Jae's shoulder, then gave me a warm look. "Siren, head on in and get comfy. Jae and I need a quick word."

He wouldn't get any complaints from me about that. I started to move past them, but Jae called out my name again.

"A shady dude came by about five minutes ago and dropped off a file for you, Danny-cat. Said it was from Carol someone?" Jae indicated to the plane. "I left it on the table."

My brows hitched. When Carol said she would get me a copy of Jude's file, I didn't realize she meant a *physical* copy. "That was quick," I commented, exchanging a look with Kai. "Thanks, Jae."

Leaving them to their "chat," I carried the box of Jude's things up the stairs to the plane and ducked inside. A quick glance around told me it was a very similar layout to Carlos's plane I'd been borrowing for the last few years. I hadn't wanted to use it since he basically told me our friendship was done, so it was lucky Kai had his own.

The thick folder of papers was on one of the tables just like Jae told me, and I placed my box down beside it. Sitting down, I glanced out the window and found Kai gripping the front of Jae's shirt in an unmistakably threatening way. Good. Jae had been giving me bad vibes ever since he "rescued" me from Sam back on the island, so I was more than happy to let Kai put him in his place. It saved me from having to break his fingers.

I set the box from Jude's office aside and reached for the file Carol's guy had delivered. It was sealed, but I ran a finger under the tab to tear it open, then pulled out the wad of paperwork from inside.

As requested, it was a copy of the Guild investigation file for the fire. I paused a moment on that first page, mentally shoring up my defenses. I needed my shields high and impenetrable, because now wasn't the time to grieve. I'd had my moment, falling to pieces in the burned-out shell of Jude's home, and again on the phone to Sabine. Now, she needed me to find her murderer and turn them into a blood eagle.

Not giving myself a chance to talk myself out of it, I started reading through the investigation notes. Page after page, the investigation addressed the entire building and every person who'd died within it. The target was clear, though. Jude was the only Guild employee living there.

When I reached the photographs, I needed to close my eyes

for a moment.

Maybe this was a bad idea. I'd already seen the building more than two weeks after the fire. Did I really need to see photos of the scene on that day?

"Here," Kai said gently, startling me. I hadn't even noticed he'd joined me, but there was a vodka martini on a little coaster on the table. "You okay?" His gaze was intense and understanding.

I jerked a nod but gulped my martini in three mouthfuls. "Yup," I croaked, placing the glass back down. "Come sit." I patted the seat directly beside me, and Kai moved around from where he'd been sitting opposite. He'd already placed my box of Jude's things on its own seat and strapped the seat belt around it. Big sweetie.

I turned my attention back to the file in my hands, angling it so Kai could see what I was looking at. He gave a grunt but said nothing else as I slowly cycled through the images.

"Jesus fucking Christ," I muttered on a harsh exhale when I reached the photos of Jude. "I didn't expect that."

Part of me had just assumed there was nothing left. Wasn't that what happened in a fire? But no, there she was. Kai had been right that she died of smoke inhalation—that was the medical examiner's consensus too. According to the notes, first responders had pulled her out relatively quickly, given she only lived on the first floor. They attempted CPR and all the rest, but she was already gone. Probably a good thing, too, as half her body was covered in horrific burns.

I sat there for a long time, just staring at the photo of my dead friend. It'd been taken on the metal table of a morgue, just like the images of the other casualties from the fire, and I found myself wishing she'd been more badly disfigured in the fire. At least if she was, I could pretend it was someone else. Like maybe they'd made a mistake in identifying her.

But no. There she was. Dead.

"Fuck," I whispered.

Kai pressed a kiss to my shoulder, and I cleared my throat. Tears wouldn't save Jude now. They were nothing but a waste of water.

Drawing a deep breath, I packed all the papers back into the envelope and stood up to tuck it inside Jude's box of things.

"I need a distraction," I said quietly to Kai when I sat back down. I took his hand in mine, linking our fingers together and feeling the solid warmth of his grip. We were already airborne. How did that happen?

He squeezed my fingers, then kissed my cheek softly. I half expected him to suggest we join the Mile High Club again, but he didn't. He just told me to get comfortable, reclining our seats together and then soothing me with legends. Stories of men who fished islands up from the sea or slowed the sun by lassoing it. My favorite would always be Pania, though, and Kai elaborated on that for me, telling me of her child who became a Taniwha.

Even legends with unhappy endings offered a measure of succor or warning in their magic. I needed both right now.

22
DANNY

Kai's team didn't mess around with snowmobiles to access Leon's house, they had a helicopter waiting at the closest airfield, and Jae landed it right beside the secluded house. I bet Leon just *loved* that, too.

I made a mental note to suggest Kai send his team elsewhere. Leon lived in the middle of nowhere for a reason, and it wasn't for the climate. It wasn't fair on my very private, antisocial Bunny to have all these strangers literally inside his home.

Leon met us at the door, not even waiting for a *hello* before throwing me over his shoulder.

I let out a yelp of surprise but didn't struggle because it was my bunny, and he clearly missed me as much as I missed him. Yet, for some reason, Eli must have seen that as a threatening move and stepped in front of the stairs before Leon could carry me up them.

"Get the *fuck* out of my way, guard dog," Leon snarled with real venom in his voice. I definitely needed to get Kai's team out of his house before they all mysteriously disappeared in the night.

I arched my back to look over at Eli, but he was focused on Kai. Silently asking his boss's permission. Fuck's sake, this was a disaster waiting to happen.

"Move, Eli," Kai rumbled. The quietly dangerous man did as he was told, and Leon muttered an insult as he took the stairs two at a time with me still over his shoulder.

As much as I wanted to fall straight into bed with Leon and show him how good it was to see him again, the mood was off. So when he kicked his bedroom door shut and tossed me onto his bed, the heat had cooled off dramatically.

"What's wrong?" he asked, frowning as he studied my face. Despite Kai's valiant efforts to distract me on the flight, the sadness and heartbreak of seeing Jude's dead body still lingered. "Who do I need to kill?"

I shook my head, offering a weak smile as I reached out a hand. "No one. Come here."

Leon still looked all kinds of suspicious and angry, but he crawled onto the bed as I asked, wrapping me up in a tight embrace. "It feels like you've been gone for a month, *mon cœur,* not a week." He kissed my neck and inhaled deeply.

"Good thing you have a photo gallery to keep you warm at night," I replied, referring to the nudes he'd taken of me while I was fast asleep that first night we'd fucked. It should have been creepy and voyeuristic, but I couldn't think of it as anything but romantic. He'd been about to kill me but wanted a reminder after I was gone. Crazy loved so much harder than sane.

Leon gave a soft laugh into my hair, his arms holding me tighter against him. "I need more. Later, though."

I wasn't in the mood to talk, and Leon didn't try to pry. Once he satisfied himself that he didn't need to kill anyone *right now*, he was content to just… snuggle. If someone had told me a year ago that I would be *snuggling* with Leon Marx, I'd have laughed my head off. And yet, here we were, comfy as all hell.

Leon must not have been sleeping a whole lot recently, because we only lay together for a few minutes before I felt his body relax and his breathing slow to the deep, even pace of sleep. As carefully as I could, I turned over in his loosened embrace, wanting to see his face.

My poor bunny had huge dark circles under his eyes, and he hadn't shaved all week. He'd probably been at his computer day and night, not feeling safe to sleep with Kai's team inside his house. Shit, he wasn't going to feel safe here anymore. I got it. I was the same way after I realized Kai had found *my* home.

The fact that it was Kai, and I trusted him, was irrelevant. It was the fact that *anyone* had found it and accessed it without my security alarms going off. If Kai could do it, someone else may be able to. So as far as I was concerned, I needed a new home. So did Leon, by the look of things, which made me sad because this house was so beautifully *Leon*.

I lay there for a long time, just staring at him while he slept. Creepy? Maybe for other couples. Considering how often Leon watched me sleep, it was only fair to return the favor. Besides, I was so calm and content lying there with his heavy arm over my waist and his soft breath feathering my skin, I just didn't want to move.

Eventually, though, I needed to get up to pee. Then, of course, I was too anxious and restless to get back into bed and risk waking him up. So, in favor of letting my bunny sleep, I tiptoed out of the room with plans to make a coffee. I paused right outside the door, though, seeing my box of Jude's belongings sitting in the corridor. Kai must have put it there so he didn't interrupt Leon and me.

Cute. Maybe they would find a balance between them, given a bit of time.

Curiosity burned hot, so I abandoned my coffee plans and picked up the box, carrying it back into Leon's bedroom. He had a small decorative armchair in the corner, so I sat myself down and carefully lifted the lid off the box. The distinctive scent of Jude's perfume made my nose twitch, and I sneezed. There was another smell mixed with hers, and I could only describe it as old man cologne.

Gross. I couldn't get past the Franklin affair. It was just so...

what the fuck, Jude?

Even so, I loved that her things still smelled like her. It made me feel warm and fuzzy but also painfully cold all at the same time. It was such a familiar perfume yet a harsh reminder that she was gone.

"Pull it together, DeLuna," I whispered to myself, glancing over to make sure I hadn't woken Leon. He didn't even stir, though, so I shook my head and pulled up my metaphorical big girl panties. I wanted to see what Jude had saved. What she valued enough to display on her desk. Yeah, I was reopening the wound, but I couldn't *not* look.

Inside the box, the investigation file was exactly where I'd left it, so I moved that aside. I didn't need to go looking through those photos again. Instead, I focused on the few personal belongings Franklin had packed up. When he said the Guild hadn't taken everything, he meant they hadn't taken anything *worthless* to them. Like the little silver paperweight in the shape of a grenade that I gave her a few years ago or her collection of novelty flamingo pens—complete with feathers.

There wasn't a lot, and most of it was meaningless, like her daily planner that she almost never used or a stack of impersonal stationery. But there was also a thick stack of photos, slightly tacky from where she'd had them stuck to the wall beside her desk at the library. I remembered seeing them there countless times when I'd visited her at work, but I was interested in taking a better look.

Glancing over to check on Leon again, I placed the rest of the box aside and put the pile of sticky photos in my lap. Jude was sentimental as hell and always tried to take at least one picture every time we got together. The ones she stuck on her wall at work were her favorites, so it was nice to look through them. Jude and Sabine were the only people I had ever trusted to take my photo, because I trusted them implicitly. Anyone else? Not a chance in hell. Too risky for a mercenary who worked most contracts undercover. Anonymous.

I lost track of time, absorbed in the memories contained within those photographs, so when Leon crouched beside the chair to wipe tears from my cheek, I startled somewhat.

"Sorry," I whispered with a sniff. "I thought you were still asleep." I swiped my cheeks with my fingers, feeling awkward. I thought I was done crying.

"Can I see?" he asked, reaching for the photos.

I jerked a nod and handed them over. He stood up, then indicated for me to get up too. When I did, he took my seat and dragged me back down into his lap.

"Tell me," he murmured, indicating the first photo on the pile. It was one of Jude, Sabine, and me as teenagers. We wore sombreros, and Sabine was dangling a mezcal worm over Jude's open mouth.

I smiled and quietly told him about that night. How Sabine

had been practicing her document forgery, so she wanted us to test out some fake IDs at a Mexican bar. Jude had ended up vomiting inside her purse later that night, then found it the next morning.

We went through all the images together, Leon listening attentively as I told him the story behind every picture that I knew. Some of them were locations or events I hadn't been at, but at least ninety percent were of me, Jude, and Sabine.

My phone vibrated in my pocket as we were reaching the last few photos, and I shifted to pull it out. The caller ID showed Carol's name, and I showed Leon before answering the call.

"Danny, please tell me you got out of Scotland safely?" she asked in lieu of a greeting. Her voice was stiff and businesslike. This was Circle member Carol, not Koen's mom.

I frowned. "Yes, I did. And I got the file. Thank you for that."

Carol released a heavy sigh of relief on the other end of the call. "Thank goodness," she murmured. "Someone released some inmates from the Castle yesterday, and I can't help my suspicion that it was linked to you being in Edinburgh."

Shocked, I scrambled off Leon's lap and ran a hand through my hair. "What, like Blanchet released them himself?"

Carol gave an irritated grunt. "Maybe. Between Leon's protection order and my publicizing you as my daughter, he would be having a hard time getting anyone decent enough to take the job. If he's desperate... who knows? I just wanted to make sure you're long gone from Scotland."

I wet my lips, considering the fact she hadn't tracked Kai's plane. Out of politeness? Or did Kai cover his tracks better than I gave him credit for?

"Yeah, I'm long gone," I confirmed. "How many inmates are we talking? That got let out of the Castle?"

The Castle was not a castle at all. Or, it hadn't been in a very, very long time. Now it was just ruins, but the extensive dungeons were still in use by the Guild as a prison. The idea that the Guild killed first and asked questions later was untrue. In some cases, prisoners were taken if they were holding onto vital information that the Guild wanted. They were placed in one of seven Guild prisons across the world and interrogated by the best of the best. Sometimes clients could pay to put someone into the prisons, too, for extended torture and questioning, and sometimes the Guild decided they might have a use for a prisoner at a later date, so they were kept alive.

Regardless of the reasons, none of the inmates within the Castle were the kind of people anyone wanted released back into society.

"That's unclear at this stage," Carol replied, sounding more than annoyed. "I'm working on finding out, though. I'll be back in touch when I have more information, but for now… stay hidden. Don't take unnecessary risks, okay?"

"Understood," I agreed, entirely unsure how to react to her concern for my safety.

Thankfully, Carol ended the call and spared me giving her an awkward thank you. Leon was waiting patiently, having packed Jude's photos back into the box and replaced the lid. I gave him the information Carol had passed on, and his expression tightened.

"I should get back to my office," he said with a sigh, standing up and pulling me closer with a hand on my waist. "I love that you're back, though."

I leaned into him, looping an arm around his neck as I tipped my head back for a kiss.

He obliged, kissing me with an intensity that washed all the residual sadness out of my head, leaving me filled with heady desire and a sense of empowerment. Kissing Leon was an addiction that I never wanted to quit, because it made me feel alive.

"You haven't been sleeping enough," I told him in a mocking scold when he released my lips. "I'm going to make coffee. Do you want me to bring you one?"

He started to shake his head—I was pretty sure he didn't drink coffee—then changed his mind. "Sure," he agreed with a half-smile. "I also have some cookies stashed in the pantry, assuming the big dumb fuck's friends haven't found them."

I gave a laugh, despite knowing I shouldn't encourage that nickname. "How do you like your coffee?" Reluctantly, I peeled myself out of his arms and exited the bedroom with him following.

Leon went the opposite way down the hall, heading to his office. "However you have it," he called back. Then he shot me a smile and a wink before disappearing into his sanctum.

23
LEON

Who in their right fucking mind would have let inmates out of the Castle? That news from Carol was a shock, to say the least. The fuckers locked up in Guild prisons weren't there under mistaken identities or false imprisonment. They were some scary motherfuckers, and I needed to know which of them had been released so we could prepare.

There wasn't a single doubt in my mind that this was done because of DeLuna. I'd pissed Blanchet off with the protection order, effectively denying access to the executioners. And no one *lower* than executioner-level was good enough to take down my woman. Especially with me by her side.

And, I guessed, Kai wasn't *totally* useless. After all, he'd gained such a reputation as Ares for a reason. Just because all I'd seen of him was a pussy-whipped bitch, didn't mean he was a liability.

In fairness, Danny had that effect on me, too. Like when she just offered to make me coffee? I didn't drink coffee. But I just wanted to accept because it'd make her happy.

I probably had five or ten minutes before she returned, so I took care of the sensitive work first, logging into my ultra-secure Circle server and checking to see if Blanchet had responded to my request for a meeting. The message had been viewed, but no reply had been sent.

Mother *fucker*.

I needed to find out what was going on with the Castle, though. Carol said she was working on it, but there was no harm in us both putting our effort into it. Funny enough, I rarely exerted my Circle powers. I'd taken the seat five years earlier after killing my mother, but I never wanted to be in charge.

Guess that was my punishment for not thinking things through when I lost my temper during a forced "therapy" session with dear old mommy. As it was, I did the bare minimum. I put together my own outer circle who basically ran my position for me, and I wouldn't be surprised if I wasn't the only Circle seat who did that.

I was already an alpha-level hacker and an established

executioner when I took my seat, so I saw no reason why that should change. It was a perfect cover, anyway. Taking orders from other Circle members gave me a free pass from suspicion that I might be anything more.

Meanwhile, it left me free to pick and choose my jobs, manipulate the system to suit my desires, and generally do whatever the fuck I wanted. Now, though, I was wishing I'd been more hands-on. Maybe if I'd worked on forging relationships with the rest of the Circle, beyond just investigating who they were, I could have cut this whole mess off before it got so out of hand.

Carol's deception—her dummy records and altered ID pictures—made me second-guess all the files I'd pulled together for the rest of the Circle. It was something I needed to put some serious work into, but it could wait until Danny was free and clear.

Instead, I used my credentials to log into the Castle's database and pull up a list of the released inmates. When I scanned the thankfully short list, an oily sense of dread curled through my stomach. Sure, they had only released ten inmates out of roughly a hundred and fifty at the Castle, but they were easily the ten worst.

"Shit," I breathed, double-clicking on the seventh name on the list. "This is bad. Very bad."

A light flashed above my desk, announcing that someone was

at the door. I didn't get up to unlock it, though. There was a pause, then the locks clicked open and the door opened to let my love inside.

"You added my prints to the lock?" she asked in shock, handing me one of the mugs she carried. She closed the door again, and the locks slid back into place smoothly.

"Of course I did," I replied, sniffing the hot beverage she'd brought me. Even I could admit that coffee *smelled* good, I'd just never been a fan of the flavor. Too bitter.

She frowned, setting her mug down carefully out of the way of my electronics and then looking around. "Why *of course?*" she asked. "This is your evil lair. I wouldn't expect you to give me free access."

I reached out and snagged her hand, tugging her closer while making sure I didn't spill my coffee on the keyboard. I didn't have another spare. Actually, I'd better put it down, just in case.

"DeLuna," I said, pulling her into my lap once my mug was safely set down. "My evil lair is up here." I tapped my temple, giving her a grin. "And I've let you in there already. So what does this office matter? I have no desire to keep secrets from you."

She shifted in my lap, getting comfy and making my dick twitch. "That's very mature of you, Bunny," she teased. "I thought you were made of mystery and soaked in secrecy. It's basically your identity now."

I smiled, cupping a hand around the back of her neck beneath her silken hair. "To everyone else, sure. But not you, *ma moitié*. That whole breakup threat you pulled in Shadow Grove gave me a wake-up call. Kai, too, if I'm being fair. It made *him* realize there were worse things than having to share your heart."

Her sapphire eyes studied my face intently. "And you, Bunny Rabbit? What did it make you realize?"

"That you are worth more than all my secrets," I confessed quietly, holding her gaze. "That I would do *anything*... I mean *anything*... to avoid hurting you like that again. I've never felt like this for anyone in my life, and I don't ever want to lose this feeling. I don't want to lose *you*. Making small concessions like allowing Kai to live—"

"*Leon*," she scolded, her eyes narrowed.

I laughed. "Okay, fine. Allow him to be a part of *this*." I gently tapped her chest above her heart. "That is a small sacrifice for me, because as much as I hate it... he makes you happy. And *that* is my new favorite thing in the whole world, *mon ange*."

My pulse was racing, confessing these things to her. It was a new experience for me, to be open and vulnerable. But I wasn't scared... not with her. She felt the same way for me, I was sure of it.

"Jesus, Leon," she breathed, running her tongue over her lower lip. "You're something else. So... no secrets at all?"

She had a calculating look in her eye. There was something she wanted to ask. But I meant what I said, so I nodded. "I have plenty of secrets, DeLuna. But none that I will keep from you, if you ask. So what do you want to ask?"

Her gaze held mine steady. "Are you on the Circle?"

Somehow, I knew that was coming. "Yes," I replied after only a tiny hesitation. Danny's eyes widened just a fraction, and her breath caught. "But I think you knew that already. It's why you never pushed me for an answer when Kai accused me weeks ago, because you weren't sure if I would lie about it."

She visibly swallowed. "That's true," she whispered. "How long have you been Circle?"

"Five years," I told her. My fingers stroked the muscles of her neck, and I couldn't help thinking about how distraught she'd looked when she arrived. How broken her expression had been while she sat in my bedroom, silently crying as she remembered her best friend. I wanted to do *more*.

She nodded slowly, then exhaled. "Okay."

My brows rose. "Okay?"

Her perfect lips tilted in a smile. "Yeah. Try your coffee. I want to see what you think."

Confused and bewildered, I did as she asked. I reached for my mug, keeping one hand firmly on her waist so she didn't do something crazy like get up.

My nose wrinkled slightly, but under her gaze, I took a sip of the bitter drink. Except, it wasn't anything like the acidic sludge I'd tried years ago. It was actually not bad.

She grinned broadly when I hummed in surprise. "You hate coffee, don't you, Bunny?"

I shrugged, putting the mug back on my desk because I'd rather have my hands on her. "I don't hate *that* one. Thank you for making it for me." I licked my lips, because now I was thinking about tasting something else. In my defense, she was straddling my lap, and I was permanently turned on while she was around. Or on the phone. Or on my mind.

"What are you working on?" she asked, glancing at my multiple computer monitors at various levels across my desk. "Layla's drives?"

I gripped her waist tighter, pulling her closer so I could grind against her crotch like a horny teenager. "Sort of," I agreed. "They mostly do their own thing, and it's just a waiting game. I was looking into the Castle prisoner release."

Her eyes widened and her mouth did this tempting little O shape. Shit, now I was thinking about fucking her throat... I wasn't going to be able to focus until I rubbed one out. Just had to keep clear of my keyboard this time.

"Did you find anything?" she asked, her eyes scanning the monitors. There was nothing displayed that would make much sense to her, in any case. Mostly code from my decryption program because I'd been checking on the progress.

I gave a small chuckle. "I was starting to."

"Well shit, don't let me distract you," she exclaimed, scrambling out of my lap and making me groan with disappointment. She heard it and gave me a rueful grin. "You're already distracted, aren't you?"

Gritting my teeth, I tried to mentally talk my dick down. "You do have that effect on me," I admitted quietly, my gaze running over her. She'd gotten changed and was wearing just a pair of black sweatpants and a dark gray tank top. No bra. Was it really such a shock I was hard as steel when her nipples had been so close to my face while she sat on my lap?

Her smile was flirtatious and sly, and she licked her lips. Was she trying to kill me?

"Well shit, Marx. If you want me to suck your dick, just say so. I thought we were being all honest and crap?" Her brow quirked in challenge, and I leaned back in my gaming chair.

"Oh really, that's how it works?"

She shrugged, but her gaze was entertained as hell. Still, she made no moves to do anything or to leave. Nope, she was just waiting to see if I'd ask.

My lips curled in a smile. "DeLuna, *mon cœur*," I purred, sliding a hand inside my pants to grip my dick. Fuck, I was so desperate for her I would probably come in seconds. "Get on your knees for me."

I spread my legs wide, giving her space. I wasn't asking, I was telling, and she loved it like that. As evidenced by the way she submissively did as she was told, resting her hands on my thighs and batting those long lashes as she looked up at me.

My breathing deepened as I tugged my own sweats down far enough to free my cock, letting it spring up, thick and proud. Danny licked her lips, her gaze hungry, but she waited.

"Open your mouth," I ordered, reaching out to run my thumb over her lips. She obliged, flicking her tongue over my thumb teasingly. I gave a small groan, my cock throbbing in need. "Shit," I whispered. "Suck me off, *mon ange*, make me come."

She wasted no time now that I'd told her what I wanted. At that first contact of her tongue on my cock, I needed to clench my teeth and tense my glutes to keep from blowing on her face. I was like a sex-starved teenager, and it'd only been a week.

I loved how she played with my piercings, not afraid to tug them with her teeth, but what I needed was a quick, dirty head job. We could play later. Right now, I just needed to get my focus back so I could work out just how deep the shit was that we were in.

So I only let her tease me for a few moments before grabbing her head and shoving her down. She gagged at the swiftness of the movement, and I groaned. I was under no illusions that she liked things gentle. Nah, not Danny DeLuna. She loved it rough, and if she wasn't gagging, it wasn't good.

There was no holding back, from either of us. I held her head with both hands, pushing her harder with each downstroke, and she swallowed me deeper like she wanted to fit my balls inside her mouth at the same time. It wasn't going to happen, but goddamn, I appreciated the enthusiasm.

I came hard, with no warning at all, and she choked on my cum for a moment. I didn't wait for her to recover fully, too eager to make sure she left my office totally satisfied. She was still coughing and gasping as I pulled her to her feet and stripped her sweatpants off, then sat her up on the edge of my desk.

Her tongue snaked out of her mouth, licking droplets of my cum from her lips, and I plunged my fingers into her hot, wet cunt, making her quiver.

"Oh fuck, Leon," she gasped, gripping the edge of the desk for balance as I pumped my hand hard and fast. "Shit…"

Her feet balanced on my thighs, and I dove in to taste her sweet pussy. She trembled and writhed, bucking against my face, and I flicked my tongue hard over her clit. My name fell from her lips in delirious moans, and I went harder, sucking that little jewel that made her thighs shudder. My two fingers fucked her pussy hard, and she was gloriously wet. So much that when I pushed my pinky into her ass, she just gasped and arched into me, begging for more.

My hand slammed into her, over and over, and I sucked her clit like that toy she loved so fucking much. She exploded, her muscles locking up around my fingers and her thighs gripping my head in a vice. Not that I was complaining, I drank in the sweet taste of her cunt and came up grinning when she eventually let go.

"Holy shit, Bunny," she gasped, sliding off the desk with shaking legs.

I sat back in my chair, all kinds of satisfied as she tugged her pants back on. "I missed you, *ma moitié*."

Her grin was wobbly but bright with post-orgasm high. "I can tell. How important is this work, again?" She nodded to my computers, and I gave a frustrated sigh.

"Too important," I groaned. "Don't go anywhere, though. I want to welcome you home properly as soon as I take a break. Understood?"

"Understood." She leaned down, bringing her lips to mine in a searing kiss. I held her tight, kissing her back with my whole soul and aching with how much I loved her. Then I reluctantly released her before I could decide my work wasn't *that* important after all.

Still, when the door closed behind her, it took me a *long* time to stop daydreaming about my white-haired angel. By the time I logged back into my timed-out server, my coffee mug was empty.

24
DANNY

Selfishly, I wanted Leon to hurry the fuck up, get *all* the info we needed, and come fuck me until I passed out from system overload. Logically, though, I knew I needed to refrain from distracting him, particularly while we were in hiding now. There was sweet fuck all that I could do from here, but Leon was in his element.

I slept in his bed that night, hoping he'd come and join me for at least a couple of hours, but I woke up alone. Kai coaxed me into the shower with him, pouting about how I'd made him sleep in a guest room, and that kept me busy for an hour or so. But then he got called away to discuss the London

meeting with Eli, and I was bored again.

Breakfast was tense and awkward, with Jae doing everything humanly possible to never get within six feet of me—clearly warned off by Kai. I entertained myself for a few hours, then decided to search out Moana. I wanted to hit the gym and figured she might like to join me for sparring.

She did, but there was something off with her. She wasn't as friendly as she'd been in our previous interactions, and more than once, I caught her scowling at me when she thought I wasn't paying attention. Eventually, I got annoyed and went back upstairs to shower.

While washing my hair, I came to the conclusion that I needed to learn some better computer skills. Or mend my relationship with Carlos. I needed to do something to contribute to saving my own ass, because relying entirely on Leon and Kai—even on Carol—was not only making me feel weak... it was *boring*.

Of course, in the middle of our current situation wasn't the best time to ask Leon to teach me basic hacking skills. So maybe Carlos was my best option. I needed to know what his fucking problem was and why he'd friend-dumped me. A sneaking voice in the back of my mind suggested it was because he was jealous of Leon and Kai. But it was easy to push that thought away, as there was *nothing* sexual between Carlos and me. Sometimes, men and women were simply platonic.

That's what I thought, anyway. Maybe I was wrong? Fuck, I

hoped not. I got out of the shower and wrapped a towel around myself. My hair was dripping, so I grabbed another one to squeeze some water out while I pondered how Stanley was doing with his caretaker.

Lost in thought, I startled when the bathroom door crashed open, and Leon strode in with a feverish look in his eyes.

"Bunny, what—" I started to say, but he cut me off with a bruising kiss. He yanked the towel off my body, discarding it on the floor and roughly palming my breasts.

I arched my back into his touch, gasping as his kiss intensified and my tongue tangled with his. He tugged my nipples, rolling them between his fingers in a way that tiptoed the line between pleasure and pain, making me moan. I didn't care what had put him in such a mood, and I sure as fuck wasn't complaining. Instead, I pushed his t-shirt up, forcing him to break our kiss just long enough to rip it over his head, then he was back and rougher than ever.

Eventually, he peeled himself away, giving me a blazing look as he ran his tongue over his lower lip. He reached over to one of the vanity drawers and tugged it open, pulling something out and placing it on the counter beside me.

Glancing down, I gasped. It was my Purple Pussy Eater and a bottle of lube.

"Use it," Leon told me in a husky voice, taking a step away to give me space while slowly tugging his sweatpants down.

I quirked a brow but eagerly grabbed the lube and sat my butt up on the counter to pour the cool liquid directly onto my pussy. Leon watched, unblinking as I turned on the Purple Pussy Eater and eased it inside, taking it slow to make sure he wasn't missing a thing.

It was easily my favorite toy, but the damn thing required a bit of concentration to get the suction mouth in precisely the right place. Leon clearly remembered that from watching me use it over video chat, and he waited patiently while I got it positioned just where I liked it.

"Does that feel good?" he asked in a rough voice, his eyes locked on my cunt and his pierced dick gripped in hand.

I swallowed hard, my breathing heavy already. "Uh-huh."

"Perfect," he breathed, stepping closer. "Turn around, keep it in place, but bend over the sink for me, *mon ange*."

Oh, hell yes.

I scrambled to do as he instructed, shivering with excitement and anticipation as he grabbed the lube and slicked it over his dick. Thank fuck for mirrors, I wasn't missing a thing.

"That's it," he praised as I hitched my hips and spread my legs apart, ready for him. "Fuck, DeLuna, the amount of times I've thought about this since Meow Lounge..."

I groaned as he pushed his lube-covered finger into my ass, rocking onto his hand and gasping when he quickly added a second. He was in a hurry, and I was more than okay with it.

When he swapped his fingers for the pierced head of his cock, I was still tight, but he didn't stop. Thank fuck.

"Yes," he breathed, forcing his way inside as I tried to open for him. "Just like that, *mon cœur*. You take my cock in this tight little asshole *so well*." A deep tremble shook through me at his praise, and he gave a low chuckle as he pushed deeper. "Does that hurt, beautiful?"

"Yes," I gasped, not lying. "Don't stop." Because of the Purple Pussy Eater sucking my clit, and the shaft of the toy inside my cunt, buzzing around in search of my G-spot, the pain was *delicious*, and I was already on the edge of a climax.

Leon huffed a laugh. "Never planned to." He pulled out slightly, then slammed home and made me howl. Then I came, unable to hold it back any longer.

He thrust into my ass with short movements as I gasped and moaned, my free hand clinging to the edge of the vanity just to keep my balance. When it started to fade, I was gasping for breath but ready for whatever games he wanted to play.

Leon met my gaze in the mirror, his lips kicked up in a smug grin as he took in my flushed, dazed expression. "We're not stopping," he told me—entirely unnecessarily, I might add— "until I fill this perfect little hole with my cum. No matter how many times you orgasm on the way there. Understood?"

All my muscles tightened with excitement, and Leon groaned in response.

"Understood," I panted, resisting the urge to pull the Purple Pussy Eater away. He wanted it there and hadn't told me to turn it off, so there it would stay… even though I was pretty sure it was already pushing me into another climax while we talked.

Leon gripped my hips, jerking me back onto his cock in an abrupt motion. "Good girl," he praised. "Count them for me."

Fucking psycho knew what he was doing. Between the mirror, the clit-sucking vibrator, the hardness of the toy in my pussy, and him absolutely *railing* my asshole… I was fucked. Literally and figuratively. I tried to get rid of the Purple Pussy Eater around orgasm four, but he just turned it up and saw me spiral into numbers five and six before finally letting himself go.

When I felt him filling my ass with cum, his motions slowing and his whole body shaking with the release, I collapsed over the sink. The vibrator dropped to the floor without me holding it, but I was fucking *dead*.

"Don't move," Leon panted, giving my ass a slap. He pulled out just long enough to scoop up his phone from the floor where he must have dropped it earlier. Then he pushed his softening cock back inside for the sake of some spank bank snaps.

He took his time pulling out, his camera documenting it all, then he made me reach back to hold my cheeks open for a few more. I could feel the wetness of his seed dripping out, and it made me beyond curious to see his whole gallery. It also made me glad as hell that he was a tech genius, because I'd bet that gallery was more secure than Fort fucking Knox.

"Are you done, Picasso?" I teased, still breathless as I looked back at him.

He met my gaze with blazing intensity. "Never done, *mon cœur*, but you can get up if you want. Or don't, I enjoy this view."

Rolling my eyes, I gave a chuckle and peeled myself up off the vanity. "Holy fuck, Marx, I'm going to be walking funny for the rest of the day."

I wobbled back over to the shower to turn it on. Apparently, it was a multi-shower kind of day.

"That was my intention," he replied with a smirk, coming to join me.

He lovingly washed my body without even being asked, and I used all my available energy to remain upright. All those orgasms had my ears ringing and my head swimming with dizziness.

"Wait, what happened?" I asked after we got out and he bundled me up in a towel. "You were all, you know…" I waved a hand, meaning how fierce and intense he'd busted in here.

Leon understood, giving me a sly grin in return. Leaning in, he kissed the tip of my nose, then brought his lips to my ear. "I cracked two of Layla's drives."

25
DANNY

Excitement at Leon's news saw me dressing quickly, then running downstairs to get Kai. I found him and Eli outside, deep in conversation with their hands stuffed in their pockets to combat the cold. Their breath fogged as they spoke, but whatever was so important to discuss out in the snow, it fell to silence as I approached.

Kai gave me a questioning look, but I shifted my gaze and bit my tongue before speaking in front of Eli. Instead, I gave Kai a small smile and tipped my head back to the house.

"Can I borrow you, Big Man?" I didn't elaborate because fuck Eli, I didn't owe him info.

Kai gave a slight frown, understanding I didn't want to talk in front of his friend, but nodded anyway. "Of course you can, Siren." He gave Eli a long look, then followed me back inside Leon's house just as the cold started sinking into my skin. Yoga pants and a T-shirt weren't appropriate attire for being out in the snow, that was for fucking sure, but Leon's central heating was elite.

"What's going on?" Kai asked once we were back inside. "Are you walking awkwardly?"

I scoffed. "What? No. Come on, Leon has something."

Kai frowned his confusion a moment, then his eyes widened. "Oh, shit, really?"

Grinning, I nodded. Then I glanced back out to where Eli was pacing in the snow with his phone to his ear. "Do they know what Leon's working on?"

Kai followed my line of sight, then shook his head. "I didn't think they needed that information. Their feelings toward the Guild... well, Mo's mostly, would make things complicated."

I understood entirely; it was exactly why I'd hesitated to speak in front of Eli. I didn't *know* Kai's team, and I sure as shit didn't trust them. Sam had already double-crossed Kai, so how could we be sure Eli wouldn't be next? Or Jae? Better they had no knowledge of the drives until we knew what they contained.

Grabbing Kai's hand in mine, I hurried back up the stairs—admittedly still feeling a bit wobbly in the knees—and Kai followed closely.

"You're definitely walking funny," he muttered. "What the fuck did he do to you?"

A slightly unhinged laugh bubbled out of me, and I couldn't help thinking about how that whole thing would have been better with Kai in place of the Purple Pussy Eater. Baby steps. Maybe we could get there one day. Not today, and probably not tomorrow, but… one day.

I wrapped my hand around the door handle to Leon's office, feeling my fingertips depress the scanners that granted me access to the room.

"I thought that was always locked," Kai commented as I pushed it open, and I just tossed him a grin. Crazy what some good news and a great fuck could do for my mood.

"Oh good," Leon said with extreme sarcasm as Kai followed me into his office, "Sasquatch is here."

Kai bristled, and I put a hand on his stomach to stop him from getting into Leon's face. "What did you fucking call me?"

Leon spun his chair around, looking bored and not even slightly threatened. "Sasquatch. More commonly known as Bigfoot, a large—"

"I know what a fucking Sasquatch is, you asshole." Kai's fists balled at his sides, and I gave Leon a hard look.

"Cut it out," I snapped. "Focus, please, both of you. Tell us what you found, Marx."

Leon kicked a spare office chair out toward Kai. "Sit down, then. I'll show you." Kai took the seat offered, and Leon pulled me onto his lap, chuckling under his breath when I shifted uncomfortably. "Alright, let's start with the boring one."

He pulled up a file folder, resting one hand on my thigh in the most incredibly *comfortable* gesture. Like we were a couple who often sat together, totally at ease in one another's presence.

"What are we looking at?" Kai asked, frowning at the screen.

"Useless trash, for the most part," Leon admitted with a grimace. "Or, it is now. Back when Layla hid the drives, this would have been considerably more valuable, but now?"

"Useless trash," I murmured, reading the info. Names, job titles, places of work, home addresses, none with any clear link that I could ascertain. "I assume they're all dead now?" Because why else would this info be trash? Also, I recognized a few names... men I'd personally killed under contract.

"Most of them," Leon confirmed. "They were all working on Project Remus, in one way or another. Of the one hundred and sixty-three people named in this drive, only five are still breathing. And I already had their names."

"So... *completely* useless, then?" Kai asked, understandably frustrated as he scowled at the screens.

Leon glanced over at him. "Not completely. I knew their names, but nothing else. These files gave me some additional leads, even if they are outdated."

"The drives are more than four years old," I commented, despite the swirl of disappointment within my gut. "It's to be expected that a lot of the data is no longer relevant."

Kai grunted his irritation. "You said this was the boring one; what else have you got?"

Leon's hand gripped my thigh a little tighter, his smile so smug I wanted to kiss it. "This one?" He pulled up another drive folder. "This… contains the location of every Guild-owned orphanage worldwide, with notes on whether they housed Remus babies or not."

Kai shot up out of his seat in shock. "What? That's—"

"Exactly what your mole has been drip-feeding you, one location at a time, for the better part of a decade? I'm aware." Leon rolled his eyes and tapped on his keyboard for a minute. "I've sent a copy of this to your business email. Do with it what you will."

Kai scowled but couldn't hide the flash of bewilderment. "How do you know what my business email is?" Leon just gave him a deadpan look back, and Kai huffed. "Fine. Then how do I know you're not just trying to get rid of me and my team?"

This time Leon laughed. "I am. Your team, anyway. You… well, I've made my peace with *you*. But just because I want *them* gone doesn't make this intel any less accurate. So, as I said, do with it what you will, but this is your one and only warning, Sasquatch. Either you get rid of your *team*, or I will."

I shouldn't find that so hot. And yet.

"Okay, don't start," I forced myself to say. "This is useful intel for your personal objectives, Kai, just… leave it at that." I almost told him to say thank you, but we *definitely* weren't there yet.

"Useful for him, sure, but doesn't really help us," Leon mused, stroking my thigh. "Other than these points of interest." He clicked through a couple of folders, pulling up two documents and placing them side by side on the screen.

I scanned them and sighed. "I'm not even slightly shocked."

"Nor was I," Leon murmured.

Kai looked confused, though, so I explained. "That one." I pointed to the document on the left. "Is where I grew up. And the other is where Sabine was raised."

His dark eyes widened and his lips parted in surprise. "Oh shit."

Before we could debate on whether Sabine might be a Remus baby, an alert on Leon's computer started beeping. He stiffened, sitting up straighter, and immediately switched to CCTV images of the entire perimeter of his house.

One of the video displays was flashing. For a moment, I couldn't see what had set it off—all the image showed was whiteness—then a helicopter descended from the sky, landing in a flurry of snow.

"Who the fuck is that?" Leon demanded, shooting an accusing glare at Kai.

I almost jumped to Kai's defense until I saw the slight wince in the big guy's expression. That was not a good wince. "What have you done, Big Man?"

His gaze was apologetic and regretful. "I fucked up, *ātaahua*, and... I needed to try and make it right again." Whatever the fuck *that* was meant to mean.

But apparently, I was about to get my answer, because the helicopter blades on the screen slowed, and the door popped open to reveal our guest.

"Carlos?" I exclaimed.

My startled gaze flicked between the guys as I rose out of Leon's lap. What the shit was Carlos doing here? The last I'd heard from him was that awkward phone call after Jude died, and then Tito—the little bitch—delivering Stanley with a big old "*fuck you*" from his boss.

"Don't look at me. I actually used to like my privacy here," Leon sulked, pushing up from his chair. "Well, come on then. Let's see what he has to say for himself."

Leon stalked out of his office, and I made to follow, but Kai grabbed my arm to halt me.

"Siren," he started to say, then gave a groan and swiped a hand over his face. "Fuck."

I drew a long breath in, then shook my head. "I'm sure it's not that bad, Kai," I reassured him, continuing after Leon as Kai's hand dropped away. Clearly, he'd been in touch with Carlos—

somehow—and had given him our location. Poor form, for sure, and Leon wouldn't be happy about it, but it was nothing to get all bent out of shape about.

"Hopefully, this shit with Stan was a misunderstanding," I commented as I headed downstairs, with Kai close on my heels. "I really want you to meet Carlos. He's been a really good friend to me these last few years. That shit Tito said... I knew he was up to no good. Jealous little bitch."

I was mostly just talking to myself, muttering under my breath, but I got down to the living room just in time to see Leon patting Carlos down for weapons. The wave of relief that washed over me, seeing my friend there, was palpable. But I held myself back from hugging him, just in case we *weren't* okay. Maybe he was here for some other reason.

"Dan! Shit, girl, you look good." Carlos dispelled all my worries in an instant, crossing the space between us and sweeping me up in a hug. "Where the hell have you been these last few weeks? You don't write, you don't call, shit, you never even told me you were coming to pick up my man Stan. Do you have any idea how worried I was when I went to have tequila with him, and he was gone?"

I shoved him away in confusion. "What? Ugh, I fucking knew it. I *knew* it. Tito, that dirty, lying—"

Carlos arched a brow at me, then flicked a wary glance at Kai behind me. "Tito told me you asked to have Stanley sent home. I take it that is not the case?"

Anger fucking choked me. I'd believed him, and that just proved to me now how broken and vulnerable I'd been feeling that day. Of course Tito had been lying; he was a slimy, manipulative shit who had been trying to get me out of Carlos's life since *before* Ricardo died.

"Your little friend delivered the plant back to DeLuna directly," Leon drawled, clapping Carlos on the shoulder, "and passed along a message that you wanted nothing to do with my girl. Which, obviously, was bullshit because you should be fucking *honored* she considered you a friend."

I shook my head, scowling. "Why?"

Carlos's gaze shifted to Kai again. There was something off in his expression. Something like... recognition?

"Siren," Kai rumbled, sounding *guilty*.

Leon just smirked like a cabaret show had just turned up specifically for his own entertainment. "Oh, *mon ange*, I bet that was Sasquatch's fault. Retaliation for imprisoning and roughing up his boss, I bet."

What the *fuck* did he just say?

26
KAI

Leon was a dead man. Dead. If Danny didn't love his sneering face so fucking much, I'd have punched him right in the teeth for that swipe. But the worst part, the part that really made my mood sour, was the fact that he was right.

In reality, I was surprised he'd kept my secret even this long, considering how badly he wanted to get rid of me *before* Danny's ultimatum.

For a long, tense moment after Leon dropped that bomb, no one spoke. Danny just stared at me with shock and betrayal in her eyes. The guilt almost choked me.

To my shock, it was Carlos who broke the tension with a laugh.

"Leon makes that sound so much more dramatic than it really was. You know what they say about assumptions, don't you?" Carlos gave Leon a pointed look, his lips curled in a sarcastic smile. "After all, *you* weren't there, and it sounds like there are a lot of misunderstandings that need correction."

What the hell? Why was Carlos covering for me? I literally held him captive and beat the crap out of him. To his credit, he'd never broken, though. Never betrayed Danny's trust even once. That was half the reason I'd released him... the other half was my certainty that Danny would skin me alive if she found out.

Danny shook her head, not buying it. "Wait. What the fuck?" Her angry gaze darted between me and Carlos, her eyes narrowed. "You two have met before?" She shifted her glare to Leon. "And you *knew* something about it?"

Smug amusement flickered through me at Leon not escaping her ire. Of course she didn't miss the fact that he'd been holding onto that information, making him *just* as complicit as me. Well, okay, maybe not *quite* as complicit, but he sure as shit wasn't innocent. Accessory after the fact, murder *bunny*.

"How about we sit down and iron things out?" Carlos suggested, swaggering over to the kitchen like he'd been here a hundred times. "You got anything to drink here, Marx?"

Leon glared daggers. "Yeah. Water."

"There's beer in the fridge," I said, giving Leon a disgusted look. "Or vodka in the freezer."

What the fuck was Carlos's angle? Was he messing with me?

"That's the spirit!" Carlos tugged open the fridge to grab two bottles of beer and one sparkling water. Then he opened the freezer to fetch the bottle of vodka that had already been in there when we arrived. "Dan, you want this neat?" He waved the bottle at Danny, and she blew out a long breath.

"Yes," she replied. "Make it a big one."

We made our way into the living room to sit, but before my butt even touched the sofa, my sister and Jae came clattering down the stairs, chatting. They cut off abruptly when they saw the four of us, and Mo's brows shot right up.

"Diaz, holy shit," Mo exclaimed, totally oblivious to my *shut the fuck up* faces I was making in her direction. "I thought we killed you weeks ago."

Carlos seemed nothing but amused by my fiery sister, though. He chuckled and saluted me with his beer. "I don't die so easily, Jane."

Mo bristled at the name—Carlos had called her that the whole time we had him captive—but just glowered in return.

"Sasquatch," Leon growled. "Now would probably be a great time to give your team something useful to do. Maybe anywhere but here?"

He had a good point, even if I was loath to ever admit when Leon had a good point. But I also didn't want to deal with my own business right in the middle of a conflict with my girl.

"We can wait," Carlos told me with a smug smile. "Dan and I need to discuss Stanley, anyway."

Moana and Jae were looking at me with confusion, and I badly didn't need them weighing in on what was sure to be a brutal smackdown from my siren. So I gave an irritated sigh and indicated for them to follow me. Eli was likely in the gym—he'd mentioned needing a workout earlier—so I took them down there to talk.

"What's going on, boss?" Jae asked before the gym door even closed behind us. "Didn't you kill that guy? What's he doing here?"

I ran a hand over my face, frustrated and exhausted. "I invited him here. And, no, we didn't kill him, Eli dropped him at home."

Eli put down the weights he'd been using, grabbing a towel to mop up his sweat. "The Colombian?"

I jerked a nod. "Irrelevant. Leon has come into possession of a list that I want you three to start investigating."

Mo frowned, folding her arms in a defensive gesture. She'd been at Leon's throat constantly and was likely to treat any information from him with extreme suspicion and prejudice, but... too fucking bad. Maybe I didn't *like* the guy, but I didn't doubt the validity of this info, knowing what Danny went through to find the damn drives in the first place.

"What kind of a list?" Mo asked.

I barely refrained from rolling my eyes. "A comprehensive, detailed list of all Guild-owned orphanages. Their training centers. Each marked with notes on whether they were involved in Project Remus or not." My whole team gaped at me, and I couldn't blame them. "I'm sending the list to you, Mo. I want the three of you in the air ASAP. It's your choice which one you head to first."

Jae muttered some Korean curses under his breath, then gave me a troubled frown. "Boss, do we think any of them are still standing?"

It was definitely something that crossed my mind, too. So many of the locations we had tried to access—to *save* those kids from being trained as child assassins—had been destroyed before we got there. Like they were tipped off that we were coming and decided to destroy the evidence.

"There's no way to know without checking them out. I don't care how, just… investigate." I gave Mo a pointed look, because this was *her* mission more than the rest of us. "You know what to do, just stay in touch."

Eli tugged his sweatshirt over his head, giving me a long look. "I take it you won't be joining us then, boss?"

As if he didn't already know the answer to that. I shook my head, already itching to be done with this conversation before I could feel any guiltier about abandoning the team that *I* put together.

"I won't. Also, keep Cyryl on the Ares clients around Shadow Grove. You'll need to touch base in London at some point, too. I made an example of Rowdy, but a few more reminders of who is in charge wouldn't go amiss."

Jae grinned in excitement at that, and Eli nodded.

Mo paused to give me a quick hug. "Be careful, little brother," she whispered as the other guys left the gym to pack their shit. "You can't trust any of them. They're *all* corrupt, don't forget that, okay?"

I frowned at the intensity of her warning but nodded anyway. Mo had more reason than most to hate the Guild, and I wasn't going to try to tell her she was wrong. Her reasons were valid, as was her pain. I just had to hope that with time, she would see—as I had—that not everyone in the Guild was the same. Not every mercenary was evil to the core. She *liked* Danny even when she didn't want to admit it.

Returning to the living room, I eyed Danny's empty glass and gritted my teeth at the casual way Carlos touched her knee while he spoke. Leon must have been thinking the exact same thing, because he met my gaze steadily when I shifted to look at him. One brow twitched up, then he gave Carlos a long look.

Apparently, I wasn't the only one with jealousy issues.

"All okay with the team?" Danny asked as I sat back down

and snagged my untouched beer from the table.

I dipped my head in a nod. "Yep, they'll be on their way in ten minutes or less."

"Thank fuck for that," Leon muttered, sipping his sparkling water.

The urge to antagonize him was so strong, but I held back. If I were in his shoes, if Leon had invited a group of Guild mercenaries to *my* home without permission, I'd be furious. Really, he'd been a shit load more patient than I would have expected, so I bit my tongue and offered a brittle smile instead.

See, Danny? We can get along.

"Well then, Kai, do you want to explain why Leon thinks you abducted Carlos and beat him up?" Danny went *straight* to the fucking point, spearing me with laser focus. Not even half a glass of vodka had any impact on her.

I swallowed. Then cleared my throat. "Because I did. And I apologize for that, Carlos. That was out of line."

The Colombian drug lord tipped his head to the side, assessing the sincerity of my apology. Then he nodded. "Thank you, man, I appreciate that." He reached out a fist, and I awkwardly bumped it with mine.

For a moment, no one spoke. Then Leon threw up his hands.

"What the fuck?" he exclaimed. "Seriously? That's it? Sorry?

And you're just, what, you're okay with that?" He glared at Carlos like he'd been robbed of something. "This is bullshit. DeLuna, baby, tell me you're gonna rip Sasquatch a new asshole for hurting your friend. Even *I* knew Carlos was off-limits, and do you have any idea how many times I wanted to kill him? How many times I *could* have? Fuck me."

The *effort* it took not to laugh was almost painful. He was so outraged... but he also had a point. I was one hundred percent expecting Danny to punch me, if nothing else.

But nope. She just shrugged and tossed Leon a seductive smile. "Maybe if you'd dropped this on me *before* the bathroom, I would have the energy to be a bit more irate."

My left eye twitched. "What the fuck happened in the bathroom?"

Leon's lips curled in a smug smile. "None of your business."

Danny felt no such confidentiality, chuckling with that distinctive, well-fucked kind of daze. "Made me come seven times, that's what. You're lucky I'm even *conscious* right now, so trust me when I say I have no energy for bashing your dumbfuck heads together."

"Seven times?" Carlos exclaimed in a hushed whisper, then gave Leon a nod of respect. Wanker. "Well, in fairness, Kai *didn't* kill me. And he brought me here when he found out how worried I was about you, Dan. So I figure it's all just water under the bridge."

I winced at that expression, remembering the bridge in Venice.

"I'm going to need you to stop giving out my address, Sasquatch," Leon drawled, hooking one ankle over the opposite knee. Now that I knew what he and Danny had been up to—why she was walking funny—it explained why Leon's temper was cooler than usual. More playful than violent.

Danny shifted her attention to her friend. "You were worried?"

Carlos just rolled his eyes. "I'm permanently worried. I even reached out to Hermes to see if he'd consider retrieving *you*. He told me no, of course, but it was worth a try."

"No shit," Danny replied with a laugh. "I wasn't lost, nor am I property. He did extend an offer to help, but I *assumed* it was one of these bozos who had contacted him and said no."

"Ouch," I muttered, but Leon just gave a shrug like he wasn't offended.

Carlos's phone beeped in his pocket, and he groaned as he pulled it out. A smile touched his lips as he read the message, then showed it to Danny. She grinned too.

"You should go," she urged him. "But thank you for coming. Do you need me to take care of Tito?"

Carlos grimaced, then drained the rest of his beer. "Nah, I'll deal with him. It's long overdue, anyway." He wrapped his arm around Danny, hauling her close for a hug. It was affectionate, yes, but non-sexual. Weirdly, this brief visit, being able to actually see him interact with Danny on a personal level, laid all my paranoia over Carlos to rest. He was a platonic friend, nothing more.

"Nice place, Marx," Carlos told Leon as he got up from the sofa. "Super secure." He was mocking. Did he have a death wish? Leon looked like he was two seconds away from snapping his neck. Or, at the very least, his hands. Clearly, Leon didn't see that Danny wasn't remotely interested in Carlos as anything more than a friend. She treated him just like she treated Sabine. Or Stanley.

Danny glared at Leon, then gave *me* a hard look. "I'm going to see Carlos out. Please make sure your team are gone, too. Then the three of us need to talk."

Ah shit. That didn't sound good.

Carlos heard it too, snickering as he grabbed his coat and headed out the door with Danny following behind.

"Don't look so panicked, Sasquatch," Leon drawled. "She wants to talk about the Circle."

Well shit, that hadn't even occurred to me. I would save my questions about that until Danny came back, though. Instead, I eyed Leon up with curiosity. "Seven times?" I blurted out without really meaning to say it aloud.

Leon smirked. "Jealous?"

"Fuck yes," I muttered truthfully. I needed more beer to

swallow this information. The jealousy crawled through my veins like acid, but I couldn't ignore the fact that I was a little bit turned-on. Was it weird that I wanted to know what he'd done to make her come *seven* times? That I wanted to *see* it?

Shit. This ménage crap was fucking with my head.

27
DANNY

Seeing Carlos, mending the rift between us, made me stupidly happy. So much so that I wasn't even mad about whatever had happened between him and Kai. Or shit, maybe that was the lingering endorphins from all the orgasms. Whatever the reason, I had a happy glow in my chest when I made my way back inside the house.

"All okay?" Kai asked cautiously as I refilled my vodka.

I arched a brow at him, and he was smart enough to look sheepish. "We're okay," I murmured, meaning *all* of us. "Miscommunication is my least favorite reason for bad blood. I'm more than annoyed that I fell for it, but that's on Tito.

Carlos will handle that."

Footsteps clattered down the stairs, and a moment later, Moana and Jae appeared with bags slung over their shoulders. Jae said nothing, pointedly *not* looking at me as he headed for the exit. Mo stopped briefly to say goodbye, but once again, she was frosty. The dirty glare she shot toward Leon might have had something to do with it, though.

"Give me a minute, *ātaahua*," Kai murmured, following his sister out of the house. They would be taking their helicopter, but we had Leon's snowmobiles if we wanted to leave.

Leon met my gaze across the room, then gave me a little nod, silently telling me to come over to him. I took my refilled drink and closed the distance. Rather than sitting back on the sofa where I'd been before, I sat directly in Leon's lap.

"You're in a very good mood, *ma moitié*," he murmured, grasping my ass and shifting me closer. "Is that because you got your friend back? Or because we finally got some *quality time* together?"

I grinned, looping my arms around his neck. "Thank you for not killing Kai's team while they were here, Bunny. I appreciate the restraint."

He tipped his head back, his gaze studying my face from just a few inches away. "Only for you."

"I know," I murmured, dipping my face to brush my lips across his. "I appreciate you."

He leaned into my light kiss, deepening it instantly and cranking the heat right up. Dimly I registered Eli leaving, but I didn't stop kissing Leon to offer a polite *bon voyage*. It was about fucking time I got my guys alone. Actually alone. We hadn't had any time for the three of us since I'd walked out on them both back in Shadow Grove.

Heat flushed through me as Leon gripped my ass, and I moaned at the ache when he pulled me against his hardening cock.

"Again?" I gasped between kisses, not even slightly against the idea. Just surprised. Then again, *he* only came once. It was me who was drained of energy and half asleep.

"Fuck yes," Leon replied, slipping a hand under my t-shirt. "I'm *permanently* hard for you, *mon cœur*. I can never get enough."

Call me whatever derogatory term was currently in fashion for sex-positive women, but I was a goner for Leon Marx. Fuck, he was addictive; I couldn't get enough. Which was why I already had my hand inside his pants and around his hard dick when Kai came back inside.

"Seven times today wasn't enough?" he growled, opening the fridge with an aggressive motion, making it slam against the cabinets.

I broke away from Leon's kisses, turning my head to look at Kai. "You could join us and give me number eight, Big Man."

Leon gave a sound of disagreement, but I stroked his cock

firmly, and his sound faded into a small moan.

Kai twisted the cap off his fresh beer, stalking back over to us with blazing eyes. "I thought you wanted to talk about the Circle, *kaikohuru iti*. This won't get much talking done."

Leon grunted, rocking his hips against me. "Not true. DeLuna loves a bit of dirty talk, don't you, beautiful?"

He wasn't wrong about that. Both of them delivered just the perfect amount of filth while fucking me, without wading into cringey porn territory. But Kai also had a good point. We should clear the air before I attempted to lure them into railing me together.

Goddamn, that was a mental image that made my panties wet, though.

Leaning in, I kissed Leon again. Then fixed his pants and climbed off his lap to deliberately put some distance between us in case my pussy overrode my sensibilities. Again.

"Is your team gone?" I asked Kai, taking a seat with plenty of space between me and *both* guys. Just because we were alone didn't mean we stripped off our clothes and started fucking like rabbits. Much as I hated to admit, we still had a lot of work to do in order to shake the killers on my tail.

Kai dipped his head in a nod. "We are clear."

"Good," I said, combing my fingers through my hair. What was I saying? Something about a threesome with double penetration? No, wait, business first. "Let's discuss the Circle. And how Leon's position on it might help us."

Kai choked on his beer.

"Excellent delivery, *mon ange*," Leon chuckled, clapping slowly. "I think some beer came out his nose."

"So it's true?" Kai spluttered between coughs. "I knew it! I fucking knew it! And you!" He pointed an accusing finger at Leon. "You looked me in the eye and *lied*."

Leon pursed his lips, and his eyes narrowed. "Did I?"

I tried to remember. "I don't think he did, Kai. But it's beside the point. The Circle only has seven seats, and one is inactive. Of the six remaining, Leon has one, Carol has another."

Kai was scowling, but he was also following my train of thought. "Then I take it the Circle often uses majority rule on anything that goes to a vote?"

Leon inclined his head. "It's the only fair way. If a unanimous decision was required, nothing would ever get done."

"So if we can get one more Circle member on our side, then we have assurance that they can't vote *against* us, should it come to that. Could it come to that? I thought Blanchet was working behind the curtain on this." Kai sat back, dropping a touch of the aggressive outrage over finding he was right about Leon being on the Circle.

"He is," Leon agreed, "but I made my allegiance clear when I placed the protection order on DeLuna. It's something only the Circle can do. Now Carol has publicly outed Danny as her daughter... it depends whether Blanchet has done his own research on who else is Circle—like clearly both Carol and I have. If he has, then he knows Danny now has some powerful allies."

I drummed my fingers on the arm of my chair, thinking. "I would have thought a power move like that might make him back off," I pondered aloud, "but it hasn't. If he's responsible for the Castle releases, then he's stepping it up."

"He's getting desperate," Kai muttered, agreeing.

"If he has a majority vote, he could issue a kill order for Danny," Leon said calmly. Just hearing that option sent a flare of panic through me, but I clenched my jaw and contained it. "Obviously, neither Carol nor I would vote in favor, but the others..." He shrugged.

For a moment, the three of us were quiet. Processing. But a kill order was every mercenary's worst nightmare. It was literally the Circle putting out a Guild-wide hit on one person. Granting carte blanche to *every* mercenary under the Guild's employ to kill that person and offering a *huge* payout for whoever succeeded. Not even the best of the best could run forever, and from everyone.

I hadn't even noticed that I was letting my panic show until Kai sat forward and pressed a gentle hand to my knee to stop it bouncing.

Startled, I met his concerned gaze and drew a deep breath. Fuck.

"Come here," he said softly, offering his hand to me. I took it without second-guessing myself, letting him pull me out of my chair and into his lap. "You're not in this alone, *taku aroha. Ma matou koe e tiaki.*" He kissed my hair as he spoke those words, and I relaxed into his warm embrace. I didn't even need to understand what he was saying, the intent was clear. He was promising to protect me, and for the first time, I felt like I *needed* protection.

Leon was watching us, but his gaze was warm. The usual anger and jealousy when he looked at Kai was nowhere to be seen, and in its place was simple, uncomplicated *caring*. He echoed with a single look everything Kai whispered.

"I've reached out to try and speak with the other Circle members," Leon told us. "Blanchet, of course, has ignored me. The others are 'taking it under consideration,' so maybe Carol will have better success."

"Who are the other Circle members?" I asked, still relaxed and comfortable in Kai's lap. "Do you have *all* their names?"

Leon gave me a sly smile. He seemed to really enjoy telling me yes. Then again, I really enjoyed it too. "DeLuna, baby. Of course I do. Erikkson is the missing member, and the deeper we get into this mess, the surer I am that Blanchet is making a power play for *that* position. Somehow."

Kai tightened his grip around me slightly, hugging me. "Could he be working to put one of his people in that seat? Maybe if he knows who is on that mysterious thousand-year-old list of legacy families, he might have cultivated a puppet. Now all he needs to do is clear the path."

"Why come at *me* in the first place?" I asked the question that had been on my mind for way too long. "I'm not a Remus baby, at least not in the sense of the experiment itself. My biological mother is already on the Circle, and she has other heirs, which makes her position—her lineage—pretty fucking secure. What is he gaining in coming after *me* so fucking hard?"

Leon tipped his head back, staring up at the ceiling for a moment while he thought about it.

"He isn't *only* coming after you, though. A *lot* of mercenaries fitting the same vague profile have been executed in recent years, and dramatically more around the time they started coming after you. That guy attacked Sabine, remember?" He returned his gaze to me, and his lips kicked up. "But things have drastically intensified around *you*, but… it's possibly just a matter of pride for him now. You escaped his first attempts—when you got set up in Prague and again in New York—so they sent you to this prick." He nodded to Kai. "Knowing that no Guild agents have ever returned from that suicide mission before."

I couldn't help smiling at that. The Guild clearly bought into the exaggeration of Ares and had no idea what a big softy Kai was on the inside. Not to say he *didn't* kill all those previous mercenaries, only that they'd been missing the mark on *who* to send.

"Then you came back with your pretty head still attached to

your shoulders," Kai mused. "Which would have pissed him off."

Leon chuckled. "The Circle are not known for being humble, that's for sure. It's my guess that you evading his assassination attempts has now become a personal vendetta. A matter of pride and proving he's *better* than a lowly honey trap merc."

I rolled my eyes. "Great. My own sense of self-preservation is the reason I potentially have escaped Guild convicts on my ass."

"Hold up a second," Kai said with an edge of annoyance in his voice. "If you're on the Circle, how come you never knew about Carol being Danny's mum?"

Leon glared daggers. "We don't get together for tea parties, dickhead. All our 'meetings' are done via a secure dark web server, using encryptions and shit to keep everyone anonymous. A few generations ago, someone started targeting Circle bloodlines to shift the power to the next families in line. They thought the same lines had held their places for long enough, and the only way to change things was to end a family line."

It made sense. "So the Circle went dark and covered their identities, making it harder to take their seat. Confusing as fuck, but I get it." I scrubbed a hand over my face. I didn't even want to think about how they managed secret meetings before the days of the internet. What a pain in the ass. Fuck, I was tired. Leon didn't look so great himself, yawning heavily as I looked over. The oddly vulnerable act tugged at me.

Kai was deep in thought; I could practically see the zap of

electricity connecting the dots in his head. "Okay, but you're *you*. There's no way you didn't go snooping about who else is on the Circle, and you just said you have all their names. So how'd you fail to notice Carol and Danny look like sisters?"

I stiffened slightly, and Leon's eyes narrowed like he was imagining how Kai would look with his organs on the outside. But he must have been more tired than I thought, because a minute later, he just sighed and rubbed the bridge of his nose.

"Because she fooled me, that's why," he muttered. "I don't want to get into logistics, but suffice to say, Carol Atwood is drastically better at this Circle shit than I am."

Kai gave a small jerk beneath me, in shock, I was guessing. "Did you just..." He trailed off, shifting his attention to me instead, and lowered his voice to a stage whisper. "Did he just admit he isn't perfect?"

I elbowed him. "Shut up, you're such a shit-stirrer. Are you okay, Bunny?"

He was wincing, rubbing his eyes like he had a headache.

"Yeah, fine," he replied with a sigh. "Just overtired, I think."

That was hardly a surprise, given how long he'd been at his computer since Kai and I had gotten back. I could imagine he'd been the same, or worse, while we were gone. My bunny needed to sleep, or he'd end up killing himself. Maybe he could rest now with us back and Kai's team *gone*.

"Come on," I said, getting up from Kai's lap and extending

a hand to Leon. "Bedtime." Kai made a sound, and I gave him a hard look. "For *sleep*. All of us need it, I think. We can continue our devious plotting tomorrow when we're fresh."

Kai pouted a bit, no doubt still determined to one-up Leon's record from earlier. But it could wait, my bunny needed to rest, and I knew he would only sleep properly if I lay down beside him.

It was codependent shit, but I loved it. I loved that Leon relaxed so much around me, that he could really rest. Even if Kai hated it, he didn't argue. He just kissed me softly at the doorway to Leon's bedroom and whispered *moemoea reka.* Sweet dreams.

28
KAI

It took me a long time to fall asleep in Leon's guest room. Way longer than I'd have liked, because it left me alone with my thoughts, and I couldn't quit picturing Danny in bed with Leon. Sure, he had looked half dead when she took him to bed, but he was also human. Red-blooded heterosexual—I think—human male, and Danny? Well, she *was* Danny.

I couldn't even convince myself that he was a lousy fuck. *Seven times?* Christ. Maybe I needed to look at piercing my dick.

Eventually, the silence of the house allowed me to fall asleep, but it meant I slept hard and didn't wake until midmorning. Groggy and hungry, I made my way down to the kitchen in search of my favorite feast. Disappointingly, Danny was nowhere to be seen, so I made coffee and toast instead. Maybe she was still sleeping too.

Munching on the last of my toast, I made my way back upstairs and paused at Leon's bedroom door. Maybe I should leave her to sleep if she was that tired. I almost walked away again when I heard a faint yell.

My body moved faster than my mind, opening the door without even pausing to knock. *Stupid, Kai. That wasn't a scream of pain.*

Thankfully, though, I didn't walk in on Leon fucking my siren. In fact, the bed was empty, just a tangle of messy sheets but no people anywhere to be seen. Maybe I imagined that cry? But then I heard it again, vaguely louder this time, followed by Leon's name.

Okay, she definitely wasn't in trouble. I should back the fuck off and leave them to it.

Should.

And yet... there I went, cautiously pushing open the bathroom door and peeking inside. Then I frowned in confusion, because the bathroom was also empty. What the hell? I pushed the door open the rest of the way to look around. Just as I was about to leave again, I glanced out the window and found the source of the screams.

There, outside Leon's bathroom, a decent-sized hot tub protruded out from the side of the house. Right out in the open air, steam rose from the hot water as snow fell in soft flakes. I stepped closer to the window, studying the scene before me.

Danny was against the edge of the pool, her back arched so much that her wet hair dangled over the side and her perfect tits pointed to the sky. Leon was between her legs, fucking her hard, with his tattooed hands gripping her porcelain waist tight enough to make dents in her flesh.

I should walk away and leave them to it. But goddamn, if my dick wasn't already hard and begging to be jerked. Danny had made it pretty fucking clear she wanted us both in bed with her, but I wasn't there yet. I doubted Leon really was, either. But I sure as shit didn't feel any guilt slipping my hand into my pants while I stood there watching them.

Who knew how long they'd already been going at it, but Danny was close to coming. I could see it even at this distance, the way her breathing shuddered and her back arched higher. Not that I was any stranger to a quick wank. Watching her fall to pieces would do it for me any day, so it wasn't difficult to get myself caught up.

Leon fucked her faster, his hand gripping her breast and pinching her nipple in a way that made her scream, and I nearly lost it. Nearly. I was holding out until she did, though. Like I was participating without either of them knowing.

She shattered a moment later, and I let myself release. My cum splattered the window, and *fuck me*, I could have sworn she looked straight at me while Leon finished inside her.

The steam off the pool might have been playing tricks on me, though. So I cleaned up and slipped back out of the bathroom like I'd never been there. A shower probably wouldn't go amiss, and that'd give them time to get out of the hot tub... granted Leon wasn't going for another fucking record this morning.

By the time I finished in the shower and got dressed, Danny and Leon were chatting in the kitchen over mugs of coffee. I eyed Leon's with suspicion, giving him a confused frown.

"I thought you didn't caffeinate yourself, *kohuru rapeti*."

Leon just quirked an eyebrow at me and sipped his coffee.

Danny put hers down, though, coming to loop her arms around my neck and tipping her head back for a kiss. I happily delivered, taking things a bit further than a simple good morning as I backed her against the pantry door.

Leon gave a fake cough, and it only made me kiss Danny harder because it was pissing him off. He coughed again, though, and this time it sounded more authentic. Murder Rabbit was such a drama queen sometimes. Most times. Maybe it was a Guild requirement to constantly act like they were the villains in a James Bond film.

"Are you okay, Bunny?" Danny asked as I released her lips. She was frowning slightly in concern as Leon coughed again with a hand over his mouth.

It took a moment, but he nodded. "Fine," he croaked. "Just something in my throat."

I scoffed. "Yeah, like jealousy."

Danny whacked me in the stomach with the back of her hand. "Cut it out. Can I trust you two to play nicely for a bit?"

I paused with my hand on the fridge door. "Why, where are you going?"

"Nowhere," she replied. "But I asked Carol if I could video chat with Koen this morning, and the fucking kid is starved for attention. He talks like he has a daily word count he needs to hit."

That was cute. Danny's relationship with her newfound brother was all kinds of adorable, but it made me so leery of Carol. Circle or not, if that woman was playing some kind of game, messing with Danny's heart, I'd cut out hers and feed it to her.

"Speaking of Carol, I should get back to work," Leon muttered. He still looked like shit, with dark circles under his eyes. Maybe less sleeping had been done last night than I gave them credit for.

Leon snatched Danny into his embrace, kissing her long and hard like he was trying to outdo me. Then he flipped me his middle finger and slouched his way back upstairs to his office.

I set about making some proper breakfast with the groceries my team had stocked Leon's fridge up on. Eggs, bacon, cheese, tomato, spinach, mushrooms... yeah, it was a good day for an omelet.

"You hungry, babe?" I gave Danny a long look, running my eyes over the puffiness of her lips and the blush of bites on her throat. "You look like you've worked up an appetite this morning."

Her smile was naughty, but her eyes narrowed in accusation. "I saw you," she confessed, then sipped her coffee. "You could have joined us. I don't *think* Leon would have objected. Much."

I gave a grunt, getting started making our food. "We're not there, yet."

Her smile spread wider, and she winked. "Yet."

The ringtone of her phone interrupted us before I could invite her to talk me into it, and she rose up on tiptoe to kiss me before answering the call as she exited the kitchen. She didn't go upstairs to hide away in a bedroom. Instead, she headed into the open plan living room and curled up in the big armchair near the floor-to-ceiling windows. It reminded me of how she used to sit in *my* chair, looking out *my* window.

Would she ever return to the island with me? Probably not, and I couldn't blame her. I'd held her prisoner there, let my team torture her. Despite how many good memories that house, that armchair overlooking the ocean, held for me... it might not be the same for her, and I needed to accept that.

I tried not to eavesdrop on her conversation with Koen while I cooked my breakfast, but the temptation was real. She was just a little too far away and a little too quiet for me to hear much, though. So I quickly ate my food alone, then headed down to

Leon's gym.

There were plenty of things to dislike about Leon Marx, but I had to admit that he knew how to set up a hell of a home gym. It was commercial standard, just without the double-ups of machines. It explained why he was so fucking ripped, that was for sure.

I hit the treadmill for a quick warm-up, then loaded up the bench press with weights. I hadn't been hitting the gym as much as I usually did, and instantly noticed the difference in my strength. Fucking hell, I needed to put more work in.

When the gym door opened only half an hour later, I was coated in sweat and aching.

With a groan, I sat up, expecting to see Danny and finding Leon instead. "Uh, Danny's in the living room," I told him with a confused frown. "On the phone with Koen."

Leon gave a tight nod, looking a little pale. "Yeah, I know. I came to find *you* for some fucking idiotic reason." He blew out a frustrated breath and ran a hand over his head, making his hair stick up in odd directions. "Come up to my office, I need to show you something."

He left the gym again without waiting for a response, and I was curious enough to do as he asked. I snatched a towel to mop up my sweat and followed, pausing only briefly in the kitchen to grab a glass of water.

Danny glanced over as I ran the faucet, but I just gave her a reassuring smile, and she returned her attention to the phone in her hand. She was giving Koen instructions on how to build a stink bomb for some reason.

Upstairs, the door to Leon's office was open for me, and I closed it carefully once I was inside.

"What's going on?" I asked the murder rabbit. "You look... stressed." I wasn't sure if that was the right word, since nothing seemed to *stress* Leon. But he didn't look good at any rate.

He scowled up at me from his chair. "You look like an idiot, but I keep that to myself most days. I cracked another drive, and this one has significantly more *relevant* data on it. I wanted to get your opinion on what to do with it."

Well, shit, color me shocked. "*You*," I said slowly, "want *my* opinion?"

Leon glared. "I did five minutes ago, but now I'm reconsidering that decision."

"Just show me, *kohuru rapeti*."

Leon huffed a sigh, then turned his attention back to the computer. A couple of keystrokes, and some documents opened on his monitors. "This is what the latest drive contained. I'm no doctor, but from what I can ascertain, these are records of genetic material being stored in a Remus lab off the coast of Wales."

My brow drew tight as I tried to make sense of the shorthand codes and notations on the documents. "And by genetic material, you mean—"

"Sperm, dickhead," Leon snapped. "And eggs. Whether they're provided willingly or not... that seems open to debate, particularly knowing what we know about Carol. Her eggs were harvested without her knowledge when she had her appendix removed at age fourteen or some shit. So it stands to reason..." He trailed off with a disgusted wince.

I wet my lips, waiting for the other shoe to drop. "Why are you showing me, not Danny?"

He gave a huff of frustration, but this time it wasn't at me. I didn't think so, anyway. He hit the keyboard a few times, finding a specific file. "Because of this." He pointed to the screen. "Donor: EA0088, harvested and stored roughly seventeen years ago."

Not waiting for me to try to guess what that meant, Leon clicked into the folder containing data on the orphanages. The same data he'd given me for my team to investigate. He found the file for an orphanage in Lyon called Maison d'Enfants du Château, which I remembered Danny pointed out as being the place she grew up.

"EA0088," I read aloud when Leon highlighted it on the huge page of similar codes within the file. "These codes refer to children..." Then it hit me why Leon was telling *me* and not Danny. "Oh shit, you think that is her, don't you?"

Leon grimaced. "Maybe. It's just a guess, but... seventeen years ago would have been roughly when they sterilized her. What if they helped themselves to some genetic material while she was under the knife? It certainly wouldn't be the worst thing I've discovered about Project Remus, nor the most far-fetched."

Holy shit. I sat heavily into the spare chair, staring at the screen. Like Leon said, it was just a guess. But it was a good guess.

"But she wasn't Remus," I said, shaking my head. "You said you'd seen the list, and she wasn't on it."

Leon shrugged. "Who says that list they gave me was complete? I could be reaching here, but I just wanted a second opinion about what to do about this. If I tell DeLuna..."

"She'll want to bomb it," I murmured, feeling confident in that assessment. "She'll be fucking *furious* and drop a missile on the whole fucking facility."

Leon gave a one-shoulder shrug. "Maybe that's the best thing to do."

"Maybe." I sighed. "Fuck me."

Leon wrinkled his nose. "I told you, Sasquatch, you're not my type. But what do we do about *this*?" He pointed at the screen, looking at me like he genuinely wanted me to make the decision. Shit, we were actually having a respectful conversation without Danny babysitting us. Progress.

I sat back in my chair, staring at the screen for a long fucking time. Then I shook my head. "We don't know for sure. It could be totally unrelated, and maybe the material stored in that lab is all legit. We can't go destroying it all without more information. That's not fair to however many hundreds of people have got their swimmers or eggs frozen there."

"If they even know about it," Leon muttered. "Which I doubt they do."

I had a feeling he was right, but I still couldn't just agree to bomb the place. Even if Danny chose to destroy anything connected to her—and that was entirely her choice to make—we couldn't make that call for everyone else involved. What if there were desperate potential parents out there who were relying on that storage facility?

"Do we know if they're *using* the material stored there? Or is it all just on ice?"

"Fuck if I know," Leon replied. "Remember, this shit is four years old *at least*. Someone might have already bombed the facility for all we know."

Surprise had my eyes widen, because that hadn't even crossed my mind. "Have they?"

He scoffed. "No, I satellite imaged it. It's fine."

"Dick," I growled.

He flashed me a tired grin. "So? What do we do about this?"

I groaned and scrubbed my hands over my face. Then I exhaled heavily. "Just... keep digging. See if you can get some kind of *proof* that this involves Danny. Or somehow work out who EA0088 is. Then we can reassess. Agreed?"

Leon nodded. "Agreed. Now fuck off out of my office, you stink."

29
DANNY

Koen was *so* bored, still on school suspension for keying his teacher's car. That was what you got for being petty, though. It was all too clear that he didn't want to end our call and go back to doing his online assessments, so I humored him. After all, I had nothing better to do while hiding out in Leon's house.

I hated hiding. It made my skin itch. Besides, there was no concrete proof that the released inmates were hunting my head... that was just a guess. An educated guess, sure, but still just a guess. Maybe they'd been released on good behavior? Then again, I'd been to the Castle. I'd placed prisoners there.

None of them should *ever* be released, regardless of their behavior.

The worst part about it was that even if the inmates had some shreds of sanity or moral code when they were locked up, the years of torture at the hands of the Guild's most depraved would have stamped it out. Nope, anyone released from the Castle would be a certifiable murdering machine.

So as much as it pained me and my desire to be active, I'd grit my teeth and remain in hiding. At least until Leon could finish decoding the drives.

I thought maybe he'd found something while I was on the phone with Koen, but he'd gone to ask Kai something instead. When I eventually finished my call to the devilish brat—he wanted to stink bomb someone from school—I went to see what the guys were up to.

Leon was hard at work in his office, and I didn't want to go distracting him *again*, so I changed into some workout clothes and skipped off to the gym where Kai was lifting weights.

"Hey, Big Man," I greeted him with a grin. "Wanna take a roll with me?"

He shot me a wicked smirk as he curled the impressively heavy weight in his hand. "Siren, I *always* wanna roll with you."

My lower belly warmed, and I didn't fight my grin. "Cute. I meant fighting. You don't mind hitting a girl, do you?" His brows rose, and I knew what was going through his head, so I laughed. "Don't worry, Big Man, you won't land any punches on me."

He gave a low chuckle, shaking his head. "Go warm up, and we'll test that theory out."

Poor darling really thought he might stand a chance against me. Not an insult to him at all—I was fully aware that he was a big scary badass in his own right—but he was *military*, not Guild. Those *rules* that got drilled into them about clean fighting were *very* hard to unlearn. By contrast, we were taught to fight dirty before anything else. Who gave a fuck about honorable if you ended up dead?

"Hey, does Leon seem different today?" Kai asked, coming over to where I'd just started a slow jog on the treadmill. He leaned his tattoo-covered forearms on the display, looking somewhat *worried*.

He was right, though. I'd noticed it too. "I put it down to not sleeping enough," I admitted. "It sounds like he has been at his desk around the clock, except for the few hours he sleeps when I make him."

Kai nodded slowly. "Maybe that's it. He just seems… off."

Last night, I'd put it down to exhaustion, because I was also wrecked. But he'd been pale and lethargic when we woke up this morning, and I'd suggested to him he might be coming down with something. He had laughed it off, then thoroughly distracted me in the hot tub instead.

"Shit," I whispered. "Now I'm worried. I thought I was reading too much into it, but if you noticed too…" I turned off the treadmill and hopped off. "Raincheck on sparring? I'm going to go check on him. Maybe he just has a cold coming on."

Kai must have been more worried than he was letting on, because he quickly agreed. If he hadn't been concerned, he'd have told me to check on him later... especially after I had all but promised we would fuck on the gym floor after "sparring" together.

I hurried my ass back upstairs and let myself into Leon's office without knocking. He was exactly where I'd left him, slouched in his office chair and scrolling through what seemed to be medical documents on the screen.

"Hi, beautiful," he greeted me with a tired smile. He held out a hand, and I willingly let him pull me into his lap. They both seemed to like holding me in their laps, not just because it put my ass near their dicks, but because they could hold me so tight. I loved it too.

"Bunny," I said with a sigh, stroking a hand over his brow and noting how clammy it was. "How are you feeling?"

He frowned slightly, looking up at me with glassy eyes. "Fine. Why?"

I pressed my hand to his cheek, feeling how warm he was. "Marx, baby, you're sick. You need to go to bed and rest. This shit can wait a few days for you to get better, I promise."

He wrinkled his nose, then laughed. "I'm not sick. I don't get sick. It's just hot in here. Kai probably fucked with my central heating."

Nope, no way. Now that I was really looking closer, the signs were all there. Not to mention how he was coughing earlier. He was definitely sick, and sitting in front of his computer twenty hours straight sure as fuck wouldn't help him recover.

My mind made up, I climbed out of his lap and grasped his hand in mine. "Come on, Bunny. You're going to bed."

The fact that I easily pulled him to his feet when he didn't want to go should have been enough evidence, but he still argued the whole way back to his bedroom. He insisted he was fine, that he'd never fallen victim to a common cold in his whole life and sure as hell wasn't about to start now.

The brighter lights of his bedroom painted a whole different picture, though. He was pale and sweaty.

"Leon, shut up and let me get you changed." I lifted his t-shirt and needed to stretch up on my tiptoes to pull it over his head.

He sat down on the edge of the bed as I went to his dresser to find a clean T-shirt. "DeLuna, my love, if you wanted to get me naked, you just had to ask. I'd never say no to quality time alone with you."

I grabbed a soft black t-shirt and turned around to give him a stern look. "Nice try, Marx. You already distracted me once this morning, and you've clearly gone downhill since then. Now, be a good boy and let me take care of you."

His watery smile widened, and I snorted a laugh, hearing

what I just said. Okay, sure, that could be taken two very different ways, and there was no question what Leon was thinking. He gave a laugh himself, then started coughing.

Then *kept* coughing. I strode into the bathroom to grab him a glass of water, but before I even filled it up, the coughing cut off with a heart-stopping thud. The glass slipped from my fingers, breaking in the sink, but I was already racing back into the bedroom where Leon was unconscious on the floor.

"Leon!" I shouted, panic ripping through me with electric waves. I carefully rolled him over, then sucked in a sharp breath when I saw the crimson stain across his lips. That was bad news. Really bad.

"Kai!" I bellowed at the top of my lungs, turning my head toward the door. I couldn't leave Leon, but *shit,* I needed help. "Kai! Help!"

Turning my focus back to Leon, I tried to remember the first responder training I'd taken years ago. Until now, I'd only ever needed to tend to my own wounds, but we couldn't exactly call an ambulance right now. So with shaking fingers, I found his pulse and almost collapsed when I found it, strong and steady under my fingertips.

Bringing my ear down to his chest, I tried to listen to make sure he was breathing properly, but it was too hard to tell. My own pulse was so loud in my ears it was all static. White fucking noise. But I heard the clatter of Kai's footsteps rushing up the stairs, and another small wave of relief rushed over me. He'd know what to do. Wouldn't he?

"What happened?" Kai barked, dropping to his knees beside me and doing exactly what I'd just done—checking Leon's pulse and breathing.

I shook my head, swallowing the thick lump of fear threatening to choke me. "He started coughing, then just collapsed. Kai, we need to get him to a hospital. Is your team far away? There's no way we can do the snowmobile trip while he's unconscious." Even if they were the ones who'd poisoned Leon—and *fuck* I hope that was just my paranoia talking—I would rather take the help and exact revenge later.

Kai swept a hand over his face, thinking. Then he shook his head. "They're too far by now. What about Carol?"

I grabbed out my phone to call, then changed my mind and dialed Carlos instead. He answered within three rings, and I babbled out what had happened in a flurry of word salad.

"Slow down, Dan, try again," Carlos interrupted, his voice hard.

I sucked in a fearful breath, then got to the point. "I need a medevac. Right now. Can you help?"

Carlos didn't fuck around asking unnecessary questions. "Give me three minutes." He ended the call without waiting for me to reply, and I stared down at my blank phone screen with tears burning the backs of my eyes. Leon hadn't moved, not even a twitch, since collapsing.

"Hey," Kai said, breaking through my panic spiral. He cupped my face, turning me to look at *him* rather than down at the blood on Leon's lips or his ashen skin. "It's going to be okay, Danny. You know it is. Leon Marx will never let *illness* take him out, he's way too stubborn and egotistical for such a mundane death."

I gave a sob of laughter, thinking how I'd had the same opinion of Jude's death. But she really was dead, so what if Leon was next? Oh fuck, I couldn't lose him.

My phone rang, and I startled before answering it with a shaking thumb. "Carlos, talk to me."

"Medevac is enroute," he advised. "They'll be there in ten minutes, maybe less. Where do you want them to take you?"

Where did I want to take Leon? Where would he be *safe*? This all felt too convenient after Carol warned us to lay low. My instincts were burning, telling me this was a trap, a way to lure us out into the open... somehow.

"I need to stay off-grid," I told Carlos in a pained whisper. "We can't go to a hospital."

"Done," he replied without hesitation. "I'll advise the crew. Call me when you're safe, understood?"

"Yeah," I replied, then ended the call and looked up at Kai. "Carlos has sent a team. Help me get him dressed?"

Between us, we got Leon's t-shirt on, then bundled him into a zip-up hoodie before Kai hefted him up off the floor. My heart almost exploded in my chest when I saw how limp Leon lay in Kai's arms, like he was already dead. I kept those thoughts to myself, though, pulling on a sweatshirt myself before racing down the stairs ahead of Kai to grab us both shoes so we didn't get frostbite when we stepped out into the snow.

Exactly seven and a half minutes after my call from Carlos, the distinctive whir of helicopter blades announced the medevac arrival. Kai carried Leon's unconscious form out to meet the paramedics, and I raced alongside. They asked questions about what had happened, and I answered as calmly and accurately as I could, leaving nothing out.

Minutes later, Leon was strapped into a stretcher with an oxygen mask over his face, and we were rising into the air. Tears started sliding down my cheeks as Leon's house faded from view, and I leaned down to kiss his sweaty forehead.

"You're going to be okay, Bunny," I whispered in a choked voice. "I swear, you're going to be okay. I can't do this without you. You're *ma moitié*." My other half, my partner in crime. This was absolutely not how our story would end. No way in hell.

30
LEON

What the fuck had happened to me? I felt like a truck had just run me over. Then backed up and did it again. My *whole* body ached. Not just the muscles, but my *skin* hurt. How the fuck was that even possible for your skin to hurt all over?

A shiver ran through me, heightening that ache, and I moaned.

Where was I? The last thing I remembered... Danny. I remembered Danny taking my shirt off in my bedroom. But not in a sexy way. It was because I was sick. Me. Sick. Of all the bullshit...

No, I didn't get sick. This had to be poison.

I peeled my eyes open, squinting at the harsh light of a hospital room. How in the hell had I gotten here? *Where* was here?

Instruments beeped steadily beside my bed, and I eyed them. Blood pressure and oxygen looked normal. Then again, I had an oxygen mask over my nose and mouth, so that had to be helping.

Raising a heavy hand, I tugged the mask away from my face. Those fucking things always made me feel claustrophobic, and I could breathe just fine on my own. Theoretically, anyway.

A large window on the side of the room showed medical staff in the corridor, and I caught a flash of white hair. Danny. My DeLuna was here. Fuck... what the *hell* happened?

The door to my room opened, and to my crushing disappointment, it was a stranger in a lab coat that entered, not my heart. The woman—doctor, I assumed—was middle-aged with glasses and a medical mask on, holding a chart.

"Mr. Marx," she greeted me with a slight crinkle of a smile touching her eyes. "It's good to see you awake. How are you feeling?"

I rubbed my throat. "Like death," I admitted. "What happened?"

"That's what we're trying to work out," she admitted. "You gave your girlfriend quite a fright when you passed out. She said you were coughing when it happened and that there was blood when you coughed?"

Was there? Shit, she must have panicked. I would have, too, if the roles were reversed.

"I have no idea," I murmured honestly. "I was feeling a bit under the weather, like I was getting the flu or a cold. Then I woke up here." If it wasn't poison, then I was probably allergic to Kai's team. Or him. Yeah, I couldn't get that lucky. So definitely his team.

The doctor nodded, tucking the chart under her arm and looking down at me with kind eyes. "As far as I can ascertain, Mr. Marx, you appear to have the flu."

"Oh," I said, blinking. "That doesn't seem serious enough to be here. Where *is* here, by the way?" And how was their security?

"You're in a private medical facility, Mr. Marx. You're entirely safe here, I promise. And you're right, we normally wouldn't keep you for the flu, but you don't seem to have any regular flu." She pulled up a chair and sat beside the bed, crossing one leg over the other. "According to the tests I've run, you have a very rare form of influenza A that, to be perfectly honest, looks a lot like the strain that killed millions of people in 1918."

I blinked at her slowly. "I have the Spanish flu? *How?*"

She shrugged. "Honestly, that's what I want to know, too. It's not strictly the Spanish flu. What you have seems to be a synthesized version of the virus with some modification, which I believe contributed to the blood in your lungs. What I find fascinating, though, is that it doesn't seem to be contagious."

Stunned disbelief combined with how utterly crappy I was feeling meant my reaction time was a little slow. "How can you be sure?"

"Because we tested your girlfriend and the gentleman she's with. Both said they've been in close proximity with you for several days, and I believe you and she have been intimate since your symptoms started? If you were contagious, she would have it. But she doesn't. Nor do any of the medical crew who brought you in." She gave me a curious look, then shrugged. "Medical mystery, Mr. Marx. But it also means that I have nothing to treat you with. We could try standard antivirals, but you're also past the forty-eight-hour window for those to be most effective. Hopefully, your body will react to this like a normal flu and you'll recover with fluids and rest, but we will keep you here just in case your condition worsens. Okay?"

All I heard was that Danny didn't have whatever I had. The relief of that statement was so intense it lightened my whole body for a few moments. Like the invisible sandbags were lifted off for a small reprieve.

"Can I see her?" I asked, clearing my throat. It was scratchy, like I'd swallowed a cactus. Was this what normal humans felt like when they fell victim to the flu? I'd survived thirty years of life without ever catching so much as a cold, and now I had a hundred-year-old illness. Great, just fucking great.

The doctor nodded as she stood up. "I'll let her know you're awake."

She left the room, and I waited for one whole, long, torturous minute before my white-haired angel came racing into the room, wearing one of my sweatshirts and a pair of snow boots over yoga pants.

"Bunny!" she exclaimed, practically throwing herself onto the bed and making me swallow a groan of pain. No way was I letting that sound escape, not when she was holding onto me like I was a broken door floating on the ice-cold North Atlantic Ocean.

She said nothing else, just buried her face in my chest and held me, so I raised a heavy, aching hand to stroke her silken hair. Fuck, it was soft.

"DeLuna, baby, I'm okay," I reassured her. "It's just the flu. Nothing to worry about."

Apparently, that was the wrong thing to say. She sat bolt upright, her glare blazing with the burning fire of outrage. "*Nothing to worry about?*" she hissed, her eye twitching slightly. "Are you fucking *high?* I thought you were *dying, you* condescending ass! You coughed up blood and passed out on your bedroom floor. I couldn't wake you up. Kai had to carry you into the helicopter, and *you looked fucking dead.* Do you understand what that was like for me?"

Speechless. That's what she made me. Utterly speechless.

For a long moment, she just glared her fury at me, then I reached up to stroke her hair out of her face, and she just fucking melted into my touch.

"I'm sorry I scared you, *mon cœur,*" I murmured.

Her eyes closed, she leaned her face into my hand, and one stray tear trickled down her cheek. I caught it with my thumb on her jaw, wiping it away.

"Don't do that to me again, Bunny," she whispered in a heartbreakingly pained voice. "I need you, so fucking much. We have to see this bullshit through and live out one of those corny happily ever after sequences."

I smiled, despite how her hoarse voice was shredding me up inside. "And instead of children, we have a six-foot-four Māori man with a bad temper?"

She gave a small laugh and nodded. "Exactly."

"Come here," I told her, patting the small space beside me. "Lie with me for a bit."

She did as I asked, getting comfy in that little gap and resting her hand on my chest, right over my heart. Like she needed that physical contact to reassure herself that I was still here with her. I understood entirely.

My arm draped over her shoulders, and I let my eyes drift shut. Fuck, I felt rough. I wasn't going to admit it to Danny; she didn't need to worry any more than she already was. But goddamn. This was the flu? It sucked.

I must have fallen asleep like that, because when I woke again, my room was dark and Danny was no longer tucked under my arm. Groggy and nauseous, I checked my own vitals on the instruments again. Still within normal range, thank fuck.

My blinds were still open, and the lights in the hallway outside had been dimmed but were still bright enough that I could see

Danny out there with Kai. He held her against him in a tight embrace with one arm, and hers were banded tightly around his waist. He held a phone to his ear, speaking with someone, but he still held my woman... *our* woman... like she was the most precious thing on earth.

I lay there staring at them for a long time, but none of my usual jealousy bubbled up as I watched Kai finish his call and tenderly stroke Danny's hair. She almost seemed to be asleep against his chest, despite the fact they were standing. For the first time since the Sasquatch had burst into her life with his big dick and anger management issues, I was glad he was here.

He was comforting her while I couldn't. He was giving her a shoulder to lean on, while I lay in a hospital bed with a century-old flu. For the *first fucking time*, I was actually grateful that Malachi Arden owned the other half of Danny's heart.

This flu was messing with my head and making me all emotional. I needed to get better soon before I went confessing to Kai that I actually respected him. Just a little bit. Christ, if that happened, I would be better off dead.

Comforted that Danny was being taken care of, I let my eyes drift closed once again. I was no use to her like this. I was no use to *anyone* like this, so I had to do what the doctor suggested. Rest and recover. Then get back to clearing my love's name within the Guild and give her that corny happily ever after she definitely didn't want. She'd be bored in a week, but at least she would have the experience.

31
DANNY

Somehow, I managed to fall asleep standing up. Don't ask me how the hell that worked, but it just did. I'd been hugging Kai, my arms tight around his waist and my face smooshed into his chest. He'd been leaning against the wall, so I'd leaned my weight on him, and the next thing I knew... zzz.

At some point, he must have finished the phone call he'd been on with Eli and eased me down onto one of the chairs lining the corridor outside Leon's room, because I woke horizontal, my head cushioned in Kai's lap and my legs tucked up on the chair I was in.

"Hey, sleepyhead," Kai rumbled when I yawned and sat up slightly.

I turned my face up to meet his soft gaze and offered a weak smile. "Sorry, I don't know how..."

"Nothing to apologize for," he told me in a quiet voice. I sat up fully, looking through the window into the darkness of Leon's room, and Kai read my mind. "He's asleep, too. The nurse just checked on him."

I let out my breath. "How is he doing?"

Kai gave a small shrug. "They've administered antiviral drugs as well as fluids. His condition is stable so far. No more coughing or blood."

Nodding, I swiped a hand through my hair, raking it away from my face. "Good. That's good. Hopefully, it stays that way."

Kai grimaced, like he wasn't so hopeful, and I squinted at him. "What do you know that I don't?"

"Let's go grab a coffee. I'll fill you in on what I've dug up." Kai stood up and offered me his hand, which I happily accepted. I'd never been a needy, clingy kind of girl before, but there was something about thinking I might lose someone I truly loved that made me crave physical contact like never before.

Kai led me down the corridor, then through some swinging doors out to the tiny reception. This wasn't a hospital in the traditional sense, it was a private medical facility. Entirely off the books and disguised as a law firm. We were on the seventeenth floor of an office building, and the people who were being treated by these doctors were the kind of people who paid handsomely in unmarked bills.

Because it wasn't a hospital, there was no cafeteria, but there was an automatic coffee machine near the elevators. Fuck it, that'd do. I was an equal opportunity coffee drinker and wouldn't turn my nose up just because it was a touch bitter.

"Alright, talk to me," I demanded while the machine loudly began producing coffee. "What's going on?"

Kai glanced around, but we were alone. "Leon's *flu*," he murmured, "I don't think it's actually a flu. Or it is, but sometime last year, before we met, my team had heard gossip among the criminal underworld about a targeted virus being created."

My eyes widened. "You think he was poisoned? How? Why?"

Kai shook his head. "It's not poison, it's a virus. But it's a DNA-specific coded virus... meaning that if anyone else came in contact with it, they wouldn't be infected. It would only bond with the coded victim."

I blinked in shock. "And... Leon is the target?"

"He's Circle, isn't he? And doesn't have any heirs? Maybe someone thought to clear the board more efficiently than just taking Erikkson's seat?" Kai looked tense and worried. "I don't know, it's just a hunch. I've got Eli working on digging up some more info, because it was quite literally just rumor and gossip when we heard of it."

Sighing, I took my cup of scalding hot coffee from the vending machine. "Where there's smoke, there's fire. If it was developed enough that rumors were leaking out, then they could have been working on it for years." I took an absentminded sip of the coffee and instantly regretted it, burning my tongue. Fuck, I hated that.

"That was my thought, too," Kai agreed. "The fact that the doctor emphasized how *rare* his flu is and that neither of us has it…"

Dread curled through me, writhing like an angry snake. "Someone is trying to kill Leon."

"I have Eli and Jae tracking down any information they can find, starting with the loose-lipped shit who told us in the first place. They'll get something soon." Kai took his own coffee from the machine and gave it a dubious sniff.

Now that my tongue was already dead, I just gulped a mouthful of the scalding crap in an effort to make my brain wake the rest of the way up. "Do we think there is some kind of cure? Or an antidote?"

Kai lifted one brow. "It's not poison, *ātaahua*," he reminded me gently. "But it seems implausible that a scientist would develop a gene-targeted virus *without* some kind of reverse button in case they fucked up and infected themselves. Maybe a matching antiviral drug?"

That gave me a shred of hope to grab onto, and I nodded enthusiastically. "Yes, exactly. If they've put all this work into coding a virus specifically to Leon's DNA or... whatever it is, then I bet they have a countermeasure for mistakes. It just seems logical, right?" Kai just stared at me with sad eyes, and it made me bristle. "Right?" I repeated firmly.

He nodded slowly. "Right," he murmured. "Eli and Jae are in Boston, questioning our lead. I've asked them to call the minute they get something concrete out of him."

I wet my lips, then took another huge, burning gulp of bitter coffee. "This could be a wild-goose chase. And we have no idea how long Leon has." My pulse was racing again, my palms sweating. Shit, what if we were chasing all over the world searching for a cure, and Leon died waiting for us?

Kai placed a gentle, reassuring hand on the small of my back, guiding me back through the innocent-looking doors beside the fake reception and into the medical suite once more. "You could stay here with him," he suggested reluctantly. "I can do the legwork with my guys."

Stay here and let him go out hunting without me? Fuck, that was an even worse idea. Sure, he was more than capable. He had his whole team; he was well trained and had infinite resources. And I'd be here with Leon. But the idea of sitting on my ass and *praying* for a miracle? It didn't work for me. So I shook my head firmly, giving Kai a hard look.

"No, no way. We both go. Leon will be fine here. They know how to keep their patients safe, and he is already looking so much better. The fluids and antiviral meds must be working at least a little bit. So long as he stays on them, he will be fine until we get back." He had to be. There were no other options. He *needed* the medical attention, there was no two ways about it. I'd call in some favors to reinforce hospital security, to guard him while he slept… whatever it took.

Kai didn't argue, just nodded silently. The light was on in Leon's room when we got back, and through the window, we saw a nurse talking to him and changing the IV bags.

A surge of hope rushed through me as I eyed Leon sitting up in bed. He still looked awful but nowhere near as terrible as when we brought him in. Maybe the medication really was working?

I waited anxiously for the nurse to finish what she was doing—I hated interrupting them while they were quite literally saving my loved one's life—then hurried into the room when she left.

"Hey, you," I said to Leon with a smile, sitting on the edge of his bed once more. "You look a little better." Holding his gorgeous green gaze, I stroked my hand over his forehead and gave a small sigh at his lack of fever.

"Sorry I fell asleep," he murmured, still sounding croaky. "Apparently, sleep is what fixes the flu, though, so I guess it's a good thing." I winced, and Leon heaved a sigh. "It's not the flu, is it?"

"We're working on it," I replied, interlinking my fingers with his on the bed. He had an IV line into the back of his tattooed hand, and tape held it in place, so I was gentle.

Leon just stared at me for a long moment, then he nodded. "When are we leaving?"

My brows lifted. "*We* aren't leaving," I corrected. "You are staying here with impeccable medical care. No one knows this facility is here, so no one will find you. For the record, you've been registered as a member of Carlos's business. Guild are *persona non grata* within these walls."

He gave a small smile. "Good to know. But I'm coming with you. Wherever you're going, count me in. I feel so much better already, anyway."

I got it. I totally understood how he was feeling. If that were me in a hospital bed, I would be attempting the exact same argument. But he was shit out of luck, because he needed more treatment, and I couldn't risk him dying on this wild-goose chase.

"Bunny," I whispered on a sigh, cupping his cheek in my hand. The bags under his eyes were so heavy they looked bruised. "You're staying here and getting better. Kai and I will hunt down whoever is responsible for making you sick, and we *will* come back for you. Understood?"

Leon shook his head, the stubborn mule. "Absolutely not."

I ignored his refusal, leaning in to kiss his cheek tenderly. "Get better, Bunny. I have so many dirty things I wanna do with you when this is over."

He groaned, and I made a speedy exit from the room before he could make me change my mind. He was too damn good at persuading me, especially when he looked all vulnerable like he did.

"We good?" Kai asked, getting up from his seat as I passed him.

I jerked a nod. "Yeah, we're good. He knows. I just need to sign some paperwork to cover his treatment costs, and we can go. Will you call a car service?" Since we'd arrived by light aircraft after switching from the medevac helicopter in Anchorage, we had no transport out of the city.

Kai pulled out his phone, already bringing up one of his own contacts for a driver. I made my way to the nurses' station and let them know that Kai and I had to go. I impressed upon them that Leon was *not* permitted to discharge himself under *any* circumstances. Because this was a highly illegal organization, they had no issues agreeing to my request.

It took a couple of minutes to finish off the documents they needed and to arrange the appropriate transfer of funds, but then Kai and I were free to go. I needed to bite my lip to keep from looking back at Leon's room. If I went back in there to say goodbye, I'd probably start crying.

Shit, what were these guys *doing* to me?

We needed to wait for the elevators, and Kai wrapped an arm around my waist when I started tapping my foot anxiously.

"The car is waiting outside," he told me. "We can go straight to Boston. Eli texted that they've taken our informant into custody."

I gave a weak smile. "You make it sound official, like you're FBI or some shit."

Kai gave a soft chuckle. "Sounds better than saying they've got him tied up and stuffed in the trunk of a car, doesn't it?"

We rode the elevator back down to the ground floor, where sharply dressed corporates were coming and going from their mundane office jobs with *zero* clue that there was an underworld hospital inside their building.

I stood out like a sore thumb in my oversized men's hoodie and snow boots, but fucking whatever. I ignored the curious glances and made my way through the foyer with Kai right beside me. A black Escalade waited at the curb in front, and Kai glanced at the plates to confirm it was his car as we approached. The driver popped open the back door for us, and I slid inside—then gave a quick gasp of shock.

"I told you, *mon cœur*," Leon said, leaning on the far window with a smug as fuck smile on his lips, "I'm coming with you."

32
DANNY

Really, it shouldn't have surprised me. This was Leon Marx, for fuck's sake. He was the dictionary definition of slippery. But stupid fucking me, I'd assumed he would actually put his own health over his stubborn pride and horrible case of FOMO.

"How?" I exclaimed. "How the fuck—"

"Holy shit," Kai muttered with a laugh, getting in behind me and pulling the door shut. "I'm a little bit impressed."

Leon gave him a nod. "Thank you."

I shook my head, anger taking over my shock. "Nope, no way. You are *sick*, Leon. What part of that are you not comprehending? Get your ass out of this car and go back to your hospital bed. We can handle this ourselves."

Leon just met my furious glare and raised one brow. "Make me."

My jaw dropped. Was he joking?

"Siren, I'm with *kohuru rapeti* on this one," Kai said with a grimace. "Sorry, beautiful, but I would want to do the same in his shoes. Besides, I bet he can still kill fuckers while half dead. He'll be fine."

Shock held me speechless. But then the car started moving, the driver completely oblivious to our conflict, and the argument became irrelevant.

"I think the fact I beat you down here proves I'm fine," Leon drawled, snaking an arm around my waist to pull me closer. "So, where are we going?"

"Boston," Kai replied. "For now, anyway. Eli might get us a new lead before we get there."

I was *pissed* that they were ganging up on me, but I couldn't seem to muster the appropriate level of determination to send Leon back to the medical facility. Especially with his arm around me and his body against my side. Dammit, I liked having him with us.

"Fill me in on what you know," Leon suggested. "What are we hunting down, or who?"

Kai gave Leon a rundown of all the information we were working off of. That he'd heard rumors about a targeted virus being developed as a new assassination tool, and we believed that was what Leon had.

I said nothing, just let Kai explain while gently resting my head on Leon's shoulder. He did seem better… certainly not one hundred percent, but he didn't look like he was dying right now.

"If it was RNA-coded to me specifically," Leon mused when Kai was done, "then they had to have collected a sample from me at some stage. Which means someone who knew who I was *and* got close enough to collect my saliva or… something."

That thought hadn't even crossed my mind. But he was right. You surely can't code a virus to hit a specific target without having that sample data.

"Who would—" I started to say, then cut off when Leon gave an angry noise.

"Carol," he growled accusingly.

I jerked. "What? No. No way, it can't have been Carol. Why would she—"

"It lines up, though, doesn't it?" Kai murmured, agreeing with Leon *again*. "She knows Leon is Circle. She's held her seat a whole lot longer, so she probably has access to experiments Leon has never even heard about, *and* she could have taken his DNA while we were at her house."

I wet my lips, searching for a plausible argument. But I wasn't naïve enough to think that just because we shared blood, she wasn't double-crossing us. I barely knew the woman, but my gut told me she was trustworthy. Was my gut wrong? Maybe.

"Why, though?" I challenged. "What would Carol have to gain in killing Leon?"

Kai shrugged. "Power? It seems to be the one thing the Circle values above all else—no offense, Marx—but human decency falls pretty low on the list of values. What if she's been working with Blanchet?"

I shook my head firmly. "No, she's not. Otherwise, she would have handed me over to him while I was sedated. She could have killed me then, too, but she didn't. There are too many flaws in this theory for my liking."

Leon pressed a kiss to my hair. "Carol Atwood is entirely capable of being a power-hungry, ruthless killer," he said softly, "as well as a great mom to Koen. The two sides of her *can* coexist, and even I can see he's been raised by a loving mother. That doesn't mean she won't sell you out, given the right price."

"What if she is working with Blanchet," Kai pondered, "but also had no idea you were her daughter? That part could have been entirely sincere, and after she found you, she changed her mind. But that wouldn't extend to Leon, and maybe she just saw an opportunity, then took it."

Fuck. Could they be right?

"I'm not convinced," I said quietly. "But you raise valid theories."

"For argument's sake, who else could be responsible for this?"

Leon asked, kissing my hair again in a comforting gesture. "It had to be someone who knew I was Circle, and that list *has* to be short."

Kai hummed a thoughtful sound. "My mole knew. Whoever the mole is, they told us you were Circle almost two months ago."

"Do you have any idea who the mole might be?" I asked, hating how much suspicion was being cast over Carol right now. Fucking hell, *she* could be the mole for all we knew.

Kai shook his head. "We didn't really care who it was until recently."

Frustrating, sure, but also understandable. The mole was handing Kai's team the information they wanted but couldn't otherwise get their hands on. I didn't blame them for not looking the gift horse in the mouth, even if it did leave us with very few leads now.

"Whoever infected Leon needed to get close to him," I said, wracking my brain for clues. "When did you start feeling sick, Bunny?"

He grimaced. "A few days ago, I guess."

Bile rose in my throat, and I swallowed hard. "So…depending on what the virus incubation period is, you either contracted it at Carol's house, on the flight home, or from Kai's team." Because those were the only people he'd had contact with that could have given it to him. Anything *prior* to Carol's house seemed too long ago to really be a possibility unless it had a delayed-release.

"My team isn't involved," Kai growled, his voice threaded with warning.

I wasn't as convinced, though. "How do you know, Big Man?

Not to go picking at old wounds, but didn't Sam put out a hit on both Leon and me not so long ago? How do we know this isn't still a part of that? Did Leon's hit ever get deleted from the dark web?"

Kai glowered at me but jerked a nod. "It's gone. I made sure of it."

"Someone might have started working on the virus for the hit, then decided to use it regardless of the payout," Leon mused. "But that only opens our pool of suspects a shit load wider, if I wasn't targeted for my seat on the Circle."

"Fucking hell," I muttered with a groan. I rubbed at my eyes, feeling a tension headache building. "So… what do we do? Go to Boston or get in touch with Carol? What about your team, Kai? We *know* how you all feel about the Circle. Particularly Mo. What if she's the one who infected Leon?"

Just that hint of accusation had Kai so angry his knuckles popped as he balled his hand into a fist. "I'll deal with them," he said with gritted teeth. "She won't lie to me about something like this."

"Fine by me," Leon accepted with a yawn. "In that case, I think we will chat with Carol. She's the prime suspect in my books, anyway. No offense, but your sister seems like she failed science at school."

Kai scoffed. "She did."

I hated *all* of these theories, but I couldn't ignore the facts. Someone had infected Leon. Someone wanted him dead. Both Kai and I would have to put our personal feelings aside to investigate all suspects.

"Are we heading to the airport?" I asked Kai, thinking through our plans. He nodded, and I pulled out my phone to message Carol and ask for a meeting. Carlos had sent his plane—the one that I'd been borrowing for the last few years—just in case we needed it. So I could go to her wherever she was.

We were stopped at a traffic light, and Kai confirmed that we were indeed heading to the airport where Carlos's plane was waiting. I turned my attention to my phone, typing out a message to Carol, but before I could send it, the front windshield shattered and blood splattered through the car.

"Down!" Leon barked, pushing me to the floor of the car. He shifted forward, awkwardly crouching behind the driver's seat and reaching through to grab the dead man's gun from his belt. Kai had one in hand already, halfway out of the car and looking around for our attacker.

Stupid fucking me, I hadn't grabbed a weapon before leaving Leon's house.

More bullets peppered the car, and bystanders screamed on the street. We needed to get the fuck out of there; we were sitting ducks.

Kai returned fire, squeezing off a handful of shots before ducking back into the car for cover.

"Multiple shooters," he informed us, "elevated positions."

"Move," I snapped at Leon, then wiggled myself through the gap to the front of the car. While trying to remain out of sight, lying almost flat below the dash, I unclipped the dead driver's seat belt. Blood covered my hoodie as I reached over him to pop open the door, then I gave the body a forceful shove to push him out into the street.

Bullets rained down on us, smashing the passenger side window and making me tense up, but I was too conditioned to being under fire to freeze. I climbed into the vacated driver's seat, yanked the driver's door shut, then slammed my foot down on the gas.

Thankfully, all the other drivers at the intersection had ducked for cover, so there was no risk of a car crash when I raced through the red light, tearing out of the ambush intersection at top speed. It wasn't until we'd made it at least two blocks away that I sat up straighter to try and see where we were going.

"We all okay back there?" I called out, glancing in the rearview mirror.

Leon was grinning, his eyes a little glassy but the gun steady in his hand as he nodded to me. Kai looked somewhat less amused, giving me a narrow-eyed glare.

"You could have warned me, *kaikohuru iti*. I nearly fell out of the fucking car when you hit the gas."

I flashed him a broad smile. "You were fine, Big Man. Come up here and kick the windshield out for me? I can't see shit like this." The bullet that killed our driver had made a hole, but the rest of the glass was a shattered spiderweb of cracks, held in place by the privacy glazing.

Kai handed his gun to Leon—too hot to stick back in his

pants—and struggled to squeeze his much larger frame through the gap between the seats. For a moment, I thought he might wind up headfirst down the footwell, but he recovered it and did as I asked.

"What is it with us and broken windshields, Danny?" He arched a smile at me, and I grinned back.

"Useless fucking things," I growled, squinting into the wind as I picked up speed. I was following the signs for the airport and praying there was only *one* airport in this city.

The lack of glass created enough noise from the wind that we couldn't really chat for the rest of the drive, but no one else shot at us. I was calling that a win. We pulled into the small airport, and I breathed a sigh of relief when I recognized my plane out on the tarmac. Thank fuck for *that*.

"Let's go," Kai barked, jumping out even before I stopped the car entirely. He circled around to help Leon out, and I loved him a little more for that, even if Leon did bat him away and muttered insults under his breath.

The two of them bickered in a friendly way as they boarded the plane, and I located my phone to finish sending my message to Carol. The car was a mess, riddled with bullet holes and the driver's seat drenched in blood, but I wasn't sticking around to clean it up.

Maybe Kai knew someone who could take care of it before local police got involved. If not, then... fuck it. Police were the least of my concerns.

33

KAI

Carol was still at her home in the Hamptons, but she didn't want to meet there and risk putting her children in danger. It was understandable, given how we'd been shot at just trying to get to Danny's plane. I knew my siren felt a lot better meeting away from Koen, too. She would never put that kid in danger deliberately.

Which was how we ended up making our way into an industrial rail yard just after dusk to meet with Carol in secrecy.

Danny was tense and anxious about questioning Carol, but Leon and I were both on high alert in case we were walking into a trap. We both had our guns out, scanning the whole area for any signs of hidden assassins. Leon grumbled under his breath about not having any spare ammo, but Danny confidently strode toward where Carol waited out in the open.

The older version of my siren rushed forward, enveloping her in a tight hug. I almost smiled at the awkward way Danny's arms flapped, like she had no clue what she was supposed to do with that hug. Carol released her before it became *too* awkward, though, and she seemed genuinely relieved to see her daughter alive.

"What's going on, Danny?" Carol demanded, stepping back to give Danny space to breathe. "I thought you were safely hiding somewhere? You don't realize how dangerous things are getting out here."

"We were," Danny confirmed. "Until Leon got sick and we needed medical help." She tipped her head to the ashen-faced murder rabbit, who just grimaced in return.

Carol was no idiot. "What kind of sick, Leon?"

He gave a brittle smile. "You tell me, Carol. Apparently, it's a new type of targeted virus that was coded specifically to make *me* ill. Do you know anything about that?"

Her brows shot up in surprise, and she shifted her gaze between the three of us. "You think I tried to kill you?" she asked in a cool voice, eyeing Leon with a flicker of annoyance.

"Trust me when I tell you, Leon Marx, if I wanted you dead, you'd be dead."

Call me crazy, but I believed her.

"RNA-coded viruses were a pet project for another member of the Circle some years ago. He dumped it, though, when he saw how slow-acting the virus was. Also, it didn't *always* kill the target, which was too unreliable for him. If I were to guess, I'd say the scientists who worked on the project must have continued their research even after Zhou pulled the funding."

As soon as she said that, Leon groaned and threw up his free hand with frustration. "Zhou. Of course. I knew someone on the Circle had involvement with medical research, I just couldn't remember who."

Danny and I exchanged a look. If that wasn't evidence of how sick Leon still was...

Carol gave a small sigh. "I can understand why you might have suspected me, but I'd be lying if I said it didn't sting a little."

I said nothing; this was none of my fucking business. She was Circle, she could still be acting. Just because she didn't infect Leon, didn't make her innocent. No one in our world was truly innocent.

"It's nothing personal," Danny said with a shrug, but I could sense her relief that Carol *seemed* innocent in Leon's illness. "How's Ko? Is he still going back to boarding school next week?"

Carol smiled warmly at the mention of her troublemaker child. "He is, thank goodness. I should be getting home to him soon." Then she gave Danny a suspicious look. "You wouldn't happen to know why I caught him making a stink bomb today, would you?"

A small laugh escaped me, and I tried to cover it with a cough. Too late, though, and Carol nodded with understanding.

"I see," she murmured with a smile. "Just don't go teaching him how to make explosives, please, Danny. Not yet, anyway. I want him to graduate high school with his limbs intact, preferably."

My girl gave a low chuckle. "No promises."

"You need to get into hiding anyway," Carol told us with a touch of a frown. "At least until Erikkson's seat gets reappointed. There's nothing I can do about the kill order now that it's passed, and with so many inmates released from the Castle, I don't like your odds of staying alive."

Shock rippled through me, and I saw it reflected on Leon's and Danny's faces.

"What kill order?" I asked, panic making my pulse race.

Carol's eyes widened. "I assumed you knew." She gave Leon a hard look. "The vote was raised on the Circle server last night. You and Erikkson, obviously, never cast a vote. Osei and Levitsky *always* vote in favor of kill orders, they don't care who it's on."

"That seems short-sighted," I muttered, and Carol flicked a glance at me.

"Of course it is, but they don't care. They're both bloodthirsty bastards and see kill orders as *fun*. Zhou, for some reason, voted against, but majority rules." Carol looked frustrated but unsurprised. "Need I remind you, there is no requirement for mental stability to hold a Circle seat, only that your blood matches the right family line."

Leon was fuming, though. "I was in the hospital last night," he growled. "Blanchet must have known. He must have known I couldn't vote; otherwise, it would have been three to three."

"Explains why we got ambushed after we left the facility," I commented, my eyes still searching the area around us. "We should get out of here."

Now that we knew there was a kill order out on Danny, plans needed to change. We needed to get her to safety. Get her hidden and out of reach of the *entire fucking Guild* while we waited out this bullshit with the vacant Circle seat.

A flicker of movement caught my eye about ten yards behind Leon, and I shot without hesitation. Whoever it was had been outfitted in a full-face ski mask, and you didn't dress like that if you were friendly.

"Oh shit," Leon murmured, spinning around to see the dead man on the ground. "Thanks, Sasquatch."

Fuck, he was too sick for this. His instincts were all dull and slow. "Let's move," I snapped.

Carol had a gun out and, when she saw Danny's hands empty, passed it over. "Don't worry, I brought spares," she said with a smile, pulling a second gun from her lower back. "Let's get the hell out of here. He might have friends."

We started back toward where we'd left our stolen car—rentals left too much of a paper trail—with guns ready. It wasn't long before another shot rang out, narrowly missing Carol as she dove for cover behind a shipping container.

"Danny, get to safety!" she yelled as I jerked Danny behind another container. Where the fuck was Leon?

Shots rang out, and I spotted Leon ducked behind a train carriage some distance away. He was returning fire on one of our attackers, but I could already see more assailants arriving in the distance. We couldn't get back to the car, no chance in hell. We needed to go the other way, deeper into the rail yard, and hopefully lose them.

Carol had her phone to her ear, barking orders to her own people. Then she put it away and drew out another gun.

Danny leaned past me, firing off three quick shots from a low angle, and a moment later, a body dropped from the top of the container Carol was hiding behind.

"You need to get out of here," Carol snapped at us. "I've got back up on their way, and I will hold them off while you run."

"Run?" Danny scoffed. "You *must* be joking."

Leon exchanged a volley of fire with someone, but no bodies dropped. Had he missed? Was Leon capable of missing?

"Danny, we need to go," I urged. "Leon isn't up for this, and we don't have anywhere near enough ammo to take them all on."

If it were just the ammo, she would have ignored me. But with Leon being as sick as he was… she didn't want to risk him. The emotions crossed her face in a flash, and she gave Carol a torn look.

"What about—"

"She's Circle," I grunted. "She knows what she's doing."

"Go!" Carol barked. "Now!"

Danny gave a frustrated growl, then jerked her head toward Leon. I read her meaning, stepping out to lay cover fire while she sprinted over to the murder bunny. She made it, grabbing his arm and exchanging a few heated words before Carol grinned and gave me a nod.

Now or never. Carol and I both opened fire in the direction our attackers were coming from, and Danny ducked low as she ran with Leon's hand grasped tight in her own. I didn't stop shooting until they were well past me, and Carol gave me a nod.

She dropped the empty clip from one of her guns and reloaded it in a smooth motion from a clip on her belt. It was impressive as hell, her left hand still firing the second gun, but then again... she was Circle.

I took off sprinting, not wasting Carol's efforts in holding off the attackers.

Danny had ducked under a dormant train, pulling Leon along with her, and I caught up to them quickly. In the distance, a freight train was just starting to move, pulling out of the depot with a long load of carriages. That was our best bet, for sure.

"There!" I said, pointing. She'd probably already seen it, though, because she just nodded and picked up the pace. Leon was wheezing, his face pale, but he kept up as the three of us bolted through the train yard. We needed to get him onto that train before it picked up speed.

A bullet pinged against a container uncomfortably close to us, and I ducked on reflex, then lost my footing and stumbled. Danny and Leon hadn't flinched at the shot, continuing to run, and I spun to shoot at whoever was catching up to us. Maybe I wasn't Guild-trained, but I could damn well pull my weight here.

I stopped, steadying my aim and bracing myself for potentially getting shot. Then lined up our pursuer and fired twice, then my gun clicked. Empty.

34
DANNY

Something was wrong. It was an ice-cold gut feeling that made me glance over my shoulder. Kai had stopped, his gun raised. He fired twice at whoever had just shot at us, then his gun clicked empty. Shit... we were seriously outgunned. Where was Kai's epic gun supply when we needed it?

He must have hit the guy, though, because he tossed the useless gun and sprinted to catch up with us. We were almost at the train leaving the rail yard, but it was steadily picking up speed, and if we didn't haul ass, we weren't going to get on board before it was gone.

Kai's long legs ate up the distance between us, and he overtook Leon and me. Just a few moments later, he grabbed onto the metal ladder on the side of the moving train and hauled himself up from the ground. Instead of climbing into the open-sided carriage, he twisted to reach out a hand for me.

I pushed my short legs harder, Leon's labored breathing twisting a knife inside me as he struggled to keep up. I stretched out a hand to Kai, and he seized my wrist in a vise grip. He pulled me off the ground, swinging me through the air all the way past him and safely onto the carriage bed. I stumbled when he released me, but otherwise I was fine.

But what about Leon?

"Leon!" Kai shouted as I hung out of the door to check. "Come on, dickhead!"

Kai had his hand extended as far as possible while hanging onto the side of the train, but Leon was too far away. Too far away, and the train was gaining speed with every passing breath. Behind him, a Jeep came hurtling out of the container yard, speeding toward us with a black-clad man hanging out of the passenger side, holding an AK-47.

Holding my breath, I took aim and waited for them to get close enough that I could be sure of my shot. Meanwhile, Kai was shouting at Leon to *haul ass*. My bunny's face etched with determination, he pushed harder, his hand finally reaching Kai's right as I opened fire on the Jeep.

The passenger with the AK-47 tumbled from the vehicle as it spun out of control with the instant loss of front tires. I ducked out of the way, allowing Kai space to drag Leon onto the carriage bed. The two of them collapsed inside, both breathing hard, and I leaned back out the door to see if anyone else had followed.

The Jeep had rolled; they wouldn't be an issue. But toward the far end of the train, I could have sworn I saw a shadowy figure jump on board. It wasn't clear enough to be certain. Maybe it was just my paranoia making me imagine things, but I couldn't rest easy until I checked it out.

"Are we all okay?" I asked, swinging back inside to check on my guys. I ran my gaze over Kai, but aside from being sweaty, he seemed unscathed. Leon looked considerably worse for wear, though, and I crouched down beside where he lay. "Hey, Bunny. We okay?"

His breathing was harsh and heavy, and sweat beaded thick across his pale brow. He gave me a nod, but I wasn't buying it.

"I knew you should have stayed in the hospital, you stubborn fool," I muttered, giving him a hard glare. It was mostly worry, though.

Leon coughed a laugh. "And miss this fun? No way."

I rolled my eyes, then looked at Kai. "I think someone

followed us. Keep him safe for me, okay?"

Kai frowned, clearly wanting to tell me to stay, that *he* would go. I was tempted to just ignore that look on his face and go before he could argue, but that wouldn't address the issue, and now was as good a time as any. If I hadn't been imagining things, our follower was still a good ten or fifteen carriages away. So I arched a brow at him in question.

He gritted his teeth, then sighed. "Just be careful, Siren. Come back to us quickly, okay?"

Well shit, that was progress. He was finally coming to grips with the fact that I did, in fact, have more experience in this area. That I was entirely capable of protecting him, rather than the other way around.

Not that I was complaining when he did shit like shooting a drunk creep motorboating my tits, but when it came to this? I was infinitely more likely to return in one piece.

Flashing him a smile, I tucked my gun—with very few bullets left—into the pocket of my hoodie so I could use both hands for balance on the outside of the train. We'd gained considerable speed now, the night whipping past in a blur as I eased myself back out onto the ladder.

I scaled the side of the train without any troubles, but once I got onto the roof of the container the boys were in, the wind buffeted me hard. Keeping low, I shimmied along to the back of the box, then climbed to a crouch so

I could make the jump onto the next container. And so on for six carriages. Then I spotted movement on the side of the next one.

Not keen to end up in a hand-to-hand fight on the top of a moving train, I decided I needed to deal with this fucker at a distance. So I slithered my way over to the side where I'd seen them and pulled out my gun. I wrapped my hand around a steel crane hook, then leaned out over the side.

He never even saw me coming, his focus on where he was putting his feet. One bullet and he was history, dropping from the side of the train and tumbling into the ditch as we sped away.

I hung out there a moment longer before hauling myself back up onto the roof and lying flat to catch my racing heartbeat. Not a moment too soon, either, because I only lay there for a handful of breaths before the train whooshed into a tunnel. If I'd still been on the side or even sitting up, I'd be dead.

"Fucking hell," I breathed out loud as the deafening clatter of the freight train echoed through the tunnel. "That was lucky."

The tunnel felt like the longest tunnel on planet Earth as I lay there waiting to emerge, but in reality, it was probably less than a minute. Life or death situations made time distort something wicked, that was for sure.

Once the sky opened up above me once more, I drew a

steadying breath and began my slow crawl and jump along the carriages back to where Kai and Leon waited. Hopefully, that was the only follower and we could have a hot second to rest. Fuck knew Leon needed it... that run was the last thing he needed while still so sick.

The whole way back to the open container, I kicked myself for not making him stay in the medical ward. The fluids and shit they had him on there, they'd been helping. What if he deteriorated faster without that assistance?

Fairly pointless questions to be asking myself *now*. The damage was already done; he was already here on this freight train to fuck knows where with us. And in fairness to Leon, he may not have been safe in that medical ward. Clearly, *someone* had known we were there; otherwise, they couldn't have attacked so quickly when we left.

I wasn't foolish enough to think one of us had a tracking device. The Guild was better than that. More connected. Leon would be the first to spell it out, if he was feeling better. They can access traffic cameras, police dashcams, and shop security footage... There were very few public locations these days that didn't have *someone* pointing a camera—innocent or not.

On top of that, if there was a kill order out on me? Anyone could call in a tip with my location for a cut of the profit. Any Guild employee who had been notified could ping my location.

Blanchet had stepped things up a notch. A big fucking notch. If Leon weren't so sick, I would be doing exactly what Carol suggested and hiding the fuck out. I'd go to a cabin in the middle of the Australian Outback and just lay low with the kangaroos until such time as a new Circle seat was announced.

Surely then, Blanchet would stop gunning for me. Wouldn't he?

It wasn't an option, though, even if it was the smart thing to do. Leon needed to get better, and my gut told me that wouldn't happen unless we tracked down the people who designed his virus in the first place.

Then I could carve out the cost of infecting Leon with it from their hides—*after* I got the antiviral to fix this shit for him.

I hadn't been counting how many carriages I'd passed, so it took me a couple of tries to find the right one to return to. Eventually, I got there though, climbing carefully back down the ladder and back inside the open container.

"Danny, thank fuck," Kai exclaimed, rising to his feet to wrap me in a hug. "Leon was worried."

I gave a laugh, leaning into his tight embrace. "Oh, just Leon, huh?"

Kai released me and gave a shrug. "I had full faith in your

abilities, *kaikohuru iti.*"

Leon started laughing, which set him off coughing violently, and I crouched down to uselessly pat his back. What the fuck I thought that would do to help, I had no clue. It was just one of those things that made a person feel less useless watching someone cough so hard.

"Did you get him?" Leon croaked when he caught his breath. He was exhausted, so I shifted to sit down with my back to the solid wall of the container and pulled Leon to rest his head in my lap.

I gave him a smile, stroking his hair. "Of course I did. What do you take me for?"

Kai gave me a heated look, like he was quietly turned-on by my killer abilities. "How much ammo do you have left?"

I pulled the gun from my hoodie and clicked the slide out. Then chuckled. "Nothing. Shit, that was lucky."

"I still have bullets," Leon mumbled, his eyes closed already. "Maybe. I think. Maybe not."

I couldn't help smiling at that and glanced up to see an amused look on Kai's face too. "Come sit with me, Big Man," I said, patting the space beside me. "Let's rest a bit and regroup when we get wherever this train is going."

He did as I asked, wrapping an arm around me as he got comfy. I snuggled into his warmth and buried my hand in Leon's hair. Connected to them both like that, how could I not feel utterly at peace? Regardless of how we got there, it was a moment to store in my forever memory bank.

35
DANNY

Time warped somewhat while we all slept on that freight train, the steady clack of the wheels on tracks and the wobble of the carriages rocking all three of us off into dreamland. Training told us we needed someone to stay awake in case there were other hostiles on board and looking for us, but after Leon started snoring in my lap, I told Kai to sleep too.

If they hadn't found us by that time, then they weren't coming. So we utilized the relative safety of our moving transport to rest. Despite waking up with a horribly stiff neck and numb ass, I felt better after the sleep.

Kai was already awake, peering out at the moving scenery, but Leon was fast asleep in my lap, so I didn't want to move.

"Where are we?" I asked quietly when Kai turned around to find me awake.

He returned to his seat beside me, giving me a shoulder to lean against. "We're coming into Erie, Pennsylvania, now. I expect the train will stop there to collect cargo, and it's a good place for us to disappear."

I nodded, then yawned. "I need a shower," I mumbled. There was still dried blood in my hair—despite my efforts to rinse it before we met with Carol—and I smelled *bad* from cooled sweat.

Kai smiled gently. "Well, you're in luck. I've got a safe house here that we can use."

I groaned, shaking my head. "We're having too much luck, Kai. It's being wasted on little shit, and then when we really need it, we'll be fucked."

He chuckled. "Alright, then you're *not* in luck. I'm just very well prepared in this region due to a crapload of demand from customers around here. And yes, that means I have plenty of stock at the safe house that we can reload with."

A happy little thrill ran through me, and the train shuddered as it started to slow. We must be on the approach to the rail yard. Leon moaned, waking up, and rubbed his eyes with the heel of his hand.

"Where are we?" he mumbled, almost incoherent as he

struggled to sit up.

"Erie," Kai replied, getting to his feet and helping Leon up as well. "How are you feeling?"

Leon did a tiny double take, squinting at Kai like he wasn't totally sure if the other man was making fun of him. But he didn't seem to be. Leon must have decided the same, because his shoulders sagged slightly as he dropped his natural defensiveness.

"Like a bag of run-over dog shit," he admitted. "Did your guys have any luck with the informant in Boston?"

"They did," Kai confirmed. "Or at least they got another lead to follow. It might take a few stepping stones to get to the answers, so they can take care of that while we get to safety."

I bet Mo was loving the diversion from checking the orphanages. And by loving, I meant quite the opposite. Or maybe that was why Kai specified that Eli and Jae were going to Boston, if Mo was continuing with their original mission of investigating Guild orphanages.

"Makes sense," Leon muttered, leaning heavily on the side of the container as he peered outside. The train was slowing a lot more now, and the presence of cranes and other trains said we were about to stop. I doubted Kai would risk contacting another car service so soon after our ambush, but we could steal another car easily enough.

We waited for the train to stop, not wanting to do a tuck and roll with Leon as rough as he was. Instead, we got off carefully and just quietly made our way out of the rail yard without running into any workers or security. It took a bit of time to avoid being seen, but much better than leaving a trail of bodies to alert our followers to where we were.

I selected a nondescript car to boost, then Kai drove us to his safe house, which was an innocent-looking family home in the middle of a suburban street. He dropped Leon and me off, unlocking the door and deactivating the alarms, then took the stolen car to ditch somewhere well away from us.

Leon was wobbling a bit on his feet but gratefully let me strip him down and push him into the shower. He made a few weak passes at me while I had him naked—I'd have been worried if he hadn't—but I brushed him off gently and focused on getting us both *clean*.

The wardrobe in the master bedroom was stocked up with fairly generic unisex clothes in various sizes, so I was able to get Leon into some boxers and a t-shirt before tucking him into bed.

I fetched him a huge glass of water and some paracetamol, then firmly told him to sleep while I worked out what we could eat.

The bathroom had been stocked with essentials, so I slowly worked a comb through my tangled hair as I made my way downstairs to check the pantry. Clearly, no one had been to the house in at least a few weeks—a thin layer of dust lay on the surfaces—but maybe they would have dry stores. Plain pasta was better than nothing and only required boiling water to cook.

Kai arrived back while I browsed the kitchen, though, and the mouth-watering smell of burgers and fries wafted in with him.

"Big Man!" I exclaimed as he strode into the kitchen with several large takeout bags in hand. "You read my mind."

He smiled in satisfaction, bending down to kiss me quickly before I snatched one of the bags out of his grip. At least seventeen fries made it into my mouth before I mumbled my thanks, and he grabbed out some plates from the cupboard.

"I got Leon some soup, too," he told me, pulling a tub from one of the bags. "Since I doubt he has much appetite for burgers."

That... was the sweetest thing I think I'd ever seen Kai do. And it was for Leon... who he called *murder rabbit*. Warmth lit me up inside, and I went all fuzzy. But I was still an awkward, emotionally stunted mess of a human, so instead of telling him how caring and thoughtful I found his gesture, I just mumbled that I'd go see if Leon was awake.

He wasn't, and I didn't want to wake him, so I returned downstairs to eat my burger with Kai while we watched Netflix. It was crazy cute and so comfortable; it would be easy to forget we were in a safe house on the run from the *entire* Mercenary Guild.

After we ate, our conversation shifted back to Leon's illness.

"Do you believe Carol?" Kai asked when we recounted what she'd told us about the virus research.

I inhaled deeply, then nodded. "I do. She has nothing to gain from killing Leon. At least not directly… and it just doesn't sit right with who she seems to be. Carol seems much more likely to have simply shot him in the head when you broke into her house than infect him with a slow-acting virus that may or may not kill him."

Kai dipped his head. "I agree. So what about this other Circle member she mentioned. Zhou?"

"If he did abandon the research years ago like she thinks, then he would still know *who* was developing the virus. I can't imagine this was completed by an entirely unrelated group of scientists, the coincidence is way too great." I tucked my feet up under me on the couch, turning to face him properly. "So if we can get in touch with Zhou, either through Leon or Carol, he could give us the names of the people who developed the virus."

"We just need to get in touch with him," Kai mused, scrubbing a hand over his buzzed hair and yawning. "And convince him to talk. Easier said than done when it comes to the Circle."

He was right. But we had two insiders now, so surely they had to come in handy for a simple favor like this?

"So…" I said, changing the subject with a sly smile. "You said you have weapons here?"

He chuckled, low and seductive. Damn, that was a sexy laugh. "Of course I do. What kind of arms dealer has a safe house without a few guns stashed around the place?"

"Well, are you going to show me? Or are we building suspense? While I'm entirely capable of killing without a gun, they are a whole hell of a lot quicker and more effective than risking my own neck in close quarters." I stood up from the sofa and looked around. "Basement?"

Kai rolled his eyes and stood up, too. He flicked the TV off, then gave me a wry glance. "Basement? Come on, *kaikohuru iti,* that's too predictable. It's in the attic."

"Really?" I glanced up, as though I had X-ray vision or some shit.

He laughed softly. "No, it's in the basement. Come on."

There was decent security on the house, nothing amazing, certainly not up to Leon's standards, but the security to access the basement was better. Still could use a little tech bunny upgrade, but it would stop bored teenagers from breaking in and finding an arsenal of weaponry.

Kai made no attempt to hide the codes from me as he punched them in, and I was too well trained not to look and memorize them.

"This is a smaller stash than London," he warned me, flicking on the lights and leading the way downstairs. "We usually bring in specific shipments through this port and offload them directly to the buyers. This is just, you know, in case of a rainy day."

"Thank fuck for that," I murmured, "because I'd say it's been pouring lately."

Kai flicked me a smile, unlocking the combination padlock on the cage door in the basement. Through the mesh, dozens of guns were visible hanging on the wall racks, but it was probably only a tenth of what he had stashed in London.

Still more than enough for the three of us, though, and that's all that mattered.

"Take your pick, *ataahua*," Kai invited, swinging the cage door open and stepping aside. "I'm arranging for some transport to arrive tomorrow, so we can take spares."

Oh, he was all over it today. First a safe house *with* guns, then burgers, now transport? Kai was quickly learning the sharpest way to my heart.

"What kind of transport?" I asked, stepping in and taking a closer look at the guns. As tempting as a good sniper rifle was, they were big and bulky and shit for improvising. Handguns were infinitely more useful for this stage of the game. Or maybe both.

Kai grabbed a couple of guns for himself, placing them down on the small table in the middle of the cage before opening a drawer to pull out ammo. "I figure we need transport that Leon can sleep in comfortably and maybe eliminate the need for safe houses. I don't know where we will need to go, but part of the info Eli extracted was that the scientists are American. I dunno about you, but I'm too paranoid to use planes. Too many *people* involved, too much scheduling to be intercepted, and far too easy to sabotage."

I spun around to face him, one brow cocked. "You got us an RV?"

His lips curved in a grin. "Not… quite. You'll see. But there's plenty of space for this whole stash, if that's what you want. Don't hold back."

A shiver of arousal ran through me, and I wet my lips. I loved a man with a plan. And guns. Big, hard guns. "Shit, Kai… I must be racking up quite a debt with Ares."

The heat in his gaze was enough to set me on fire. Or my panties, at the very least. "Lucky for you, Siren, Ares accepts many forms of non-cash payments. Pick out what you want, then we can talk *finances*. Deal?"

I couldn't wipe the stupid grin off my face. "Deal."

36
LEON

Waking up in the safe house, I knew I was dying. For all my stubborn reassurances that I was *fine* when Danny asked, I was not, in fact, *fine*. I was dying. If we didn't track down the scientists who manufactured this virus and cling to the hope that they could reverse it... then I was as good as worm food.

How'd I know? When I woke briefly at some point, I could hear the faint but distinctive moans of Danny getting thoroughly railed by Kai and his big old dick. I must have drifted off again, because when I woke up, dawn was breaking and Danny was lying beside me. Her hair was messy, and her lips held the evidence of some rough kisses, making it all too obvious that I hadn't imagined those moans in the night.

None of my usual jealousy and competitiveness flooded my veins as I watched her sleep, though. Instead, I was *content*. I was *pleased* that Kai clearly knew how to take care of my woman.

That was how I knew I must be dying.

Leaving Danny to sleep like a fucking angel, I mustered up a flicker of strength to get up and use the bathroom. My head spun dangerously as I staggered down the stairs to get some water. Logically I knew I needed to eat something, but my stomach rolled in protest at even the thought of solid food.

So far, I'd been lucky enough to escape the vomiting and shits that usually accompanied a normal flu. It was all just fever, headaches, dizziness, lethargy, and that goddamn bloody cough. *So far.*

Grimacing, I checked the fridge and found a takeaway container of smooth chicken soup. Fuck, Danny really was an angel; that was exactly what I needed to eat.

I put the whole thing into the microwave to warm up and poured myself a huge glass of water. Danny had found aspirin somewhere when we arrived, and I badly needed some more. My head was pounding so hard it was almost about to pop.

"Hey, you should have woken me up," Danny said, entering the kitchen as I located the aspirin above the fridge and dry swallowed a few. "I could have gotten that for you."

I pasted a smile on my face, despite how much it hurt, and held out my arm for her to come closer. "You look so peaceful when you sleep. If I wake you up, *mon cœur*, it'll only be to fuck... and I don't think I have it in me right now."

She gave me a sharp look, clearly not missing the subtext. That I felt a whole shit load worse than I was letting on. But she didn't call me on it, instead just wrapping her arms around my waist and hugging me close. Her face buried into my chest, and I gave a long sigh as my own arms locked around her. Who knew I could become so fond of these intimacies that *didn't* involve swapping fluid?

If my mother could see me now, she'd probably kill herself and save me the trouble. She told me from a *very* young age that I simply lacked the capacity for love in any form. That my brain just wasn't wired to sustain any long-term relationship, healthy or not.

I thought I'd proved her wrong with Layla, but I knew better now. Layla had been sleeping with Lee Sheridan—he claimed they were in love—and had accepted a deep cover honey trap that saw her enter a relationship of sorts with Kai. She'd been a friend but never a *lover*.

Danny DeLuna, though. She was the real deal. The sadness that coiled through me at the thought of leaving her *permanently* sat bitter in my mouth. She had Kai, though. He would comfort her, protect her, *love* her.

"Hey, Bunny." She gently leaned away and touched a soft hand to my face. "It'll all work out. You're indestructible, remember? We'll get you better. Then we'll slaughter anyone who has remotely looked at us sideways. When this is done, not a single one of our enemies will be left breathing... but we will."

I had nothing to say to that, because while I believed *she* would avenge me... I no longer believed I would be around to see it.

"I'm going to shower and dress quickly," she told me. "You eat that soup. Kai is packing our truck with enough weapons to take down a small nation. If we need to, then we have to get moving. Staying in one place too long will—"

"I know," I cut her off gently. "I'm sick, not a civilian."

She pursed her lips, then gave me a soft kiss on the cheek. "Sit. Eat. I won't be long."

I did as I was told, taking my soup to the dining table and sitting heavily. For a few minutes, I needed to just rest my head on my folded arms to catch my breath. Cold sweat coated my skin, and every muscle ached. I couldn't survive on water alone, so I slowly forced myself to eat the soup.

It was good soup.

Kai stomped back and forth through the front door and down to the basement several times while I sat there, carrying duffle bags full of guns, ammo, knives... I wondered if he had anything cool in there. Like a missile launcher. Or nerve agents. It made me wonder whether his Ares business dealt in poisons and chemical weapons or if that was a different specialty and Kai stuck to just plain old bullets and blades.

He lugged them all out to a boxy truck parked out in front of the house, a Mercedes Unimog. Smart thinking, if that was Kai's idea. It would double as accommodation and transport, and was rugged enough to go off-road when necessary.

Danny came bouncing back down the stairs as Kai seemed to be securing the last of his supplies in the back of the truck. She had tightly braided her long hair, and I had a weak thought about how much I loved to wrap that braid around my fist while fucking her from behind.

My body ached too much for the thought to reach my dick, though, and I just gave her a watery smile instead.

"We good to go?" she asked me with a probing look.

I nodded, carrying my empty container back to the kitchen to throw out. I'd used a plastic spoon, so I threw that out as well. Less mess for whoever Kai used to service his safe house.

"Here," Danny offered me a pair of boots as we exited the house. They were only a half size too big for me. "I figured these would be more comfortable than those too-small sneakers you stole from the hospital."

I gave a soft chuckle, but she was right. I'd snatched clothes and shoes from the patient in the next room over from me back at the medical center, and the shoes had been so tight my toes were covered in blisters.

Danny had tucked some socks inside one of the boots, so I sat down on the front step of the house to put them on. The sun was only just peeking over the horizon, and we would be long gone before the residents of this very suburban street woke up. The house across the street had a trampoline on the lawn, and two houses down, there were kids' bikes left dropped on the driveway.

Definitely best if we didn't linger too long here.

Putting boots on was a harder task than I really anticipated. Just the act of bending over had my head swimming so hard I thought I might fall over. I gritted my teeth and squinted to focus, tying the laces carefully.

A screech of tires made me jump as I finished lacing my second boot up. I looked up—my reaction time was shot to hell—but Danny was already on her feet and screaming at Kai to get off the road.

She was too slow, though. I sat there, utterly frozen, as the speeding Escalade slammed right into Kai's solid body. He got thrown on impact, flying through the air for at least twenty feet before hitting the tarmac like a broken rag doll. The car that'd hit him didn't slow, it just sped right past his body and disappeared out of sight in a heartbeat.

The scream that escaped Danny's throat was unlike anything I'd ever heard. Unlike anything I *ever* wanted to hear again, full of horror and heartbreak as she threw herself over Kai's crumpled, unmoving form.

Shock rippled across me in palpable waves as I pushed to my feet and staggered over to where she sobbed. Even before I got there, I could see it was too late. Kai's neck was at such an awkward angle, it was most definitely snapped. His eyes were open, staring sightlessly at the ginger cat licking itself on the lawn nearby.

"Danny," I forced myself to say, "we need to go. They might come back and—"

Before I could get the rest of my sentence out, the Escalade came speeding back down the block, and this time a black-clad assassin hung out of the passenger window with an AR-15 aimed right at us. I grabbed Danny, trying to force her to run for cover, but she brutally shook me off. Her grief over Kai was so intense she didn't even see the threat until bullets began ripping through her body. One after another, the bloody holes tore her perfect back open, and she collapsed across Kai's twisted form right there in the middle of the street.

I screamed in pure agony and disbelief, then glanced down when I felt burning heat spread across my abdomen. Oh good, I'd been shot too. At least I wouldn't suffer in this world without her.

Dropping to my knees, I let myself go limp and crashed onto the rough, blood-soaked road right alongside Danny and Kai.

Just as my eyes started to close, a dark shadow filled the sky. A burning ball of light shot across the sunrise. Holy shit. That was a meteor. Too late, universe, we were already dead.

Everything went dark. Of course, it was dark. There was no white light waiting for me… not after the life I'd led. But that was perfectly okay with me; I wouldn't want to spend eternity with a bunch of *wholesome* individuals. Talk about my idea of Hell.

Then the strangest thing happened. Someone slapped me.

My eyes snapped open, and I glared up into the dark brown eyes of the slapper. "What the fuck?" I growled. "Can't you let me die in peace?"

"You're not fucking dying, *rapeti*," Kai told me in an exasperated voice. "Get up, you're going to scare the neighbors."

Who cared? They would all be dead when that meteor landed anyway.

"Leon, baby, get up," Danny urged, and I sat up quickly at the sound of her voice. "Come on, let's get in the truck. We need to get out of here." Her gaze was pure concern and love, and… *what the fuck?*

I snapped my head around, looking at the street. No blood stained the road, no speeding Escalade was to be seen, and most of all… Danny was all in one piece. Frantic, I grabbed her shoulder, turning her around so I could check her back, but sure enough, not a single bullet hole.

"Oh fuck," I breathed. "I think I'm hallucinating."

Kai scoffed. "You think? Come on, let's go before you start screaming again." He gripped my forearm and pulled me to my feet. I wobbled as the whole world tilted again, and Kai steadied me.

That hallucination had seemed *so* fucking real; I was actually relieved to see he was alive.

So I hugged him.

Yeah, I was definitely still dying… just slower than from a drive-by shooting or meteor strike.

Kai awkwardly patted my back and helped me climb into the back of the Unimog, where beds were all set up along with all the supplies we could possibly need. He deposited me on one of the beds and muttered at me to quit being weird, then got out to take the driver's seat.

From the window, as we drove away, I locked eyes with a ginger cat sitting on the lawn. Creep.

37
DANNY

Leon's hallucination had me all kinds of rattled, and I couldn't stop checking on him as we drove out of Erie. He hadn't said much, but he had staggered out into the middle of the street like he was looking at something distressing. Then he'd screamed in horror and just collapsed to the ground like he'd been shot.

The scariest part of it all was the way he hugged Kai. Did he just hallucinate us all dying?

His freak-out was making me freak out, and eventually, I just climbed into the back and curled up in bed with him. He was half asleep and feverish but held onto me tightly.

Kai made no comment, just drove in silence while Leon held me like his favorite teddy bear and mumbled things in his sleep about broken necks, shootings, and meteors. And ginger cats. More than once, I caught him muttering about an evil ginger cat.

It took more than an hour before he relaxed enough to sleep properly, and I very carefully peeled myself out of his sweaty embrace.

"How is he?" Kai asked as I clambered back into the passenger seat beside him.

I gave a shrug, because I didn't want to say the answer out loud. But he certainly wasn't getting better.

Kai didn't bother with empty platitudes, instead just reaching out and lacing our fingers together as he drove. I held onto his hand like a lifeline, even as I shifted my gaze out the window and went to the happy place in my mind. The place where I played out in vivid detail all the ways I would make Blanchet pay for hurting my bunny. Every cut, every hit, it was all so easy to imagine.

The only frustrating thing about it was that Blanchet was still faceless, and not because I'd messed it up so bad. Because he was still just a *name* and not a face to us. So far.

Sometime later, Kai pulled into a gas station at my request so I could pee and get snacks. I always found huge Fritos on a drive so much more enjoyable, and I was so restless and anxious that I needed the distraction of doing *something*. Even if it was just eating corn chips.

Kai was on the phone, standing outside the truck when I got back from paying, and I offered him a corn chip. He smiled but shook his head.

"Thank you, Eli," he said, deliberately letting me know who he was speaking to. "That's very helpful. Tell him to call me as soon as he gets the location." He ended the call, then clasped a hand on my waist, pulling me close.

Rising up on my toes, I pressed my lips to his for a kiss. "You look pleased," I murmured.

He licked his lips and hummed. "Spicy. And I am pleased. My team is making progress. Cyryl is currently interrogating someone—a Guild merc—who supposedly worked on this project several years ago. I would assume while Zhou was funding it. But she surely will know the names of whoever is still developing it."

Hope flared hot within my chest, and I smiled. "That *is* progress." I studied his face, sensing there was something more. "How is Mo?"

Kai gave a small sigh. "She's not answering my calls. Eli said he will check in with her, though. She's… not happy with me for diverting the team onto this virus research."

That wasn't surprising. I also didn't feel particularly bad about it, given the urgency in saving Leon's life versus Moana's ten-year-old vengeance plan, so I shrugged. "She's a big girl, she'll get over it." Eventually.

Kai grimaced like he wasn't so sure. His phone rang, and he

glanced down at the screen. "Ares business," he told me. "I'll keep it quick."

I pressed another kiss to his lips as he answered the call, then climbed back into the truck to check on Leon. He was awake, but just barely. Lying on his side, eyes glassy, skin like a fish belly, he looked worse than ever.

"I'm okay," he croaked.

I sighed and sat down beside the bed, fishing a huge bottle of Gatorade out of my bag of snacks. "Kai's team has another lead," I told him, helping him to sit up. The last thing we needed was for him to choke trying to drink while lying down. "We should have the name and location of the head researchers soon."

Leon took a small sip of the Gatorade, then winced. "Who is interrogating?"

"Cyryl, I think."

He frowned. "I didn't meet that one."

I smiled. "I bet they moved him before you got back so you wouldn't slit his throat for touching me." Leon sucked a sharp breath, and I placed a hand on his chest. "Calm down, I'm fine. He's Agencja Wywiadu trained, so… take from that what you will."

Leon scoffed a laugh. "Got it. Do we think he's actually going to get answers?"

"Eventually, I hope. Kai seems hopeful." I shifted, so I was sitting beside him, my back to the wall and my shoulder against his. "I'm hopeful too. I have to be, Bunny. Saving you is my only focus now."

He leaned against me, turning his head to kiss my hair. "I'm fine, *mon cœur*."

"You're a fucking liar, *dur à cuire*." I tipped my face to kiss him softly. "But I love you anyway."

A strange look passed over Leon's face when I said that, but then he turned away as a cough rattled through him. He covered his mouth with a tissue, and I caught a glimpse of blood before he hid it. Our time was running out all too quickly.

The driver's door opened, and Kai climbed in with a satisfied look on his face. "I've got a name and possible location," he announced.

"Good work, Cyryl," I murmured, somewhat surprised but not at all disappointed. "He must have improved his interrogation techniques."

Kai flashed me a knowing grin. "He said he would like some tips from you, when you're willing. But for now, he got the info we needed."

"What's the name?" Leon asked, his voice rough.

Kai gave him a long look, then frowned. "Drink that Gatorade, *kohuru rapeti*. You look like death."

Leon grunted, then took a huge swallow of the brightly colored drink. "Happy?"

"Ecstatic," Kai drawled. "Dr. Rupert Granger. One of the

two head researchers on the virus. Cyryl also got the last known location of their research lab, which is a few hours' drive from here."

"That's great news!" I exclaimed, sitting up straighter. "Even if they moved to another location, there could be another lead. In the meantime, can we get someone working on tracking Dr. Granger?"

Kai nodded firmly. "Eli is getting Mo onto it. She's the best at research since we had to remove Sam from the team."

Leon started to say something, then set off coughing again. I took the drink from his hand while he coughed, passing it back when he reached for it.

He took another long swallow, then sagged back against the wall of the truck, seeming exhausted. "You're wasting your time."

Anger and panic surged through me. "Bullshit. We can still save you, you're not that far gone yet."

"I'm not a quitter, *mon ange*. I meant you're wasting your time on Dr. Granger because he's already dead." He groaned and lowered himself back down to horizontal on the bed. "I killed him last year."

Kai and I locked eyes, both equally as startled.

"You did *what*?" Kai exclaimed, slamming his hand against the steering wheel in frustration.

Leon released a pained sigh and closed his eyes. "He was a geneticist," he muttered, "and worked on Remus. I was tasked with cleaning up all traces of Remus. If I'd known we would need him *now*, I might have made another choice. Sadly, I never graduated from Xavier School for the Gifted, so I couldn't see this coming."

Kai's expression was bewildered, and I bit my lip to hold back a smile. Fucking Leon.

"Get some rest, Bunny," I told him as I stroked his hair. "We'll work something out."

He mumbled under his breath, something that sounded a whole lot like *je t'aime, mon ange,* and I kissed his sweaty face before climbing over to the front passenger seat once more.

For a few minutes, Kai just drove silently, and I stared out the window, thinking. Plotting.

Eventually, I sighed and glanced back to see if Leon was fully asleep. I hadn't wanted to keep him awake with conversation around strategy. His face seemed peaceful in sleep, despite how deep the shadows lay beneath his eyes.

"Why does he use French with you?" Kai asked quietly. "Nothing in my research said he is native to France."

I smiled, warmth radiating through my chest. "He isn't, but I am."

Kai cast a sidelong look at me, then nodded. "That's actually really sweet. I didn't know he was capable."

"Neither did he, I think." I looked back at Leon fondly again, then shifted my gaze to Kai. "Don't worry, Big Man, I like your language too. Don't go changing on me now."

He shot me a heated look but kept his thoughts to himself as he drove. "So, if Dr. Granger is dead, what do we do now?"

I'd been wondering the same thing, but we had more than just a name. "We go to check out this address Cyryl got. Maybe luck will be on our side, and they're still using the same lab for the research. In the meantime, I want Carol—and Leon when he wakes up—to lean on Zhou for the name of the other scientist. If Leon killed Granger last year, then someone *else* had to have manufactured the virus for Leon's DNA."

Kai nodded, and I pulled out my phone to check whether maybe Carol had reached out. There was a message from Sabine, instead, and I opened it with a small rush of panic. Everyone I cared about seemed to be dropping like flies, so I was counting on Sab to stay off-grid and *safe*.

Sabine: Don't panic, I'm safe. Are you?

She may have been masquerading as a stripper—and more— for the last few years, but she was still a mercenary. She wouldn't give away her location by text.

3982: Within reason, yes.

The cabin she'd been staying in had no reception, which meant she'd moved. Why? Dammit, Sabby, don't make me worry about you too.

Sabine: Can I do anything to help?

I ran a hand over my face. Of course, she left the cabin; she'd have been going *insane* there with no contact. I didn't blame her, either.

3982: *Please, just stay safe. I can't lose you, too.*

There was a pause before her reply came through, but when it did, I could breathe a little easier.

Sabine: *I will. I hate this so much. I want to help, Dan. But I'm going ghost tonight. I won't become a liability, just coz you love my sexy ass.*

I gave a small laugh, imagining her sassy smirk as she said that.

3982: *I'll miss you.*

Sabine: *Make them pay, Dan. For Jude.*

Damn right, I would.

"Sabine," I explained to Kai at his curious look. "She's defecting from the Guild. Erasing herself in order to hide."

His eyes widened. "That sounds extreme."

I nodded, propping my head on my hand as I looked out the window. "It is." But I couldn't help feeling envious that she had that opportunity. She could disappear, start over. Once Blanchet was dealt with, I would make sure Leon and Carol wiped Sabine from Guild records. She never needed to be hunted like this.

All I could hope was that one day our paths might cross again.

Fuck, it hurt, though. She was safe, but she was lost to me.

38
DANNY

Over the next few hours, Leon woke a couple of times. I coaxed him to drink more Gatorade and take pills to manage his fever, but otherwise, he just slept like the dead. Eerily like the dead. Far too much for my liking, but Kai scolded me to leave him alone to rest.

So I ended up back up front in the passenger seat, jittery with anxious energy and bouncing my knee in a way that I *knew* was pissing Kai off.

He was on the phone to his team, getting an update on what Moana had dug up on Dr. Granger, which wasn't much. He was found dead in his home about eleven months earlier, a single gunshot wound to the head. The case was closed as suicide, but we knew better.

Granger had no family, and his house had been settled by the state already, so there were no leads to chase there. Mo was able to give us some business names of places the doctor frequented, and all seemed to be located near the lab we were going to investigate. Kai and I agreed that we could stop by some of those businesses and ask around. Maybe someone would be able to ID one of Granger's associates if the lab was gone.

Kai took a few more calls unrelated to all the Guild bullshit we were dealing with, but I guessed he still had a business empire to run. If an arms dealer like Ares just *stopped work*, then it opened a gap in the market for some other fucker to slide in. So, I kept my mouth shut and drummed my fingernails on the windowsill.

After a while, Kai pulled us into a gas station to refill the truck. We'd covered a lot of miles, and I could do with a bathroom break anyway. Anxious energy prickled my skin as I slid out of the truck and stomped over to the restrooms. It would take Kai ages to refill that thing, and Leon was *fast* asleep, so I took my sweet time in the bathroom.

Washing my hands, I peered at myself in the cracked mirror. I looked rough, but I was going to blame that on my worry for Leon's health and a whole day on the road. Still, I splashed some water on my face and dragged my fingers through my hair before braiding it.

I looked marginally better when I was done, tossing my braid over my shoulder as I left the restroom. Kai was stalking toward me with a determined look on his face, though, and before I could say anything, he clamped a hand around my throat and shoved me back into the tiny restroom.

"Kai, what the—"

"Quiet," he snapped, spinning me around to face the mirror and yanking my sweatpants *and* panties down to my ankles. "You're stressed, anxious, and annoying the *shit* out of me with all the fidgeting." His hard cock breached my pussy, and I gasped at the intrusion. "You need to fucking *relax*, Danny, and you know what always chills you the fuck out?"

He pushed harder, stuffing himself into my tight cunt with determination, and I grasped the edges of the sink for balance. "Your cock?" I guessed, already breathless.

He grunted, pulling out slightly just to push in deeper. "Orgasms," he corrected. "But it just so happens I could also do with some stress relief. So shut up, hold on, and let me unlock some endorphins for you."

One of his hands was clamped on the back of my neck, the other on my hip, and he wasn't wasting time. He fucked me hard and fast, my hips smacking into the pink porcelain of the sink with each vicious strike of his cock inside me.

I pushed back against him, riding him right back, and ended up pressing my face to the dirty, cracked mirror while he railed me. Eventually, he dropped his hand from my hip to find my clit, pinching it hard and making me come just seconds before he did.

His thrusts slowed, then stilled. For several moments, we just stayed locked together like that, bent over the restroom sink. Then he slowly withdrew and fixed his pants. With a groan, I bent over to fetch my own, and Kai dragged his fingers up my inner thigh, collecting his cum where it'd leaked out of my pussy already.

I straightened up, getting my pants back in place, and he locked eyes with me in the mirror. Then he brought his slick fingers to my mouth and made me suck them clean. Dammit, I nearly came again.

"Next time you start fidgeting that badly," he told me in a low voice, kissing the side of my neck, "I'll get my dick out and fuck your throat. While driving. Clear?"

A deep shiver of post-orgasm arousal zapped through me, and I just nodded my understanding. But if he thought that was a deterrent, he was dead wrong. Then again, with Leon still fast asleep in the back of the truck, it might make me think twice. Time would tell.

Kai went inside to pay for our gas in cash, and I made my way back to the truck with wobbling legs, flushed cheeks, and wet panties. I had to hand it to him, though, I wasn't anywhere *near* as anxious and fidgety when we hit the road once more.

He was all kinds of smug, too, giving me a satisfied grin as I relaxed into my seat and got comfy. I just rolled my eyes, not taking the bait, then glanced over at Leon in the back. He was still fast asleep, not looking any better. But he also didn't look *worse*, so that had to be worth something.

"How long until we get to this lab?" I asked sometime later.

Kai checked the GPS coordinates on his phone. "Maybe another hour," he told me, then gave me a tender look. "Take a nap; I'll wake you up when we get there."

I shook my head. "I'm not tired, just curious." But I then yawned and felt the weight on my eyelids. Maybe a tiny nap wouldn't hurt. Sometimes a good fuck had that effect on me… I went straight past *relaxed* and into *sleep*.

It was no great shock when I found myself being gently woken up by Kai an hour later because we had reached our destination. I sat up with a groan, and Kai gently kissed my cheek.

"I was tempted to let you sleep," he confessed, "but figured it was more urgent to get another lead on this antiviral shit for *kohuru rapeti*."

He was right about that. I climbed over into the back to check on Leon, but he was sleeping soundly. I put a fresh bottle of Gatorade out along with some aspirin where he would see it if he woke up while we were gone. Then I unzipped one of the bags of weapons that we'd brought from Kai's safe house. No way in hell were we going in there unarmed.

Briefly, I considered putting a gun within reach for Leon too, but his hallucination freak-out made me second-guess myself. If he needed one and was lucid enough to shoot the right people, he could get one out of the supply stash.

It was bad enough that the lab may or may not be in use for Guild experiments, but we were in a warehouse area on the outskirts of a no-name kind of town. It was enough that my instincts were screaming at me, so I over-armed myself. A basic Glock 19 under each arm in easy access holsters, extra clips on my belt set up for quick changes, and an M4 slung over my neck.

No such thing as being *too* prepared when there was a kill order out on my head.

Kai gave me a long look. "Are we expecting trouble?"

I smiled and shot him a wink. "Always. Ready?"

He gave a small frown, then ducked back into the truck to grab more weapons for himself. Smart man. He popped back out a moment later and closed the door carefully—so he didn't wake Leon, maybe?

Before we walked away, though, Kai gave a troubled frown at the truck. "He'll be okay asleep in there, right?"

I quirked a brow. "Where was that concern for Leon while you were fucking me into a broken mirror back at the gas station?"

Kai gave me a sly, sexual smile. "We were quick. Besides, I have no doubt he will make up for lost time when he recovers."

Fuck, I hoped so. "He can't come with us, not like that. Just lock the truck up so no one steals it with Leon in the back, and we will try to make this quick."

Kai nodded his agreement, locking the truck up and tucking the keys into his pocket. Then the two of us approached the door that *should* take us into Dr. Granger's lab. Or the space that used to be prior to his death. According to Mo's research, he lived in this area and had still been sighted at the coffee shop two blocks away as recently as the week of his death. Surely that meant he'd still been using this lab?

Kai and I spotted two security cameras on the outside of the building, and Kai shot them both out with a silenced pistol. Then I tried the front door. It was locked, shocker, but I immediately went to work with the picks I'd found in Kai's weapon stash.

It clicked open a moment later, and we silently entered the building. Instantly, my hopes plummeted. I could *smell* the dust, and the building just had that unmissable *abandoned* vibe to the air.

Swallowing my fears—for what this meant to Leon—I flicked on the overhead lights.

Kai gave a small sound of protest, but the fluorescent bulbs flickered to life and displayed exactly what I expected. We were inside a warehouse, complete with a rolling door large enough to take trucks, but the rear of the warehouse was all set up with laboratory equipment. Clear plastic-created walls and a roof over that specific area, but inside, it was a mess. Like it'd been cleaned out in a huge hurry.

"There might still be something here," Kai said, trying to stay positive. "Maybe they missed a computer or, shit, I dunno. A letter addressed to someone *other* than Granger? There has to be something here, *ātaahua*, don't give up yet."

He strode forward to the plastic enclosed area, and I followed with a heavy heart. If the Guild had cleared out this lab, there would be nothing left. Nothing useful.

Kai was utterly determined, though. He started searching through every drawer, turning over every piece of paper left on the desks... everything. I loved that he cared so much. He and Leon, now that they'd stopped trying to kill each other or make me hate the other, were *actually* forming a friendship. Maybe neither of them would admit it, but it was there.

Kai *cared* if Leon died of this virus. Leon had hugged Kai when he hallucinated that we all died. The sparks were all there... I just needed Leon to get better so we could fan those flames a little more.

Right now, though, seeing that stubborn determination all over Kai's strong features, melted my heart into a puddle of agonized goo.

Then a muzzle flashed from somewhere outside the room, and I dove at Kai to knock him to the floor. Before he could even register what was happening, I had popped up from behind the table and was returning fire.

Bullets ripped through the plastic by the dozen, and I ducked back out of sight, turning to Kai with wide eyes. "Are you okay?"

I asked him with a gasp.

He nodded firmly, checking his own gun and holding it ready. "What the hell is happening?"

I grimaced, bracing my muscles with tension as more bullets peppered the plastic. "This was an ambush," I gritted out. "Someone knew we were coming here, and... we're seriously outgunned."

Where were Carol and her sharpshooters when I needed them?

39
KAI

An ambush. It was a fucking ambush. Had this whole thing been a setup? The informant that Cyryl squeezed could have fed him curated intel to put us in the right place at the right time for an attack like this. Whatever. The how, who, and why were irrelevant while we were actively under fire.

A brief break in the gunfire gave Danny and me both a chance to return fire, and I caught her counting our assailants while I dished out a barrage of bullets to protect her.

"At least fifteen," she told me with a grimace when we ducked back behind the metal cabinets. "Maybe more coming."

She popped back up to fire again, then straight back behind cover.

"This cabinet won't last forever," I muttered, even though she was probably already well ahead of me in assessing our surroundings. "Can you see any other way out of here?"

Her eyes darted around the enclosed area we were trapped in. "Cover me," she barked, moving almost instantly. I quickly shot off a spray of bullets as she darted across the abandoned laboratory space, diving behind a blocky piece of equipment.

"There's a fire escape at the back," she shouted across to me. "I can't see if there's anyone—"

She cut off what she was saying as something hit the plastic at the back of the enclosure, and an explosion detonated. Danny hit the ground, and I winced, clapping my free hand over my ear.

"Never mind," Danny shouted, barely audible over the ringing in my ears, "they have that covered, too. We just need to shoot our way out the front and hope like hell the truck is still there."

The truck, *and Leon.*

Had they already found him? Fuck... I hoped not. And that in itself weirded me out because I genuinely cared whether the little psycho was alive or not.

"Now?" I asked, reloading my gun. Thank fuck for Danny's instincts on coming in so heavily armed.

She shot me a lopsided smile, her eyes shining with a hint of excitement. "Now or never, Big Man. Just shoot anything that moves and get to the truck. Clear?"

There was no time to second-guess or debate pros and cons. I just had to trust that she knew what she was doing. And I did… trust her, that was. So I gave a firm nod back and silently cursed myself for not putting on a bulletproof vest.

"Clear," I agreed.

She flashed me a smile. "We got this. On three? One… two… *three*."

Simultaneously, we emerged with guns blazing. The tattered plastic sheeting enclosing the lab proved no obstruction as we darted forward. My aim was good, very good, but goddamn, Danny was *excellent*. Every single shot out of her gun found a mark, and bodies dropped from the rafters as we moved through the warehouse, forcing our way closer to the exit.

The roller door started cranking open, and a tiny flare of hope lit me up inside. Only to be doused instantly when at least ten more heavily armed assailants ducked under the rising roller door with guns trained on us.

They weren't actively shooting, which made me think they wanted to take us alive. Or one of us. I glanced at Danny in question, but she just narrowed her eyes and shot three of them. They dropped but weren't dead. The heavy vests and helmets they wore meant it would just be a nasty bruise.

"Drop your weapons!" one of them shouted at us. "You're outnumbered, and you know it, Danny."

A flicker of recognition passed over Danny's face, but it

wasn't the good kind. "That you, Frederick? I didn't take you for such a fucking coward."

She didn't lower her gun, but she *did* stop shooting. I took her lead, keeping my own weapon in hand and ready for her command.

"It's a fine line between cowardice and common sense, Danny," the same guy replied. I couldn't even see which one was talking, their helmets were so dark. "You know there's a kill order out on you?"

Danny gave a fake gasp. "There is?" She shot another armored assailant, dropping him to the floor. "Here I was thinking you just missed me."

Frederick, whoever the fuck that was, just laughed. "Thanks to the kill order, there are some *very* lucrative contracts out for your capture. I was tempted to just claim the kill, but if you saw what Nero is offering for your capture..."

Nero. I knew that name but couldn't put my finger on why.

Danny snorted a sarcastic laugh. "Lazy fuck," she muttered, then shot down another of Frederick's men.

"Move in!" Frederick barked in response. "Take her alive, dispose of her friend."

Fuck.

His troops only made it one step forward when loud music cut through the tense air and an engine revved. That was all the warning we got, and I threw myself at Danny on instinct, dragging her out of the way as a truck smashed through the half-open roller door at high speed, plowing down Frederick and his men.

Chaos erupted, and Danny immediately rolled out from under me, her gun aimed at the shooters above us on the catwalks. I joined in, popping off shots and watching bodies drop while Leon swung down out of the truck cab with a glazed look in his eye.

He held a gun in each hand and seemed to skip a little as he wrecked utter carnage on our attackers. When one of his guns clicked empty, he tossed it aside and pulled a long dagger from his belt. One by one, he grabbed the already fallen mercenaries, jerking their helmets off and slitting their throats.

It was all over in less than a minute, but Leon was thorough. Was he—fuck yes, he was *whistling* along to the *blasting* music from the truck as he meticulously checked that every single one of our attackers was dead.

Danny and I just stared, watching him as he slit throat after throat, and a slightly sick laugh started bubbling up in my chest.

"What's funny?" Danny asked over the music.

Adrenaline was ebbing out of me, leaving me all loose and loopy, so I curved a grin at her. "Little bunny foo foo, hopping through the forest, scooping up the field mice and—"

"Slitting their little throats?" Leon finished for me, coming over to where we stood. Blood splatter coated his t-shirt and face, and his hand clasping the dagger was *dripping*. The most disturbing part was the feverish look in his eyes, like he wasn't fully on the same plane of reality with us.

I arched a brow. "Exactly." I had to admit… he'd just saved our asses. Even half-dead, Leon Marx was a fucking *force* of nature.

"Bunny," Danny exclaimed, her eyes wide. "Are you okay?"

He blinked slowly, like he was trying to make his eyes focus on her. Then gave a wobbly smile. "Yeah, of course. Why wouldn't I be?"

I narrowed my eyes at the blood coating his hand and arm and splattered across the rest of him. Then glanced around at all the dead bodies littering the warehouse.

"Uh, okay, here's a better question," I said when Danny seemed torn on how to reply. "Why Taylor?"

Leon's smile brightened and he bopped his head a couple of times to the still booming music. "It just felt right for the moment," he replied, waving his bloody dagger around the room. "Don't you think?"

In a way, he had a point. Taylor Swift's "Red" was oddly appropriate given how much *red* he'd just shed.

Before Leon could explain his crazy any further, he started coughing. Then coughing *harder*, and Danny rushed forward with a sharp inhale to somehow offer support. She got her shoulder under his arm just in time as Leon's coughing cut off with a rattle, and his eyes rolled back into his head. His body sagged, and Danny grunted as she caught his unconscious form.

I grabbed his other arm, taking the weight from Danny, and she shot me a panicked look.

"Let's get him back in the truck," I suggested with a grunt, shifting my grip on Leon so I was carrying most of his dead weight. "Then I think we need to get him some medical attention."

Danny nodded, wetting her lips. "Agreed. I'll call Carol and see if she knows anyone in this area. Failing that, I'm sure Carlos will know someone."

Leon was heavier than he fucking looked, but I managed to manhandle his unconscious ass back into the truck and drop him down on his bed. Danny grabbed a towel and cleaned up as much blood as she could from his body while I slipped into the driver's seat.

"He fucking hot-wired the truck," I said out loud.

"You took the keys," she reminded me from beside his bed.

"He hot-wired the truck, smashed through the doors, ran over a bunch of dudes who were about to capture you by any means necessary, then slit the throat of about twenty mercenaries... while feverish and dying of a manufactured virus." I turned in my seat to stare at Danny. She just smiled down at the blood-stained murder rabbit in bed.

"Don't forget how he selected a soundtrack for it all, too."

I gave a chuckle. "Is he the Terminator? What the fuck?"

Danny just smiled back and shrugged. "He's an executioner.

Get us out of here before anyone else shows up. I'll call for help."

I had no arguments with that plan whatsoever, putting the truck into reverse to get it out of the warehouse full of bodies. Thank fuck it was built like a tank, because other than a few paint scratches, there didn't seem to be any damage to the vehicle.

Turning the blasting music—Taylor's version of the *Red* album—off, I listened as Danny relayed our ambush to Carol in vague details. She skirted the sensitive information about where we were but asked Carol if she had any medical assistance within the city.

There was a tense pause as Danny listened to Carol's reply, then she gave a frustrated sigh. "How? Leon's unconscious, and who knows when he might wake up again. I need—"

She broke off, listening again and smoothing a hand over her braided hair. When I glanced in the mirror, it was plain to see how frustrated and worried she was. Apparently, Carol wasn't giving good news.

"Fine," Danny growled a moment later, "I'll figure it out. What about—" Another pause, then she sighed. "Done. Thank you, I'll be in touch soon."

"Where am I heading?" I asked, meeting her eyes in the mirror.

She grimaced, then gave me an address. I stopped briefly to type it into the GPS, and the estimated time of arrival showed it should take us twenty minutes from where we were.

Danny climbed over to the passenger seat, a deep frown set

on her face, and I arched a questioning brow.

"Zhou responded to Carol's message," she told me with a frustrated sigh. "Apparently, he doesn't appreciate Carol *inserting* herself into Leon's problems. If we want his help, he needs to speak directly with Leon."

Shit. I glanced over at the unconscious Circle member in the back of the truck, then grimaced. "That won't be easy."

"Let's hope we can wake him up with some medical attention," she said softly, pain etched across her beautiful face, "because we're running out of time."

Danny needed him. That would wake him up. If nothing else, Leon Marx had proved to be a relentless murder rabbit where our woman was concerned. And fuck if I didn't admire him for it.

40
DANNY

Carol had given me an address and a phone number. On her instruction, I called when we pulled up in front of a modest brick home, and the woman who answered told us to wait in the truck. We waited, anxious, for what felt like an hour, but when I saw the woman hurrying across the lawn with a huge bag over her shoulder, I realized it'd only been a few minutes.

I jumped out of the cab to meet her, opening the back of the truck up so she could climb in while Kai took her medical bag.

She didn't introduce herself, just asked pertinent questions about Leon's symptoms and medical history. Working quickly, she checked all his vitals, then inserted an intravenous line to hook up several bags of fluids.

"Listen," the doctor said with a sigh, sitting back on her heels, "this is just a stopgap. It won't magically cure him, it'll just... sustain him. Mrs. Black gave me the vague rundown of the virus when she called, so... this is all I can do."

Mrs. Black must be one of Carol's aliases, not that it mattered. She probably had dozens. As badly as I wanted to scream and shake the doctor, demanding she do *better*, I wasn't a moron. If she could fix him, she would. Right now, we just needed *time*, and that seemed to be what she was providing.

"Thank you," I murmured, wrapping my arms around myself.

The doctor just gave me a sympathetic smile and pulled out four more bags of fluid from her bag. She gave us clear instructions on when to change them, then packed up and exited the truck.

For several moments after she was gone, neither Kai nor I spoke. Then I sank down onto the bed opposite Leon and rested my head on my hands.

"What do we do now?" Kai asked quietly, coming to sit beside me.

I inhaled deeply, watching the IV line deliver medication directly into Leon's veins. He was still unconscious, but the doctor said he would wake up on his own. I needed him to eat something when he did.

"We need him to contact Zhou. So for now... I guess let's just get out of here, so we aren't putting the doctor in danger. We just wait until Leon wakes up and go from there." Saying that out loud, admitting to the fact that we had *no* plan... *hurt*.

Kai didn't make me feel worse about it, instead just nodded and slid back into the driver's seat to get us moving once more. A moving target—even as obvious as a Unimog—was better than a stationary one.

I sat there for a while, staring at Leon like a creep, then finally gave myself a mental slap and climbed over to the cab once more.

"Let's stop and pick up some food," I suggested. "We need Leon to eat something when he wakes up, and us too. We can't shoot straight if we're starving."

Kai shot me a grin. "Cute. I bet you could still shoot straight even if you were drunk off your ass."

True. I pulled out my phone to send Carol a message of thanks and asked her to send me the bill. Nothing came for free, even from my recently discovered biological mother. Not that it fazed me, such was the way of mercenaries. Everything had a price, and there was *no* price too high to save Leon. Or even just to buy him time, like the doctor had done.

We needed that extra time... because every single lead seemed to be a dead end, and I was quickly running out of ideas.

"Why don't you lie down with him?" Kai suggested, giving me a knowing look. "There's nothing we can do until he wakes up. Take a minute to rest, I'll keep us moving."

He was just as exhausted as I was, but I didn't argue. I just crawled back through to where Leon lay hooked up to his drip and slid into the space beside him. Yes, there were other beds, but I wanted to be near him. To touch him. Because who knew how long we might have left?

At some stage, I fell asleep, unsurprisingly, but when I woke, Leon's arms were around me. My face was buried in his chest, and he gave a small groan when I sat up with a gasp.

"Bunny, you're awake," I exclaimed.

He squinted up at me, but the corners of his mouth turned up. "I had the *weirdest* dream, *mon cœur*."

I smiled back, stroking his cheek with my hand. "What was it about?"

He wrinkled his nose. "I dreamt I was skipping through a meadow of red grass, bopping field mice on the head while Taylor Swift played a live concert."

A chuckle bubbled out of me. "As odd as it sounds, that wasn't a dream."

Kai opened the back of the truck, climbing inside with several grocery bags in hand. When he saw Leon awake, his face split with a wide, *sincere* grin.

"Little bunny foo foo! You're awake. Have you contacted

Zhou yet?"

Leon narrowed his eyes. "What the fuck did you just call me?"

"Long story," I quickly interrupted. "But we need you to contact Zhou through whatever Circle network you use. Carol said Zhou will *only* speak with you directly because he doesn't appreciate her involvement. For whatever reason."

Leon grimaced and sat up. I helped him resituate himself so he could lean on the side of the truck, and he eyed the IV lines curiously.

"He's just being cautious," he muttered, wincing as he shifted his position. "Carol might be asking about the virus because she wants to kill me, not save me. Where's my phone?"

Kai grabbed it out of a drawer and handed it over.

Leon mumbled a thanks, unlocking the device with his thumbprint, face scan, then password. Never could be too secure with as many secrets as Leon Marx had. "I'm starving," he commented while his phone booted-up. Then immediately switched off. "Uh, did anyone bring a phone charger?"

I looked to Kai, who rolled his eyes. He snatched Leon's phone to check the connection type, then sighed and handed it back.

"Fucking Android user. I'll be right back," he told us, climbing back out of the truck once more. A quick glance out the window showed we were parked outside a Walmart, so Kai was going back in to buy a charger for Leon's phone.

"It's a superior operating system," Leon commented, scowling after Kai.

"I'll get you food," I told my sick bunny, rolling out of his bed and checking the IV fluid. The bag wasn't due to be changed for a few hours yet, though, so I went to see what Kai had picked up for us. "Ah, perfect. Here, eat this while I make you a sandwich." I handed Leon a container of fruit salad with a fork, then unpacked the sandwich supplies onto the little kitchenette bench.

"Gross," Leon mumbled with his mouth full. He was scowling into the tub of fruit salad like it'd personally offended him but still ate another piece of strawberry.

"Something wrong?" I asked, biting back a smile. He was still sick, so I was going plain on his sandwich. Bread, butter, cheese. It was quick to make.

Leon sighed, pouting up at me. "There's kiwi in this salad."

"Um…" I glanced into the container. "Yeah, there is. Last I checked, it was a fruit, and that is a *fruit* salad…"

Leon rolled his eyes and stabbed an offending piece of green fruit. "But it's revolting and makes my tongue all fuzzy." He put the chunk of kiwi in his mouth and ate it while shuddering.

I grinned, on the edge of laughter. Seeing him awake and eating, joking even… it gave me hope that we could still cure him.

Or maybe his energy was just a result of the fluids in his IV.

"Why are you eating it then?"

He quirked a brow at me, then gagged as he swallowed another piece of green fruit. "Because they're a rich source of vitamins and antioxidants, DeLuna."

"Smartass," I muttered, placing his sandwich on a plate and handing it to him. "Eat. You've barely had anything in days."

He already had a mouthful, so he just smiled at me with stuffed cheeks and bobbed his head. Kai returned a minute later, ripping open the plastic packaging of a new phone charger. He plugged it into the socket near the front cab and held out his hand for Leon's phone.

I handed the device over, and he connected it up, the display showing the battery charging symbol.

"We should move location," I told Kai softly. "We've been here too long already."

He nodded his agreement, sliding back into the driver's seat without a word. Leon wobbled as the truck started up but otherwise kept eating his food. He patted the bed beside him, and I took the invitation to snuggle against his side while Kai relocated our truck somewhere less conspicuous.

The fact that no one *else* had ambushed us seemed to imply that our truck was still off the Guild radar. Probably thanks to Leon ensuring there were *zero* survivors at the lab. No one left alive meant no one was able to report back to the Guild.

"So, Zhou wants to contact me directly, huh?" he asked between bites of his sandwich. "Hopefully, that means he has something worth telling. What's my percentage at?"

I glanced over to his phone and wrinkled my nose. "Three percent. Vehicle charging is always so slow."

Leon shrugged. "That's okay. I feel alright now." Then he paused and shook his head. "I mean, less like I'm dying. But I would kill for a shower."

"I got you, *kohuru rapeti*," Kai said from the driver's seat. "I saw a truck stop not far from here, so I grabbed toiletries and towels with the groceries."

Leon grunted as he swallowed his mouthful. "Thanks, Sasquatch." Then he frowned at his IV line. "Though how I'm going to shower with this..."

"I'll help you," I said without hesitation. "I can hold the bags while you shower."

Leon looked down at me with a smirk. "If you're offering to hold something while I shower, *mon ange*, I can suggest something else."

It really shouldn't have shocked me, this was *Leon,* after all, but it still rendered me speechless for a hot second. Maybe because he was basically on death's door, so sex was the last thing on my mind. Then again, if it made him feel better...

Kai pulled our truck into the rest stop a moment later and

collected our supplies as I unhooked Leon's IV bags from where the doctor had suspended them. Kai handed us a towel, and I used it to disguise the whole medical setup while he paid for our showers.

It wasn't the easiest task, getting Leon showered, but with some patience and gentle scolding, we managed. Then I made him sit down and wait while I showered myself. He watched me with longing, his eyes running all over my naked body while I washed, but there was no way he had the strength for anything more than watching.

"I'll make it up to you," I said softly, bending to kiss him while I toweled dry. "When you're better, I'll be all yours to do anything you want."

His eyes lit up at that, and he licked his lower lip. "Anything at all, huh?"

I tipped my head to the side and narrowed my eyes. "Within reason. You try to shit on me, and we have problems."

Leon's laughter quickly shifted to coughing, and it was like a bucket of ice water over me. I hurried to finish getting dressed, then helped him back out to the truck, where Kai was already waiting for us.

"Everything okay?" Kai asked, giving Leon a worried frown.

Leon just gave a tight smile back. "Would have been better if I'd talked DeLuna into a blow job, but I guess it'll wait until I'm less… *this*." He flopped down on his bed once more, and I hooked his IV bags up on the wall.

Kai handed Leon his phone—with a whopping twenty percent battery now—and Leon yawned as he powered it up and unlocked it.

For a minute, Kai and I just sat there in tense silence, waiting for Leon to log into whatever program he used for Circle business. Right when I was so anxious my skin was itching, Leon grinned.

"Bingo," he murmured, then held the phone out for me to take.

Startled, I accepted it and read the message on the screen. It'd been run through a decoder, but Leon left the finished version there for me to see.

"This…" I gasped as I continued reading, using my finger to scroll down. "Leon, this is exactly what we needed to know! Look, Kai. The lead researcher, Dr. Morgan Harris. Confirmation that the virus was coded specifically to kill *Leon*, and a last known location for Dr. Harris." Zhou also gave a short apology that his funding had been used against another member of the Circle and made it perfectly clear that Zhou offered no loyalty or support to someone who attacked their Circle peers.

"We believe him?" Kai asked, skeptical.

My stomach dropped. "What other choice do we have?" I replied softly. "This is our only lead. It's this… or giving up." And I *refused* to give up.

Kai knew it, too, nodding his understanding.

"So, road trip to Seattle?" Leon asked on a yawn.

Smiling, I leaned down to kiss his forehead. "You know it."

41
DANNY

It took two days before we were ready to make a move on Dr. Harris. First, we needed to drive all the way to Seattle, then we needed to get all the ducks in a row to make our hastily pulled together plan work out. Because, of course, Dr. Harris wasn't just chilling in a low-security house where we could walk straight in for a chat. Nope, he *knew* there was a target on his back and had decided to put himself in the safest place he could access.

"Remind me again why we can't just shoot everyone that gets in the way?" Leon muttered from his bed. We'd just had a visit from another doctor—this time one of Carlos's people—

and Leon was drowsy with whatever they'd given him.

Kai was being surprisingly patient, despite Leon asking questions we'd already discussed while he was sleeping. "Because he's not hiding out with criminals and people who can be paid to look the other way. He's hiding out with celebrities and billionaires and fucking *royalty*. Not the corrupt kind, either."

"Or if they are corrupt," I added with a sigh. "And they probably all are, it'd just take us too long to build enough blackmail on *all* of them to just stroll in guns blazing. No, we need to do this quickly and *quietly*. Harris knows exactly what he's doing, hiding out in the middle of one of the most heavily guarded, high-profile *retreats* in North America."

Rumor had it that Wellington Manor was a rehab facility disguised as a hotel, but the security was impressive. The only chance we had at getting close to Harris was to *not* arouse suspicion from the security. Which was why I was fixing my hair underneath a brunette wig. I was already wearing a designer dress and sheer silk pantyhose, and my makeup was done.

"How do I look?" I asked Kai, holding up my new fake ID beside my face and smiling.

He scowled. "Gorgeous, as always. This plan—"

"Is as good as we've got," I cut him off before he could protest. In fairness, if he and Leon had been happy to send me off into danger without at least *trying* to be the big man and protect me, I'd have been disappointed. All that really mattered was that they did, deep down, trust that I was the only one who could pull this off.

"I prefer your white hair," Leon mumbled, pouting. "But it's a decent disguise."

I gave him a smile. "That's all that matters. We can't risk someone tipping off the Guild before I get our antivirals."

"I'd feel better if you had some kind of weapon on you, *ātaahua*." Kai folded his arms over his chest, leaning against the kitchenette counter.

Leon gave a sleepy chuckle. "She does, dickhead. Her whole body is a weapon. A deadly one, too." To me, he blew a kiss. "Make it quick, *ma moitié*, or the worry might kill me."

I rolled my eyes, trying to ignore the pang of fear at his words. "Play nice while I'm gone, boys."

Bending over, I kissed Leon softly, then stopped in front of Kai to give him a hard warning look.

He scowled back at me, then grabbed me around the waist. His face dipped to kiss me ferociously, but I ducked out of the way before his lips could land. "Lipstick," I scolded him. "I don't have time to waste fixing it."

Frustration flashed over his face, but he reluctantly released me. "Stay safe, *kaikohuru iti*, come back to us."

Us. Goddamn, that made me all warm and fuzzy inside. Warm and fuzzy, and *so* determined to get Leon well again. So I gave them both another reassuring smile and jumped out of the truck.

It took thirteen steps to get from the truck to the car that Carlos's men had delivered—along with my cover identity and disguise—but only three steps to slip into my new personality. For the first time in the dozens, maybe hundreds, of times I'd disguised myself as someone else… this one came easy.

After all… she was my sister.

"Carolina Atwood," I murmured, sliding into Carolina's stolen Maserati. Well… not so stolen. Borrowed. "Thanks for the coke habit, little sister."

When Carlos had compiled a list of women that could be accepted into Wellington Manor, Carolina was the obvious choice. Carol had been more than happy to fill in the paperwork and leave the keys in Carolina's car for us.

The drive to Wellington Manor—well outside Seattle itself— took me around half an hour from where I left Kai and Leon. They would follow in the truck, but with enough of a gap between us, we wouldn't be connected. I spent the drive solidifying my cover story in my head, really *feeling* like I was climbing into Carolina's skin. This time, I had the added advantage of actually meeting the girl, albeit briefly.

As I pulled into the valet area in front of Wellington Manor, a familiar face appeared from the lobby. What the shit was he doing?

Firmly in character, I turned the Maserati off and climbed

out, handing the keys to the valet attendant before turning to face Carlos with my bitch face in place.

"Baby, you made it!" he called out before I could speak. "I knew you'd get lost. She's hopeless with directions," he tossed this remark to the smartly suited man at his side.

I pursed my lips and tipped my chin higher, oozing Carolina's entitlement from every pore. "I told you I didn't need you here," I snapped, because I seriously doubted Carolina would be *happy* to check into Wellington Manor. Even if it was more country club than rehab facility, and she was only scheduled for a two-night stay. It was what the manor called their *Refresh* program. It basically consisted of a high dose of vitamins and electrolytes delivered via IV. It was a rich girl's party detox.

Carlos just smirked, draping an arm around my shoulders as I approached. "I know, sweetcheeks. This is Darren Levine, the general manager of Wellington Manor. He was just giving me the whole rundown of their security measures, so I know you're totally safe here." He gave me a conspiratorial look, lowering his voice to a loud whisper, "In case someone tries to kidnap you again, pumpkin butt. We can't be too careful."

Fucking Carlos was improvising, but his story held merit. By suggesting Carolina had been targeted for ransom kidnapping, it made it entirely plausible that he wanted to know exactly what security they had and where.

So, I batted my lashes and gave him a ditsy in-love smile.

Carlos had an easy fifteen years on Carolina, but I'd seen way, *way* worse in my previous contracts. Little rich girl dating an older drug lord? Old news, another nothing to ever glance twice at.

"Lovely to meet you, Miss Atwood," Levine gushed, holding his hand out to shake mine. His grip was limp and made me shiver in disgust. There was something so repulsive about a weak handshake from a man to a woman. Condescending. "Please, follow me. We can talk further in my office, and then my staff can show you around and take you to your room."

Just two steps inside the main doors, we needed to pass through metal detectors, and I made sure to look utterly insulted when they asked me to surrender my phone. It was to be expected; they valued their security and privacy here, and the last thing they needed was tabloid journalists sneaking in to take pictures.

Once the manor security was satisfied that Carlos and I were totally unarmed, Mr. Levine led the way to his office. I sat there in the uncomfortable chair, looking like I was bored out of my mind, while he outlined the security measures in place to keep guests *safe* within Wellington Manor.

Carlos asked pertinent questions, though, and by the time we left the office, we had a much better understanding of what we were dealing with.

"Why the change of plans?" I murmured to him as one of the staff directed us to some seats in the bar lounge. "I thought I was running this alone."

Carlos, the shit, just smirked and shrugged. "You usually have more prep time. It didn't feel right letting you waltz in here totally unarmed and without backup. You don't even have any comms to communicate if you get into trouble."

Because nothing we could get on short notice would have made it through the metal detectors, but theoretically, Leon would hack into the manor's own security feed so they would at least have eyes on me, even if I couldn't speak to them.

"I'm surprised Kai let *you* take the job," I commented, arching a brow. "Or did you not tell them either?"

Carlos just smiled again, then thanked the waitress who delivered us each a glass of champagne. Wellington Manor wasn't going to go depriving their highbrow clientele of alcohol, which was generous of them. It would also make my job easier when I tracked down Dr. Harris. Drunk men were much easier to manipulate than sober, suspicious ones.

"He has the subtlety of a bull with a bee sting, don't you think?" Carlos mused, sipping his champagne.

I bit back a laugh, glad Kai couldn't hear us. Carlos and he had their own issues, but the fact that Carlos had brushed it off when given the opportunity to call him on it? Said it was none of my business. Hopefully, whatever went down between them, Kai had accepted that Carlos and I were *friends* and nothing more. Carlos was not a threat... at least not sexually.

After our drinks, we were shown to our room—apparently, Carlos was staying with his *girlfriend* for her safety—and a nurse came to install my IV line while I lay on the bed with the TV on. We double-checked the recipe with Carlos's doctor, and he'd assured me it was perfectly safe, even without *needing* it.

After the nurse left, I gave Carlos a long look and flicked my eyes to the corner of the room. Hidden in the edge of a wall lamp was a discrete camera aimed at the bed. It would seem, that Wellington Manor had more visual surveillance than the manager had let on.

"Why don't you go take a look around, snugglepuff?" I suggested with a simpering smile. "I'll be fine here on my own." I was willing to bet those cameras had audio, so I wasn't risking blowing my cover so soon. Nope, I would wait patiently while Carlos browsed around and hopefully located our target.

Easier said than done. Sitting there for the next hour of my life, watching TV, and feeling the camera on me was enough to make my skin itch. Luckily, when Carlos returned, he had a satisfied glint in his eye that said he'd found something. Maybe it had been a good thing he tagged along uninvited after all.

I met his gaze with my unspoken question, and he gave a slight head dip.

Impatient, I reached over and pressed the intercom to call the nurse back to our room. When she arrived, I complained that my arm was aching and I needed a break. I could see she thought I was being a drama queen, but she was clearly paid well enough to just do whatever the clients wanted. So she detached the drip and said we would "try again later."

With the nurse—and the IV line—gone, I crooked a finger at Carlos seductively. "Come here, hot stuff."

He cringed slightly, and I held back my laughter as he climbed onto the bed, pretending like we were about to make out. He held himself too stiff, though, and I wrapped my legs around him to pull him in close.

"Make it believable," I whispered in his ear, then tossed my head back and moaned like he was already rocking my world. Somehow.

He was wildly uncomfortable, I could tell, but so long as our voyeurs were buying it, this was the easiest way to talk. "This is so creepy," he muttered, burying his face in the pillow beside my neck, making it seem like he was kissing my throat. "It's like making out with my sister. I'm going to be scarred for life, I hope you know."

I laughed, then covered it with a sexual moan, raking my nails over his shaved head. "If you make it out alive. Depends on whether Leon hacked this camera."

Carlos inhaled sharply and probably would have leapt off the bed if I hadn't used my legs to roll us and push him into the mattress.

"Calm down, I'm just teasing. What did you find?" I asked in a hushed whisper, letting my brunette hair fall in a curtain beside our faces.

"Your doctor," he confirmed, making me smile. "I asked around—very subtly, of course—and heard he follows routine. Dinner at seven-fifteen, drinks in the lounge until ten."

"Perfect," I breathed, rolling my body to keep things looking natural, and Carlos fake gagged, making me laugh again. "Quit it. You'll make me break character. Shit, it's already seven!"

Carlos was no fucking help, giving me a clueless, wide-eyed look as I shifted around and pretended to ride his undeniably flaccid dick through his pants. If Kai or Leon ever needed proof Carlos and I were platonic, it was right there.

"Okay, how are we going to—" Carlos started to ask, but I already knew how to end this charade.

"Oh my god!" I exclaimed, sitting up and swiping a quick hand over my mouth to smear my lipstick before flipping my hair back. "Did you just come? What the hell, Carlos, I thought you were taking medication for that!"

His jaw dropped in horror, and he struggled to sit up. "What? No, I—" The coin dropped, and he cringed. "Yes... I guess I did. Sorry, snookums, you just get me so... hot... I can't help it." The look on his face promised retribution, but I bit back my laughter, pasting on outrage instead.

"Ugh, this is getting so old," I snarled. "Go and clean yourself up. I'm hungry now, seeing as I'm clearly not getting any dick."

Carlos glared at me but stalked into the bathroom and ran a tap, pretending to clean up his premature ejaculation while I fixed my makeup in the mirror right beside the hidden camera.

"Ready to go, Care Bear?" Carlos asked as he exited the bathroom.

I smiled wide. "Absolutely. I can't wait to see what dinner is like here." I quickly checked the hidden pocket in my bra, making sure my supplies were still secure, then slipped my high heels back on while Carlos held the door open.

The hidden camera in the room was unexpected and made it somewhat more difficult. But it wasn't a deal-breaker, and I was desperate enough to take *any* risk to secure the antidote to Leon's illness. It just meant I needed to be more subtle, even in private.

Tricky, but not impossible. Hopefully, before midnight, I would be back in the truck and administering Leon's cure.

42
DANNY

Carlos directed us to the dining room and gallantly held out a chair for me to sit down. I quirked a brow in question but didn't object when he scooted my chair in for me. The waitress came over almost before Carlos even sat down himself, rattling off all the specials from the menu.

My mouth watered when she mentioned the filet mignon with red wine jus, potato puree, and garlic sautéed brussels sprouts. So I ordered that—medium-rare—and nodded to Carlos to order his own meal.

"Brussels sprouts?" he asked with a smile as the waitress

walked away. "You're not still utterly sick of them?"

I gave a low laugh, remembering a time—while Ricardo was still alive, before things turned nasty—when the new cook accidentally purchased ten pounds of brussels sprouts. She'd been so embarrassed, and she felt like she needed to use them all up before they went bad. So we had eaten all kinds of different, somewhat creative dishes containing brussels sprouts for the better part of a week.

"Never," I replied with a nostalgic grin. "She made me love them. So, do you see anything else interesting?"

He tipped his head slightly to the side. "Eleven o'clock," he said quietly. My eyes drifted oh-so-casually to that point, and I instantly recognized Dr. Harris sitting at a table alone.

Relief washed through me. We were so fucking close. If this turned out to be another false lead, another dead end... I would scream. Literally scream. Then probably blow the place up in rage.

"Got it," I murmured, then turned a polite smile to the waitress, who returned with the drinks that Carlos had ordered for us.

He lifted his glass, waiting for me to take mine. "To... brighter futures," he toasted, and I tapped my glass against his.

"So, how are you going to do it?" he asked so quietly, there was no way anyone could hear us. "And when? Do I need to cause a distraction?"

I gave a small laugh. "Don't stress about it, amateur. I can handle things. Let's eat first, though. I've had so much junk food lately, I'm starting to smell like a French fry."

Carlos huffed, not liking being the amateur for once. "Is that what that smell was? I just figured you had a yeast infection."

I choked on my champagne.

"Fuck you," I croaked between coughing fits, and Carlos pretended to look *super* concerned. Luckily for him, though, there was a doctor just a few tables away. My target came rushing over to offer a Heimlich, but I waved him off, red-faced and still spluttering.

"I'm fine," I gasped, looking up at my mark with big watery eyes. "Just inhaled my champagne. I'll be fine."

The middle-aged man frowned his concern, his hand still resting on my bare shoulder. "Are you sure?"

I nodded quickly, making sure I oozed embarrassment. "Yes, thank you, though. You're too kind."

Dr. Harris sent a judgmental glare at Carlos—probably for not getting up to help me himself—before patting my shoulder. "If you change your mind," he murmured, his eyes more calculating now, "I'm just over there." He pointed to his table, and I nodded like an airhead.

"Thank you again. I'm so sorry to interrupt your meal, sir."

The doctor gave me another long look, then his gaze dipped to my cleavage briefly before he returned to his own table once more. I dabbed at my mouth with a napkin, turning my attention back to Carlos, who looked somewhat shocked.

"Holy shit, *Carolina*, even I thought that was real. You're smooth as fuck."

I narrowed my eyes. "That was real, you asshole. You made me choke on my drink. I just used it to my advantage. Fucking yeast infection. I'll have you know, sir, that I take meticulous care with my vaginal hygiene." I needed to, especially when Kai kept putting things like gun barrels in there. The risk was well worth the reward, and it was nothing a solid wash out with a vaginal cleanser couldn't handle.

Carlos made a gagging sound, covering his mouth with a napkin like he'd just tasted shit.

"Sorry," he grimaced. "You just made me think way too hard about your fine china, and that's not... nope. Da— um *Carolina*, never talk to me about your... you know... your meat wallet again. Please."

Laughter was bubbling up inside me, but I had to maintain the illusion that he was a *shitty* boyfriend, so I couldn't let it escape. Still, the effort required to hold it back had my eyes watering and my voice tight as I replied, "Did you just call my vagina *fine china*? Like... coz it rhymes? Oh my god. Just say *vagina*, Carlos. It won't bite you."

I was careful to keep my voice quiet enough not to be overheard, but *damn*, it was hard not to cackle out loud at Carlos's quirk. As far as I knew, he hadn't been involved with anyone since his late wife... and even then, she had been unfaithful, so who knew how long it'd been since he explored anyone's *fine china*.

"Okay. You're not allowed to talk anymore," I told him with a firm shake of my head. "This is why I run these jobs alone, I swear."

The waitress arrived with our food then, perfect timing, and Carlos only grumbled a little about how mean I was to him. For the head of a drug cartel, he was a big teddy bear.

While we ate, I asked him about Victor. It was a safe subject, because it wouldn't betray me as anyone I wasn't. Carlos wasn't in disguise, so there was no harm in talking about his real life, and I loved hearing how his son was doing.

"Oh, that reminds me," Carlos said as the staff cleared our empty plates. "I arranged for Stanley to be transferred back to my island. The guy Kai had looking after him did a great job, but I just trust my people more."

I quirked a brow. "I don't."

He sighed. "Tito has been... dealt with. That won't happen again."

I pursed my lips but didn't push the subject. Instead, I dabbed my lips with the linen napkin and drew a deep breath. "Alright. You ready to finish this?" Carlos sent a longing look at the desserts being delivered to the table beside us, and I rolled my eyes. "You can order room service dessert. It'll probably take me that long, anyway."

"Fine," he agreed. "Then yes. What do you need me to do?"

I flashed a quick smile. "Just react naturally." Then I threw my glass of water all over him.

He jerked backward with a gasp. "What the *fuck*, Carolina?" he snarled the question, remembering to use my fake name. Maybe he wasn't so shit at this after all.

"You *promised me*," I shrieked, rising out of my chair and waving a finger in his face. "You said you would leave her if I let you put it in my butt! And now you're telling me she's *pregnant*? Why? You said you loved me!"

"Carolina, baby, not *here*," Carlos pleaded, so I picked up my champagne and doused him in that too. Fuck off, Carlos. Go change. He got the point, shoving his chair back so hard it tipped over. Instead of just storming away, he came around the table and grabbed my upper arm, jerking me close like he was furious.

"You have an hour, then I'm coming to find you. Clear?" He whispered the words in my ear, and I trembled as though I was being threatened. When Carlos released me, stalking out of the dining room with every eye on him, I wobbled on my heels a moment.

Then I sniffed away my tears and smoothed my hands down the front of my dress like I was embarrassed and shaken up. Rather than sitting back down, I made my way over to the bar to order another glass of wine.

The bartender gave me a sympathetic smile and overfilled the glass for me. I smiled my thanks, letting more tears trail down my cheeks to make me look really broken and fragile. But to my irritation, Dr. Harris wasn't making any moves to approach.

Shit. Maybe I hadn't laid it on thick enough earlier?

I allowed myself a covert glance in his direction while sipping my wine but found him on the phone. What the fuck? So much for no phones permitted inside the manor.

Then again, I had to assume some allowances were made for their permanent residents. Especially those who were still actively working on medical research. Dr. Harris must be paying a fucking *fortune* for this safety.

Almost fifteen minutes passed, and I started wondering whether I needed to fake another choking incident to catch his attention once more. Nah, too obvious. If I didn't make a move soon, though, Carlos would come looking for me before I could get the answers—and antidote—that I'd come for.

So I ordered another glass of wine, then slid off my stool to leave the dining room with my wine in hand. As I approached Dr. Harris's table, my heel wobbled and my ankle rolled, making me stumble. I gave a drunk girl gasp and grabbed the edge of Harris's table for balance before I completely hit the ground.

"Oh no," I groaned, looking down at the wine that had spilled all over myself. "Oh, gosh, I'm such a mess." Tears pooled in my eyes, then spilled out as I started to sob.

Dr. Harris quickly ended his call, standing up to offer me his napkin with a concerned expression. I just kept crying, making no effort to mop up the wine all down my front.

"I-I c-can't go back to my room," I sniffled pathetically. "My boyfriend will be there, and we just had a big fight."

Harris gave a small, slightly unkind smile. "Yes, I heard. The whole dining room heard."

Oh, I misread the *kind* Dr. Harris. He was a bit of an asshole. Not that it mattered, I just needed to dial up the brazen vixen a notch and ease off on the distressed damsel act.

I wet my lips with a slow swipe of my tongue. "Is there somewhere else I can get cleaned up?" I asked in a husky, tear-filled voice. "Maybe somewhere I can shower, so I don't smell like wine?"

Harris gave me another long look, his gaze catching on my cleavage and his lips kicking up in another mean smile. "Yes, I think I can help. Miss...?"

"Atwood," I supplied. "Carolina Atwood." Thanks to the Circle's dumb secrecy, that name rang no alarm bells for Dr. Harris, not even after all the noise Carol made in outing me to the press. Look at that. He *gallantly* guided me out of the dining room with his hand resting on my lower back. The further we walked from the dining room, though, the more that hand shifted from my back to my ass.

Excellent. Hook, line, sinker.

I had forty-five minutes, but this should only take thirty. Maybe less.

Harris led the way up to the fourth floor where his suite was located and unlocked the door with a downright sleazy look on his face. He indicated for me to enter ahead of him, and I made sure to hesitate like I was nervous.

After a moment, I acted like I'd talked myself into it and headed inside the suite. Harris closed the door behind us, and the lock clicked shut with a heavy sound. Followed by a deadbolt *and* a chain.

I widened my eyes and blinked at the doctor like an owl. "Um, maybe this wasn't a good idea," I murmured with a nervous laugh. "I should probably get back to my boyfriend. He will be worried."

Harris smirked. "No, he won't. Why don't you take that wet dress off, Carolina?"

Oh, too fucking easy. Why were they always so easy to manipulate? Then again, the Guild rarely employed good, morally clean, upstanding individuals. The doctor himself had actually lost his medical license *years* ago for malpractice. I was going to take a wild guess now and say it was more likely a sexual assault case.

"Um, no, thank you," I whispered, all timid and *weak*. "I should go."

Harris gave a cold laugh, then grabbed me by the back of my neck. He shoved me against the wall of his hallway, his breath hot against my cheek. "I wasn't *asking*. Don't worry, sweetheart, no one will believe you if you call security later. If you're good for me, I'll give you a bag of coke before you leave. Deal?"

I gritted my teeth and forced my body to tremble.

"Deal," I whimpered, but inside I was already doing a victory dance. He was as good as dead, he just didn't know it yet.

43
DANNY

Honey trapping unsuspecting men and women, even in a quick con like this one, came to me like second nature. I was good at my job, and *this* was my job. Without the distraction of a comms unit in my ear, it was effortless to slip back into my old skin. To play the role of a stupid, drunk, rich girl caught in the clutches of a depraved man intent on getting his dick wet by whatever means possible.

Yes, it meant I had to let him get a little further than I was entirely happy about, but that was the job. I wouldn't have been able to access the tiny syringe in my bra without him stripping my dress off. And I needed to reciprocate enough that he didn't notice the prick of the needle in his upper thigh as he ground his sea-cucumber dick against my hand.

The drug was one of my favorite concoctions, and I was crazy appreciative that Carol had access to some that Carlos's people could deliver in time for this job. It took a few minutes to kick in, though, so I maintained the illusion that Dr. Harris was *actually* going to fuck me.

He manhandled me over to his bed, pushing me down with a firm shove before grabbing my tits in two greedy handfuls. His motions were becoming more sluggish, though, and I took my opportunity to turn the tables. Acting like I was suddenly turned-on—for some inexplicable reason—I wrapped my legs around his waist and flipped our positions. For whoever was spectating on the hidden bedroom cameras, it wouldn't be so obvious that he was drugged if he was already lying down.

"Oh, I knew you were hungry for it," he snickered with a leering grin. "You want me to fuck your ass like that big, tattooed boyfriend of yours, huh? I bet you love that."

I shuddered, thinking of my *actual* tattooed boyfriend fucking my ass. Yeah, I did love that. But not from Dr. Harris and his chode. But I gave a flirty laugh and tugged off his tie, using it to loosely bind his wrists just for appearances.

"It's so quiet in here," I commented, wrinkling my nose. "We need some background noise, don't you think?" I grabbed the

TV remote from his bedside table, pressing the "On" button. The flat-screen facing his bed—where I'd spotted the hidden camera located just above—flared to life, and the forced moans of hard-core porn filled the room.

Well shit. Here I was hoping for a western movie or something to drown out my questions, but porn would work.

Dr. Harris tried to say something undoubtedly disgusting, but it came out in a slurred mumble. I watched his face carefully as panic flashed through his eyes. His hands gave a tiny twitch as he tried to move, but that was it.

Perfect.

I smiled as I climbed back on top of him, keeping up appearances, so the manor didn't send security to come breaking down the door at the sight of a generous donor in trouble. Nope, as far as Wellington Manor was concerned, Dr. Harris had just picked up a kinky new friend and was lying back to enjoy being fucked.

"Don't worry," I told him softly. "The drug is just making its way through your body. It's a strange sensation, isn't it? Being totally paralyzed and unable to even cry out for help? If it's any consolation, you won't lose consciousness. Not yet, anyway. And you can still *feel* your body, you just can't move it. Isn't that fun?"

Just to prove my point, I grabbed one of his hairy nipples and twisted it hard enough that it *had* to hurt. Pain flashed through the doctor's eyes, but only a low moan escaped his voice box. Perfect.

"Now then, Dr. Harris, we will make this quick and painless.

The fact you're hiding out here tells me you *knew* someone would be coming for you, sooner or later. It also tells me you're a fucking coward, so I don't think we need to get crazy with torture... do you?"

More muffled noises from Dr. Harris that I took as agreement. I needed to get to the point before the drug started wearing off. He'd only been shot with a tiny dose, so it wouldn't hold for long.

"You developed an RNA-targeted virus recently. I want the antiviral. Now. And I won't be leaving here without it, no matter how many pieces of you I need to detach from your bones." I smiled, batting my lashes to make that statement even more unhinged. It was more than just the threat of violence that motivated fear in my victims, it was the unpredictability of a pretty, smiling face combined with death threats.

Harris blinked several times, which again I took as acceptance, so I nodded.

"Good. Let's keep this simple. Is the antiviral here in your suite? Blink once for yes, twice for no."

One blink. *Finally,* things were working in my favor. I sat up to look around. He must have an office or something. Giving Harris a long look, I slid off the bed and pretended to do a bit of a striptease while I looked around. Then, because I was getting frustrated with the camera watching my every move, I took off my bra and casually tossed it to land right over the tiny lens.

"That's better," I murmured, peering out into the living area. There was bound to be another camera there, but I took the chance, darting across to the second bedroom in nothing but my thong and pantyhose. The door was locked, but it was a flimsy one and broke with an aggressive twist in the right direction. Inside, I struck gold.

Dr. Harris didn't just have an office, he had a whole *lab* in his suite. How fucking long had he been hiding out in Wellington Manor?

The medical team that Carlos had called in to revitalize Leon before I started this mission had given me some vague information about what I should be looking for, so I quickly located a glass front refrigerator. Inside, there were dozens upon dozens of vials, all containing different colors of liquid. But only one was labeled with Leon's name.

I snatched it up, then raced back through to where I'd left Dr. Harris paralyzed on the bed. My bra still covered the camera, and the porn on the TV was loud enough that the next room could probably hear it. Good.

"Is this it?" I demanded, showing Harris the vial of yellow fluid. He blinked once. I narrowed my eyes in a glare. "Are you *sure*? I don't think you want to know what I'd do to you if this wasn't the antiviral."

Harris seemed genuinely terrified, blinking firmly once again.

I was torn on whether to believe him or not. What if the vial I'd grabbed was just more of the virus, and it ended up killing Leon? I didn't have the time to send it away for testing, and we only had one shot at administering it to him. Shit. The pressure to get this right was making me sweat.

The sound of the suite's front door opening made me stiffen, but a moment later, Carlos came rushing into the room with a phone in his hand.

"Hurry," he hissed at me. "Your boys have taken control of the security and are looping camera feeds, but they will figure it out soon. We need to get the fuck out of here."

He snatched my bra off the camera and tossed it to me. I quickly slipped it on, then took the phone from his hand. "Do I even want to know where you found a phone, Carlos?"

He just smirked. "You're not the only one who can seduce dumb rich people. Hurry!"

I put the phone to my ear and smiled when Kai's familiar voice rumbled down the line. "*Kaikohuru iti,* is that the cure in your hand?"

Smiling, I crossed over to the hidden camera where Kai and Leon were clearly watching. "This? I think so? I can't be sure, but Harris says it is."

"Roll the dice, DeLuna," Leon said in the background, sounding *rough*. "You and Carlos need to get the fuck out of the manor soon. When security shifts change, they will notice—" He broke off with coughing, and panic zapped through me.

I tucked the vial of liquid into my bra and hurried to get my dress and shoes back on.

"What are you going to do with *him*?" Carlos asked, pointing at Dr. Harris.

Kill him was the obvious choice. I never enjoyed leaving loose ends that could come back to bite me in the ass later. But I hesitated on this one, because *what if* I had the wrong medication for Leon? What if I needed Dr. Harris alive?

"Kill him," Kai growled in my ear, "and cut off his fucking hands for touching you like that."

I flashed a smile at the camera. "I don't have a knife. Also, what if we need him to—"

"Kill him," Leon croaked. "Carlos has a knife. Make it hurt for me, *mon ange*, then come back to us."

I arched a brow at Carlos. "You've got a knife?"

He smiled and pulled a folding tactical knife from his pocket. "I stole it from one of the security guards I passed on my way back from dinner."

Swapping him for the phone, I flipped open the blade. It wasn't huge, but it was sharp. I could make it work. Frowning at the camera, I gave the boys a head shake. "Fuck, I hope we don't regret this later. But for you, Bunny... he's gotta pay."

Straddling Dr. Harris again, I ignored his panicked eyes and weak moans as I pinned one of his hands to the mattress. Kai told me to cut his hands off, and Leon wanted me to inflict pain. No reason why I couldn't do both.

For the record, it wasn't an *easy* task to cut a man's hand completely off with a short blade. But it was doable. Shockingly, he was still alive when I finished with the second hand. Not that he would stay alive for long, not with how fast his blood was pooling on the bed around his wrist stumps, but we couldn't risk him having a miracle survival and biting us in the ass later. So I smothered him with a pillow to ensure the job was done.

When I climbed off the doctor's corpse, my hands and arms drenched in sticky red blood, Carlos looked like he was barely containing the urge to vomit.

"Oh my god, don't act like you've never tortured anyone," I muttered, rolling my eyes. I hurried my ass through to the bathroom and rinsed as much blood away as possible, just in case we ran into anyone on our way out. Glancing in the mirror, I gave a small laugh. My wig was still perfectly in place, and I managed to only get a few splatters on the front of my dress. Not too shabby, for an out-of-practice mercenary.

"We gotta go, Dan," Carlos called out, and I towel dried my forearms.

I double-checked that the antiviral was still tucked into my bra, then led the way out of the suite. The best way to exit a place like Wellington Manor with all its security? Straight out the front door. Leon managed to keep the cameras looped long enough that I even collected Carolina's car from the valet.

"What about the lab?" Carlos asked. "Do I need to—"

"Leon will," I answered. Or Carol. We'd send a team to

sanitize it. Either way, we would make sure no one else accessed Dr. Harris's research and virus technology.

Carlos and I drove away into the night without even one hitch. I relaxed once the facility disappeared from view in my mirror, then cast a long look at my friend and unexpected partner in crime.

"You okay, Carlos?"

He glared back at me. "No, I think I need a vacation. Is that what you do on every job?"

I just shrugged, because it certainly wasn't out of the ordinary.

Carlos grimaced and shook his head. "That was disgusting, Dan. I never want to see that again, okay?"

I barked a laugh. "You afraid of a little blood, Diaz?"

"Blood? No, that part was fine. I meant your bare-ass tits. Warn a guy next time he's going to walk in on his best friend wearing nothing but a thong, alright? Fuck. I feel all creeped out like I've seen my mom in the shower."

My laughter continued right up until we reached the truck at our rendezvous point. Hell, I was still chuckling as I climbed into the back of the van... though my smile slipped fast when I found Leon pale and lifeless on the bed.

Kai bent over him, slapping his face to try and wake him up, and the look on his face nearly fucking killed me. Elbowing him aside, I jabbed Leon with the needle that would *hopefully* save his life.

Time would tell. There was nothing else we could do.

44
LEON

Carol Atwood had taken a considerable risk, exposing Danny to the public eye. Not only had she claimed her as an heir to her Circle seat, but she'd also destroyed Danny's career as a covert mercenary. It was hard to play the role of Danielle, the bank teller, when Danny Atwood, heiress, was in the tabloids.

Initially, I'd been furious. Then I'd quickly seen the benefits of what she'd done. How much safer Danny would be *and* as an added bonus? Danny would never be inviting strangers between her thighs just for the sake of secrets. That payoff appealed to me. I had only just accepted the idea

Kai's hands on her—and only then, because I *knew* how much she cared for him—but I couldn't suffer a stranger touching her. Not now. Hell, I'd already lost my patience before Danny and I ever got together... it was why I'd killed Ted back in New York.

Then I saw her back in action. *The* Danny DeLuna doing what she does best.

God *damn*, she was impressive. Beautiful, deadly, professional... it reminded me of when I used to simply watch her at a distance.

My whole body ached with fever chills, but I managed to hack into the Wellington Manor security feeds so we could get eyes on Danny. Seeing that Colombian prick, Carlos, playing the role of her boyfriend made my blood boil... The only saving grace was that Kai seemed equally pissed. Common enemy and all that shit.

Not that Carlos was an *enemy* exactly... except when it looked like he was making out with DeLuna. Then I could have skinned him alive while singing nursery rhymes.

At some stage, I fell asleep. It was unacceptable and unprofessional... but it also spoke to just how sick I was. Kai didn't fucking wake me, either, at least not deliberately. He barked a laugh at something he'd seen on the screen, and I jerked awake.

Danny had thrown her drink all over Carlos in the restaurant, but I couldn't hear what she was saying. My ears were ringing. Fuck.

"Give me a pen," I mumbled at Kai, blinking hard in a vain attempt to wake myself up.

"I don't have a pen. Who the fuck carries a pen around?" Kai gave me a look like I was having delusions again.

Grunting with the effort, I leaned over to grab Danny's eyeliner from her makeup bag. "Dickhead," I groaned, "give me—" I broke off, coughing.

Kai handed me some tissues, and I grimaced to see blood on them. Again. The sand through his hourglass had almost run out.

The computer screen still displayed the restaurant bar where DeLuna was drinking wine and assessing her target. He wasn't coming to her easily, but she would get him. She always got her mark. Meanwhile, though, I might expire... so I needed to take a leap of faith and seriously hope it was the right one to make.

Grabbing Kai's arm in my pathetically weak grip, I carefully started writing on his skin with Danny's black eyeliner. "Fuck me, you can barely read this," I croaked. Stupid Kai and his stupid black tattoos on brown skin. What the fuck. Why make this simple dying act so fucking difficult, asshole?

He glanced down and grunted a sound of agreement. "Write it on the window."

I shook my head. This was too important to write on a fucking window. I started coughing again, my whole damn chest rattling as I tried to suppress it.

"Jesus Christ," Kai muttered. He stared at me for a long moment, then shook his head. "Here." He yanked up his T-shirt and exposed some un-tattooed skin on his abs. "Don't get any ideas; you're not my fucking type, alright?"

I gave a laugh, but it set off more coughing, and I blacked out. Only a little bit, but enough that when I regained consciousness, I was horizontal on the bed, and Kai was watching the cameras while Carlos ambushed a security guard and divested him of his phone and weapons.

"Shit," I croaked, pushing myself back up. "Where's—"

Kai held up the eyeliner pen for me without a word. He understood it was important and wasn't going to be a little bitch asking questions. He just sat back and waited while I carefully wrote numbers and letters onto his stomach. When I was done, I collapsed again.

"What is it?" he asked in a low rumble, holding his shirt up to let the eyeliner dry.

I scrubbed a heavy hand over my face, literally feeling the last of my strength sap away. "It's my access codes," I gasped. "To everything. The Circle... all of it. If I die..."

Kai jerked a nod. "Got it. You'll be fine, though, *kohuru rapeti*. Have some faith in our woman; she's the best for a reason."

Fuck. I hated that I didn't hate that he called her *ours*.

I sagged against the bed, watching the security feed. Carlos was on one. Danny and that leech were on the other. The doctor had her pinned to the wall, his greedy hands undressing her, but I'd seen enough honey traps to not be concerned. Kai, on the other hand, looked like he was about to break the screen. Thankfully, his phone rang before he could punch anything.

"What?" he barked, then instantly sighed in relief. "Carlos. Hurry up and get in there. Dr. Harris is getting far too handsy."

On Danny's screen, the doctor had her on his bed. She wrapped her legs around him, and I gave a weak smile. She had things totally under control.

My vision blacked as my ears rang once more, and I slipped back into unconsciousness.

When I woke again, Kai was speaking to Danny on the phone as she looked into the camera.

"Kill him," he growled, "and cut off his fucking hands for touching you like that."

Danny flashed a deliciously sexy smile at the camera. God, she was beautiful. "I don't have a knife. Also, what if we need him to—"

"Kill him," I croaked, hoping that was loud enough for her to hear me. "Carlos has a knife. Make it hurt for me, *mon ange*, then come back to us." Then I passed out again.

"Make it hurt for me, mon ange," I sighed. *"Then come back to us..."*

"What?"

I snapped my gaze to the present and the woman seated across from me. Dressed in a perfectly pressed, white-linen pants suit and jacket, she presented a slender, ice-cold figure. From her frosty gaze to the cool blonde of her hair pulled taut into a chignon, she was a slash so severe she bisected the world around her.

We were her playthings, her toys, the people from whom she pulled the wings off and enjoyed watching us flop around. In no way did I ever make the mistake that I counted for something more as her son and heir.

No, she'd well and truly disabused me of that notion.

"I said nothing," I answered her when it was clear we would not continue with the session until I said something.

"That's my point." She clicked one razor-sharp nail against the whiteness of her desk as if to underscore her sentence. "You are not speaking."

Steepling my fingers together, I kept my expression bland and my gaze empty. Twenty-three years of diligent practice under her vicious tutelage had given me an unbreakable mask. Dr. Marx would only *ever* see what I allowed her.

"You haven't asked any questions." The bored tone didn't require affectation. These sessions bored me. They had since the day I mastered shutting her out of my mind entirely.

Physical torture I'd overcome by puberty.

Emotional torture I'd neutered before my eighteenth birthday.

The mental, however, could only be endured. She didn't have to know that. In fact, I'd die before I let her know she could still get to me. It certainly helped me in my work to keep my reactions in check.

"Leon," she practically tsked my name. "Put your hands on the desk."

Eyebrow quirked, I stared at her. I hadn't put my hands on the desk in over a decade. Why would—

A hand closed over the back of my neck and jerked me forward. "Hands on the desk."

Three things struck me at once. The hand holding me belonged to a much larger man. The woman behind the desk suddenly seemed ten feet tall. And fear clawed inside of me.

Real fear.

I didn't feel...

Pain lashed across my hands. The slap of the ruler cracking my knuckles. Why the fuck did that—

A whip sliced into my back.

"Again," she said, her tone cool and detached. She sat in a chair just a few feet away. I couldn't look anywhere but at her.

Leather stroked over my skin like fire, splitting it open and spilling blood out.

"What did we learn…"

The chains dragged at my arms, keeping my shoulders at an unnatural angle. "Torture," she said as she sat behind her desk, "begins with the body—why?"

"Because it is the easiest to break."

"What happens when the body is broken?"

"The mind unlocks."

"Very good." She seemed almost pleased.

Electricity scalded my nerves.

Like I said.

Almost.

Rising from behind the desk, she circled it to approach me. "I said, hands on the desk, Leon."

Sparing her a long look, I smiled. "No."

"Exc—" I didn't even think about it, I just moved. The knife was in my hand and sliding across her pale, porcelain throat and sending a fountain of crimson to splash over the painful whiteness of her suit, her desk…

Her hair?

Danny clasped a hand over the gaping slice where I'd severed the jugular. The blood pumped from between her fingers, staining them and her hair. Shock rippled in her eyes. Shock.

Pain.

Betrayal.

Only this time, instead of flipping me off and fighting me across my house, she staggered and dropped to the ivory carpet, and her eyes went still and cold.

"No," I said, dropping to my knees. "No. No. No."

I didn't just kill her.

I didn't just—

"So weak, Leon. Why don't we ever try to break the heart first?"

Because I didn't have a heart. It was bleeding out in front of me, painting my world red.

A seagull squawked. I fucking loved seagulls. Ballsy bastards were not afraid of anything when they had their eyes on some food. I respected their dedication. But why was I dreaming about seagulls? Or was I already dead, and now there were seagulls in my afterlife? Seemed plausible, since I did like them.

But would I be able to actually *smell* the sea in a dream?

Blinking my eyes open, I squinted at the daylight. Shit. I hated daylight... maybe this wasn't the afterlife. White gauze curtains billowed softly with the cool ocean breeze from an open window, and I frowned at the cheerful seashell painting on the wall opposite where I lay.

Where the fuck was I?

I raised a hand to rub my face, then peered at that hand. Well shit, I might be alive after all.

Where was Danny? Where was *mon cœur*? Did she make it out of Wellington Manor?

The door to the room opened, and my pulse raced. My palms went sweaty in anticipation of seeing her, *mon ange*… but it wasn't her, and my heart dropped to the floor.

"Oh shit," Kai muttered, his eyes wide in surprise. "You're awake. I was just coming to check your meds." He indicated to the IV bags hooked up on a pole beside my bed. Crap, was I in a hospital? No… no, this wasn't a hospital.

"Sasquatch," I murmured, my throat like razor blades. "Where's DeLuna?"

Kai gave me a blank look, then sat down cautiously beside the bed… like he had bad news.

"Where is she?" I demanded, struggling to sit up.

"Take it easy, Leon," he said, putting out a hand in a placating gesture. "You've been asleep for a long time. A lot has changed."

Wait. He called me *Leon*. He never fucking called me by my name.

Panic flared, and my heart beat so hard I could feel it in my throat. "What the fuck do you mean? How long? Where *is she*?"

Kai grimaced. "Leon… it's been two years. You were already so far gone when Danny gave you the antiviral medication… it was just too late. They put you in an induced coma for a year and then…" He spread his hands, trailing off and looking apologetic. But he still wasn't telling me where the fuck Danny was, and I was getting pissed.

"Malachi, I swear to all that you hold dear, if you don't tell me where the *fuck*—"

"Leon, she's gone." Kai issued those words with cold detachment, making bile rise in my throat. "Danny's gone."

45
DANNY

The sound of Leon's voice had me running back toward his room. I'd been out for a walk on the beach—Kai made me because I was driving him nuts pacing inside—and I heard them talking the moment I stepped back into the house.

"Leon, she's gone," Kai said right before I got back to the bedroom. "Danny's gone."

Frowning, I pushed open the door and beamed when I saw my bunny sitting up and *awake*. Whatever scolding I was about to deliver Kai was forgotten with the embarrassingly girly squeal I let out, throwing myself onto the bed to hug

Leon tight.

"Bunny, you're awake!"

Leon wrapped his arms around me, slightly hampered by the IV lines in his left hand, but he held me tight, nonetheless. "I sure am, baby. Kai was just telling me that you were *gone*..."

"Gone for a *walk* on the beach, of course." Kai was smug as fuck when I glanced over at him in the armchair beside the bed. "So dramatic, *kohuru rapeti.*"

One of Leon's hands lifted from my back, and I suspected he might be flipping Kai off.

"You have no idea how good it is to see you awake, Marx," I told Leon sincerely. "How are you feeling? Kai, can you call Katie and let her know?"

Kai nodded and stood up from his chair. "I'll get her back here to sort out the rabbit. He probably needs to stretch his legs after so long in bed."

He said it with a smirk at Leon before leaving the room, and I sat up with a confused frown. "It's been a week, not a fucking year. I'm thinking Kai is the dramatic one of the three of us."

Leon muttered something about kicking Kai in the balls next time he saw him, then pressed a kiss to my forehead. "DeLuna, *mon ange,* I have questions. Where are we, for one, and who is Katie?"

Smiling and damn near floating on my relief to see him awake, I shifted into the chair in order to give him some space. "Katie's the nurse who has been looking after you this week. She's—"

"Right here," the woman in question announced, strolling into the bedroom with a warm smile. "Nice to see you awake, Mr. Marx." She cocked her head at me in question, and I sighed.

"I'll give you a minute," I reluctantly said, standing up. "But I'll be right outside."

Leon looked confused, and his protest was written all over his face. But he'd been unconscious for a week... The nurse needed to remove his catheter, and I doubted he would appreciate an audience for that whole situation. So, I slipped out of the room before he could tell me to stay, then just lurked awkwardly outside the room.

I wanted to go make Leon some food and maybe a coffee or something. But I said I would be right outside, and the fear of losing him was still so strong that I couldn't force myself to even go that far away. So I just lurked.

Danny DeLuna, alpha-level mercenary and internationally renowned badass, assassin, seductress, spy... *lurking* outside a man's bedroom, fretting over his well-being. Oh, how the mighty can change. Not fall, just change.

Katie opened the door again just seven minutes later, giving me a smile and a nod. "He is making a good recovery. He'll be weak, so take it easy for a few days, clear?"

I nodded firmly, and she narrowed her eyes. "About my fee..."

"It's handled," I quickly responded.

Her brow raised. "You haven't even asked what it is. What if all I wanted was a night alone with your Kiwi?"

I scowled. "You have better respect for your own life than that, Katie. Whatever your price, in *dollars*, it's handled. Leave your banking details with Kai on the way out."

Cheeky bitch. She was lucky I knew she was joking. Mostly. Regardless, I slipped past her and into the bedroom, smiling wide when I saw Leon sitting up on the side of the bed.

"Bunny, you look better." I gently ran my hand over his hair, softly squeezing the back of his neck as he looked up at me with tired eyes. "How do you feel?"

"Like I was poisoned," he admitted with a groan, leaning back into my hand.

I bent down to kiss him softly. "It was a virus, Bunny, not poison."

He grimaced, his hands resting on my hips. His grip was weak but still a hundred times stronger than it had been in the last few weeks. Thank *fuck* Dr. Harris hadn't screwed us over.

"I've been unconscious for a week. It's safe to say I need a shower," he murmured, his hands moving down to grasp my butt cheeks. "Join me?"

"Tempting," I replied with a chuckle, "very tempting. But Nurse Katie says you need to rest. So you go shower *alone*… The bathroom is fully stocked, and I'll put clean clothes out for you. When you're done, food, water, more rest."

Leon pouted, and it nearly broke my firm resolve. So I tugged him to his feet and held onto his arm the whole way into the bathroom. He didn't protest, which spoke volumes about how weak he still was.

Still, I couldn't help myself. "Good boy," I teased as Leon meekly allowed me to undress him.

His gaze flared hot, his hands finding my waist and spinning us until my back hit the wall. His body pinned mine in place, and his lips rested warm on my throat. "Careful, *mon cœur*, I'm weak, but I'm not dead. I can still bend you over and smack this lush ass while sitting down and resting."

Oops, maybe I pushed that too hard. Aw damn, now I was all turned on too.

"You're lucky I want that shower," he murmured, kissing my neck. "And to brush my teeth. Fuzzy teeth are not my favorite."

He released me and slipped out of his pants, showing off his rising erection. Damn it all to hell, I licked my lips. I missed my Bunny and his magical pierced dick. Riding that dick was easily one of my favorite pastimes.

"Give me three minutes," he ordered. "Don't go anywhere. Maybe I don't have the energy to fuck you into seven consecutive orgasms, but I think I can handle one. At least."

Dragging my lower lip through my teeth, I tried *really* hard not to take the bait. "Marx, you nearly died. Maybe give it a day."

He shrugged, stepping under the shower spray and giving a moan. "That feels good," he murmured in a *way* too sexual tone of voice. "Pass me that toothbrush?"

Clenching my jaw, I snatched the new toothbrush and toothpaste from the vanity and held them out to him. He took them from me slowly, letting his wet fingers caress mine while his eyes promised that if I joined him, the shower would get very dirty, very quickly.

"I'll go find your clothes," I told him, forcing myself to leave the bathroom before I gave in to his intoxicating allure. Damn Leon Marx was too sexy for his own good, especially now that his life was no longer hanging in the balance.

It took me all of one minute to put together a stack of clothes for Leon. Then I paced the bedroom another three minutes while trying to convince myself that I *wasn't* going back into the bathroom to take Leon up on his offer.

"Siren, you never mentioned that part of Nurse Katie's payment," Kai said, striding into the bedroom with a puzzled look on his face. "I wouldn't have complained, but a heads-up would have been nice."

That jerked me out of my pacing. "Huh? What did she ask you for?" That sneaky shit better not have—

"She bit my ass cheek. Really hard, too." He turned around and tugged down the waistband of his pants. Sure enough, there was a set of teeth marks on his left butt cheek. Well, shit. Katie was a kinky bitch. "Oh, and she gave me bank details to transfer the rest of her payment. Five hundred thousand."

I let out a low whistle. "Nurse Katie knows her worth. Good for her."

Kai nodded to the bathroom, where the shower was still running. "Is he going to be okay?"

The genuine concern in his eyes warmed my chest. "I think so, yes. But we won't be if we stay here much longer." We'd already stayed in one location for too damn long.

"I'll call my team and make arrangements for our next move," Kai told me, pulling out his phone as he left the bedroom once more.

Leon gave a pained groan from the shower, and I rushed back in there without a second thought.

"Marx, are you—" My panic cut off as quickly as it'd started, realizing my mistake. "Oh, I see."

He gave me a lazy grin, his hooded eyes full of lust. "I'm glad you do. Want a closer look?"

Nurse Katie had set up a shower stool, knowing he would be

weak when he woke up. Leon was using it, slouched against the shower wall with the spray on his chest while his fist stroked his hard cock. That wasn't a *pained* groan, it was a moan.

"Bunny," I scolded, not strong enough to look away, "you're meant to be *resting*."

His hips rocked, pushing his dick up into his grip. "This helps me relax. Maybe you can lend a hand so I don't expend too much energy."

I licked my lips. "Cute. You really are feeling better, huh? I'm still not letting you fuck me until you rest some more. You need strength if we're going to escape my kill order."

He tilted his head playfully. "Oh? Is that why you just took your top off?"

I glanced down. Oops, so I did. How did that happen?

"And there go the pants. I like how this day is turning out." He spread his legs wider, his wet hand sliding down to grasp the base of his shaft.

Laughing, I stepped into the shower and sank to my knees between his legs. "Leon, Bunny? Shut up and fuck my mouth."

A lazy, sexy grin crossed his lips, and he gathered my hair up in his fist. "Yes, ma'am."

I smirked. "Good boy." Then he punished me for that remark by making me nearly suffocate on his pierced dick and then ordered me to make myself come while he watched. Then he unloaded all over my tits.

46
DANNY

Despite Leon's best efforts to lure me into more, I could see he was exhausted. I bullied him back into bed and set him up with fruit juice and a grilled cheese sandwich. Not exactly the ideal post-illness food, but I couldn't say no when he asked with those big bunny eyes.

His blinks grew slower and deeper around halfway through his sandwich, so I drew the curtains and left him with strict instructions to sleep.

In the living room, Kai was on the phone to Moana. His gaze locked with mine as I came closer, and he set a hand around my waist, pulling me in tight.

"That's good news, Mo," he was saying. "Have you got things handled with new management? They'll need support while—"

She must have cut him off, but he smiled as she spoke. He kept me against him as he gave a murmur of agreement with something Mo was saying. I leaned into him, tucking my hands into his back pockets and pressing my cheek to his chest.

"Alright, alright," Kai said with a laugh. "You know what you're doing. Stay safe, okay?" He ended the call and tossed his phone down on the couch closest to us.

"Good news?" I murmured, tipping my head back to look up at him.

He leaned down to kiss me gently. "Very good news. Mo linked up with some allies on the ground in Germany. The orphanage there was still operational."

Shock and a touch of dread made my eyes widen. "That's great," I murmured. It was. But just thinking about how many Guild orphanages were still out there... it made me sick. Knowing how I'd been raised, how Sabine had been raised, we foolishly assumed ours were the only facilities like that.

"It really is," he replied, grinning. "Somehow, the Guild has *always* been a step ahead of us on these. I assume now, that our mole was just toying with us or something. I don't know, but this is a huge win. Mo is ecstatic."

"I bet she is," I commented, stretching up to kiss him again. This time he deepened the kiss, and it quickly turned heated.

Within moments, we were horizontal on the couch with our shirts off, then his phone rang again, buzzing underneath me.

"Ignore it," I suggested, claiming his mouth with my own once more.

He let me distract him while the call rang out, but then it started again, and he chuckled. "I need to take that, *ātaahua*. My team is organizing our next safe location."

I pouted but got up so he could retrieve his phone. Now I was all annoyed and edgy, but his arrangements were important. As soon as Leon woke up, I wanted to move.

He'd likely sleep a few hours though, so I tugged my shirt back on and mimed to Kai that I was going for a run. The recent ambushes and attacks had made me realize I needed to get my fitness up to scratch, so while waiting for Leon to recover, I had been running on the beach.

When I got back, sweaty and puffing, I found Kai and Leon both sitting at the dining table with a laptop open, and half-empty mugs of coffee beside them. They seemed... comfortable.

"Marx, you were meant to be sleeping." I crossed over to him and delivered a kiss when he tipped his face back. His arm wrapped around my waist, holding me close.

"Sleep is for the weak," he muttered.

"And dead," Kai agreed. "Besides, our invincible *kohuru rapeti* has valuable intel to unlock for us."

Leon nodded, then shifted his eyes to Kai. "Speaking of

which…"

Kai flashed a grin and lifted his shirt. "All gone. Like I never had it."

"The access codes?" I asked, smiling. "He kept re-inking it after every shower so it wouldn't wash off until you woke up."

Kai gave a bashful shrug. "He said it was too important to write down anywhere else." His phone buzzed with a message, and he checked it. "Truck's here. Siren, do you want to change before we go?"

I glanced down at my sweat-drenched shirt, my sand-splattered legs, and wrinkled my nose. "I'll be quick."

"I'll move this onto the truck," Leon murmured. "My decoding software had cracked several more of Layla's drives. I'm just trying to download the data from my cloud. Not a quick process on a weak mobile signal."

I kissed him again, then left them to relocate all our stuff to the truck.

After getting changed, I took a few extra minutes to sweep the house, making sure we hadn't left anything behind. It was a Hestia property—I used my discount—so they would clean it thoroughly for us when we were gone, but we still didn't need to take chances.

Stepping out of the house, I smiled to see our familiar Mercedes Unimog sitting at the curb. It'd had a makeover in the last week; Carlos's guys had given it a full paint job and replaced the plates.

"Still not subtle," I commented with a laugh as I climbed into the passenger seat, tossing my bag into the back. "But it's a clean slate."

"It's better than that," Leon replied from behind my seat. "Carlos hooked us up."

I twisted to see what he was talking about, while Kai started up the truck. In the back, instead of a kitchenette, a full tech desk was set up. Multiple screens were positioned on the desk, and Leon looked happier than a pig in shit as he connected his laptop up to it all.

"Cool," I murmured, climbing over from the front to take a better look. "You said your systems decoded more drives? How was that possible while you were on your deathbed?"

Leon smiled and shook his head. "Come on, *mon cœur*, you know me better than that. Want to see what we've uncovered?"

"Fuck *yes*, I do," I enthused, taking a seat directly in his lap. "Show me, Tech Bunny."

He gave a light chuckle, wrapping his arms around me and kissing my neck. "Fuck, I missed having you in my lap. Alright, let's crack open Pandora's box."

Reaching around me, he went to work on downloading and opening the huge files he'd accessed on a cloud server. For a while, I was at a loss for what we were looking at. Strings of code and jumbled letters that Leon genuinely seemed to understand. It didn't bother me, though. I was more than happy to just sit in Leon's lap and watch his long fingers flying across the keyboard.

"Holy shit," Leon whispered eventually. "Tell Kai to pull over somewhere. He'll wanna see this."

Instead of getting up, I just called out to relay the message to Kai, then turned my attention back to the information on the screen. "What am I looking at, Bunny?"

"IVF records," he said softly, brushing another kiss over the bend of my neck even as he sighed. "Unedited IVF records for Project Remus. This… is probably the reason Layla was killed."

"I thought I was the one who killed her," Kai muttered, dragging over a spare seat and sitting heavily. He wasn't picking fights with Leon, just stating facts.

I glanced over at him. "You were just the weapon, Big Man. If it wasn't you, it would have been someone else. Layla was in some sticky shit."

Kai just grimaced. "So, what have we got here? Looks like thousands of medical files dating back decades. How relevant are these now?"

It was a good question, but Leon seemed to have some idea. He twisted to give Kai a long look but said nothing in response. Just typed a few keys, bringing up a search box and typing in AE0088. He paused a moment, his other hand moving to my waist in a gesture of comfort, before he hit enter.

I was confused for a moment, reading the first file that popped up. It was for a surrogate, a woman named Sandra Wildeboer. Leon clicked a link within the file, and I sucked a gasp.

"Carol Atwood," I murmured aloud, reading the *egg donor* information. Though if Carol was telling the truth, she was a less than willing donor. "Is this...?"

Leon gave a sigh, clicking the next link. "And Martin Erikkson. The seventh Circle member... the one with *no heir*."

"I want to say I'm surprised," Kai murmured, "but I'm not. This explains a lot, doesn't it?"

Shock rippled through me, a little delayed. "You think this is me? My file?"

Leon's hand on my waist gave a small squeeze. "If my hunch is right about Carol, it should be easy to check." He brought up the search field again, typing in ATWOOD. The same file that was already open dinged, but nothing else came up. Search results also showed no other files using her "donations" whatsoever. This was the only one.

Bile rose up in my throat, and I pressed my fingers to my mouth. "That's me, then."

"Dates line up, don't they?" Leon said softly, returning to the original file. The one that outlined an embryo transfer to Sandra Wildeboer almost thirty years ago.

I swallowed hard. "What about Erikkson? If this whole thing has been about killing me so I can't take his seat..."

Leon followed my train of thought, typing the missing Circle member's name into the search box. The computer dinged with *hundreds* of results, and I gave a small gasp.

"That can't be right," Leon muttered, frowning.

"Some of these date back too far," Kai murmured, sitting forward.

Leon sighed. "That makes sense, I guess. Project Remus was started by the Erikkson seat back in the 1940s." He narrowed the search field to *Martin Erikkson*, and the results filtered down dramatically. There were still dozens of files, though, meaning that I *wasn't* his only heir.

"This explains the widespread culling of mercenaries, I guess," I commented as Leon flicked through the files, confirming they were indeed all IVF files using Martin Erikkson's swimmers. "Talk about a fucking god-complex. So, someone knows that the Erikkson seat not only has an heir, it has *dozens*, and they decided to... clear the gameboard? Why not just keep it quiet until the time runs out on Martin's hold? If no one ever knew about his heirs, then no one would dispute the seat passing to the next family on the list. Right?"

Leon shifted me in his lap, banding his arm around me once more. "Theoretically, yes. But Martin isn't dead, which means I bet he's put safeguards in place to ensure his seat passes to a chosen heir and not to another family. Whoever is behind this—Blanchet or someone else—they've decided that the only way is to kill *that* heir."

"But they don't know who it is," Kai mused aloud, looking thoughtful, "so they're killing *all* the Remus mercenaries."

It was a heavy-handed approach, but I could see the logic.

Sometimes, to catch one fish, you needed to use a net and fuck the collateral damage.

"No wonder Layla was paranoid enough to hide these in a dead drop," I said with a sigh. "Why in Shadow Grove, though? Who was she leaving them for? Someone else must have had a key to that drop location and just never collected the data."

Leon pressed a kiss to my neck. "I suspect she never got a chance to tell the other party that there was intel waiting... and that person was not in the best mental state to search for it under her own initiative."

I stiffened. "Why do you sound like you know who has the other key?"

"Because he does," Kai rumbled. "Spit it out, Marx. The three of us are well past secrets now."

Leon flipped Kai his middle finger, then turned his attention back to the computer screen, double-clicking the IVF surrogate's file. "Sandra Wildeboer," he said, "was Layla's mom." A few more clicks brought up the file he was searching for, confirming his announcement.

"Holy shit," I breathed. "Wait, it says Sandra herself was the egg donor for Layla?"

Leon nodded. "It seems to be common, if the Guild saw genetic traits in their surrogates that were worth experimenting on. I would guess that the carriers never got told whether they were implanted with their own embryo or someone else's to keep their emotional connection as low as possible. Considering they would hand the babies over to the Guild on birth, it makes sense."

I reached out, knocking his hand from the mouse so I could click *sperm donor*.

"She was my half-sister," I whispered, reading *Martin Erikkson* on the screen. "Explains why you two are both so into me. Must be the genetics."

Leon pinched my waist, sensing I was joking. Sort of. "Funny girl."

"We should keep moving," Kai murmured, glancing out the window. "Our next safe house is still a good five hours away."

On reflex, my gaze skipped over to the back of the truck, where several heavy-duty plastic boxes sat full of guns and ammo. Carlos had restocked us from one of Kai's stockpiles, so we were ready for another ambush.

"There's shit loads of data here for me to comb through," Leon murmured, kissing my neck again in a gesture that seemed more self-soothing than anything else. "It's nearly five years old, though, so it might just take some time for me to compare against Guild records for who is still alive."

Kai rose to his feet, clapping Leon on the shoulder. "Take it easy, Marx. If you nearly die again, Danny will finish you off herself."

Leon just grunted an amused sound, and I shifted in his lap to cup his face in my fingers. "He's not wrong," I growled, then kissed him hard. He returned the enthusiasm, hauling me closer so that my legs straddled him and his hand slipped under my top to stroke my back.

His dick was already hard, it had been the whole time I was sitting in his lap, and the way he ground against me was so tempting. Tempting enough to forget the massive information bomb he'd just uncovered? It *shouldn't* be, but… shit. I missed my bunny. I wanted to lock myself in a room with him for a month, no clothes allowed.

Okay, him *and* Kai. They seemed to be getting along so much better now… almost like they had found some kind of mutual respect for each other. Would it extend to sharing a bed?

"DeLuna," Leon groaned against my kiss. The truck rocked slightly as Kai started the engine and got us back onto the road. "You're quickly making me forget what I was meant to be doing…"

Shit, he was doing important work… work that could potentially uncover the bigger plot at stake and save my ass in the process. Meanwhile, all I could think about was unzipping his jeans and—

"*Ma moitié,* what do you think you're doing?" he asked with a deep chuckle as I slipped out of his lap. I didn't leave him to go back to my seat, though, instead sinking to my knees between his legs.

I wet my lips, popping the button of his fly and dragging the zip down. "Helping you focus, Bunny. Now hush, I'm starving."

Leon gave a groan as I fisted his cock, but I heard no complaints as I teased his tip with my tongue. Quite the opposite. His hand moved to the back of my head, and he shoved my face down, making me choke on his dick.

"Don't play with your food, DeLuna. It's rude."

47
KAI

Listening to Danny sucking Leon's dick while I drove was pure torture, but it no longer filled me with the violent need to put his head through a window and cut his dick and balls off. I couldn't pinpoint when things had changed between us. Maybe when Danny decided she would rather break her own heart to avoid choosing between us. Maybe it was when she'd forced that first three-way while I was handcuffed to the bed at Carol's house.

Shit. Maybe it was when I genuinely thought Leon was dying... and realized I didn't *want* the annoying little fuck to die.

But it didn't matter when it'd changed... only that it had. I no longer wanted to murder him for fucking my siren's mouth. I wanted to join in. I wanted to pull over onto the side of the road and climb over there. Maybe strip her knickers off and fuck her from behind while she blew him.

I even glanced over my shoulder when the temptation became almost too strong, but despite what was undoubtedly an elite blow job, Leon *was* still working. One hand navigated the computer mouse, clicking file after file as he read the information. His other hand was on the back of Danny's head, guiding her pace and petting her hair.

With a huff of frustration, I turned my attention back to the road. Multitasking bastard.

She finished a few minutes later, or I should say *he* finished a few minutes later, and they exchanged some quiet, warmth-filled words that I tried really hard not to eavesdrop on. We might all be in this together, but it didn't mean either Leon or I had relinquished our right to private moments with her. If I wanted him to respect that, then I needed to lead by example.

A minute later, Danny leaned over to tell me she was going to take a nap. Good. She'd barely slept all damn week while we waited for Leon to recover from that fucking virus. I grabbed her elbow before she could disappear, dragging her back so I could kiss her without stopping the truck.

She gave a surprised sound, then kissed me back deeply. Yes, I was fully aware she'd just taken a load of Leon's cum in her mouth, but I found it hard to care. I wasn't sucking his dick, just dealing with a little crossover, which was simply inevitable in a menage relationship. So, fuck it. Better get used to it now.

"That was hot," she confessed in a heavy whisper when I released her lips to avoid crashing our truck. "I love that you're playing nice."

She hesitated, like she wanted to say something else, but then changed her mind and went to crawl into the bed opposite where Leon worked. Soon, the only sound in the truck was the click-clack of Leon's mouse and keyboard while he worked through the files he'd unlocked.

Settling in for the drive, I turned the stereo on low. Just enough to keep me awake on the long, boring drive to our next safe house location. In no time at all, I zoned out and just concentrated on the drive, ignoring Leon working and Danny sleeping. Hours passed, and I stayed in my little solitary bubble while the scenery whipped past.

That was, until I caught movement in the corner of my eye right as I took the on-ramp for our next highway. Leon was standing up from the computer desk, stretching his arms over his head. He must have needed a break, which was understandable.

He didn't climb over to the passenger seat, though, which made me glance in the mirror again.

"Leon!" I exclaimed, seeing him peeling Danny's panties down her legs while she remained dead asleep.

He shot a look over at me, a sly smile on his face. "What? Eyes on the road, Malachi."

My teeth ground together. "Let her sleep. She's exhausted."

"I know," he replied, smirking as he rolled her onto her back, spreading her legs apart. "She took a sleeping pill. I won't wake her up."

Outrage—and arousal—flooded through me, but I needed to watch the fucking road. We were on a highway; there was nowhere to stop. When I glanced back in the mirror again, Leon had his own pants off and was pushing inside Danny's pussy. Fuck, she barely even stirred.

"Leon, this isn't—"

"Shut up, dickhead," he grunted, thrusting into our woman's sleeping body. "It was her suggestion."

Oh. That… changed things.

"Just don't fucking crash us, and maybe you can have a turn." He hitched one of her legs up, increasing his pace and making me certain she'd wake up any second.

I couldn't deny how hard I was, so I clenched my jaw and shifted my eyes back to the road. "At least make her come, selfish dick."

Leon's husky laughter was my only response, but a few minutes later, Danny gave a sleepy moan, and when I glanced in the mirror, her back was arched as Leon pushed her into an unconscious orgasm. Fucking hell… trust Leon to make up for lost time even while Danny slept.

He finished himself a moment later, then grabbed his phone out to take pictures. Sick fuck.

When he finally climbed over into the passenger seat, his smile was wide and satisfied. Unsurprising. It was *her* idea? I shouldn't be surprised—this was Danny DeLuna we were talking about.

"Stop scowling, Sasquatch," Leon teased, getting comfy in his seat and rearranging his junk. "Just pull over at the next truck stop, she'll appreciate it."

I cast a suspicious sidelong glance at him, not totally sure if I was buying that story.

Leon rolled his eyes. "I'm not making that up. She literally said she wouldn't be unhappy if she woke up dripping with cum. The request wasn't specific to *my* cum."

Wetting my lips, I glanced in the mirror again. She was still dead asleep, her bare legs askew on the bed and her hair splayed out like a white halo.

"You're being awfully *accepting*," I commented, still suspicious as fuck. Was he setting me up?

Leon just gave a heavy sigh, looking out the window. "Nearly dying will have that effect on priorities, Malachi. She loves you. I'd be blind not to see that and an idiot to try and fight it."

I had nothing to say back to that, because it was pretty much the same conclusion I'd drawn in the recent weeks while Leon clung to life. So I just kept driving in silence, but when a sign advertised there was a truck stop and gas station at the next exit, I changed lanes and indicated for the exit.

Leon smirked. "That's the spirit."

I didn't entertain him with a response, just followed the signs toward the rest area. We needed gas, anyway. And food. But still,

I parked us away from the other vehicles already stopped at the rest area, because there was only one thing on my mind as I killed the engine and unbuckled my seat belt.

"I need to stretch my legs," Leon announced, popping his door open. "Take your time, Sasquatch. Make her come."

I flipped him off, but he was already slamming his door shut and strolling away from the truck, leaving me alone with my Sleeping Beauty. I was fucking lying to myself if I wanted to pretend I wouldn't do exactly what Leon had just done. Use her. Fill her up with my cum while she slept peacefully.

Groaning, I climbed into the back to where she lay. She was a damn angel, just like Leon liked to call her. I may not speak French, but *mon ange* wasn't a hard one to work out. He'd left her naked from the waist down, and her top simply pushed up to bare her breasts. He hadn't done it out of disrespect, he'd done it for me. Sly little bastard, he knew I wouldn't be able to resist.

Kneeling on the small bed, I cupped one of her full breasts, rolling her hard nipple between my fingers. She gave a quiet moan, arching into my touch and her lashes fluttering. That sleeping pill must be wearing off, because she was waking up.

Not giving myself a moment to second-guess what I was doing, I pushed my pants down just far enough to free my cock. I was already so fucking hard I could have easily come in my pants, and she was slick with Leon's cum... I tried to ignore *that* fact as I slid inside her warm cunt, but it was impossible. She was so wet, and I couldn't shake the knowledge that I'd just seen Leon fucking her, but I didn't stop.

"Kai," she moaned, her lashes fluttering again as I thrust deep. "Mmm... yes..." She trailed off, her breathing deep, but I was already gone. I gripped her thighs, spreading her wide as I had my way with her perfect pussy. But I wasn't so far gone that I couldn't be a gentleman, so when she stirred again, I bent down to kiss her.

She was still more asleep than awake, her lips relaxed as I kissed her mouth, and my hand snaked between our bodies to find her clit. My tongue thrust into her mouth in time with my cock, and my fingers rubbed her already swollen clit with feverish need. I was going to blow soon but needed her to finish first. It was only polite.

As relaxed as her whole body was in sleep, the orgasm seemed to steal over her in waves, her limbs trembling as her pussy walls clenched tight, making me moan. I didn't let up on her clit as her trembles increased, wanting to make her fall apart even harder.

Trouble was, I couldn't stop myself. I came abruptly, shooting hard inside her as she pulsed around my cock. But she was so close to coming again, I could sense it. I'd become so attuned to her body cues, and while she slept, she didn't hide them anywhere near as well. So I just remained buried inside her as my fingers rubbed her over the next crest.

This time she cried out as she came, rocking on my already spent dick. It was perfect.

Reluctantly, I pulled out, then groaned at the creamy mess

between her thighs. Maybe Leon wasn't such a sick fuck for his perverted photo collection.

"Big Man," she murmured, her voice still thick with sleep, "take a picture, if you want."

Shit, was it *that* obvious what I was thinking? Grunting, I tugged my pants up before I could be tempted to push my half-soft dick back into her. "No need," I muttered. "It just gives me incentive to recreate the scene. You should go back to sleep."

Danny yawned, stretching out like a cat. She made no attempt to close her legs, knowing full fucking well how much I was appreciating the view. "I slept *very* well," she told me with a smile. "Best sleep I've had in forever. Where are we?"

"Truck stop," I told her, sweeping a hand over my face, then snagging her panties from the floor. "Probably about an hour or two from the next house. We needed gas and..." I trailed off, taking another long look at her dripping cunt.

She just grinned back at me, holding out her hand for the panties bunched up in my fist. "You gonna give me those? Or hold them hostage?"

Hostage, my mind quickly decided. But she would want to go into the store, and it was a hard choice between wanting her to suffer without panties, knowing all that cum would be sliding down her thighs... versus letting her put the panties on to keep it all in place.

Slowly, I handed them over and watched as she threaded her legs into them like some kind of reverse striptease.

Sitting up, she reached over to her bag and pulled out a skirt to put on. Tease.

"Where's Leon?"

I sighed, turning away before I could totally lose my brain and throw her back down on the bed for round two. "Went for a walk," I told her. "He's been working on these files the whole trip so far." I tapped the computer desk, and the small motion woke the screen up. I stiffened in shock when I saw the files he had left open.

"What's wrong?" Danny asked, instantly seeing the shift in my mood. "Do you know him?"

I nodded slowly, letting out a breath of relief when I saw the bold red font of DECEASED beside the mercenary status. That would have been way too fucking creepy.

"Yeah," I muttered, "or I did. Once. That... is *Timothy*."

The file said his name was Justin Brancott, but the fact that this prick had supplied Mo with a fake name was no great shocker. What had me stunned, horrified, and filled with dread was that Leon had matched the Guild personal file to one of the IVF records.

"Oh shit," Danny breathed, realizing what I was saying. "Mo's baby would have been my nephew."

Because Timothy, the lying son of a bitch who'd seduced my sister, got her pregnant, then stole her baby? Was Danny's half-brother. Thank *fuck* he was deceased.

48
DANNY

My first question to Kai had been how sure he was that *Timothy* was dead, but he was confident. Apparently, his team had been tracking him several years ago, and Mo had gotten the pleasure of shooting him herself, then blowing up the building with C-4.

I was happy for her that she was able to get that closure. And I was selfishly glad I didn't have a sick fuck half-brother out there somewhere.

Kai brushed it off with a sigh, climbing out of the truck and lifting me down. The rest area contained a gas station, a diner, and a bar with a whole shit load of motorcycles lined up outside, making me think this was more of an MC territory than a truck stop. Whatever, though. We needed snacks, and I needed to pee, so we headed over to the sleepy little diner—next door to the biker bar—where Leon was already seated near a window.

He gave us a knowing smirk as we approached his table, his heated gaze running over me from head to toe. "DeLuna, *mon ange*, did you sleep well?"

Grinning, I leaned over to kiss him deeply. "Best nap of my life. Order me a burger?"

"Already done," he replied. "Where are you going?"

I just rolled my eyes, not answering his teasing question as I headed for the restroom. My panties were already a sodden mess, but I cleaned up as best I could after I peed. Back at the table, our food had already arrived. Leon had guessed well, and my stomach rumbled as I eyed the greasy burger and fries.

"I figured you'd have an appetite when you woke up," he told me with a wink, and I just grinned back.

"You were right," I murmured, then yawned. Sleeping pills always left me drowsy when I woke up, but it was worth it. My pussy ached and my limbs were all loose and relaxed, the surefire sign of multiple orgasms while I'd slept. It wasn't something I'd ever done before, but the idea popped into my head right after taking the sleeping pill, so I'd casually dropped the suggestion to Leon.

Of course he'd listened. What I was surprised about was Kai

taking a turn. It was so hot I was tempted to drag them back into the truck for a proper three-way right here and now. God knew they were giving me all the right signs. Weren't they?

"Did Kai tell you about Timothy?" I asked instead, distracting myself with some fries. Yum.

Leon arched a brow at the big guy sitting opposite him, and Kai quickly relayed the discovery he'd just made, thanks to the file left open on Leon's computer screen. Leon listened attentively while eating his own burger, then sat back with a well-fed groan when he was done.

"What are you going to do about it?" he asked when Kai finished explaining the whole Moana and Timothy story. "Will you tell her that her baby daddy was Danny's half-brother?"

Kai grimaced. "I'd rather not. Mo has been... she doesn't *love* my sudden involvement with the Guild. I can't see this information as helping that situation."

That surprised me. I got the impression Kai and Mo didn't keep many secrets from one another. But Leon just nodded.

"Good choice," he commented. "She's already a frosty bitch, and it's irrelevant anyway. Danny is related to half the Guild thanks to her sperm donor's generosity."

I winced. "Thanks for the reminder."

He wrapped an arm around my shoulders, bringing me closer. "It's not as bad as it seems... I found another familiar face in the files when I cross-referenced. Someone that I think you'll be *happy* to be blood-related to—compared to some of the others."

I studied his gaze for a moment, then my eyes widened with understanding. "Sabby?"

Leon smiled. "Two peas in a pod. Literally, when you look at the sperm donation dates."

That filled my heart with warmth, even though she was long gone by now. She'd enacted a ghost protocol that we set up a long, long time ago. A desperate bid to disappear off the face of the earth if we ever needed to leave the Guild. I should have used it myself, but by the time I realized how deep my shit was, it was too late. I was glad she had been smarter than me.

"You think Martin Erikkson named one specific person as his heir?" Kai asked, munching on his own food. "How will we work it out?"

Leon shrugged. "I think Martin left a safeguard to ensure his seat stayed in his family line. Whether it is one heir named or just the existence of blood heirs at all... hard to know. Also, it looks like the Erikkson family tree is seriously widespread. More so than Blanchet must realize, because there is no plausible way he could wipe out *every* last apple from that tree. Remus was started by Martin's grandfather. That's why there were so fucking many IVF babies using Erikkson DNA. Apparently, they were keeping the bulk of experimentation within the family line."

I frowned, no longer hungry. I'd finished most of my food, though, so that was something. "Playing god, huh? So why has

Martin all but abandoned his Circle position if he is continuing the Remus research?"

Leon cocked his head to the side. "Because he's not. Martin inherited the project and wanted *nothing* to do with it. He's the one who tasked me to clean it up before I took my own seat."

Kai scoffed a sound of disbelief. "For someone who wanted to clean up the project, he sure donated a lot of sperm."

"I thought the same," Leon agreed, "until I was studying Danny's file for the six hundredth time, and it occurred to me, Carol's *donation* was taken from her under the guise of an appendectomy or some shit, wasn't it? So who's to say that Martin's genetic matter wasn't also harvested without his consent? He's the same age as Carol, so would have only been fifteen or so when Danny was conceived—so to speak—which seems young to be the diabolical mastermind."

I wrinkled my nose, considering the logistics of that and then deciding I really, *really* didn't want to work it out. But Leon had a good point. Maybe when Martin inherited the sick little project, he uncovered what had been done and decided to shut it down.

But... Sabine was my half-sister. I loved that so much. Fuck, I hoped she was safe and already starting a new life.

"So now we know the *why*... we just need to get access to the *who* so we can stop the *how*," I mused aloud. "I guess we should keep moving. That fucking kill order could get us attacked at any moment." I glanced around the diner, then self-consciously pulled up the hood of my sweatshirt to hide my distinctive hair.

Kai swiped the last few fries from his plate, tossing them in his mouth as we all slid out of the booth. Leon headed for the counter to pay, and Kai said he would go fill the truck up with gas. I lurked with Leon, leaning into him when he wrapped his arm around my waist as we waited for the bill.

"We should grab some extra snacks," I murmured with a yawn. "So we don't have to leave the house once we arrive. The less time we spend in public, the better."

He nodded, then kissed my hair. "Good idea. Then we can just leave our clothes at the door and spend some quality time together."

I chuckled, but my thighs clenched with excitement. "I'll grab energy drinks, if nothing else. Meet you back on the truck." Leaving Leon to deal with our bill, and probably visit the restroom, I wandered back outside to grab some money off the truck. We were paying for shit in cash to reduce our paper trail, but it was inconvenient at best.

Kai was filling us up with gas, which would take a while, so I climbed inside and grabbed the black bag full of cash. I was too lazy—and still sleepy—to unzip it and count out the few bills I needed, instead just slinging the whole thing over my shoulder. I yawned heavily as I climbed back out, hovering for a moment to ask Kai what he wanted from the store.

I took my time, filling a basket with snacks and drinks, then waited near the checkout counter while Kai finished filling our truck up. When he was done, I paid for everything from the cash in my bag and glanced out the window to see Kai had disappeared. He was probably back in the driver's seat, waiting for us.

Leon was strolling out of the diner when I stepped outside, so I paused for a moment to wait for him.

Then the truck exploded.

It was there one second, then a ball of flame in the next. Leon threw me to the ground, his body on top of me before I could even fully comprehend what the fuck just happened.

"Kai!" I screamed when it all clicked together in my sleepy brain. I shoved Leon off me, scrambling to my feet and trying to run right at the ball of flame that used to be our truck. Leon's strong arm banded around my waist, hauling me off my feet to prevent my progress, but when he spun me around, I sagged in his grip.

Kai was standing there, untouched. Holy *fuck*.

Leon released me, and I launched myself at Kai. My fist struck him in the jaw, and his head snapped to the side, his eyes wide.

"Danny, what—"

"I thought you were *dead*!" I shrieked. "Don't fucking scare me like that!"

A smile tugged at Kai's lips, and he grabbed me in a tight embrace, his lips dropping to mine. "I was taking a leak, Siren. I'm fine. Our transport, though…"

"Guys, we should go," Leon prompted. "That was a mini-drone missile. Whoever was controlling it can't be more than five miles away, and they'll probably be coming to finish the job."

I grimaced. "And all our guns were on the truck. Fuck."

The gas station attendant was staring through the window with a *horrified* expression on his face, and the severity of the situation struck me like Thor's fucking hammer. "Kai, make sure everyone gets the fuck out of the gas station, *now!*" I gave him a shove to get him moving. If the flames ignited the gas, the whole station would explode.

"Leon, evacuate the diner," I barked. "I'll get us transport."

Not waiting to make sure they were doing as they were told, I jogged over to the biker bar and shoved through the front doors. Somehow their music and noise had been loud enough that they hadn't heard—or hadn't cared—about the explosion from our truck. But they all fucking paid attention when I strode in like I owned the damn place.

"I need three bikes," I announced, my voice hard with authority. "First three to toss me their keys, gets this." I reached into the bag, still over my shoulder, and pulled out three thick wads of cash. I slapped them down on the pool table closest to me and spun to face the bikers. "*Quickly.*"

The wads of cash contained much more than the bikes were worth; they'd be idiots not to take the offer. Thankfully, the bikers closest were smart enough to see that, and a minute later, I was back outside with three sets of motorcycle keys in hand. A young, acne-covered kid accompanied me to point out which ones they were, and his jaw dropped when he saw the flaming pillar right beside a gas pump.

"I suggest you tell everyone inside to fucking run," I advised the kid, tossing keys to Leon and Kai both as they jogged back over to us. "This whole place is going to explode."

I was right, too. The three of us had barely made it a hundred paces down the road when a deafening explosion roared through the night, making the bike under me wobble dangerously. We were far enough, though, and didn't spare a glance behind us.

Fucking kill order was really starting to piss me off now.

49
DANNY

About five minutes after the gas station exploded, a maroon-colored soccer mom van passed us on the road, heading in the direction of the fire. I barely gave it any thought until two minutes later, when I spotted the very same mom van following us.

"Marx," I called out, accelerating to pull up beside him. He glanced over at me, and I tipped my head to indicate our tail. Kai was out in front of the three of us, but he glanced back, signaling his understanding.

"I'll handle it," Leon told me, his expression confident despite how recently he'd nearly died. Fucking hell, maybe he was part Terminator. "Just keep going and steer clear if they start shooting."

Normally, that warning would get my bristles up, because I didn't *need* saving. But shit had changed a lot, and I was coming to recognize that it wasn't a bad thing to rely on my men every now and then. Especially now, while I had no weapons on me. I'd been more concerned with the slick mess of cum between my legs when I got out of the truck, not thinking about making sure I was adequately armed. Lesson learned.

Leon accelerated hard, racing ahead of us, and Kai dropped back level with me. The frown on his brow said he didn't understand Leon's plan, but I had a vague idea. Chances were, he analyzed and strategized the same as I did, which meant—

Yep, a minute later, he reappeared, flying toward us at top speed. Kai and I sped up slightly, and Leon whipped past us, swerving into our lane right in front of the mom van tailing us. He gave them no opportunity to get out of the way, leaving it right to the last possible second as he dropped his bike and jumped free of the collision.

The van slammed into the sliding bike, making the heavy vehicle jerk and swerve, barreling into the ditch beside the road and hitting a tree with a sickening crash.

Kai and I had slowed the moment Leon passed us, and I kicked out my stand to climb off as the van smoked against the tree, its hood all caved in.

Leon was already back on his feet, stalking over to the van

and just narrowly avoiding getting shot by the driver, who leaned out the broken window with a Glock 19 in hand. Leon ducked low, his back to the wreckage of the van, then swiftly disarmed the driver through the window.

"Holy shit," Kai muttered, standing beside me to watch the show. There seemed to only be one mercenary in the van, so we really weren't needed. Leon had it handled. Literally handled, as he reached through the broken window and hauled the middle-aged woman out by the front of her cashmere sweater.

Leon threw her down into the dirt, but she was already in bad shape based on the blood pouring from her head and the twisted mess of her left leg. So really, Leon was doing her a mercy when he snapped her neck with one vicious twist. Smart choice, not wasting bullets since we had none to spare.

Kai and I waited by our bikes as Leon patted down the soccer-mom mercenary, taking another Glock 19 from her, then checking the back of the mom van for more weapons. He returned with an AR-15 slung over his shoulder and handed the two Glocks to us.

"Mind if I ride with you, *mon cœur?*" he asked with a grin. "I seem to have lost my bike."

Kai muttered something under his breath about Leon being insane, then climbed back onto his own bike. I tipped my head to Leon, telling him to get on behind me. For one thing, it meant he had his hands free to shoot if anyone else was on our tail, and for another, I liked how he felt against my back.

We got the hell out of the crime scene before some well-meaning cop could stumble past us and end up dead. About twenty minutes later, we pulled over to reassess our plans.

"Any thoughts on how she found us?" Leon mused as we climbed off the bikes. "Do we think someone at the rest stop reported seeing you? Seems... unlikely, doesn't it?"

I grimaced. "Not really. The Guild could have access to any kind of security footage combined with facial recognition software... You know this better than I do."

Leon gave me a long look. "I do. That's why I'm asking the question. The cameras in that diner weren't operational. I checked when I first entered. They were just dummy security, so either a physical person saw you, recognized you, and called in a tip..."

"Or someone we trust has betrayed us," Kai finished that thought with a heavy sigh. "Which isn't a comfortable thought. And not a narrow net, either. My whole team knew where we were and where we were going; Carlos's guys worked on the truck, so could have planted a tracker; Hestia company could have tracked us from the safe house... the list is long."

Leon inclined his head. "Or not long enough. Which then begs the question, where do we go now? If anyone on that list has sold us out, it would be suicide to continue to that same arranged safe house. But the *predictable* thing would be for us to go the opposite direction."

He was right. "So we go in the same direction but pick a motel at random. Regroup there. I believe we can trust Carlos. Maybe not his men, but *him* we can trust. And Carol too." I cast a glance at Kai. I wanted to say we could trust his team, but I wasn't as confident. I just didn't know them well enough to make that assertion. "Good thing I grabbed our bag of cash, huh?"

Kai gave a chuckle. "Very good thing. The fewer bodies we can leave in our wake, the longer we can stay hidden."

"Alright, let's go," I said, giving a slight shiver. I'd put on boots before getting out of the truck earlier, but I was still only in a skirt and thin long-sleeve top, no bra. The cold was starting to set in, so I was glad for Leon's warmth wrapped around me while I drove. "We'll continue toward Shelly Cove."

An hour later, we pulled into the parking lot of a beachside motel called The Pirate's Booty. It wasn't the *worst* motel in the area, but it was far from the best. Shelly Cove was a popular destination for the beautiful beach, so vacancies were low across every property we passed.

I left the boys with the bikes and went into the tiny office to rent us a room using the cash in my bag. I requested just one room, not wanting to split up right now. Not that we had another choice. The bored old lady at reception grunted that the key she handed me was the last room available anyway.

Really, the heart-shaped keyring should have clued me in. I hadn't been paying attention, though, so the gaudy, eighties vibe honeymoon suite that we ended up in was unexpected at best.

"Something you're trying to tell us, DeLuna?" Leon teased, peering at the huge mirror on the ceiling directly above the enormous, circular bed. "Oh, full service kinda accommodation." He picked up a pump bottle of lube from the nightstand and waggled his brows at me.

I wet my lips, trying really hard not to go *Girls Gone Wild* and just live my best life in The Pirate's Booty honeymoon suite.

"It was their only room available," I muttered, defending my room selection. In the corner, a pink heart-shaped bathtub faced out to the ocean view. The view was pretty awesome, I had to admit.

"It's fine," Kai agreed. "I can sleep on this thing, I guess. Seeing as our *kohuru rapeti* is still recovering." He indicated the crushed velvet chaise lounge with some questionable stains.

I cringed as he sat down on one of the stains. Gross.

"I'm going to call Carol," I decided, pulling my phone from the pocket of the hoodie I was wearing. Thank fuck I'd grabbed it when I grabbed the bag of cash, or I'd be doubly annoyed right now. As it was, Leon had lost all that computer equipment, which was less than ideal. Good thing he backed up everything to his own secure cloud server.

"Good idea," Leon said with a long yawn. "I'm just going to lie down for a minute."

Kai watched Leon climb onto the bed fully clothed, then stood up himself to grab some cash out of the bag. "I'll go into town and get us some replacement supplies," he said, kissing me quickly. "I'll be quick."

"Be careful, okay? Maybe put on an American accent or something, so you're less easily identifiable." I quirked a brow, and he grinned back.

"Can do," he agreed, then grabbed the heart-shaped key as he left so I could lock the door behind him.

Leon already seemed to be asleep, so I headed into the attached bathroom for a quick shower to warm the hell up—and wash my cunt—then had to re-dress in my dirty clothes. Ick.

Grabbing a spare blanket from the end of the bed, I made my way out to the balcony—it was enclosed on either end, ensuring it was highly unlikely that I could be randomly seen and identified--and got comfy in one of the sun chairs to call Carol. It really was a nice view, and the late afternoon sun gave the whole beach a nice golden glow. I didn't want to keep Leon awake, either, so I closed the door behind me.

"Danny, perfect timing," Carol said on answering my call. "I have good news for you."

"Thank fuck for that," I muttered, running my fingers through my hair. I winced when I snagged on some knots and silently hoped Kai would pick up a hairbrush for me. "What have you found?"

"You mean *who*," Carol replied, sounding like she was smiling. In the background, I heard Koen calling out for his mom, then the line muffled as Carol probably put her hand over the speaker. I could still hear them, in any case.

"Is that Danny?" Koen asked. "Lemme talk to her!"

"Ko, *go away*," Carol replied, annoyed but affectionate. "She doesn't call just to talk to you."

Koen laughed. "Yes, she does. Gimme the phone, Mom. I want to tell Danny about Carolina's car being stolen."

Carol gave a vexed sound. "She already knows. Now, go *away*. I promise I'll give you the phone when we're done."

The phone line muffled again, then Carol came back to me with a sigh. "Koen wants to talk to you when we're done. I'm sure you've already worked it out, but he idolizes you."

I laughed, all warm and fuzzy about that fact. "So, don't tell him that it was me who stole Carolina's car?"

Carol snorted a laugh. "He most definitely just worked that out for himself. Maybe just don't tell him the *why* of it all. Anyway, back to the important things. Are you safe? How is Leon?"

I breathed a long sigh. She'd stayed in contact through the week that Leon was recovering—Nurse Katie was one of Carol's people. "He's doing great. Tired and weaker than normal, but I think that's normal. He will get stronger every day and otherwise seems to have made a full recovery."

"That's a relief," she replied, sounding genuine. "That must be a huge weight off your mind."

I relaxed into my seat, pulling the blanket up around my legs. "It is. Big time. Now I just need to deal with this kill order, so I can live my happily ever after, just like a Disney Princess."

Carol laughed. "Bullshit. You'll close the kill order, then go straight back to taking contracts, and you know it."

I grinned. "Yeah, exactly. Happily ever after, doing what I do best. Anyway, what's your good news?"

"Blanchet," she replied. "My people tracked him down and got in touch. He's agreed to meet with me in person tomorrow."

Shock made my jaw drop, and words failed me for a hot second. "What?" I finally squeaked. "That sounds like a terrible idea, Carol. He must know about our connection by now, and I need to tell you what *else* we've discovered."

"Well, shit, Danny, don't keep me in suspense," she murmured. "Tell me."

I only hesitated a split second. She had a right to know, just as I did. "We unlocked a file with all the IVF records for Project Remus… and found my file. My biological father is Martin Erikkson. He has fathered *hundreds* of Remus babies."

There was a shocked pause on the phone, and then Carol gave a small laugh that seemed to be edged in disbelief. "Of course he is," she murmured, seemingly to herself. "That actually makes a lot of sense. Fucking Martin. Well, all the more reason for me to take this meeting with Blanchet."

I frowned. "What? No, Carol, he could just be luring you in to—"

"Danny, sweetheart, as much as I *love* that you're worried about my well-being, please don't underestimate me. I might present as non-threatening, but I've been on the Circle for nearly twenty years. Trust me when I say that I can handle myself."

Okay. She probably had a good point there. The number of Guild mercenaries who lived to Carol's age—young as she still was at forty-five—was shockingly low. But when we started killing before our tenth birthday, it was just a matter of probability. Only the very best survived *every* job thrown at them, year after year. I could imagine being on the Circle was even more dangerous.

"I'll be in touch as soon as I've met with him," she assured me. "Hopefully, it can get us some traction in the right direction. Maybe if he knows you're not the only Erikkson heir, he'll give up."

We could only hope. "Sounds too easy," I muttered, "but it can't hurt to try. Are your other children all safe? If someone is trying to kill off Circle lines, you could be a target too."

"Sweet of you to ask," she replied with a sigh. "Yes, they're fine. The twins are in Slovenia for an equestrian camp, neither of them any the wiser about our family business. Bram is still in training with General Landers, but I've increased security around that compound."

I winced, feeling sorry for the half-brother I'd never met. "General Landers is a bastard, Carol. Why would you send him there?"

Her answering laugh was low and warm. "He's a bastard, but he's good at what he does. If Bram is serious about one day taking my seat on the Circle, he needs to be a lot better than he currently is. Perhaps when this kill order is handled, I could ask you to spend some time with him?"

I hadn't expected that, but I also wasn't *against* the idea. "Maybe," I murmured, noncommittal. I'd have to meet Bram… If he was an entitled prick, I would just as soon kill him than teach him.

"Alright, I better go give the phone to Ko," Carol announced. "I'll be in touch tomorrow, though."

"Actually, maybe we should meet in person," I suggested. "I kinda need some more guns… could you hook us up? I feel like I'm draining Kai's resources something awful at the moment, and he still has a business to run."

Carol chuckled. "I'm sure he doesn't mind. But yes, of course. I'll sort it out and text you a time and place."

She went in search of my little brother to give him the phone, and I spent the next hour talking to him about god only knew what. For a pre-teen boy, Koen sure could talk. I was in no hurry to end our call, though. I kept hearing Carol's voice in my head, telling me that Koen idolized me. I'd done nothing to deserve that, but I also didn't want to fuck it up.

While Koen chatted about his school, sports, and what his friend Stell was doing this week, I made myself a silent promise to set a good example for Koen. And to teach the mischievous little shit how to protect himself, because I'd bet anything he got into his fair share of fights at school.

After we ended the call, I headed back inside. The sun had set, and Leon was fast asleep, but Kai wasn't back yet. So I just kicked off my shirt, shoes, and skirt and crawled into bed beside my Bunny.

50
DANNY

Either I was having a very realistic dream, or someone had their hand inside my panties. They were both good options, but I knew which one I preferred, so I was very pleased when I cracked my lids open to find Leon awake and smiling slightly as his fingers gently teased inside my underwear.

I gave a small sigh and rocked my hips, giving him permission to continue. The room was dark, the only light streaming in from the full moon over the ocean.

"Shh," he breathed, his index finger finding my clit and rubbing ever so lightly. "Sasquatch is asleep."

A warmth at my back told me he'd decided the chaise lounge was a crappy option, especially considering how huge the bed was. The fact that he'd chosen to sleep in the bed with Leon and me both made me stupidly happy, and I didn't try to hide my smile from Leon.

"Take them off," Leon whispered in my ear, tugging on my panties.

I did exactly as I was told, lifting my hips and wriggling my panties down my legs as carefully as possible without waking Kai. Just as I kicked them off my feet, Kai gave a deep snore and rolled onto his side, making me laugh silently.

Leon wasn't paying Kai any attention, though, rolling me onto my side to face him and dipping his fingers back down between my thighs now that there was no fabric to hinder his movement. At some stage, he'd taken his jeans off and was just wearing his boxer briefs, the pierced tip of his hard dick poking out of the waistband.

Gasping as he plunged his fingers into me, I tugged on his boxers to free him.

He groaned softly as I wrapped my fingers around his hardness, biting his lip to try and remain quiet. It was too late, though. The mattress rocked as Kai woke up behind me and propped himself up on an elbow.

"Seriously?" he growled in a sleepy voice, peering over at my fingers wrapped around Leon's erection. "I thought we were sleeping."

Leon gave a slightly delirious chuckle. "You can keep sleeping if you want, but I'm much more interested in *this*." He flicked his thumb over my clit, making me moan as my hips rocked forward. "You can join in, if you want. I know DeLuna wouldn't say no… would you, *mon ange*?"

Words failed me. Hell no, I wouldn't complain, but I also didn't want to go pressuring Kai into a three-way that he wasn't ready for. So I just bit my lip and held my breath in anticipation.

The silence that stretched was long. Too long.

"Fuck," Kai muttered, then grabbed my jaw in a forceful grip, turning my head and crushing his lips to mine in a bruising kiss.

I moaned against his mouth, parting my lips to kiss him back deeply while Leon gave a sultry laugh.

"Good choice, Malachi," he murmured, his fingers sliding in and out of my already soaking cunt. His thumb circled my clit, playing with me. My hips rocked, eager for more, and my fingers tightened around his cock, sliding down to the base and back up to the pierced tip.

Kai held my jaw in his grip, taking his time kissing me while Leon toyed with my clit. Then when Kai released my face, Leon captured my lips in a kiss just as sinful and delicious. Oh yeah, I could get used to this.

I was still on my side facing Leon, and Kai shifted slightly to strip out of his own clothes. When he settled back in, his hard dick prodded the small of my back, proving he was more than okay with this scenario. Thank *fuck*.

Leon released my mouth, then shot me a wink before shimmying up to sitting, his back resting on the headboard and his ass on the pillow. "You know what to do, beautiful." He gripped his erection, tapping it on my cheek teasingly, and I licked my lips.

"Careful," Kai muttered. "She'll bite it off if you make her angry."

I grinned but shifted onto my stomach between Leon's spread legs, licking up the length of his cock. "Bunny doesn't mind a little teeth, do you?" Just to prove my point, I took his tip in my mouth, sucking lightly, then scraping my teeth ever so gently across the smooth skin as I withdrew.

Leon grunted and hissed a breath, then threaded his fingers into my hair. "Get on your knees, Danny. Give Kai some better access while I fuck your face."

Who was I to argue when he spoke such sense? Casting a sly look at Kai, I shifted to my knees, arching my back as I bent to take Leon in my mouth properly.

"Fucking hell," Kai whispered, smoothing a strong hand over the curve of my ass as I tugged on Leon's jewelry with my teeth. The hand in my hair pushed me down harder, though, so I took him deeper, sucking on as much as I could fit in my mouth.

Kai's petting hand suddenly smacked my bare ass, and I

jerked, my jaw tightening up ever so slightly before I could catch the reaction. Leon hissed through his teeth as I relaxed my mouth around him again, but I'd definitely given more bite than he might be comfortable with this time.

"Careful," Leon growled at Kai but pushed my head down harder, his studded tip striking the back of my throat.

Kai's response was just a mocking laugh as his thick fingers slid into my pussy, and I moaned. I rocked back onto his hand, encouraging him to give me more, and his thumb searched for my clit.

"Fuck, you do that well," Leon whispered, his hand guiding my head as I bobbed up and down on his cock. "I missed the fuck out of this mouth."

Kai moved on the bed, his warm hands moving my knees wider apart, then his mouth was on my cunt, and I nearly died. His hands gripped my inner thighs, holding me open as his tongue lashed my core, and my whole fucking body trembled with the heady waves of pre-orgasm euphoria.

"You like that, huh?" Leon asked, his voice husky. "Having dickhead eat you out while I fuck your throat? I can feel the way you're shaking right now, *mon cœur*. Are you gonna come on his face?"

Probably.

It was a rhetorical question, because his hips bucked, pushing more of his huge cock down my throat and making my eyes water. There was something about that illusion of danger, the pretense that he could actually choke me with his dick, that got me all worked up and hot. Saliva dripped down his balls as he pushed his way past my already impressive gag reflex, really upping the intensity as Kai added his fingers to the mix.

His tongue stabbed into me while his fingers pinched and rubbed my clit, making it utterly impossible to hold my orgasm at bay. Hell yeah, I came on his face. Hard, too, with my thighs gripping onto him and my hips rocking as I rode the waves.

When the climax started to ebb, Kai peeled himself away. But only to straighten up and reposition. The head of his thick cock pressed into my still tensed pussy, and I moaned.

Leon used his grip on my hair to pull my head up, bringing my face to eye level with his, and he grinned. "I wanna see your face as he enters you."

Panting, I licked my swollen lips as Kai gripped my hips, pulling me back onto him. My internal muscles were still clenching and spasming, but he was relentless. A heavy puff of air escaped my lungs as he sheathed himself entirely within my cunt, and Leon held my gaze with hungry eyes.

"Is this what you wanted, DeLuna?" Leon asked in a sultry whisper, his eyes darting to the mirrored ceiling. Curiosity gripped me, and I couldn't help looking up as well. The image reflected down at us was pure filth, and I gave a small, helpless whimper of delight. "You wanted us both in bed with you, using your body, making you come?"

"Yes," I gasped out as Kai started to thrust into me, his grip on my hips firm and demanding. "Yes, exactly that. This."

I switched my gaze back to Leon, licking my lips as he stroked his cock right in front of my face. I was balancing on my hands, or I would have taken over for him.

"What else, *ātaahua*?" Kai rumbled, grunting lightly as he fucked me in hard slaps of skin against skin. "You want more than this, don't you?"

I swallowed hard, but Leon was watching me close enough that I couldn't bullshit. "Yes..." I moaned the word, already primed and ready to come again.

"Go on, *mon amour*," Leon coaxed. "Tell us what you want, and it's yours."

I believed it, too. He didn't even just mean during sex; he meant *anything*. There was nothing these two would deny me, even if I told them to slaughter an entire nation for my amusement. That feeling of power was intoxicating.

"Both," I gasped out, then moaned as Kai drove deep and paused there. "I want you both. Together."

Leon smirked, because this wasn't news to him. Kai gave a thoughtful hum, then pushed a finger into my cunt alongside his already sizable cock.

"Together in here?" he mused, wiggling a second finger in and making me gasp loudly. "Or..." He pulled those fingers out, then pushed one into my ass. "One here?"

I moaned, rocking back onto his cock and hand. "Either, both, I don't care."

Leon gave Kai a long look over my head, but I was too excited to pay much attention. They clearly needed to have a silent man chat about where their personal boundaries were, so I distracted myself by lowering my mouth back over Leon's dick.

"Shit, Danny," he murmured, but bucked up into my mouth anyway.

A few moments later, they seemed to have come to their decision, because Kai withdrew and climbed off the bed. I gave a sound of protest, but Leon chuckled and manhandled me to turn sideways, still on my hands and knees but facing the side of the bed where Kai stood with cock in hand.

He tossed Leon the bottle of lube that the motel had generously supplied, then stepped closer to offer me his dick to suck. I eagerly swallowed him deep, shivering as Leon squirted cold lube down the crack of my ass.

Kai distracted me, fucking my mouth while Leon carefully prepared my backdoor with his fingers and copious amounts of lube. When he pushed a third finger into me, I spontaneously shuddered with another orgasm. He felt it, giving a deep chuckle and pushing fingers from his other hand into my pussy, pushing me over the edge.

I quaked and moaned obscenely around the thick shaft filling my mouth, then Leon gave my ass cheek a teasing bite as my orgasm ebbed off.

"I reckon she's ready," he commented, amusement threading thickly in his voice.

"Thank fuck," Kai grunted, withdrawing from my mouth with a groan. He climbed back onto the circular bed, positioning himself where Leon had been earlier, his back against the pillows and his glistening erection saluting the porn mirror above us.

Leon gave my butt a swat. "Sit on him, Danny," he ordered. "Facing me. Let him have that lush ass for once."

Kai had a handful of lube now and was slicking it up and down his huge appendage. My breath caught as I sucked it in, but I quickly moved to do as instructed, positioning my legs on either side of his hips and lying back on his chest.

"This mirror should be illegal," Kai commented, glancing up as I shifted my weight to get into the right position. He didn't get distracted for long, though, reaching down to guide the head of his cock to my lubed-up ass.

I gasped as he increased the pressure, arching my back as I tried to force my muscles to open for him. It was an awkward position, but the look of rapture on Leon's face as he watched was well worth it.

"She's tight, bro," Leon muttered to Kai. "You're gonna have to force it."

Oh shit, why did that instantly make me wetter? Because he

told Kai to *force* it? Or because he called Kai *bro?*

Kai kissed the side of my neck, then gripped my hips, holding me firmly in place as he pushed deeper. I cried out, and he hesitated, but Leon was quick to offer encouragement. There was enough lube between us that it wasn't *painful*, just... perfectly uncomfortable.

"Holy shit," I gasped as he pulled out slightly, only to surge back deeper. "Did your dick just get thicker?"

Kai huffed a laugh, his breath warming my skin, then forced the rest of his way in and made me scream a little.

"God damn, that feels amazing," he growled, one of his hands snaking up my front to caress my throat. My muscles burned and ached, but I was also shaking with heady arousal, so my only response was a sensual moan as he started to move, giving shallow thrusts as I lay back on his chest.

"Mind if I join in?" Leon asked with a grin, stroking his cock as he watched hungrily.

He was calling the shots like he was in charge, and a devious little thought wormed through my brain. "Marx, baby," I moaned, reaching out a hand for him.

He responded, leaning down to kiss me deeply as I threaded my fingers into his short hair. Then I pushed him down, my intentions crystal clear. "Make me come again, then you can have my cunt."

Oh good. I shocked him. One of his eyes gave a slight twitch, and his brow dipped with the tiniest of frowns. But right when I thought he was going to deny me, he shrugged and bent forward to lick my pussy.

I jolted, giving a shocked gasp, and Kai's teeth gently sank into my shoulder. "Holy shit, Leon—" I exclaimed in a strangled voice, but he was taking me at my word. His lips closed over my clit, sucking it just like my Purple Pussy Eater, and his fingers shoved into my soaking core.

"Kai, don't stop," I gasped when he paused.

"I can feel his breath on my balls," he complained in my ear, sounding equally turned-on and horrified.

In response, Leon gave a chuckle, then did *something* that made Kai jerk violently. "Marx, I swear, I will castrate you," he snarled, and Leon just grinned up at me in pure mischief.

I rolled my eyes, amused as hell. "Leon, just eat *me* out so I can have your dick again. Leave Kai's balls alone."

"Yes, ma'am," he replied, angelic as a demon, but then delivered me another toe-curling orgasm within less than a minute. He seriously knew his way around my lady garden, that was for damn sure. "Now can I fuck this?" he asked, thrusting two fingers into my pulsing core.

Kai had slowed the hell down when I came, and now seemed to be waiting for this interaction to play out. There was no forgetting he was there, though. He would have me walking funny for *days*.

"Please," I gasped, licking my lips because, holy crap, I was panting hard. Sweat slicked across my brow and along the hard lines of Kai's abs at my back, but this was too good to quit. "Leon, *please.*"

"Well, when you ask so nicely," Leon teased, moving closer on his knees and nudging Kai's thighs wide.

Kai grunted, spreading his legs, which in turn spread me open even more, but it gave Leon the space to maneuver his pierced cock against my pussy. He was still playing with me, though, sliding his tip up and down my throbbing center and watching the way I tensed and shivered when his piercings rubbed my swollen clit.

"Quit fucking around, Marx," Kai barked, his fingers tensing where they rested around my throat still. "I'm losing my grip."

Leon held my gaze, watching me intensely as he pushed into my pussy ever so fucking slowly. My lips parted in a silent cry as my body stretched to accommodate and the intense feeling of fullness choked me. Panic welled up a second later, a small part of my brain screaming that it was all too much.

He saw that moment of indecision—I was sure of it—and pushed deeper, obliterating my worry as he stuffed me full. His mouth crushed against mine, his tongue lashing at mine as he pulled back and pumped forward again.

I trembled and whimpered, turning to fucking jelly between them as they silently found a rhythm. One out, one in... it was hypnotic and overwhelming and made all the worse when I tipped my head back and looked up.

"Oh shit," I gasped, watching Leon's firm backside flex as he thrust in and out of me. My limbs were a pale contrast beneath Leon's tattoos and tanned skin, and splayed across Kai's naturally dark complexion. My white hair was a tangled mess all over the pillows, and my lips were a puffy, red splash on my blushed face. Kai was right, this mirror should be illegal.

Closing my eyes, I moaned and writhed, really exploring the new sensations of having them fuck me together. Kai's heavy hand still rested on my neck, seemingly forgotten as his hips rocked beneath me, his cock sliding in and out of my tight ass with determination. Like he was in some kind of competition with Leon. Shit, they might kill me if this turned truly competitive.

"Kai," I gasped, tipping my head back to gently bite his earlobe. "Big Man... choke me."

Leon's rhythm faltered, but Kai just grunted and licked his lips. A second later, his fingers tightened, and the familiar build of pressure started filling my head.

I moaned, expelling more air from my lungs than I really should, but *shit*, I was in heaven. Maybe next time, I could get them to tie me up while we did this.

Kai squeezed harder, and black spots danced across my vision. Both he and Leon fucked me hard, more ferociously, as I stared up at my reflection, watching with dizzying darkness as my face turned red. Right as my own reflection faded out, the most insanely intense orgasm ripped through my body.

It curled through my limbs, making my muscles spasm and lock. My back arched, my feet cramped, and the scream that tore through me was like something out of an exorcism. Kai and Leon kept going, fucking me with bruising force.

Leon came first, his hot load filling my drenched pussy up and seeping out while Kai kept going in my ass. He finished only a few moments later, shooting deeply inside and gasping curses under his breath.

For the longest time, none of us moved. Neither one of them seemed interested in pulling out of my body, so I reached up and brought Leon's mouth to mine. I took my time kissing him, really exploring the shape of his lips, the taste of his mouth, then released him and did the same to Kai.

"Thank you," I whispered to the big guy beneath me.

Leon took the hint and groaned as he pulled out of my pussy. It took me a second to gain enough strength in my legs to climb off Kai, and even then, I just ended up on all fours as I tried to crawl over the bed.

Both guys gave a groan as I turned my back on them, and I was pretty sure I knew what they were staring at. After all, I could feel the drip.

"I'm going to run that stupid eighties porno bathtub," I told them. "Then we're gonna have a bubble bath together, and you can take turns soaping me up."

I glanced back to find them staring at each other in another one of those silent dude conversations. Then Kai gave a smirk and tipped his head toward me. "I'm in."

"Me too," Leon enthused. "What's the record? Six?"

"Seven," Kai corrected.

I groaned, already second-guessing my life choices.

Ah, shit. Who was I kidding? This was the shit of dreams. Wet ones, that was.

51
LEON

Had I been asked a month ago, would I be okay watching another man shooting his load all over my woman's face? Whoever asked me would have had their throat ripped out just for asking. But now...? Well, let's just say that nearly meeting my maker had shifted my priorities and perspectives in a whole host of ways.

Which is why, rather than putting a bullet in Kai's head as he glazed Danny's face like a Krispy Kreme the next morning, I just grinned and continued rearranging her guts.

Carol had made contact an hour earlier, setting a meeting for this afternoon, but neither Kai nor myself had been willing to let Danny out of bed without at least one more game of naked twister. But now she was getting impatient, so I tweaked her clit with my fingers, making her come *again* while I painted her insides white.

Her phone alarm went off before I could even pull out, and she wriggled out from the middle of the bed. "Time to go, sex addicts," she yelled at us both on her way to the bathroom. "Don't even think about joining me in the shower, or we will be *late*."

Kai gave me a narrow-eyed glance, and I grinned back. "Better not. She hasn't killed anyone in a while."

I'd already showered before falling back into bed with Danny and Kai, so I just gave my dick a quick man-whore bath in the heart-shaped tub before getting dressed. Thanks to Malachi's visit into town, we all had clean clothes to put on, even if my underwear was tighter than I'd have liked.

Otherwise, no complaints. The jeans fit, as did the gray t-shirt and black jacket.

"Kai!" Danny shouted from the bathroom. "Did you get me any panties?"

I glanced over at the smug fuck, who was following my example and washing his dick before getting dressed. "Oh shit, sorry, Siren, I forgot!" The smirk on his face said he did not, in fact, forget.

Silently laughing, I put out my fist and bumped knuckles with him. That was the kind of teamwork I could get behind.

Danny looked less than impressed when she stormed out of the bathroom, though, her hands on her hips. "Fine, where are my panties from yesterday? I'll wash them in the sink."

Kai and I both glanced around, and I spotted the scrap of black fabric just near the edge of the bed where the blankets were falling off.

"Those jeans fit you nicely," Kai commented, crossing over to her and grabbing two handfuls of her ass while I quickly kicked her panties further under the bed where she wouldn't see them. "You don't need underwear, *ātaahua*. You're not wearing a skirt. The only people who will know you're bare under here are the three of us."

"Kai—" she started to protest, but he distracted her further by boosting her legs around his waist and pinning her to the wall as he kissed her breathless. Okay. That made me want to punch him, because I wasn't getting any.

But at least I *only* wanted to punch him. That wasn't life-threatening. Progress.

"We should go," I prompted. "We don't want to keep Mama Atwood waiting." Because she was scary as hell, and I, for one, did not want to get on her bad side. Friends in high places and all that shit. Especially seeing how Danny was warming to the idea of having her in her life. *Our* life.

Not trusting anyone with our travel plans, I'd taken a

stroll in the early morning and had a stroke of good luck when I found a car parked a few blocks back from the beach with a "For Sale" sign in the window. I'd woken the owner up by hammering on her door, then paid twice the asking price in cash.

In fairness, the old bird had no idea how low she'd priced the convertible '62 Studebaker Lark, and I still got it for a steal. Yeah, it needed a bit of restoration work, the turquoise paint was chipped and scratched in places, but I knew the best garage to take it to if it survived this adventure.

She already had a fresh tank of gas, so we were good to go as soon as Danny accepted her lack of underwear.

"Fine," she grumbled, peeling Kai's hands from her ass. "We better be getting coffee on the way, though. You two barely let me fucking sleep an hour straight."

I smirked, sharing a smug look with Kai as we gathered up our few belongings. I could safely say I had underestimated how well we could work together when provided the right incentive.

"Hold up," I said as Kai opened the door to our seedy sex suite. "Phones." I held out my hand and waited.

Danny shrugged and handed hers over. She, like most mercenaries, had her data all backed up so she could easily duplicate it onto any device. Kai frowned and looked less willing, though.

"Hand it over, Big Man," Danny prompted. "Someone sold us

out yesterday. We need to eliminate the question of our phones being traced. Leon will set us up with new ones when we get to the next bigger city."

She knew me so well. Adorable little murderess.

Kai scowled but pulled his phone from his pocket and handed it to me nonetheless. Danny had him firmly around her little finger, and it would be entertaining if I weren't right there with him. Snared.

I took our three phones into the bathroom—where the floor was tiled—and used the heel of my boot to smash them as much as possible. Then dropped the broken devices in the sink and poured three cans of Coke over them.

"Honestly, destroying phones used to be so much easier," I muttered, returning to where Danny and Kai waited near the door. "Remember back when you could just put the whole thing in water, and it would be dead in seconds? Now you have to smash it to ensure the liquid actually reaches the internal mechanics, and *that* is harder than ever thanks to this toughened glass bullshit."

Danny laughed, wrapping her arm around my waist as we left the honeymoon suite. "Good old days, huh, Bunny? Back when phones were fragile and easy to dispose of."

She was teasing, but I knew she knew what I was talking about. Waterproof phones were a pain in the ass. Except, I guess they had their merits when we were forced to take an unexpected swim.

"This is the car you bought?" Kai asked when I stopped in front of the Lark. "I thought we discussed *subtle?*"

I rolled my eyes. "We discussed available for cash sale, which this was. Besides, she's got a V8 engine and can hit some decent speed if necessary."

Kai looked skeptical as fuck, but too damn bad. I popped the tiny trunk and threw our things inside before closing it heavily. "Get in, loser."

Danny snickered a laugh, muttering under her breath, "We're going shopping," then climbed into the small back seat. I'd have rather had her beside me in the front, but I doubted I could deal with listening to Kai complain for the next four hours about the lack of legroom in the back.

A few minutes later, we were driving out of Shelly Cove and headed toward our meeting point with Carol. She had flown to Montreal to meet Blanchet, but we didn't have time to drive across the country. So, to save time, we were meeting her at a private airstrip north of San Francisco so that we could drive there from Shelly Cove. If we timed it right, we should arrive just before her plane landed.

Danny sat in the middle of the bench seat, and as we hit the open road, I reached back to place my hand on her leg. I was addicted to the feeling of her skin against mine, and a small jolt of disappointment ran through me when I touched denim instead.

I took us through a Starbucks drive-thru and let Danny order for me. Then we settled in for what turned out to be a shockingly *pleasant* drive. The weather was nice, which was lucky because I hadn't tested the soft top, and Danny picked up a pair of Hollywood Glam kind of sunglasses when we stopped at a gas station for a pee break.

When we pulled into the deserted airstrip several hours later, we were ahead of schedule. There wasn't a building or tree for miles around—the airport terminal long gone—so there was no way for anyone to sneak up on us or set another ambush. Danny took advantage of the quiet by reclining across the bench seat, her legs hanging over the side of the car, and taking a nap.

Kai glanced over at me, then gave a sigh. "So, I know you like grenade launchers, but what's your gun of choice?"

I squinted at him suspiciously. "Are you... trying to get to know me better?"

He glared back, utterly unimpressed that I was questioning his olive branch. "You licked my balls last night, Marx. I figured maybe we could make an attempt at finding common ground that doesn't involve Danny's cunt."

A mocking laugh rolled out of me at that, remembering the horrified look in his eyes. "Calm down, Sasquatch, I was just messing with you in the moment." I paused, then sighed.

"I don't play favorites with my guns, as I've lost more than I can count, so usually just take basic, anonymous weapons on jobs."

Kai gave a nod but had nothing much to say back. I hadn't really given him anything to work with, considering his business literally was weapons.

"Occasionally, though, if I'm confident it's an easy job, I'll take something with a touch more sentimentality. Like the Beretta M9 that I made my first kill with." Hopefully, that gun was still secure back at my house in Alaska. Not that I could ever go back there permanently... it was a compromised location. I'd need to buy something new. Maybe I could let Danny choose since her house was also compromised.

"How old were you," Kai asked, "when you made that first kill?"

"Eight," I replied, matter of fact. "Same as Danny. Despite being the heir to a Circle seat, my mother didn't ever coddle me. I was trained just like any other lifetime merc."

"Fucking hell," Kai murmured, giving me a look that bordered on pity. "No wonder you're so fucked-up."

That made me laugh. "What about you, *Ares*? What age did you draw first blood?"

His lips twitched in a self-deprecating smile. "Eighteen."

I chuckled and shook my head. "Fucking ancient. No wonder

you're so moralistic. Let me guess, it was within lawful conflict, too?" I didn't need his answer to know I was right. "You're basically a saint, Malachi."

He joined me with a quiet laugh of his own. For the next half hour, we conversed amicably about weapons, torture, and warfare. I'd never in my entire life been able to talk about my interests with someone who understood and wasn't trying to psychoanalyze my level of fucked-up... It was a really strange feeling. Was this what it was like to have a friend?

Right on schedule, Carol's Gulfstream G150 appeared in the distance, descending to land on the empty runway in front of us. I leaned over to gently wake Danny, who yawned and stretched her arms over her head. My angel was wrecked, but I didn't even feel slightly guilty. She'd loved every second of not sleeping last night, just like we had.

"She better have something good for us," Danny grumbled, climbing out of our car—which I'd named Lark—and leaning her butt on the hood. "I'll be *pissed* if this is yet another dead end."

Kai gave her a smile, slinging his arm over her slim shoulders and kissing her hair. "Just think, *ātaahua,* if this wasn't so difficult, you'd be complaining that it all came together too easily and that it must be a trap."

He had a good point. The fact that we *were* hitting so many dead ends gave me hope that we were staying ahead of our enemies.

Danny just grumbled and yawned again.

Carol's plane taxied down the short runway toward us, and I pulled a gun out. Just in case. Kai had his hand on the piece at his lower back, too, clearly thinking the same as I was. If anyone other than Carol Atwood stepped out of that aircraft, they were going to get shot.

It was a tense few minutes as we waited, but Danny let out an audible sigh of relief when the older version of her stepped through the door after the stairs were lowered.

Carol's expression was severe as she descended the stairs and briskly crossed over to us. Two of her men followed but maintained a respectful distance as Carol pulled Danny into a hug.

My woman stiffened at the unfamiliar affection, but after a slight hesitation, she hugged Carol back. It confirmed my suspicions about Danny's softness toward the older woman, and it made me uneasy. My own mother had used her power to abuse me... I hated the thought that Danny could be opening herself to being hurt.

"I'll keep this brief," Carol said, releasing her eldest daughter with a soft smile. "Blanchet is not behind this. He's been a red herring all along. He has had no prior knowledge of Danny, Project Remus... nothing. Your enemy has been hiding behind his name, using his credentials, and he had no clue."

Well, *shit*. What was that Danny had just said about dead ends?

52

DANNY

Carol was joking. Surely. She *had* to be joking. I was on the run from Emmanuel Blanchet... *he* was the one who oversaw my contracts. *He* was the one who sent me on those suicide missions—including the contract to kill Kai—and *he* was the one who'd put out a kill order on me. Wasn't he?

"I don't understand," I confessed, shaking my head in disbelief. "How? Why? What? No, that's not... you said only a member of the Circle could enact a kill order, which means—"

"Which means someone has access to Blanchet's Circle account, his passcodes, probably also his DNA for those random screening tests," Leon finished for me, sounding thoughtful. His brow was pulled in a deep frown as he thought it through, but I was still playing catch up.

"How is that even possible?" I demanded, my gaze flitting between the *two* Circle members on our team. "How the fuck does someone steal a Circle seat's identity?"

Carol grimaced. "It's a major drawback in the whole secrecy shit that the Circle has been running for generations. Our forefathers became *so* paranoid that their competition would kill them, or their heirs, that they started hiding even from one another. Now, in the digital age, it's left a gaping hole in security that *someone* has utilized to their own benefit."

I blinked my disbelief. "Is this a joke? You're the fucking Circle, not a World of Warcraft guild who live in their parents' basements. How the hell is there such a *massive* flaw in your security?"

"This could be a good thing, Siren," Kai spoke up, touching his hand to my elbow to draw my attention. "If Blanchet *now* knows someone is using his access, he can cancel the kill order and kick them out of his system. Right?" That was aimed at Carol and Leon, who exchanged a troubled look.

"Theoretically," Leon murmured, but Carol shook her head.

"For one thing, whoever has taken over Blanchet's identity has locked him out of the account. He can't access any of his Circle control whatsoever, nor can his son, who had been in transition to take Emmanuel's seat when the old man dies." Carol pursed her lips, clearly irritated at the news she was delivered. "And for another, he is a prick of the highest degree and outright said he doesn't give a fuck about the kill order. His only concern is in securing his power, so even if he does regain access, he won't remove the kill order."

My jaw dropped. But then, this was the Circle we were talking about; the callous cruelty shouldn't shock me in the least.

"Okay," I said, trying *really* hard to remain calm. "Okay, this isn't the worst. Now that Blanchet knows, he will be actively working to find this person and kill them. Right? So, this is a good thing." Somehow. This had to be a step forward, or I would *scream*.

Carol inclined her head. "That's true."

"Whoever it is, has to have had access to Blanchet or his son. Someone gave them those access codes, someone handed them the key to the door." Leon paced away from us, thinking it over, then turning back to us. "The son, the one preparing to take over. What do we know about him?"

"We know he has a daughter that he abandoned," I muttered, thinking of cute little Estelle, who thought her parents were both dead.

"I've kept a close eye on Stell; he's made no attempt to contact her. So we have nothing of use regarding Clement," Carol replied. "He's mid-forties, balding, unemployed. As Danny said, he let his father fake his death to protect the Blanchet line. Lives off Daddy's fortune and gambles too hard. He was there at the meeting with Emmanuel and seemed just as shocked to hear someone was using their seat to further their own agenda. Truthfully, Leon, you have the best leverage to force him to take any kind of action."

Leon scowled. "Because his pretender tried to assassinate another Circle member? Sounds like he will shirk responsibility there, and I have no stomach for politics."

"Can either of you access the list?" Kai asked, raising a great point. "When we questioned the archivist, he mentioned there is a list of hierarchy. Families in line to take the next available Circle seat. That should be our focus, surely. Only someone who will benefit from a seat being vacated stands to gain anything."

He was one hundred percent right. I nodded my agreement. "Surely one of you two can access the list."

"Quite the opposite," Carol replied. "We are the last people allowed to look at the list for reasons such as this. If the current Circle knew who was next in line, it would be all too tempting for some of us not to stack the deck."

Leon scoffed. "Doesn't mean we couldn't just break in and take the list."

Carol rolled her eyes. "You think I haven't already tried that? It was the first thing I thought of when *you* became a target, Leon. The archivist isn't *stupid*, though. He doesn't just keep it on display in the library."

Leon threw up his hands in frustration, and a heavy feeling

of defeat settled on my shoulders.

"How long until Erikkson's seat is reassigned?" I asked, trying hard to swallow this bitter pill of disappointment. "How long do I need to keep watching my back?"

Carol grimaced. "A month."

"Shit," I breathed. Then nodded. "Okay. Stay alive for another month."

Leon grimaced, too, shaking his head. "Something tells me that won't be an easy feat."

"I agree," Carol said regretfully. "They will only increase in intensity the closer we get to that vote. We now know that Martin *has* named an heir, but we don't know who it is. Which means that no matter who that person is, unless they are verified as deceased, *they* will inherit the seat. Think of the lengths your enemy has gone to already; they won't take that risk."

Sabine was in trouble, too. And countless other Erikkson progeny who never even knew who their donor was. Because the magical disappearing Circle member had named a damn heir, no one could come forward to claim it until he was dead, or declared dead, and we found out if his heir survived him or not—Circle secrecy with a fine dusting of bullshit.

"We can't wait it out," Kai rumbled. "We need to find them before the month is out, or no one will be left alive."

"Dramatic," Leon muttered. "But true, in a way."

Carol glanced between my two companions, both taller

than her as well, considering she was only slightly taller than me. "Gentlemen, do you mind if I speak with Danny alone? We'll be brief. I need to get back to deal with Koen." She tipped her head to me, indicating for us to move away from the convertible, my guys, and her backup.

For a minute, we just walked in silence side by side, aimlessly wandering down the abandoned runway. It wasn't an uncomfortable silence by any means, but I had so much on my mind that I was becoming impatient.

"What's going on with Ko?" I asked, glancing at Carol.

She smiled. "Nothing out of the ordinary. His suspension is over, so he needs to return to school, and I know my son well enough to know he will cause trouble unless I personally drop him at the front door."

I laughed. That seemed accurate. "So... what did you want to talk about privately?"

She paused, turning to face me with a cryptic expression on her face. Then after a moment, she gave a small sigh and shook her head. "Nothing. It's... never mind. It's none of my business."

Well shit, now I was curious. "What?"

Carol gave me an apologetic smile, glancing back to where Leon and Kai were accepting a trunk full of guns from Carol's guys.

"I'm way overstepping, so I apologize. I just wanted to say that I'm happy for you, Danny. Since I last saw you, things have changed between the three of you. You seem... content."

My brows lifted. Then my cheeks heated. Could she tell what I'd been up to all damn night long? Was I really walking awkwardly? "Um. Thanks? I am. Things were a bit uncertain right when you and I met, but… it was just teething pain. I think."

Carol smiled, reaching out to give my upper arm a little squeeze. "They both adore you. It's written all over their faces. I'm a little envious, to be honest. I've only ever loved one man, and he left me."

I tipped my head, curiosity over Carol's life pricking at me. "I thought you said your husband died?"

She gave a dark chuckle. "He did. But he was just a husband, never a love."

We strolled back toward the plane, and this time Carol looped her arm through mine. I didn't pull away, because it was… nice.

"Can I give you a lift somewhere? That little car looks like it's three miles from a breakdown."

I smiled at the description of our Lark. Leon was already attached to the beaten-up old car, I could tell. "No, we're fine. Thank you, though."

The guys had heard Carol's question as we drew closer, and Kai nodded his agreement. "If we need it, my jet is in Shadow Grove right now."

Carol frowned. "What happened to that truck you were telling me about? The one with beds and everything?"

I gave a groan, combing my fingers through my wild hair. "The kill order happened."

When I said nothing more to explain, and neither Kai nor Leon added any information, Carol gave an understanding nod. "You have a leak," she murmured. "In that case, I'm flattered you trusted me enough to meet in person. It means a lot."

"Don't get all emotional, Atwood," Leon muttered. "It's unprofessional. We should go, *ma moitié*."

He was right. Lingering anywhere too long was risking more attacks. "Thank you for the guns," I told Carol with sincerity. "And the information. I wish your visit with Blanchet had been more fruitful, but I can't say I'm all that shocked."

"I'm not giving up, Danny," she told me with a determined frown. "My people will keep digging, focusing on younger Blanchet. He's my best guess for a security breach, especially with his vices."

The guys murmured polite thanks and climbed back into our Lark. I hesitated awkwardly for a moment, then put my arms around Carol in a stiff hug. It was a start, right?

Carol gave a soft laugh and hugged me back in a *much* more natural way, which only reminded me that she, unlike me, was comfortable offering affection. She was used to hugging her children, while I was an emotionally stunted dumpster fire. Martin Erikkson and Project Remus had a lot of damage to answer for, but there was no use crying over spilled milk now.

I bid her farewell, then climbed over the side of the Lark to take my seat in the back once more. We drove away from the airstrip as the sun started setting, and I glanced back to see

Carol's plane preparing to leave. A pang of anxiety shot through me, and I swallowed the sharp fear of danger.

Carol wasn't vulnerable like Jude had been. I *would* see her again and couldn't let myself think any differently.

"So, what's our plan?" I asked, sliding my sunglasses back onto my face and sitting forward to talk over the wind. "Do we have a plan?" Because I didn't.

Kai and Leon exchanged a long look, like they were already arguing about something. Then Kai clenched his jaw and shifted to look back at me. "The mole," he rumbled. "That's our next lead... which means we need to speak with Mo."

"Question her," Leon corrected, and Kai glared hard at the side of his face.

"*Speak* with her," he reaffirmed. "My sister is *not* our leak. But I will make it clear that we want to see her alone... if you're worried it might be someone else on my team."

A sour feeling of dread curled through my guts. If he was willing to make that admission, then a small part of Kai must also suspect his team. And I hated that for him, especially after Sam had already betrayed his trust. I badly hoped it wasn't them. That the attack yesterday had simply been a lucky break for the assassin who saw us drive past or some shit.

Kai deserved to keep the family he already had. I never wanted to be the one to take that away from him, even if I had taken *him* from them.

53
DANNY

Since we were already in California, we decided to head back toward Shadow Grove to meet up with Moana in person. Kai was utterly determined that *if* the leak came from his team, it wasn't from her. Leon wasn't so sure, though, and it would be easier to get a read on her if we could see her face to face.

Even if Kai didn't want to push her for answers, Leon and I could get the job done. We'd cracked much harder nuts in our time.

After the mess we'd left in our wake last time we'd visited Timberwolf territory, I made sure Kai arranged our meeting with Mo away from the main populace. Funny enough, the area he decided on was intimately familiar.

"Here?" I asked in slight disbelief as he directed Leon to the neighborhood within Shadow Grove that was totally abandoned. Several years ago, a wealthy businessman gambled his fortune on a dirty deal to *rejuvenate* the city of Shadow Grove. He'd built a university, bankrolled mansions, and invested in businesses, but karma had caught up with him for all his sins before he could finish. Meaning there was an entire six-block neighborhood left empty and condemned.

Kai shot me a sly grin as he got out of the car, holding out a hand to help me out. "Why not? The only *innocent* bystanders who could get caught in our mess are already gangsters and drug runners. No one truly innocent ever uses these houses."

I eyed the dilapidated house, remembering Halloween night. When Kai had brought me to this very house, he tried to scare me, then fucked me with his gun on the stairs. Good times.

"Not for long," Leon grunted, slamming his car door and coming to join us on the sidewalk. "I heard Hades has been negotiating an affordable housing development deal with Shadow Grove City Council. By this time next year, this area will look drastically different."

"Good," I murmured. The resurrection of the Timberwolves in their new home had only been a good thing for Shadow Grove. Their leader genuinely *cared* about the locals.

There was a light on in one of the rooms, and I smiled when I remembered how delighted I'd been to find the lights worked when Kai and I had been… playing.

"Looks like she's already here," Leon murmured, pulling his gun.

"Seriously?" Kai growled, glaring at the weapon in his hand.

Leon flicked his eyes to mine, and I shrugged as I pulled my own piece out. One never could be too careful with a worldwide bounty on my head. Technically speaking, I *should* be safer than anywhere while in Shadow Grove since the Timberwolves didn't take kindly to external conflicts in their territory. But I doubted the mercenaries coming for me really gave a shit about local gangs.

Which wasn't shocking. I barely paid attention to their rules when I was in town either. The Guild was a step above, and *we all* carried that edge of elite arrogance.

"My sister isn't selling us out," Kai snapped, clearly pissed off as he stalked up the decaying front stairs and pushed open the front door. "Mo! It's us!"

"Little brother!" she called back, emerging from the room with its lights on and launching a huge hug at Kai. "I missed you!"

Kai hugged her back warmly, and I eyed them curiously. Then someone else moved into view.

Leon and I both snapped our guns up in preternatural synchronicity, and Jae threw his hands up in the air as he froze.

"Whoa, it's just me," he said with a shaky laugh. "Relax, killers."

"So much for Moana coming alone," Leon muttered, not lowering his gun even though I did.

I had to agree, though. Why the fuck was Jae here?

"I know you said to come alone," Mo said, stepping back from Kai's embrace, "but I figured you wouldn't care if Jae came to watch my back. You never can be too careful in an area like this, you know?"

I was tempted to snap at her that *that* was exactly why we wanted her to come alone. But I suspected she already knew that and brought Jae to show us that she didn't take orders from anyone. Gritting my teeth, I held my tongue. This was for Kai to handle, not me. Not yet, anyway.

"We need to talk about the mole," Kai told her, cutting straight to the point. "Have you had any contact with them recently?"

Mo's eyes widened ever so slightly. "The Guild mole? No. Not since they gave us Danny's location in Iceland months ago."

There was something... off with her tone. The glance she flicked at me was colder than usual... When I'd previously interacted with her, I'd thought we were almost friends, but that all seemed to be forgotten now. We were strangers again, and I wasn't sure how that had happened.

Mo's gaze flicked to Leon, and her expression twisted with violent rage, and I understood. She was still consumed by her hatred of the Guild, and my involvement with Leon had become unforgivable.

She wasn't going to tell us anything useful when Leon was standing right there. If we wanted any truth from her, it'd have to be on Kai alone.

I tugged on Leon's arm. "Bunny, put the gun away. Let's give Kai and Mo a minute to talk privately."

Leon reluctantly lowered his weapon and let me lead him further into the house. I flicked on some more lights as we went, because fuck letting someone jump out of the shadows at us, and Jae took the hint to follow along with us.

"So, Danny, you're looking good," Jae commented when we reached the dirty old kitchen.

I stiffened, spinning to face him in disbelief. "Seriously?" I exclaimed. "That's what you're going to open with? Leon was ready to shoot you a moment ago, so... what? You thought you'd take your life in your hands by flirting?"

Jae's brows rose and his gaze darted to Leon, then back to me. "Calm down, girl. I didn't exactly grab your ass and ask you to blow me."

Smack.

Leon's fist slammed into Jae's face, and he staggered backwards, crashing into the wall. Jae was taken so off guard that it took him a hot second to recover. Then he launched at Leon with a roar of anger.

"Oh, for *fuck's sake*," I muttered, watching as the two of them hit the floor. Jae was on top, but Leon was in control, his sharp punches slamming into Jae's ribs with a sickening thud. He would be lucky to walk away without anything broken if—

Crack.

Alright, too late. He definitely had broken ribs now.

"What the hell is going on in here?" Kai roared, stomping into the kitchen like... well, like the God of War. Hot.

I shrugged and put my hands up. "Don't look at me. I tried to warn him."

Kai scowled like he wasn't buying my innocence, then grabbed Jae by the collar and hauled him up off Leon. He needed to physically restrain his team member; meanwhile, my bunny just casually got to his feet and brushed the dirt and dust off his clothes without a care in the world.

"Talk shit like that about Danny again, *Jae*, and I'll mess up your pretty face next time." Leon inspected his knuckles, then seemed satisfied that he hadn't taken any damage.

I leaned back against the cracked laminate counter and eyed the guys. "This might have been a bad idea. Then again, we *did* ask you to come alone." I aimed that at Moana, who was staring wide-eyed at the still furious Jae.

Mo's gaze snapped to me, and her eyes narrowed. "Excuse me for not wanting to get mugged in this shady fucking neighborhood. Why the fuck did you even want to meet? You could have asked this on the phone."

Because we needed to see for ourselves that you're hiding something, Mo.

"We need access to the dark site that your mole uses for contact," Kai told her, ignoring the question. "Log-ins, passwords, whatever."

She frowned. "Why? It changes all the time. They never use the same web address twice."

"How do they send you the location?" I asked, folding my arms.

Mo scowled. "Email. Just a link with a new access code whenever there is something new."

"Then we need access to that, too."

"Screw you, I'm not giving you access to my emails. What the fuck do you think—"

Kai cut her off. "Do you have something to hide, Mo?"

She hesitated, licking her lips. "Of course not. But you won't find anything useful. The pages are erased once I've accessed them. They're dead ends."

Leon gave a cool smile. "No such thing as totally erased, Moana. But why don't you leave that up to us? Just provide the access, then walk the fuck away."

Mo bristled, her lip curling in hatred as she looked at Leon. "How about you—"

"Moana," Kai growled. "This isn't the time or place. Did you forget that Leon's intel gave you the opportunity to save dozens of children recently? I understand your feelings toward the Guild, but you owe *him* a debt for furthering your mission."

Her mouth fell open, and she looked up at Kai in shock. "You mean *our* mission?"

Kai shook his head. "Just give us the details, Mo. You have more work to do using Leon's intel. We're just wasting time here."

Fury burned through her eyes, but the flames seemed to die out after a minute and her shoulders sagged. "Fine. I'll send it through to you."

Kai gave a small sigh. "Thank you, Mo."

She shot another glare at Leon. "Now we're even."

Leon just laughed. "Not even *close*, but I admire your arrogance. Now take your horny guard dog and *fuck off* before I decide to shoot him just for fun."

Jae scowled, but at a sharp look from Kai, he stalked out of the kitchen. A moment later, the front door slammed and Moana gave me a sad look.

"Your inability to choose is going to get my brother killed, you know?" she asked with a bitter twist to her words. "Why can't you just let him go? Your fight with the Guild is nothing to do with us."

Even if I had a good response to that—which I didn't—Kai didn't give me an opportunity to offer it. He grabbed Mo by the elbow and marched her out of the house to follow Jae. They exchanged some words at the door, but I didn't listen as I crossed over to Leon and grabbed his hand in mine.

"You didn't have to do that, Bunny," I scolded, brushing my thumb over his red knuckles. "Jae poses no threat to me."

Leon shrugged, then cupped the back of my head, tilting my face back so he could kiss me deeply. He was in no rush, stealing the breath straight out of my lungs and making me tremble with desire before letting me go.

"I didn't have to," he agreed, his voice husky. "But I wanted to. Kai would have done worse if he'd heard him." His glance over my head was warning, and a moment later, Kai had spun me around to face him.

"True statement," he rumbled, then kissed me himself. "And for the record, no one needs to *choose* here. We're perfect just the way we are. All three of us... even if Murder Rabbit tests my patience every damn day."

Leon gave a dramatic gasp. "*That's* what you've been calling me? Fuck. I like it."

Dammit, I was so in love with both of them it made me sick.

54
KAI

None of us wanted to hang around a city so full of criminals and morally gray citizens, so we didn't bother trying to find accommodation in Shadow Grove. Instead, Danny suggested heading back to Echo Creek, and I agreed. If the past few weeks had proven anything, it was that her pursuers didn't give two shits about collateral damage.

We had stopped earlier to pick up new phones and a laptop for Leon, so we just grabbed food from a drive-thru on the outskirts of Shadow Grove and continued inland toward Echo Creek. It was as safe as we could be, as remote as possible without losing mobile signal for Leon to work on peeling back the layers of that darknet site that Moana had been accessing.

"I don't suppose there's still power in this town?" Leon asked as we rolled into the silent, abandoned main street of Echo Creek.

Danny grinned. "None. Although maybe one of these buildings has a backup generator if you need it for the computer."

"I might," he murmured, looking around. "This place is *creepy*. In the best kind of way. How have I never been here before?"

I shared a knowing grin with Danny, tipping my head to the church where we had *reconciled* after her escape from my island. "This is just a walk down memory lane, huh, Siren?"

"If you two fucked in that awesome old church, I'm going to want a repeat," Leon announced, squinting at the two of us. "Except, you know, me in place of Sasquatch."

Danny grinned, rising up on her toes to kiss him teasingly, then whispered something in his ear.

"Or that," he grunted. "So... where to?"

Danny glanced around, thinking. "Let's check the logical places for a generator. Police station, hospital, library..."

"Good idea," I agreed. "*Kohuru rapeti*, stay here and keep working in case we can't find power."

Leon scowled. "I want to tell you to go to hell... but the battery life on these things is shitty at the best of times. Go find us a generator. If you get distracted inside DeLuna's jeans, I'll cut you."

Danny chuckled, but I was pretty sure he wasn't joking. I mean, it wasn't going to stop me from getting her alone in a dark corner somewhere in this creepy town, but at least I knew what I was in for when we got back.

I popped the trunk of the Lark, handed Danny a loaded M92 from Carol's stash, and took a Heckler & Koch UMP for myself. Carol *also* didn't buy from me, which was irritating, to say the least. We would have to change that.

Admittedly, prior to all of this, I probably would have refused to even meet with anyone who even slightly smelled like Guild. Selling to them would have been laughable. But I never would have known corporate CEO Carol Atwood was Circle, so my irritation stands.

"Are you going to be okay here?" Danny asked Leon as he settled himself back into the passenger seat of our Lark with the laptop open.

He was already sucked into his work, though, and waved a hand to assure us he was *fine*.

Danny shrugged and indicated for me to follow her along the street. The bright moon lit our way, which was convenient. Without it, we would be fumbling around in pitch blackness, thanks to the lack of streetlights or... *any* lights.

"There are always candles in the church," I reminded her

as we headed into the library, which was closest to where we had parked. "If we can't find a generator. It won't help Leon's computer, but it'll give *us* light."

She glanced over at me, the sexy smile on her lips telling me that my suggestion wasn't even slightly subtle. Fuck it, she knew I was crazy about her. There was nothing to hide here.

We both used the flashlight on our phones to light the way as we entered the old Echo Creek library. Shelves were all still lined with books, like the residents had just disappeared one day without taking anything with them. Hopefully, that meant Danny was right about the generator.

"Being this far into the middle of nowhere," she said softly as we made our way to the fire escape stairs, "I would expect many of the businesses would also have generators. High winds and falling trees are a pain in the ass for power outages."

I almost asked how she knew that, but then I remembered her cozy home on the edge of a cliff in Iceland. It was poor form for me to go there and steal Stanley, which was something I needed to apologize for. But at the time, I had been so utterly consumed by my need to find her again, there was nothing I wouldn't have done. And I kept Stanley safe, dressed him up for the holidays... I'd say he enjoyed the vacation.

"Alright, cross your fingers," Danny told me in a dry voice as she twisted the door handle for the maintenance room in the basement. It didn't budge. "Fuck's sake," she groaned. "It's locked, and I have nothing to pick it with."

She frowned at the problem door for a moment, then glanced back at me with that glitter of an idea in her eyes.

"Stand back," she said, giving me a little push so I backed up a few steps. Then she fired three bullets at the door lock, splintering it from the frame. "Now kick," she instructed.

I arched a brow, my ears ringing, but did what she asked and planted my boot in the middle of the door to finish the job her gun had started.

"You could have kicked that," I commented, giving her a side-eye as we entered the maintenance room. "It was barely hanging on by a thread."

She grinned. "I could have. But watching you do it was hot. Oh, look! We're in luck tonight!" She shined her light past me, lighting up an old diesel generator. "Hold the light for me."

After handing me her phone, she pried open the old fuse box and started switching off all the various zones of the library that we *didn't* need to power, so we weren't wasting fuel. If there even was fuel in the tank, that was.

Keeping one phone light aimed at the fuse box for her, I used the other to inspect the generator for a fuel gauge. "Looks like it has maybe a quarter tank already in it," I told Danny. "But how old it is… fuck knows if it'll work."

She shrugged. "One way to find out." She tugged the choke

button out, then gripped the pull cord. Planting a foot against the generator, she ripped the cord out with practiced ease. It took three pulls, but then the generator gave a spluttering rumble as it started up.

Danny's grin widened as the light above us flickered to life, and I swept her up in a hug that lifted her feet from the floor. "Nice work, *kaikohuru iti*. I'm impressed."

She hooked her hand around my neck, pulling me down to kiss her. "I'm very good with my hands, Big Man."

I smirked and kissed her back, resisting the urge to pin her down on this dirty concrete floor and make her scream my name. It took more willpower than I really wanted to admit. "Oh, I know you are," I chuckled, releasing her reluctantly.

"Well, it won't be worth much unless we can get some more diesel, though," she sighed. "Let's go tell Leon that we have power so he can plug in, then go hunting for more fuel."

She looped her arm around my waist, happy to maintain casual contact as we headed back upstairs. It was a small thing, something normal couples took for granted, but it meant the whole fucking world to me. That she had grown so comfortable with me, that she actively sought out those so-called *normal* displays of affection.

"Is that electricity I see?" Leon asked, strolling toward us with his laptop under his arm. We'd barely made it out into the street, so I held the front door open for him to head inside. "Nice work." He palmed Danny's face and kissed her, then continued inside to find a working wall socket for his computer.

"Stay here with him," I suggested to Danny, nodding in Leon's direction. He was setting himself up at the main desk where the librarians would have worked, muttering under his breath. "Maybe see if you can find us somewhere to sleep. I'll find more fuel and be back soon."

She hesitated briefly, but I indicated my guns, then headed back outside before she could fuss. I was more than capable of navigating this ghost town alone, and we would hear another car coming a mile away with how quiet the night was.

The task of finding more diesel wasn't as hard as it seemed. Last time we had passed through Echo Creek, I'd seen a gas station on the other side of town. Based on the way all the other businesses had been left totally abandoned, I took a gamble that they still had fuel in their tanks.

Luckily, my gamble paid off, and half an hour later, I was returning to the library with two full gas cans and a bag full of candles that I'd found in the gas station store.

I was almost surprised *not* to find Danny and Leon in the middle of a quick fuck, but instead, Leon was exactly where he'd been when I left, frowning at the bright screen of his laptop. The only lights on were small reading lamps, which was smart. It saved power and didn't light the whole building up like a beacon.

"Where's Danny?" I asked quietly as I glanced around.

"Sleeping already, I think," he replied, not even looking up from the computer. "Back there, in the kids' section. She said there were pillows." He jerked a thumb over his shoulder.

I decided to deliver my fuel down to the generator, then washed my hands to clean off the diesel stink before going in search of Danny. Sure enough, she was curled up in an adorable ball among a pile of floor cushions. She looked so peaceful I didn't want to disturb her.

Returning to Leon, I glanced over his shoulder to see what he was doing. It was all gibberish to me, in any case. "Making any progress?" I asked, kind of bored. I was too paranoid to sleep, though, so I figured I could stand watch and annoy Leon in the process.

"Yes and no," he murmured. "Your sister lied about hearing from the mole."

My brows shifted up. "What?"

Leon glanced up at me with a *you heard me* look on his face. "She said the last time the mole reached out was to give you Danny's home location, right? Well, that must have been what, early December? Ish?"

I nodded, frowning. Why would Mo lie?

"Well, she did a good job of clearing her cache, but there were at least two more contacts since then. The site itself is proving harder to peel back, but it got me thinking... who knew where Danny lived? Because I looked into it *extensively* and couldn't get a location." He sat back, his fingers linked behind his head as he stared up at me.

I shook my head. "Wouldn't that information be accessible to the Guild? Like... a personnel file or something?"

Leon scoffed. "Fuck no. We're mercenaries, not government agents. Our homes are meant to be *safe* places, which means we carefully guard the location. No way in hell did she register her address on her files with the Guild. However... when I *did* track her down, it was through Carlos's property records. It looks like she has bought and sold the same land to herself several times over the decade she lived there, and most recently, it was one of *his* shell companies that purchased it."

Jesus, was he suggesting Carlos was the traitor? Surely not. I beat the crap out of the guy, and he remained loyal to Danny.

"Carlos cares about her," I said carefully.

Leon shrugged. "Yeah, I can agree on that. But what about the prick who delivered Stanley and bullshitted about Carlos sending him?"

My eye twitched, remembering how broken Danny had been when she thought her friend was dumping her. Also, how *guilty* I'd felt, thinking it was because of what I'd done. "Tito,"

I growled. "Entirely possible, but he wasn't Guild. How would he have all the inside information?"

Leon just arched a brow. "Wasn't he?" He yawned heavily. "Look, I'm falling the fuck asleep here. You mind keeping watch for an hour?"

"An hour? Fucking hell, sleep longer than that, Marx. You're not actually half a machine, no matter how much you like to act like it." I jerked my head toward where Danny had created a cozy nest. "Go. Sleep. I've got this."

I patted the strap of the assault rifle still slung over my shoulder, reminding him that I was more than capable of standing watch. He grunted something in French but didn't hang around to argue my capabilities. I appreciated that from him too. He trusted me.

Damn, we'd come a long way.

Taking my job seriously, I made my way back to the front doors of the library to keep watch. What I thought I was watching, I had no clue. The town was utterly deserted, like something out of an apocalyptic movie. I wasn't on watch for long before I started imagining shit. Movement in the corner of my vision, random shadows moving that turned out to just be my own.

"Fucking hell," I sighed. "Ghost town has me suddenly believing in spirits."

Those words barely passed my lips when something hard

slammed into the side of my head. Blinding pain filled my skull, my vision darkened, and my body crumpled. Then... nothing.

55
DANNY

Something woke me up. My eyes snapped open, and I drew a sharp breath, that familiar sense of danger coursing through me. Leon was curled around me on the pile of dusty library cushions, but he was still breathing steadily with sleep.

But still, *something* had woken me.

I checked the time on my phone, frowning when I saw we'd only been asleep for a little over an hour. No wonder I was all disoriented. That first hour and a half was the deepest I'd ever slept, so when I got jerked out of it, my brain took a second to catch up.

Carefully shifting onto my back, I listened for any sounds that might have woken me. The library was silent, though. Just the low, steady hum from the generator in the basement and nothing else.

"Bunny," I whispered so softly I could barely hear myself.

He heard me, though. His arm over my waist tensed, and his breathing quickened as he surfaced from sleep.

"What is it?" he replied, just as quietly, his lips right over my ear.

I gave a tiny shake of my head to indicate I wasn't sure. "Kai?"

"Door," he replied, shifting his eyes in that direction.

We took another moment to assess our surroundings, then moved slowly and silently to get up and retrieve our weapons. I'd kicked off my shoes before falling asleep, so my steps were silent as I crept back toward the front of the library. Leon's laptop was still plugged in, charging, and a reading lamp was on at the desk.

Kai was nowhere to be seen.

I shot a worried glance at Leon, creeping through the shadows a few paces away from me. He gave me a clueless shrug, though, so I prowled closer to the front door. Maybe he was outside on the street?

My bare foot touched down on something wet. Warm and wet and dark.

Sucking a breath of dread, I peered at the sole of my foot, shining the light of my phone to confirm my sickening suspicion.

"Blood," I said aloud, letting Leon know.

We weren't alone in Echo Creek, and Kai was hurt... at best. I couldn't let myself think about the possibility that he might be dead, but *shit* that was a lot of blood on the library floor.

Swallowing deeply to contain my panic, I shifted out of the open and flicked the safety off my gun. I needed to switch my personal feelings off and treat it as a job. Forget that Kai's blood was all over the floor and just slip into mercenary mode.

Leon had disappeared into the shadows on the other side of the foyer but stepped into the moonlight from the front door just enough to give a few quick hand signals. Instructions on what we needed to do. Split up. Find whoever was in here with us. Kill them.

As carefully as possible, I wiped the blood off my foot on the opposite leg of my jeans. Only an idiot wandered around, leaving bloody footprints for the bad guy to follow.

Leon was closest to the stairs leading down to the generator, so he would go down. I would sweep the ground floor, then go up. There was no doubt in my mind, that our uninvited guest was somewhere in the building. They hadn't come for Kai; they'd come for *me*.

No lights were turned on deeper into the library floor, and I wasn't keen on announcing my location by using my phone. So I let my eyes adjust to the darkness and barely blinked as I slowly, carefully, made my way through the aisles.

I had a nearly full clip in my Beretta, but the spare ammo and guns were out in the car. Leon and I were getting complacent and sloppy, being out of work for so long. Or maybe the dead silence of Echo Creek had lulled us into a false sense of security.

A shadow flitted across the end of the aisle, and I shot without hesitation. Whoever—*whatever*—had caused that movement was too quick, though. As I drew closer, I found my bullet had landed harmlessly in a stack of non-fiction autobiographies by politicians. Phew. Luckily I hadn't shot any real literature like the romance section.

Movement in my peripheral had me spinning around with my gun raised, ready to shoot. But again, there was nothing to shoot at. What the *fuck* was going on? Was this a ghost? Had I gone crazy?

I padded down two more aisles without finding anything. Then a blinding flash of light lit up the windows, coming from outside. A flare? What the hell was going on?

As quickly as possible, I made my way back to the front door of the library and peered through the dirty glass doors. Sure enough, in the middle of the street, a lit flare had been dropped like...

Fuck. Like a diversion.

The air displacement near my head was the only thing that saved me from having my skull cracked open with a metal baseball bat. I ducked just in time, sending my assailant's bat slamming into the window and shattering it. The sound of breaking glass in such silence was almost painfully loud.

I twisted, firing two shots off at the cloaked assailant, but the bright light from the flare caused spots across my vision when I turned to the darkness. I missed, and they were gone like a fucking wisp of fog.

This wasn't right. Something… something was delaying my reaction time, more than just sleep haze or light flare. There was no possible way for an assailant to be *that* quick, and I knew I wasn't imagining it, because the shattered glass of the doors served as evidence.

Stepping carefully to avoid the broken glass, I got the hell away from the light to try and… think. Plan. Because right now, it felt like I was fighting a ghost, and there was no winning that. Ducking low behind some study tables, I checked my ammo. Then peered around and waited for the blind spots in my vision to fade. It took too fucking long, but I no longer had the confidence to go after this guy—or girl—blind. They were too quick.

Leon would have heard my shots, so he was probably already back up here looking for me. He wasn't dumb enough to announce his location by calling out, though, so I just needed to be careful not to accidentally shoot him.

After what felt like a year, my vision returned to normal, and I slipped out of my hiding place. Sinking my headspace back into mercenary mode, I blended with the darkness as I slipped past each row of bookshelves, searching for our assailant. Or… assailants? It was entirely possible we were dealing with more than one person; that could explain how they seemed to be so quick.

As I moved to clear the fifth aisle, a whisper quiet sound of clothing moving gave me the microsecond warning that I needed to avoid getting stabbed. This time, my eyes had adjusted to the darkness, and I didn't let my attacker go so easily. I dodged the stab but grabbed their wrist before they could retract.

He was bigger than me, but that was nothing new. With my height and weight disadvantage in nearly every combat situation, I had to lean on my elevated *skill* instead. So I acted on my lifetime of training as I twisted and pulled, forcing his center of gravity to shift off-balance.

He sailed over my curled back with a slight grunt, hitting the library floor with a thud as I brought my gun up to shoot. Whoever he was, he was highly trained, though. His foot snapped out from his vulnerable position, kicking my wrist in just the right place to send the weapon flying out of my grip.

Fuck.

He'd retained the knife, and now I was unarmed. Quick as I could, I scanned him from head to toe, searching for a weakness or *anything* that could be used to my advantage. He was head to toe in black tactical gear, complete with a hood and a mask that covered his mouth and nose. The only part of his body showing was his dark eyes, which gave nothing away.

Not sticking around for a chat, he launched at me, going for my legs. I darted out of reach, but it didn't take long for him to close the gap and catch up. I muffled a grunt as his knife slashed the denim on the back of my leg, and I tripped when his hand caught my other foot in mid-step. Keeping my body loose, I hit the carpet well, instantly rolling to fight off the advancing attacker.

Once again, he was moving faster than he should. Or I was moving slower. One of the two. But it was unquestionably giving him the advantage as we grappled, rolling around on the carpet as I fought to keep his blade away from my flesh.

Eventually, I sank my teeth into his gloved hand, making his fingers spasm just enough to drop the weapon, and I used my elbow to push it out of reach.

Unfortunately for me, hand to hand, we were far from evenly matched. I landed blow after blow as we wrestled, but none seemed to deliver any kind of real pain. Worse still, the disguised bastard seemed to be Guild-trained. Of course he was. There was a kill order out on my head. Anyone catching up to us now wouldn't be some half-rate idiot that fancied himself a killer.

Some moments later, he got a lucky break as I tried a sloppy chokehold. He turned the tables, twisting around me like a black-cloaked snake. The next thing I knew, he had me in an arm lock submission where the only way out was to break my wrist.

So that's what I did.

The pain ricocheted through my arm, making me cry out as I slithered free of my attacker's hold, but I was too slow. Too sluggish. His elbow met my temple, and I went crashing into the closest bookshelf.

56
LEON

The sound of breaking glass followed by two gunshots had me racing back up the stairs to the ground floor where I'd left Danny, but before I exited the stairwell, I spotted a bloody handprint on the railing leading *up*.

Pausing a moment, I waited to listen for more conflict. But everything was silent. Dead silent.

Making a decision, I continued up to the next floor, following the occasional drops of blood on the concrete stairs. If Danny had shot someone, this could be them trying to escape and regroup. Better to catch them unawares if it was.

Or, worst case, if it were Danny that was bleeding, I needed to help her. With that in mind, I raced up the rest of the stairs to the upper floor and pushed through the heavy fire door that showed some bloody finger marks.

As soon as I stepped through the door, I noticed the air smelled different, and it made me stiffen with shock and worry. *This* floor smelled like dust and stale air. It smelled like you'd expect a library to smell and like how the ground floor *had* smelled when we *arrived*. But the fact that I *noticed* the difference in smell now seemed to suggest that the scent downstairs was different... and dread rolled through me.

Muffled thumps below me jerked my attention, and I abandoned the blood trail. Someone was definitely still downstairs.

This time, when I raced down the stairs, I yanked off my t-shirt and tied it around my face as a filter. And I paid better attention as I slipped through the door to the ground floor of the library.

Somewhere deeper into the stacks, Danny gave a cry of pain, then more muffled thumps followed, and I hauled ass in the direction her voice had come from. Now that I was aware, I could taste the slight sweetness of the air. Someone had been pumping gas into the library... and that gave me chills of memory.

Prisoners had recently been released from the Castle...

there was a kill order out on Danny... but I only knew of one former executioner who used a gas like this. It was designed to dull the senses, just subtly slowing reaction times and making it appear as if he were moving supernaturally fast.

He called himself The Sandman, and I was the one who'd put him in the Castle.

"*Le-on*," a disembodied voice sang out, echoing through the dark library. "I've got your girl."

Fear coursed through me, unlike anything I'd ever experienced. The last time I'd taken on The Sandman, I had nothing to lose. I was there on a contract and simply did my job, just like any other. I'd been lucky to come away with my life on that encounter, but this time? I had everything to lose. I had Danny... and if *he* had her...

Shit. This was bad. *Really* bad.

"Leave her," I called back, stalking carefully and slowly through the library floor. His voice had been bouncing around, so I was going in the direction I'd heard Danny cry out. "Your score is with me, Sanders, not her."

His laugh seemed to come from five different directions, and I strained my ears to pinpoint the right one. "My score with *you* is exactly why I can't let her go, Marx. You know that."

I groaned inwardly, cursing the past version of me. Because I knew there was no sense in begging for Danny's safety... not when I'd killed Sandman's sister in my pursuit of him.

"Stop hiding, you coward," I snarled instead. "Or are you still too scared to face me without the games?"

His laughter was the only response, but I had a feeling I knew where to find the unhinged motherfucker. So I ignored the distraction of his laugh bouncing around the room and made my way back to the children's section. Sure enough, there he was, still tying Danny to a heavy wooden chair dragged over from the study area. The few small lamps we had turned on lit the space with a dramatic glow, casting long shadows.

"Uh-uh," he warned, bringing a blade to DeLuna's throat as I raised my gun. "I wouldn't if I were you. That t-shirt won't be filtering all the gas out. Your aim might be off... what if you shot your girlfriend?"

I swallowed hard. He was right. I didn't lower my gun, though. I just didn't fire. Yet.

"What do you want, Sanders?" I demanded, keeping my breathing shallow through the makeshift mask I'd created. "I'd have thought you'd have taken your second chance at freedom and disappeared. Yet here you are, doing the Guild's dirty work."

His laugh sent chills through me, because it didn't touch his eyes at all. "Is that what I'm doing? The Guild wants this pretty princess dead." He gripped Danny's jaw with his gloved hand, raising her face up toward me. She was unconscious, blood dripping from her eyebrow, but she was alive. "And they're willing to let a deranged serial killer like *me* out of the Castle to get the job done. Yet she's still alive... for now. So, am I doing what they want, Marx? Or am I getting revenge?"

To drive his point home, he sliced his blade down the side of Danny's neck from ear to collarbone. A deep red line of blood welled up, flooding me with panic and blinding rage. It was an unfamiliar sensation for me, genuinely fearing for someone else's well-being.

"So kill me and be done with it," I told Sanders, desperately trying not to react to the sight of Danny's blood. She moaned in pain as she slowly regained consciousness, and I choked back the desire to reassure her.

Sanders laughed. "Kill you? Now, why would I do a thing like that? I said I wanted revenge... and you didn't kill *me*, did you?"

"No," I murmured my response with the acid of regret burning my throat. "I put you in the Castle instead. Under orders from the Circle, because someone thought you might come in handy one day. Today, apparently."

Sanders's eyes narrowed at me from his position behind his DeLuna shield. Coward.

"You condemned me to eight years of *torture*," he corrected, then punctuated his point by dragging his blade down Danny's breastbone, stopping only when he reached the collar of her top. She moaned again. This time her dark lashes fluttered, and she squinted over at me.

"Shoot him," she mumbled, her voice slow. From the hit to the head? Or the gas that she'd been breathing. It was hard to tell. But either way, it wasn't good. We needed to end this soon, or Sanders would just wait it out and let the gas do its work. Then, when he had me incapacitated like he had Danny, not even my wildest delusions could guess what sort of torture he'd put her through... purely to hurt me.

I would never let it get to that point. Not now, with Sanders, not ever.

But I also wouldn't risk shooting Danny with sloppy aim. I needed to draw Sanders out from behind her. I started to shift to the side, intending to ease around behind him.

"Don't fucking move, Marx," he snarled, pulling a second knife and stabbing it straight through the back of Danny's hand where it lay flat on the arm of the chair.

I sucked a sharp breath, my whole body tensing as fury choked me wordless. Danny was utterly awe-inspiring, though. She winced, giving a small grunt of pain. But otherwise gave Sanders no satisfaction of a reaction.

"Marx," she growled, "I told you to *shoot him*."

"Hush, *mon cœur*, I have this handled."

I did not. I absolutely had no clue how in the *fuck* I would best

The Sandman for a second time. The first had been a stroke of dumb luck. Another executioner had also been hunting him, and between the two of us, we'd captured Sanders in a tiger cage. Of all the fucking things. And I didn't see any tiger cages around the library.

This guy... this was one of the few targets I'd ever lost sleep over. I knew I should have killed him when I had the chance, and now I was living to regret that choice. Fucking hell, this was what I got for blindly following my poisonous mother's orders all those years ago. Shit, it had been her idea to kidnap and mutilate Sander's sister to draw him out. Sick bitch that she was.

My mother, I meant. Not Sander's sister. *She* had been a sweet girl who didn't deserve anything done to her.

"Face it, Marx," he sneered, still crouched behind Danny where I couldn't get a clear shot at him. "You let your guard down, and now I'm going to carve the last eight years of torture from Danny DeLuna's flesh. Won't that be fun?"

He wrenched Danny's head back, exposing her bloodied throat, and her eyes rolled like she was fighting off the haze of unconsciousness.

She whispered something, but it was too quiet to make out. Sanders frowned, though.

"What'd you say?" He licked her cheek. "Speak up, princess."

"Kai," she croaked, flicking her gaze to me with intent.

I frowned, shaking my head to show I didn't understand. She was the one who'd stepped in his blood to start with.

"Your military watchdog?" Sanders asked, thinking she was talking to him. "Dead. Caved his head in with one smack of my bat. Dropped like a sack of rocks, too."

Well, fuck. Hearing Kai was dead actually hurt. I didn't expect that, but evidently, the big moron had grown on me. Like mold.

Danny, though? She started laughing. Shock must be setting in; it was the only explanation.

The gas was slowly starting to affect me, because Sanders moved far too fast when he cut her again. He sliced across her ribs this time, cutting through her top and spilling more of my heart's blood.

Fuck it, I needed to take the chance to shoot him. I couldn't just stand there like a helpless asshole while he cut her up.

Right as I made that decision, the shadows warped and swelled, the darkness becoming sentient as it surged toward Sanders and Danny both. Fear shot through me, and a wordless shout escaped my lungs. I fired. It was the first time in my *life* that I'd fired a gun without knowing what I was shooting at.

Sanders hit the floor heavily, the shadows smothering him, and Danny bucked against her bonds. Her chair tipped to the side, and I strode closer, firing two shots into Sanders's head the moment I had a clear line past the shadows.

Fuck. Not shadows. Kai.

Kai just saved our love, and I shot him for it.

Fuck. Not shadows. Kai.

Kai just saved our love, and I shot him for it.

57

DANNY

It all happened so damn fast. I saw Kai lurking in the shadows behind a display of books about unicorns pooping rainbows. I tried to give Leon the heads-up, then... what the hell happened next? My chair tipped, and I whacked my head again. Not so hard, this time, but enough to disorient me.

Leon crouched down, using Sanders's bloody knife to cut the zip ties holding me to the chair. He said something to me as he gripped the knife still protruding from my hand, but the rush of my own pulse was creating too much static to hear.

It was likely a warning, though, because in the next breath, he had yanked the knife out. Searing pain rippled up my arm, and I ground my teeth together hard to choke back a scream.

"Gas," I gasped out, my ears ringing so loudly I couldn't hear myself.

Leon helped me to my feet, and I cradled my broken, bleeding wrist to my chest. The masked executioner—or ex-executioner, I guess—was dead on the floor, a dark puddle of blood spreading across the carpet. On top of him, was another body.

"Kai," I gasped out, horrified.

Leon gave me a firm push toward the exit. "Outside," he mouthed clearly and firmly. "Now." He pushed me again, and I staggered with indecision. But Leon turned his back on me, stooping down to lift Kai's lifeless form. He wouldn't leave him here.

That hope boosted me, and I hauled ass out of the library, barely even noticing the broken glass under my bare feet as I lurched out into the night.

Clean air filled my lungs with painful gasps, and I sagged to the pavement as Leon carried Kai out with him. He'd tied his t-shirt over his face to filter the gas that Sanders had been pumping into the library; something that'd been made clear while fighting Sanders. I'd punched him in the face and realized his mask was a filtered gas mask, not just a dramatic costume.

"Kai," I gasped, staggering over to where Leon was placing the big guy down gently on the pavement. "Is he okay?"

Leon grimaced, checking Kai over with professional touches. "Yeah, I think so. I, um, I shot him, though." He flicked a guilty look at me when he said that, and I bit my tongue to keep from yelling. "It's just a flesh wound, though." Then I could have sworn I heard him mutter *thank fuck* under his breath as he used his t-shirt to apply pressure to Kai's upper arm.

The big man groaned, flinching from the pain, and his long lashes fluttered. "What the fuck, bro?" he mumbled, almost incoherent.

"Leon shot you," I offered, because I was pissed about that fact, even while I was mostly relieved Kai was alive. "But I'm more concerned with your head." He was drenched in blood; all over his scalp, neck, shoulders... I could imagine Sanders genuinely thought he was dead and had left him to bleed out on the floor, creating that puddle I'd stepped in.

Kai hissed a breath through his teeth as I gently probed his skull with my left hand. To my shock, it all seemed in one piece. Just a long gash in his scalp that provided all that blood.

"He said you were dead," Leon said, shifting to sit on the pavement while keeping pressure on Kai's arm. "Should have known you wouldn't die that easily. Was that your blood I was following upstairs?"

Kai huffed a laugh. "Yeah, I needed to clear my head—no pun intended—and get away from the gas while I worked out what the *fuck* to do. He underestimated how thick my skull is, I think."

Leon's shoulders started shaking, and for a panic-filled moment, I thought he was having a seizure. Then I realized he was *laughing*… at Kai's joke. Wow.

"We need to get out of here," I told them. "Kai needs stitches, and I don't want to risk hanging around in case that bastard has friends."

Leon winced. "He doesn't. No one would be insane enough to align with The Sandman. But I agree on getting out of here. Check if the Lark is okay?" He tipped his head to me, and I scrambled to my feet. I hurt all over from the fight, and my various cuts were dripping blood freely. The worst damage was to my right hand, though. The wrist was broken, and fuck only knew what damage had been done with that knife piercing through my palm.

"Looks fine!" I shouted back to Leon as I approached the Lark. "Wait while I check for bombs, though." Because *that* would be a shitty twist. Survive one of the Guild Boogeymen only to get blown up in a car bomb. How embarrassing.

Lark was small, though, so it was quick enough to check her over while Leon covered his face and sprinted back inside to retrieve our few belongings—most importantly, the bag of cash. When I was satisfied the car hadn't been tampered with, I gave them a left-handed thumbs up.

Leon half-carried Kai as they staggered over to the car, and I popped open the passenger side door so he could drop Kai straight into the seat.

"Shit, this blood is going to stain," Leon complained as Kai sagged into the seat with a groan. "Suppose it needed a deep clean anyway."

He circled around to the driver's seat, then gave me a sharp look as I closed Kai's door and awkwardly climbed over into the back without moving my right arm more than necessary.

"*Ma moitié,* is that broken?"

I just nodded back, fumbling for my seat belt. Harder than it might seem, left-handed.

Leon muttered some curses under his breath but leaned over to buckle me in. Then he buckled Kai in, too, because the big guy was holding pressure on his gunshot wound.

"Where are we going?" Leon asked, starting the car up.

"Dogwood," I told him, letting out a long, pained breath as I relaxed incrementally into the seat. The cut down my neck throbbed, the one along my breastbone merely stung, but the one across my ribs felt deeper. My stomach was wet and sticky, and I didn't want to take a look. "Vega owes me, and we need medical supplies."

It was also the closest town to Echo Creek.

None of us seemed in any mood to chat as we drove back down the mountains toward Dogwood, but every five minutes or so, Leon would give Kai a gentle prod to keep him awake or simply ask a pointless question.

He was taking care of Kai, and I loved the hell out of him for it. Because I kept zoning out as I pushed all my pain aside and mentally debriefed myself on what'd just happened. It was something I needed to do out loud with both guys, but for now, I needed to go through my process and analyze my own mistakes objectively.

Leon set a good pace, and we arrived in Dogwood right before dawn. Vega—leader of the Dogwood Death Squad—would be asleep. But too fucking bad. Leon drove us right up to his house—clearly, I wasn't the only one who researched the Shadow Grove region gangs and players—and leaned over to help with my seat belt.

"Wait with Kai," I told him with a grunt, climbing out of the Lark. "Just in case." Because one of Vega's men had come for me once before.

Leon handed me a gun, and I thanked my own ambidextrous shooting ability as I held it in my left hand.

Vega lived in a nice house. Not a mansion like some gang leaders I knew, but it was far from low-income housing. There were no security gates or anything, though. I walked straight up to the front door and hammered on the wood with the butt of my gun.

I waited impatiently for a few minutes—okay, probably thirty seconds at best—then banged on the door again.

Heavy footsteps sounded on the stairs, then a moment later, the door jerked open and a shotgun stared me in the face.

"What the fuck—" Vega snarled, then must have realized who was waking him up and lowered the gun. "Oh shit. You look—"

"Fucking terrible," I grimaced. "I know. You still fucking that filthy ER surgeon from Rainybanks?"

Vega and I had shared a few vodkas when I was in town last year. He'd been chatty. Real chatty.

"Maryanne," he corrected. "Yeah, I am." He glanced over his shoulder, and I breathed a sigh of relief. She must be here, in bed. Thank fuck.

I nodded. "Good. Go wake her up. I'll get my friends." Vega shook his head, protesting, and I glared daggers. "You *owe* me, Vega."

"You stole my Stingray," he accused, "and got it written off."

I shrugged. "Shit happens. But your man tried to kill me, and that's worth more than a car. Go wake your girlfriend up, and we can be out of your house in no time."

Not waiting for his response, I hurried my ass back out to the street where the guys waited, giving Leon a wave to bring Kai up. I tried to offer my help, but they both waved me off like I was insulting them.

Back inside Vega's house, a beautiful Asian woman was yawning as she hurried down the main staircase, tying a silk robe over her skimpy pajamas. Vega trailed after her, carrying what looked to be a medical supply bag.

"Come through here," she ordered as we crossed through the foyer, following her into the large open plan kitchen with stainless steel counters. "I'm Maryanne." She flashed me a smile, her eye contact confident. I liked that.

"I'm Danny," I introduced myself, then nodded to the guys. "Leon and Kai... who has been shot."

Maryanne was all business, giving a curt nod and clearing off the stainless island. "Two seconds," she murmured, grabbing a bottle of isopropyl alcohol from under the sink and using some paper towels to sterilize the whole surface. "Up here," she ordered Kai while pulling on a pair of latex gloves.

Leon helped him up onto the counter, and Maryanne directed him to lie down so she could access him easily from her standing height. She peeled Leon's wadded-up t-shirt away from Kai's arm and poked around for a minute before nodding to herself.

"Vinnie, pass me a roll of gauze," she ordered, holding out a hand to Vega.

I quirked a brow at him, resisting the urge to tease him because his girlfriend was currently patching up one of my loves. Maryanne quickly, and tightly, bound the bandage around Kai's arm, then moved around the counter to inspect his head.

"I can stitch up the arm in a minute," she told him in a

distracted mutter. "A flesh wound like that won't kill you. I'm more concerned with this."

Kai remained stoic, his jaw clenched while Maryanne poked and prodded. Part of me suspected that he was clutching his man-card so Leon wouldn't think he was weak, but hell, maybe he could compartmentalize pain like I could.

"Vinnie, baby?" Maryanne said after a few moments.

He shot me a glare before responding to her. "Yes, possum? What do you need?"

Okay, this time, I snickered a little.

"Coffee," Maryanne replied. "For our guests, too. And orange juice, too."

Vega scowled but didn't protest. He just moved over to the coffee pot and started doing what he was told. Good for him. Maryanne seemed like a catch. And I really wanted that coffee now that she'd mentioned it. I was swaying slightly on my feet, and Leon must have noticed. He looped an arm around my waist, gently nudging me to sit down in one of the dining chairs.

"Do you want painkillers?" he asked softly, crouching down beside where I sat to examine my neck.

"Hmm? Oh. No, I'm fine. Just looking forward to that coffee."

He gave me a worried frown but smoothed my hair back and kissed my forehead reassuringly. "I'm so sorry, DeLuna," he whispered.

"Hey, Leon," Maryanne called out. "I need an extra pair of hands over here. Wash your mitts and put some gloves on."

He kissed my hair, then went to do what Maryanne instructed. I just sagged in my chair, putting my gun down on the table. I zoned out a little, slipping back into the planning space inside my head. One thing was for fucking sure, we couldn't keep going like this. Not for another month... especially now that we were injured.

"Danny, do you want cream and sugar?" Vega called out, and I mumbled my affirmation. A moment later, he delivered the coffee in front of me, then plonked down orange juice beside it.

He put out coffee for Maryanne and Leon, then returned to sit opposite me with his own mug. For a long time, he just stared across the table at me, then broke eye contact to sip his hot beverage.

"Someone came at you pretty hard, huh?"

I snorted a little laugh. "Gee, what gave it away?"

Vega glared back at me, but I didn't flinch as I sipped my coffee. It was awful but better than no coffee at all, so I didn't complain.

"I take it they're dead now," he said, not rising to my childish bait.

"Very," Leon confirmed, holding some supplies for Maryanne. "Like he should have been eight years ago when I had the chance. Like he *would* have been if someone on the Circle hadn't thought

The Sandman might be broken into her personal puppet."

The bitter twist to his lips told me that he was speaking about his mother. It was a very specific look he got when thinking of her.

Vega grunted with surprise. "The Sandman? I thought he was a myth. Like a boogeyman made up to scare wannabe gangsters." None of us responded to that, and he let out a low whistle. "No wonder you're all fucked up. I need to call this in... we're supposed to be staying out of Guild business right now."

He gave me a slightly apologetic look. Or was it nervous?

I just gave a weak shrug, knowing who he would call it in to. They would look the other way.

"Run down to the bakery and pick up some pastries for breakfast, Vinnie," Maryanne ordered. "This one lost a lot of blood, he needs sugar. And I'm hungry."

Vega scowled, shaking his head. "I'm not leaving you alone, Mar."

I rolled my eyes. "Cool your jets, Vinnie. We won't hurt your girlfriend."

Maryanne was finishing up on Kai's head and pursed her lips as she glared across at her partner. "Vinnie. Go. They always have the freshest pastries at this time. Do you like apricot Danish?" she asked that question to Leon, who nodded.

"If they have those snail things with sultanas, get me one of those," Kai told Vega with a smirk. "They're the best."

Vega glared at all of us a moment, then grumbled complaints under his breath as he slouched out of the kitchen. A moment later, the garage door clanked as it opened, and a motorcycle rumbled out into the street.

"Thank you, Maryanne," I said with a yawn as the sound of Vega's bike faded. "We really appreciate this."

She glanced over at me with a frown, her gaze flicking down to my wrist where I cradled it. "I need to call for a portable X-ray machine," she announced, checking the time on her watch and frowning. "My friend can probably drop one over. Give me a second." She stripped off her gloves and grabbed her phone from the pocket of her robe.

A couple of steps away from Kai, she paused and turned back to address Leon. "Help him sit up to drink some orange juice. I'll be back to sort out his arm in a moment."

Rather than leaving the room, Maryanne just moved into the dining area and put her phone on speaker while she called her friend. She very clearly instructed her friend to drop off the equipment on the front porch, then leave, and I appreciated how she was putting our paranoia at ease. This was a woman who'd patched up more than one criminal in her time.

"Right then," she announced after ending her call. "Where were we?"

"Right then," she announced after ending her call. "Where were we?"

58
DANNY

Maryanne made quick work of cleaning up Kai's arm, then got him set up on the sofa with a sedative to help him rest. Then she moved on to my cuts. She cleaned and patched them while waiting for the portable X-ray machine to arrive. When the doorbell rang, she gave me a reassuring smile.

"I'll be right back. Vinnie will be back any minute now, too."

I gave her a tight smile. "Good. You really sold those pastries. Now I'm starving."

She laughed as she went to fetch the machine from her

front porch, then returned to set it up on the dining table. It only took a few minutes to prepare, and I finished my coffee while waiting.

"You must be in a lot of pain," Maryanne commented when I winced as she guided my arm into position. "But you handle it well. Any tips?"

"Meditation," I replied, holding still as she took the X-rays. I knew my wrist was broken, but she needed to see *how* it was broken in order to set it. The last thing I needed was for it to heal badly and impact my ability to shoot.

Her brows arched over the machine at me. "Seriously?"

I smiled. "No. But decades of practice dulls the sensation. How does it look?" Maryanne was inspecting the images on the digital display, eliminating the need to wait for physical prints.

She shrugged. "Looks broken, but we already knew that. But nothing seems horribly out of place in the break, so I can set that without needing to pull it into place, thank fuck. My concern would be how that wound will heal..." She trailed off like she was mostly talking to herself. "This needs to be thoroughly washed, assessed, and closed, ideally in a sterile environment."

I just blinked at her, and she sighed.

"In a hospital, Danny. But I'm guessing if you came here, then you won't go there?" She gave me a hard look, and I just nodded. Her lips pursed as she thought, then she cleared her throat. "Alright, I'll do my best here, but so we're clear, I won't accept *any* responsibility if this gets infected or heals badly. It's my *professional* advice that you should go to a hospital."

I smiled, appreciating her no-bullshit attitude. "Understood."

She shook her head with a heavy sigh. Then turned to her bag to pull out a couple of painkillers, dropping them into my palm. "Non-negotiable, Danny. This is going to hurt like a bitch, even with those in your system."

I sighed and did as I was told, washing the pills down as Vega's motorcycle rumbled back into the garage. At least breakfast was here to accompany what sounded like a whole lot of fun to fix my hand.

"Give me a minute to sterilize the bathroom sink," Maryanne murmured. "Best we do the wash out in there. I should have enough saline, I think." She hurried down the hall, and I waited patiently with my arm flat on the table.

Vega slouched back into the room with a cardboard box in hand. He peered over at Kai, asleep on the couch, then looked at the X-ray machine set up on the table. "Looks fun," he muttered, pulling out a plate for the food. "Is that the muscle that saved my bar a few months ago?" He indicated to Kai, and I smiled at the memory.

"Yeah, he dragged me out of there before I could break too

many tables."

Vega huffed. "Suppose I owe him, then. Here." He placed the plate of assorted pastries on the table. Leon helpfully handed me one to eat while we waited for Maryanne to summon me into the bathroom.

"Damn, these are good," I mumbled around the food.

"So, now what's your plan?" Vega asked, eyeing us with a frown as Maryanne returned to the room, peeling off another pair of gloves.

Leon scoffed. "Like we're sharing that with you."

I kicked him under the table. "What Leon means is that we respect Hades's desire to stay clear of Guild business. While we appreciate your assistance, Maryanne, *greatly*... we will be on our way when you're done patching me up."

Vega's eyes narrowed. I could tell he wanted to argue, but his hands were tied. He'd clearly been told to keep his nose out of whatever trouble we were in, so a moment later, he pushed his chair back and stalked out of the room. Not before swiping one of the pastries for himself, though.

"Don't worry about him," Maryanne murmured, giving us a warm smile. "He doesn't like being excluded from things. But I still have a lot to do on that hand, and you need to rest before you go anywhere."

Leon shook his head. "We need to keep moving. If The Sandman found us, I dread to think who will be next."

Kai gave a loud snore from the couch, and Maryanne arched a brow. "I don't think you have a choice, unless you have a bigger vehicle than that cute convertible out in front."

"Fucking hell," Leon groaned, throwing his hands up.

Maryanne smiled at me, gesturing that I follow her. "Come on, Danny. Let's see how far that pain tolerance will hold up."

She wasn't joking. Washing out that wound through the middle of my hand with copious amounts of saline—and I mean a small ocean worth of the salty acid—tested me. Next time Kai's team needed to torture someone, they should take tips from Maryanne.

"We're almost done," she reassured me as she led me back to her sterile work surface to take a better look at the wound. "Do you need a break?" Glancing up at me, she gave a chuckle. "Of course not, silly me. Leon, could you sort us out with some fresh coffee?"

I smiled at that. "Maybe don't ask him. He only just started *drinking* it recently. I don't think he would know how to make it."

Leon apparently took offense to that, though, shooting me a narrow-eyed glare. "I can figure it out, thank you. I'm not just a pretty face."

Maryanne stitched up both sides of my hand with quick, neat stitches, working with the smooth confidence of practice. It made me all kinds of glad that we'd come here instead of trying to attempt our own first aid. My stitching was nowhere *near* that tidy, and I probably wouldn't have done anything more than douse the wound in vodka.

She applied a dressing over my stitches, then set up to plaster my broken wrist.

"You'll need to take this off in a week or so to remove those stitches and check how it's all healing," she murmured as she worked methodically, wrapping my wrist with gentle touches. "I can do that for you if you're in the area. Or you can see someone else, but just don't forget."

I bit the inside of my cheek to hold back my cynical suggestion that I'd be lucky to still be alive in a week. But she didn't need to hear about that, and Leon was worried enough without me showing I was losing hope. He was pacing the kitchen while waiting for the coffee to brew, and a deep line furrowed his brow.

He was beating himself up over The Sandman, I could tell. He thought it was his fault, when in reality, it was his bad blood with Sanders that had *saved* me. Without that animosity and Sanders's desire for revenge, I'd have simply been dead. So, really, I needed to thank him. I'd take a few cuts and a broken wrist over being *dead* any day.

The room was silent as Maryanne worked on my plaster cast. Then when she was finished, she went to check on Kai, who was snoring softly.

"Alright. I think my work here is done for now," she announced, then pushed the plate of remaining pastries closer to where I sat, inviting me to eat more. "Leon, come with me. You need a shower and a shirt. I'll get you one of Vinnie's."

"Go," I told him, helping myself to Kai's *pain aux raisin*—or sultana snail as he called it, which was so cute—since he was asleep. "We're fine here."

Leon's brow furrowed with worry. "But for how long?"

I couldn't answer that, and he didn't expect me to. He followed Maryanne out of the room, and I groaned as I stood up to pour my mug of coffee that Leon had started. The cut on my ribs had needed stitches, the others just glue and dressings. My hand was the worst, throbbing where it was stitched, but it was nothing I couldn't survive.

"He's taking a shower down the hall in the guest room," Maryanne told me, returning to the kitchen fully dressed herself and carrying another stack of clothes. "Clean clothes for you, too, if you want them. You can't get the dressings wet, but I have no doubt you'll manage. I need to go and convince Vinnie that he can go to work without worrying you will kill me while he's gone."

I snickered a laugh, leaning against the counter. "Old school gang leaders are so paranoid. I promise we will be out of your hair the second Kai wakes up."

She gave me a nod, then left the room. Her soft footsteps sounded on the stairs, heading up, and I gulped my coffee. Kai needed rest, but I needed a plan.

When Leon returned from his shower sometime later, looking fresh as a fucking daisy compared to how rough Kai and I were, I was pacing the kitchen with my mug in hand.

"You look like you've been plotting," he murmured, looping his arms around my waist and kissing my hair.

I tipped my head back to give him my lips. "I have. Give me five minutes to wash up, and I'll tell you what I think our plan needs to be."

Leon's brow dipped. "*Needs* to be? That sounds ominous."

It was. But I needed to clean some of the dried blood off my skin and put on a clean shirt before I could fully focus on the planning aspect of what came next. So I handed Leon what was left of my coffee and made my way to the guest bathroom to clean up without wetting my cast.

Maryanne was small like me, so her long-sleeve top and V-neck sweater fit me well. I still had my own blood-splattered jeans on—with no panties *still*, dammit—and my bra was damp from the wash I'd given it in the sink. But I felt a million times better when I headed back out to the kitchen-dining area where Leon was on his phone.

He ended the call as I approached, turning to gather me up

in his arms but being ever so careful of my injuries. "DeLuna, *mon cœur*, I can't even begin to apologize. This is all—"

"Martin Erikkson's fault," I finished for him, ignoring the fact he was trying to accept blame for a situation that technically I had put him in. "I totally agree. If that prick wasn't playing stupid games with naming his successor, we wouldn't be in this mess. If I ever get my hands on him, I intend to make him pay. But for now… we need to discuss next steps."

Leon released me, indicating that I sit. Which was good, I needed to sit. Fucking hell, I was all dizzy and crap. Maybe I could do with a nap after all.

"What are you thinking?" he asked, studying my face intently.

Kai gave a moan from the couch, and I glanced over to see his eyes cracked open. "What's going on?" he slurred, trying to sit up.

Leon went to help him, and I relocated to the couch beside him. It felt better discussing this with both of them, even if Kai was still groggy. To stitch up his head, Maryanne had needed to shave a thick strip out of his already short hair, which just made the injury stand out more prominently. It'd be a badass scar when it healed, and I was still shocked that his skull hadn't been cracked.

"We were just talking next steps," I told him, leaning into his embrace as he wrapped his good arm over my shoulders. "The Sandman was one of the prisoners released from the Castle, right?"

Leon nodded. "Yes, one of a dozen. And unfortunately, not even the worst of them."

Kai grunted an angry sound. "Why the fuck anyone thought it was a good idea to imprison and torture *already* deranged killers…"

"You can thank my mother for that idea," Leon muttered. "Marx seat has quite the sadistic legacy on the Circle."

I swallowed hard. Leon was only confirming what I already suspected. "We barely made it out of that library alive," I said softly. "Three of us against *one* merc… and we nearly died. For once in my life, I need to admit when I'm in over my head. And right now? We're *way* over our heads. The Sandman didn't kill us, but he has made it a whole *shit* load easier for the next guy." I held up my casted wrist, which would take a good six weeks to heal.

"What are you suggesting, *taku aroha*?" Kai rumbled, his lips brushing my shoulder where the sweater had slipped down.

Drawing a deep breath, I ignored the anxiety and dread curling through me. "We need to stop running," I told them softly. "We need to stop *reacting* and start taking matters into our own hands."

Neither one of them spoke, but I got the feeling they knew what I was about to say. Or, shit, maybe not. But it didn't change the fact that this was our *best* chance of survival right now.

"This won't stop for us until I'm dead. So... you need to kill me."

"This won't stop for us until I'm dead. So... you need to kill me."

59
KAI

My gut reaction was to disagree. Firmly and fervently disagree with Danny's suggestion that our only course of action was to *kill her*. But I'd learned a thing or two about how her brain worked over the past four months, so I bit my tongue and forced myself to *listen*.

Leon was already on the same page as her, their strategic minds ticking over in such similar ways, and he nodded thoughtfully.

"Kill you to collect the kill order bounty," he murmured. "That would draw out whoever is hiding behind the curtain. After everything you've put them through, they'll want to confirm the kill themselves and not trust photos that could be so easily manipulated."

Danny leaned into me, soothing me with her warmth. "We'd need to know the exact parameters of the confirmation. Where, how…"

"Wait," I exclaimed, unable to bite my tongue any longer. "Can someone explain how we plan on killing Danny without *killing* Danny? I thought you were talking about a bit of Photoshop and fake blood, but—"

"That won't be enough," Leon commented, pacing the carpet in front of the couch while he thought it over. "If it were me, I'd be asking for physical proof. Either a body or a head."

"A *head*?" I exclaimed, my whole body rejecting that idea with a physical shudder.

Danny snorted a laugh, despite this not being anywhere even close to funny. "I think a body will be easier. Unless we could get our hands on a really realistic prosthetic head that looked like me on short notice?"

Leon genuinely seemed to consider it, then sighed. "Not short notice. My guy would need months to get it realistic enough to pass kill order inspection."

"So, we need to deliver me… dead. Of course, we still need to work out where the inspection point would be, then come up with a plan for how to kill whoever reveals themselves as the Wizard of Oz when we get there." Danny tipped her head back, resting against my chest, and it took all my willpower not to wrap her up in my arms and carry her back to my island.

We could hide there. We could wait it out... the place was a fortress. With enough weapons, we could hold off a siege for months. I didn't suggest it, though, because I already knew what their response would be. What the Guild's response would be. If they had us trapped, cornered on my island, they'd just drop a bomb on it from an airstrike.

"How exactly do you plan on appearing *dead*?" I rumbled, barely containing my hatred of this plan. She knew what she was doing, though. So did Leon. They wouldn't even be entertaining this if they didn't think it could work.

A small cough interrupted our conversation, and Maryanne stepped into the room. "I apologize for listening in. Blame it on curiosity. But I think I can help with that problem... if you'd let me?"

Leon scowled, distrust written all over his face, but Danny straightened up to give Maryanne a chance to explain.

"You know how to simulate death?" Danny asked with a slightly feral grin. "I knew I liked you."

Maryanne gave a laugh. "Of course. But more than that, if you'll extend an element of trust to Vinnie, he can reach out for the details of the hit on you. It might be a lot less suspicious than if one of your lovers asks around, don't you think?"

Now that she said it like that, she had a good point. I looked over at Leon, and he met my gaze with that shrewd, plotting look in his eye. Then he switched his gaze to Danny and gave her a slight nod of understanding.

"We're listening."

Maryanne shook her head. "*You*, I can plan this out with. My patients need rest." She crossed to a cupboard and pulled out pillows and blankets. "Please, *rest*. You're safe here for the day, and I'll need some time to get the drugs you need anyway. Leon can help me on logistics, seeing as he seems totally unscathed from whatever messed you two up. But you both need to *sleep*. Understood?"

Danny started to protest, but a yawn interrupted her sentence, and I swallowed back my own desire to argue. She needed to rest, which meant *I* needed to rest. No way in hell would she stay here and sleep if both Leon and I were off making plans to kill her together.

"Understood, Doc," I rumbled, tugging Danny closer.

She started to tell me to get fucked, so I gently put my hand over her mouth to muffle the complaints while giving Leon a *now or never, dickhead* kind of glare.

Thankfully, he was smart enough to understand and quickly disappeared out of the room with Maryanne to talk murder, drugs, and a kill order bounty.

"Big Man, if you hadn't nearly died last night, I'd punch you in the nuts," Danny snarled when I removed my hand from her mouth.

I smiled, tugging her head back so I could kiss her lips. She moaned into my kiss, and the fight drained out of her between heartbeats. That's how exhausted she really was. Planning her fake death could wait, or Leon could run point for just a few hours. Our girl needed to press pause.

Gently, I eased off the couch and coaxed her to lie. Then I grabbed one of the pillows and blankets Maryanne had set out, tucking Danny in and kissing her softly.

"Sleep, *kaikohuru iti*. I'll be right here beside you." I grabbed the second pillow and blanket, making a bed for myself right there on the floor in front of the couch.

She gave me a sleepy smile, cradling her casted arm to her chest as she got comfy and her eyelids drooped. "What about..." Her words mumbled, and I didn't catch what she said. But whatever it was, it could wait.

"Sleep," I told her again, stroking her hair. "Leon will keep us safe."

I meant it, too. A year ago, if someone had told me I was trusting a member of the Guild Circle to *keep me safe*... to keep the woman I *loved* safe? I'd have laughed so hard I peed myself. Then punched the person who asked right in the face. With a grenade.

Now? Now, I sat there on the floor, stroking Danny's hair until she fell asleep, then lay down without a fraction of hesitation in my mind. Leon *would* protect us. Both of us. Even if he did shoot me.

Two days later, we were thirty thousand feet above the Atlantic, enroute to deliver Danny's "dead" body to whoever was masquerading as Emmanuel Blanchet. We were all nervous, even if none of us were willing to admit it out loud. The amount of trust our plan required us to place in others sat like a lead weight over our shoulders.

Not the least of which had been the decision to use one of Carol Atwood's private jets to transport us between countries without the red tape of customs and immigration. Not that the three of us didn't have our own work-arounds for that inconvenience, but Carol's was a step above.

And her jet was better suited to long-haul travel.

"How confident are we in Carol's trustworthiness?" I muttered to Leon when Danny went to the bathroom. "We could be flying into yet another ambush."

Leon looked up from his computer, taking my concern seriously. "I'm more confident in Carol than I am in your team, Malachi. Or even mine for the time being. She's had countless opportunities to kill Danny herself or have someone else do it if she wanted to keep her hands clean. But she hasn't. Quite the opposite, she's gone out of her way to *help,* and that in itself is a rare thing for anyone on the Circle."

I scowled. "So shouldn't that make you *more* suspicious of her motives? What is she gaining out of all of this, Marx? Despite the face she likes to show the world, Carol Atwood is no Martha Stewart."

Leon cracked a grin. "Nah, Carol's too smart to go to jail. Look, I get what you're saying, and I agree, to a point. But after all the digging I've done and purely based on gut instinct, I think Carol only wants one thing out of all this... and yes, I believe it's important enough to throw all her considerable assets into helping us."

Shaking my head, I studied his face for any sign of deception. He'd withheld information from me before, but this didn't seem like one of those times. "What's that?" I asked. "What does she want, worth all this?"

"A relationship with her daughter," he replied softly. The sincerity was unmistakable in his eyes, and it made me uneasy. "Her oldest daughter, that she never knew existed, who can actually relate to Carol's *real* life. When I see her with DeLuna, I don't see a manipulative shrew plotting to further her own power and reach. I see an older version of Danny... one silently grieving for lost opportunities and trying to make amends." He cleared his throat and turned his attention back to the laptop in front of him, like he was done with the conversation.

I mulled over his opinion for a few minutes in silence, then studied Leon more closely. "Your mother was the manipulative shrew, wasn't she?"

He didn't look up, just sighed. "The worst type. Not a day goes past that I'm not glad I slit her throat. Now, even more so than ever, because she can't get her poisonous claws into DeLuna. Dr. Marx was the very definition of the Circle that you hate so much, Malachi. All that and more."

I winced, feeling sorry for Leon. That was an emotion I'd never anticipated feeling toward my girlfriend's other boyfriend. My boyfriend-in-law? Ick.

Whatever I might have responded evaporated out of my brain as the woman at the center of *both* our universes exited the jet's luxurious bathroom wearing... nothing.

"Um." I gulped a breath as she met my eyes with a smirk. Well... the only things she wore were her wrist cast and the dressing over her sliced ribs. That was it.

"What?" Leon asked, glancing back up from his computer. His back was to Danny, and he had no idea she was standing there totally naked with a clear invitation written all over her face.

She licked her lips, then winked and turned to head toward the back of the plane. To where there was a full queen-sized bed tucked into a private cabin. Oh. Hell. Yes.

Danny disappeared into the cabin, and I scrambled to get out of my seat, almost forgetting to unbuckle my safety belt. Leon squinted at me like I was having a fit, but fuck him. *You snooze, you lose, sucker.*

Totally ignoring Leon's question about my sanity, I all but ran down the aisle of the jet and slipped into the little cabin. Danny was waiting, wearing nothing but a grin, splayed out across the bed like an offering to the gods.

"You know what I was thinking we should do before I die?" she asked in a sultry voice, watching as I awkwardly tugged my shirt over my bandaged arm.

I grinned back at her, unbuckling my pants. "Tell me."

"Get a platinum membership to the Mile-High Club," she replied, her casted arm resting on the pillows above her head. Her left hand cupped her breast, playing with her own nipple. "I think a filthy three-way should secure that, though."

I kicked my pants aside, climbing onto the bed and closing my lips over her other nipple. "I'm yours to command, *taku aroha*."

Now… and always. Nothing would change that, not even her impending death.

60
DANNY

Words failed me as Kai sank his thick cock into me, an incoherent moan escaping my throat instead. He'd already worked me up so much with his mouth that I was soaking, but he was big, so it took a hot second for my muscles to adjust.

Not that he was being patient. He grabbed one of the pillows and tucked it under my ass, bringing me up to an angle that was all kinds of amazing for *both* of us, especially given the limitations of our injuries. My wrist was fine, so long as I didn't do something stupid like whack it on stuff, but the wound in my hand ached painfully, and the stitches across my ribs itched.

As for Kai, his arm was bandaged where Maryanne had stitched his gunshot wound, and his head was sporting a seriously badass line of stitches. So, as much as I wanted to get up to all kinds of crazy shit in this aircraft bed... we needed to be careful.

"Yes," I moaned, as Kai lifted my hips higher, then added a second pillow—they were admittedly pretty flat to start with—and drilled into me deeper. "Fuck me, Big Man. Fill me up."

"Hello..." Leon drawled, slipping into the little cabin and closing the door behind him. "What do we have here, hmm?"

Kai gave a dark chuckle under his breath, thrusting into me so hard I was seeing stars. "Our girl wants to get double-teamed at thirty thousand feet, and I sure as hell won't tell her no. You bring any lube?"

Leon gave a scoff, already stripping out of his clothes. "Did I bring lube," he muttered under his breath as he tossed a bottle of my asshole's best friend onto the mattress. "Do I look like I'm stupid? Honestly. I don't go anywhere without that now."

His wink at me was pure filth, and I dragged my lip through my teeth, panting hard as my tits bounced with Kai's thrusts.

"Bunny, you gonna come closer so I can suck that pretty dick of yours?"

Kai laughed. "See? She asks so nicely."

Leon stroked himself, eyeing our position and giving our injuries calculating looks. Then he climbed onto the bed and straddled my chest, holding his weight up on his knees.

"Open up, beautiful. I'll do all the work." He prodded my lips with his pierced tip, and I flicked my tongue over his slit before opening wide. He pushed in just a shallow thrust, letting me get used to the angle for a minute. I sucked on his spongy head and ran my tongue across the tight band connecting to his shaft. Then he was pushing deeper, and I sucked a deep breath through my nose.

Kai slowed his motions while Leon fucked my face, and I was crazy curious to know if he was just distracted while watching.

Leon popped out of my mouth a few moments later, though, and he looked down at me with a thoughtful expression as I licked around his piercings.

"Are you feeling adventurous today, DeLuna?"

I grinned back. "Always."

He chuckled and climbed off. "Make her come, Sasquatch."

Kai grunted and slammed back into me harder again, his thumb finding my clit like a magnet. Leon grabbed the bottle of lube and squeezed some into his hand, then stroked it down his cock. He shot me a smirk as Kai drove me up to the precipice of orgasm, then lifted my left hand and wrapped it around his lubed cock.

The pleasure knotted up in my belly, my legs tensing up as Kai pushed me harder, and I stroked Leon in time with the thrusts in and out of my pussy.

My whole body quaked as I came, my toes curling into the bed and my hips lifting higher while Kai remained buried deep, riding it out. Then before I was even done coming, Leon was giving directions to switch things up.

Flutters of orgasm aftershocks still quivered through me as I sank back down on Kai's shaft, this time with him on his back and me riding his fat cock.

"That's it," Leon purred, still casually jerking his own cock as he watched us reposition. "Lean forward, baby, get that arm comfortable in the pillows." His hand on my lower back pushed me into the position he wanted, with my tits pressed into Kai's hard, tattooed chest.

Kai's hands gripped my cheeks, spreading me wide as Leon drizzled lube down my crack. "You okay, Siren?" he rumbled, kissing my throat. He was asking for my injuries, not the sex. The sex was *always* okay in my book.

"Uh-huh," I groaned, rocking back as Leon slicked the lube around.

"How wet is our girl?" Leon asked, positioning his knees on either side of Kai's legs. "Soaking?"

Kai just grunted as I rolled my hips, rising and falling in small movements, keeping him deep.

Leon gave a soft chuckle. "I know you're straighter than a fucking arrow, Malachi, so just shut your eyes and roll with this, alright?"

My eyes widened, and I sucked a breath as I realized what Leon meant. He pushed two fingers into my pussy alongside Kai's thick cock, and a strangled cry escaped me. Briefly, a little voice in my head panicked that this wasn't possible; they'd tear me in half. But then my sensible logic kicked in, reminding me that women were capable of squeezing whole formed humans out of there. And the average circumference of a baby's head was nearly fourteen inches.

My boys had big dicks, but even combined, they weren't going to have a fourteen-inch circumference. We'd be just fine. Great, even. The female body was fucking amazing.

"Shit," Kai muttered, so I kissed him. *Hush, Kai, I want to try this.*

Leon used his fingers for a few moments, making Kai jerk and shift beneath me. Then the tip of his pierced cock was right there, *pushing*.

"Oh my god," I gasped against Kai's mouth. "Fuck, *fuuuuck*. Leon!"

"Relax, baby," he grunted, holding my hip firmly. "You can do it. Tell us how it feels."

I gave a pained moan, but the ache was already warming into

intense pleasure. "It feels like I kinda wish you two had thinner dicks."

Kai laughed, kissing my throat. "Don't lie."

"Leon..." I moaned, trying to relax my cunt as he pushed deeper.

He was taking his sweet fucking time, though. Probably admiring the view and wishing he'd grabbed his phone to record it. "So pretty, DeLuna," he purred, his fingers flexing on my hip. "You take us both so well. Your pussy was made for this, wasn't it?"

A wordless mumble escaped me as trembles of pleasure and pain rolled through me, turning me to jelly. Kai was still gripping my cheeks, his fingers digging into my flesh, and his lips were at my throat. Fuck, he was probably going to leave a hickey at this rate, but maybe it was distracting him from the fact he was rubbing dicks with Leon right now.

Shit. That image was *hot*.

"Are you gonna come for us like this, baby?" Leon asked, his breathing rough as he pushed in the rest of the way. I was so fucking full of cock I couldn't speak. Holy *shit*. Luckily, Leon didn't seem to need an answer. He gave a few shallow thrusts deep inside me, like he was reminding my pussy to stay open like that.

"Shit's sake," Kai growled. "Can I move now, or what? This is like the worst test of patience—"

"Yes!" I gasped. "Yes, *fuck*, move! Fuck me, both of you, just..." The rest of that trailed off as Kai found my mouth again. He kissed me deeply as he started to move, fucking me in alternating strikes with Leon. It meant I was constantly full, and it was almost embarrassing how easily I came. Wetness slicked between us, and it only spurred the guys on.

Leon shifted his grip, pausing his thrusts while buried deep. "Keep going, Kai," he ordered, circling his index finger over my asshole. "Yeah, just like that. Get rough, she can take it. Can't you, *mon ange*? You love taking it." He pushed his finger into my ass as Kai fucked me harder from beneath. Fucked *both* of us, technically, since Leon's dick was right in there with him, feeling every thrust and slide.

I cried out, rocking between them, and Leon added another finger. He fucked my ass with his hand while Kai punished my over-full pussy, and I shattered again. Holy shit, I was going to pass out soon if we kept going like this.

"Shit, I'm gonna come," Kai grunted. He only lasted another three strokes, and then he erupted inside me. His cock twitched, and cum flooded my pussy, and Leon gave a startled laugh.

"Okay, that was different," he muttered. Then he started his hips moving again, fucking my pussy hard—with Kai still buried inside—and kept pace with his fingers in my ass. He finished with a grunt a few moments later. Then I spontaneously came again as their combined seed dripped out between us.

It was filthy but so fucking hot. This was how every long-haul flight should be.

Leon waited out my orgasm before sliding out, then went to grab a wet towel from the bathroom as I rolled off Kai. My legs were too weak to hold my weight; I could already tell. So I just lay there like a rag doll while Leon cleaned me up—as much as one could with a wet towel.

"We should discuss our plan," Kai said, reclining on the bed, totally unconcerned with his nudity. *I mean, fair call.* He'd essentially just fucked both of us, so...

Leon nodded. "I agree. We need to get our plan tight. Failsafe. If it's not..." He shook his head, frowning at me. "It needs to be tight."

I gave him a lazy, sex-soaked smile. "How tight?"

His answering gaze was so hot I was almost sweating. Maybe we weren't finished making the most of this bed after all.

Oh. We *definitely* weren't finished. Leon took that hint of flirtation and ran with it, sinking down to his knees beside the bed and hooking my legs over his shoulders. I gave a yelp of surprise as he dragged me closer, slamming my pussy against his face.

"I love flying," I moaned, threading my good hand into his hair and lying back to enjoy getting eaten out at thirty-thousand feet.

61
LEON

The waiting was the worst part of the plan for me. In order for me to slip into the meeting site unnoticed, I needed to get there well *before* the appointed time. It meant that while Danny and Kai were getting ready to finally end this era of our adventure, I was stuck in my hiding place. While Kai administered the drug cocktail that Maryanne had provided us, the drugs that would slow Danny's heart rate so dramatically it would simulate death, I was sitting with the crows in the rafters of the ancient building.

I hated it. I hated waiting, hated not knowing what was going on, hated feeling *useless*. I wasn't, though. I was the one with the drugs to bring Danny *back* to life, and for our plan to work, I needed to remain undetected until after her "death" was confirmed.

But still, I hated it. What if Kai fucked up the drugs somehow? What if Danny reacted to the mixture and died for real? I wouldn't *be there*.

Getting angry about it wouldn't do much now. I'd been becoming one with the crows for hours already. Kai should be arriving in an hour, which probably meant the *other* side would be putting their people in place any minute now. Or they should be, if they had any common sense when dealing with mercenaries and killers.

When Vega had sent us the location for the handover, my team had visited in person to examine every inch of the building. It was an old church, because *of course it was*, in a small village near the French Riviera. The town itself had a new church built sometime within the last century that the parishioners used. This one was a relic from the past, crumbling and decaying. The perfect location for this kind of meeting.

As bitter as the pill was to swallow, we'd ultimately decided Kai was the right one to deliver Danny's body. He was *Ares*, the infamous arms dealer and boogeyman of the Guild. He'd already gained a reputation for killing any mercenaries sent after him, so this wasn't such a stretch to think he'd killed Danny. After all, it was what I'd feared when she got assigned his case all those months ago.

To the best of our knowledge, Ares hadn't been linked to Danny since she accepted and completed her contract on him months ago. We'd have to cross our fingers and hope no one on the bad-guy side had worked out that Ares was Kai, who was crazy in love with Danny DeLuna.

On top of that, I'd kicked up a fuss when I put Danny under a protective order. No way in hell would anyone believe I flipped on that now. And as we didn't trust anyone else... Kai simply had to sell it.

As expected, a half dozen mercenaries turned up a few minutes later. They performed their due diligence in sweeping the church for traps, bombs, and hiding assailants... but they never looked up into the rafters. Fucking amateurs. That told me a lot... if it were a Circle member behind this whole farce, they'd have brought more experienced backup.

They finished their sweep in a pathetic five minutes, radioing in the confirmation that the location was secure. I strained my ears to listen for the response and caught the reply telling them to move to the *secondary location*.

Good. They were following the predicted script flawlessly so far.

I pulled out my phone and sent a text to let Kai know that we were good to proceed. He didn't reply, but I didn't need him to. So long as he did his part and convincingly sold the illusion that he'd killed Danny DeLuna.

Some minutes later, a car pulled up outside the church. I waited with bated breath as the engine shut off and a car door slammed. Then the trunk. Then the crunch of heavy footsteps over gravel as the person approached the doors of the church.

There was a momentary pause, then the doors opened with a squeak, and Kai strode in, carrying an oversized black duffle bag.

He glanced around, then slowly made his way down the old aisle, heading for the front of the church, where he carefully placed his bag down on the raised dais. The black coat he wore disguised his bandaged arm—though he carried the bag with the other one—and a knitted cap covered the fresh wound on his scalp. He looked every part his alternate persona, Ares. Especially with the guns he made no attempt to truly conceal.

I smiled at that. Danny and I had been in agreement that we didn't want to alert his team to our plan, so he'd been forced to choose weapons from one of *my* stashes. He was beyond salty about it, too, bitching about how I had probably paid way overprice for the pieces I had purchased from a competitor of his.

He waited less than a minute before the front doors opened again, telling us that he'd been watched on arrival. Three men entered. Two were heavily armed, the protection detail. The middle one was short and stocky, wearing a black hat and spectacles.

"*Bonsoir, Ares,*" the short man greeted Kai. "Is this the package?" He nodded to the bag, and Kai shifted in front of it slightly.

"Who are you?" he rumbled, oozing threats of violence like I never really saw from him. Then again, I only ever saw him around Danny, who'd tamed this beast as effectively as a ringmaster in a circus full of tigers.

The small man whipped off his hat. "Of course, you're suspicious, and rightfully so. I'm Dr. Phillipe Eniss, tasked with confirming the identity and condition of the, er, package. Once things are in order, my associates here will take you to collect payment from the client."

Kai stared the little man down, and I ached to yell at him to *hurry the fuck up*. Maryanne had given us a very specific timeframe to work within, which left no margin for fucking around.

"Fine," Kai grunted a moment later, making me release my frustrated breath. He bent over the duffle bag and unzipped it entirely, revealing the curled-up body of a dead woman.

The doctor clicked his tongue and reached into his bag for a stethoscope. "Could you, *s'il te plaît...*" He indicated for Kai to uncurl her, and I swallowed hard as Kai removed her from the bag, laying her flat on the dais.

Fucking hell. She was like a wax doll, her pale skin ashen and her white hair like a halo around her body. Sitting where I was above the scene, there was nothing to block her from my view. It was a vision that would remain etched into my memory for a very long time, because even knowing what I knew... even sitting there with a syringe of drugs in my pocket that would revive her... I almost believed she *was* dead.

The doctor was thorough but quick in his examination, confirming for his armed friends that no signs of life were detected. He then took a photo of her face and lifted one of her limp hands to press her fingerprints into a device. It scanned for a moment, then beeped twice. Danny's Guild file appeared on the tablet screen, confirming her identity.

We'd been right not to use a replacement corpse; they weren't taking chances.

"Are we done here?" Kai asked, sounding irritated and impatient. Rightly so, too. The timer on my watch was dwindling.

"Yes, I believe we are," Dr. Eniss confirmed. "The client will be very pleased. This target has been quite elusive for some time."

Damn right she had, and she still would be if they could just *leave* the damn room.

Kai just grunted, folding his arms.

"Ah, you're in a hurry. Let's go, then."

Kai gave Danny's body a quick glance as the doctor and his

goons started to leave the church. "What about the body?" he asked, hesitating.

"We have no further need now that identity and death are confirmed. Leave it there. I'll send someone to take it down to the incinerator shortly." The doctor continued out of the church, not giving it another thought.

Kai followed slowly, glancing up into the darkness of the rafters ever so quickly. He wouldn't be able to see me, but he knew *I* could see *him*. The message was received loud and clear. *Be quick.*

I barely waited two breaths after the doors closed before grabbing the ropes my team had secured with bolts to the wall and rappelling down to the church floor. I closed the gap to Danny in just a few long strides, already flicking the cap off my syringe.

"Hang in there, *mon cœur*, I've got you." I gently took her wrist, shuddering at how *cold* her skin was. Maryanne had been crystal clear that the second dose needed to go directly into a vein, so I pushed up Danny's sleeve to try and locate one. Trouble was, with her heart rate slowed to the point of passing a death inspection, it was impossible to raise a vein.

"Shit," I breathed aloud, tipping her arm into the light. Time was running out, and all I could see was smooth, pale skin. Panic welled up inside me, and I pulled a zip tie from my pocket, hastily tightening it around Danny's upper arm.

The display on my watch started flashing at me, signaling that we were out of time.

"Come on," I whispered. "Come on, please work." Sending up a quick prayer to... *anyone*, I slid the needle into what I desperately hoped was a vein and not a shadow in the crook of Danny's arm.

Bile curdled in my throat as I depressed the plunger to push vital drugs into Danny's bloodstream and—if all went to plan— bring her back to life. Fuck me, why had I agreed to this plan? This was too much, even for me. Putting DeLuna at risk like this made me feel physically ill. She couldn't defend herself when she was barely even alive.

"Wake up, baby," I whispered as gunshots rang out through the night somewhere close by. "Come on, DeLuna, please..." I smoothed her hair back from her lifeless face, my lips brushing over her cold cheek.

More gunshots rang out, and I checked my phone. Shit, there was a message from Kai, sent probably right before that first gunshot. All it said was *trouble*.

Fuck. If I ignored it and Kai got killed...

"Dammit, Sasquatch," I snarled out loud. I knew I had to go help him, though. The drugs should have already started working in Danny's system. So long as she woke up before someone came to toss her in the incinerator, she'd be fine. There were guns stashed in Kai's duffle bag, too.

I pressed a quick kiss to her lips. "I will be *right* back," I whispered. "I promise."

The gunfire ramped up outside the church, and I strode down the aisle. I was already heavily armed, and my guys had stashed additional ammo and weapons around the church grounds. I swung my HK433 around from my back as I kicked open the doors and then stepped out, already firing.

Fuck these bastards. Whoever they were, they all deserved to die.

Tonight was the night we ended this shit. One way or another.

62
DANNY

Lying back, watching and *allowing* Kai to inject me with a cocktail of drugs that would, for a short time, make my body imitate death... it was the biggest leap of faith I'd ever taken. He was nervous about it, even if he was doing a great job of maintaining his stoic expression.

Sweat glistened on his brow, though, and he'd already stalled several times.

"Kai," I cut off his latest hesitation. "It's now or never. Do I need to do it myself?"

He glared. "No. I've got this." Clenching his jaw, he carefully slid the butterfly needle into my vein and slowly depressed the plunger.

I hissed as the drugs burned up my arm, and a chemical taste flooded my mouth. It was quick-acting, like Maryanne had warned us. We needed to move fast now.

Kai set the timer on his watch, then lifted me into the bag before I *totally* lost consciousness and made it all the more difficult. I curled up to fit, and he gave me a worried frown.

"I love you, Big Man," I whispered as the world faded around me. His lips moved in response, but I was already falling under.

The next thing I knew, a low, slow drumbeat woke me up.

Thump. Thump. Spaced out so far, I wondered if it might stop entirely. But instead, it gradually got faster.

Oh shit, that was my heartbeat. Thank *fuck*, I was still alive. Sort of.

Kai must have pulled off our con and had my "death" verified already, and Leon had administered the counter-drug. Someone was here with me; I could hear whispered words. Leon, maybe?

Little pops of sound cut through the almost deafening silence in my head, joining the slow beat of my heart. Anyone might think that a town nearby was setting off fireworks, but I automatically heard it for what it was. Gunfire.

There was no way Leon would leave Kai in a firefight and stay here with me. He *knew* how serious I'd been when I told them to protect each other at all costs. If Kai was in trouble, Leon would do what he needed to save him.

So… who the fuck was here with me in the dark old crumbling church? There was definitely someone, whispering and… *crying?*

The recovery from my simulated death was a slow one. So far, all I had was a slow, painfully slow heartbeat, shallow, undetectable breathing, and cognitive brain function. It would take longer to regain control over my body, including my eyelids, to see who was here with me. Probably a good thing. If this was just a random person, a passing innocent who saw the dead body of a woman left in an old church, then I couldn't suddenly lurch back to life.

Ever so slowly, the dullness in my head started to dissipate. The gunshots grew louder, and the whispers gained clarity.

"…so sorry," the person was sobbing, "…never meant for it to go this far…"

Wait. What?

More weeping, the real soul-deep, gut-wrenching kind that could never be from a stranger. This was the kind of grief you could only experience when someone you truly loved was dead and gone.

"Danny, I'm s-so s-sorry," the crying person moaned. "I loved you so much. This doesn't change the fact that I loved you."

What the fucking fuck?

The drugs must be making me hallucinate. That was the *only* explanation… because I knew that voice. I knew that voice just as well as I knew my own.

"Why did you have to make this so hard?" she whispered, choking on sobs. "It would have been so quick and painless if you'd died in Prague like you were meant to."

I was glad I couldn't move. Couldn't see. Couldn't speak. If I could... I didn't know what the hell I would do. My whole world was imploding, my heart shredded into ribbons, and blood just pooled inside my chest cavity.

Please let this be a drug delusion. Please don't let this be real. Please...

"I swear, DeLuna, I'll make you proud of me... somehow. I'll make this all count for something. The Circle needed fresh blood on it, babe. You *knew* that better than anyone. I can make a real change when I have a seat. I can finish getting rid of the orphanages, wipe the rest of Project Remus off the face of this earth and *start over*." She was fervent as she whispered her bullshit excuses over my corpse, like she was trying to convince *herself* that she wasn't the two-faced, backstabbing bitch that put out a kill order on me. For what? Power. Greed.

Nausea rolled through my whole body, the oily slick of betrayal and disgust coating me from head to toe. She continued crying, sniffling, and moaning while I *raged* internally.

"Why?" she wailed after a few moments. "Why did you make it come to this? Why did you have to be so fucking *stubborn*? If you'd just... *let Leon die*, like he was supposed to! Why did you have to go off on that *insane* mission to save him? If he'd died, then you didn't need to. I could have called this whole thing off, and you…y-you'd s-still be here. With me."

My head ached worse than any migraine I'd ever experienced, and it was purely from the electric shocks of puzzle pieces connecting. She'd been the one to infect Leon with that virus. Of course, she had. She must have known he was Circle and lifted his DNA in person. But how did she—

A clear memory flashed through my brain. The box of personal items from her desk that Franklin had given me. Her perfume mixed with what I'd *assumed* to be Franklin's cologne… I'd sneezed while I was looking at those photos and thought nothing of it. She'd used me as a Trojan horse to deliver the virus right to Leon.

Fuck. My best friend almost killed a man I loved, and I had unknowingly facilitated her plan.

"It's almost over," Jude wept, her hand grasping my undamaged one and squeezing. "It's almost over, babe. I promise it will all be worth it. It has to be, right? This *has* to be worth you dying for." She dissolved into more gut-wrenching sobs, her tears falling on my skin as she leaned over my corpse.

I could feel that wetness, though. I could feel her fingers clutching desperately at mine… like she was seeking my forgiveness or reassurance from beyond the grave. I could *feel* those physical touches… which meant I was coming closer to regaining my body.

Which also meant my heart rate was returning to normal,

as was my breathing and core temperature. It wouldn't be long before Jude noticed I was suddenly less dead than I'd been five minutes ago.

The church doors slammed open, and Jude gave a small gasp, sniffling.

"Ma'am, you need to get out of here!" a man shouted. "They came prepared. This is getting bloody. It's too dangerous for you to stay."

"No. I need five more minutes!" Jude snapped back, her voice still tight with anguish. "I need to say goodbye."

"The boss says you've gotta go!" the guy called back, his footsteps crunching on the floor as he approached. "Now."

Jude gave a furious hiss, then a gunshot cracked through the air. Close enough to make my ears ring. "I said *no*." Her voice was cold as ice as a body crumpled to the ground with a heavy sound. "Fucking idiot."

While I was fairly sure she was looking at the man she'd just shot—and not me—I cracked my eyelids ever so slightly. Just testing whether I could control that motion. I could, but it wasn't easy.

Jude sniffed again, turning back to me, and I let my lids softly close once more before she could notice they were open. She sighed heavily, the click of metal on stone telling me she'd set her gun aside. Good.

"He thinks he can push me around, tell me what to do like

I'm one of his fucking soldiers. He forgets that it was *me* who uncovered Project Remus in the first fucking place. Without *me*, he wouldn't be in this position, ready to take a seat on the Circle *alongside* me. No, to him, I'll always be weak. Crippled." The bitterness in her voice was unlike anything I'd ever heard from Jude. Even right after her accident, when she realized she would never be an active mercenary, she hadn't been bitter.

Apparently, she'd fooled me, and that hatred had festered in the worst kind of way. She'd killed her whole family. This wasn't even just about me, or Leon. She'd had her *whole* family slaughtered. I would never in a million years have thought Jude capable of an act like that.

She was gutting me. Slicing me up inside, far worse than any of the hired assassins had ever managed. Her words cut deeper than The Sandman's knife, and the blistering agony of truth struck a thousand times harder than a broken wrist.

He. Who the fuck was *he*? Someone else was pulling strings here; it wasn't all Jude alone. She was working with someone else. Blanchet's heir? Franklin?

Gunfire peppered through the night, closer than ever, and Jude sucked a deep breath.

"I have to go, Danny. I can't let anyone see me alive, not until this is all done. It would ruin everything... but I had to see you one last time. To s-say g-goodbye." She was crying again, and a cold fury settled over me. How dare she mourn me. How *dare* she grieve like I'd grieved over her.

Her hand smoothed over my hair as she sobbed. "I'm so sorry, Danny. I love you so much. I'll never forget what an amazing person you were. My heart sister. My *best* friend. I can't believe you're gone."

She bent down, her lips pressing to my cheek in a kiss, and I knew I couldn't let her leave. If she walked out of this church now, it wouldn't end. She wouldn't stop, and Leon would be her target once more. I couldn't let that happen.

Curling my fingers inward, I slipped the hidden stiletto blade out of my wrist cast and gripped it as best I could in those fingers. Keeping the handle inside the cast helped. It was now or fucking never, so I simply needed to hope for the best.

As close as Jude was to my face, she must have noticed something amiss. She gave a small gasp, jerking back a couple of inches. I bet she'd heard me breathing. Well... fuck it.

I opened my eyes, meeting her terrified gaze, and stabbed my blade into her side—aiming upwards with the long, thin dagger so the tip would strike her heart. Her lips parted in a silent scream, tears still rolling from her widened eyes as she realized what I'd just done.

"Danny," she croaked, shock setting in as she brought a hand to her side where my knife remained buried deep. Maybe it hadn't struck her heart—it was an awkward position, and my grip was weak—but it would be enough. "H-how?"

I swallowed the acidic taste of betrayal and hatred, not gracing her with an explanation. Instead, I sat up with monumental effort and reached for her gun that she'd helpfully placed down near my good hand.

Jude slumped over, slouched on the edge of the dais as she looked up at me with pleading eyes.

"I'm sorry," she whimpered. "I never wanted this."

I had to shove my emotions aside, because I refused to give her the satisfaction of seeing my tears. Surely she must have known how her death would have broken me, though. This betrayal was a thousand times worse. And I would never let her see how internally I was *screaming*. I was beaten and bleeding; I was torn to pieces and pleading for mercy. But as far as she was concerned? I was a goddamn robot. Or good enough.

"Yes, you did," I whispered, standing on jelly legs and aiming the gun at my best friend. "You could have stopped this… at *any* point. But you didn't. You put a bounty on my head and then felt *relief* when you thought I was dead. Save the bullshit apologies, Judith. Consider this karma catching up with you. Once and for all."

I fired.

63
KAI

Thank *fuck* for Leon Marx and his paranoia. That was all I was going to say about the situation we were currently balls deep in, bullets smacking into the grass, the headstones, the trees all around us. He had instructed his guys to leave stashes of ammo and weapons at strategic points all around the church meeting site for a solid five-mile radius.

A day ago, I'd called it overkill. Now? I'd happily eat crow.

He flashed me a feral grin, tossing me a fresh magazine for my M13. He hadn't needed to reload, coming prepared for this party with a hundred-round, double-drum magazine on his HK433. Smartass would be rubbing that in later, for sure.

"Is Danny okay?" I called over to him. We were shooting from a defensive position after I'd come within a bee's dick of being executed when Doctor Dickhead had escorted me out to claim my so-called bounty. That slimy fuck had died in my place after I used him as a human shield until I got behind a mausoleum.

Leon peered out from his hiding spot—right over one of the ammo stashes, because apparently his guys buried ammo literally *in* graves—and fired off a half dozen shots. A moment later, a shooter dropped from a tree. Thank fuck, that asshole had us pinned down way too effectively.

"I think so," he replied with a scowl. "But the sooner we get back in there, the better. I don't trust them not to toss her into the incinerator before she wakes up."

That idea sent a ripple of panic shooting through me. She was so vulnerable right now, but we had a new objective. Because I had spotted someone I recognized right before these bastards opened fire on me, and I wasn't leaving until he was captured or dead.

"Up on the rise, beside the crying angel statue," I barked at Leon. "That's the ringleader. Don't let him escape."

Leon popped out from his hiding spot, laying down cover fire as he took a look at who I was talking about. One thing was fucking lucky—that bastard was confident enough that he wasn't tucking tail to run. He was just waiting it out, figuring that thirty against two would see both Leon and me eliminated sooner or later. Probably sooner.

Of course, he had underestimated us and severely underestimated Leon's marksmanship. Holy *shit*, he was accurate. The only reason we were still locked in this firefight was that our attackers wore Kevlar, and we did not.

"Got it," Leon replied, giving me a nod.

"Let's take him alive," I clarified. "We need answers, for Danny."

Leon rolled his eyes and grumbled, muttering something about me being a spoilsport, but he agreed, nonetheless. "Fine," he snapped. "Let's get this rolling, then. Before he realizes that he's losing and tries to run."

I nodded back, in total agreement with that assessment.

Working together, we pushed forward from our sheltered positions. Now that Leon had dispatched the shooters in the trees, it was easier to gain ground through the cemetery. We leapfrogged it, one moving while the other laid out cover fire.

It didn't take long for the bastard on the rise to figure out we were coming for him.

He tried to retreat. Of course he did. Leon was a step ahead, though. He sprinted toward a stone obelisk and snatched up a grenade launcher that had been hidden behind a bunch of flowers. A second later, the SUV that'd been waiting as an escape vehicle exploded in a ball of flame.

"Nice shot," I complimented him as I tucked and rolled to get behind a low headstone as shelter from the returning fire.

Leon's smirk was pure arrogance, and it made me laugh. Crazy fuck was actually having fun. Maybe I would be, too, if I wasn't nursing my fresh injuries from The Sandman's attack.

"He's making a run for it," Leon advised. "I'll cover. You go hog-tie that motherfucker."

He didn't wait for my agreement before popping up and squeezing off round after round to pick off the remaining goons still shooting at us. Now that we were closer, he had a much better line of sight for headshots. It made me glad to be *on* his team, not against it.

Sure enough, our quarry was sprinting down the street. Not that he was going to get far now. Not unless he had another vehicle stashed somewhere, which I wouldn't put past him.

I put my fate in Leon's hands, ignoring all the shooting and focusing on catching our runaway. I dropped my gun, letting the shoulder strap catch it as I sprinted out of the cemetery.

The bastard glanced behind him, blindly firing a few shots from a handgun, but they went wide and barely made me miss a step in running him down. I didn't shoot him, because it would be way too easy for the shot to hit something vital. Too many people needed a chunk of this motherfucker's flesh before he could be allowed to die.

When I closed the gap between us, I kicked out his feet from under him and watched as he ate gravel. I winced as he rolled, blood running down his face from a nasty graze.

"Hey, *brother*, long fucking time. I thought you were dead." I stomped on his knee, hearing a satisfying crack that would prevent him from running again.

He howled but was already reaching for the gun he'd dropped when he fell. I kicked it out of reach, then knelt down to straddle his chest. Gripping his shirt, I lifted him up slightly to meet my fist, not holding back even slightly.

"Fuck you, Kai." He spat blood at me. "You don't have the balls to—"

Whatever he thought I didn't have the balls to do, boy was he wrong. But I also wasn't interested in listening to more bullshit, so I punched him again and let his head hit the road, knocking him out.

"That's enough of your mouth, *Timothy*," I sneered at the unconscious man beneath me. The very same man who'd given me a nephew... only to tear him away from Moana and disappear.

Flipping him over, I zip-tied his hands and patted him down for weapons. The arrogant piece of shit had seriously come out to an ambush like this with only a handgun and one knife? Jesus, he'd really let his training slip in the past decade.

My arm fucking ached—thanks, Leon—so no way in hell was I carrying this son of a bitch back with me. The continued gunshots behind me said Leon was still dealing with the last of Timothy's guys, though, and I couldn't just *leave* my capture lying in the street. I grabbed his ankle in my good hand and started dragging him.

So what if he took a few deep grazes? They wouldn't kill him. Not before we were good and fucking ready for him to die, anyway.

As I drew closer to the church and cemetery, I spotted a shadowy figure lurking through the shadows, sneaking up on Leon. Dropping Timothy's weight, I grabbed my gun and shot the sneaky fuck before he could kill our murder rabbit.

"Thanks, dickhead!" Leon called out, giving me a broad grin. "I didn't see that one!"

I couldn't help smiling back. *Kohuru rapeti* was a whole other species—I seriously wouldn't be surprised if he started skipping and singing any minute now. He casually, systematically, made his way around every fallen assailant, shooting them again at close range, making sure to cross all our t's so no one could pop up and shoot us in the back.

Before all of this, I'd have definitely thought that was both overkill—literally—and a waste of bullets. Now, though? I respected how thorough he was.

"Is that our fake Blanchet?" he called out, rolling over a body with his toe and firing a bullet into the already dead man's face.

I reached down and grabbed Timothy's ankle again, dragging him over the rough ground toward the church. "Yep, sure fucking is. How he's been doing it, I have no clue. But considering he is an Erikkson heir, I think his motive is clear."

Leon strode over and peered down at Timothy with a confused look. "Who the fuck is he? Oh, shit, that's the guy who knocked up your sister and stole the baby?" I grunted my confirmation, and Leon nodded. "There's more to this, though. How he accessed Blanchet's Circle server, for one thing. Danny will extract the info... Good thinking on keeping him alive."

He clapped me on the shoulder, making me wince because that was the side he'd fucking shot me in just two days ago. Dick. He knew it, too, snickering as he checked his ammo and pulled out his phone. "I'm going to call Carol for a clean-up crew," he told me.

"Why Carol?" I asked, still dragging Timothy through the cemetery behind me. "Why not call in your team, if they're so trustworthy?"

He glanced over at me from his phone. "For one thing, *my* team doesn't know they're the bad guys, and this many bodies to clean up will raise some eyebrows. For another thing, cleanups are expensive. Why not let Carol foot the bill and feel useful?"

I don't know why I found that so fucking funny, but I did. The way he made it seem like he was doing Carol a *favor* by letting her clean up our mess. He put the call on speakerphone too.

"Where's Danny?" Carol asked after Leon had made his request for a cleanup crew. "Is she okay?"

"I fucking hope so," Leon muttered, running a hand over his head, then grimacing when he realized there was a glob of bird shit in his hair. That's what happened when you lurked in the rafters for several hours. "We're heading back to her now. I'll have her call you soon."

Carol gave a vexed sigh. "Thank you, Leon, I appreciate it. I've made a few discoveries of my own here, but they can wait until you finish... whatever the fuck you're doing there." She was still irritated that we hadn't given her the details of our plan, but tough shit. That had been Danny's call, and we would respect it. All of us.

He ended the call, then glanced down at my prisoner and the awkward way I was dragging him.

"Fuck's sake, Sasquatch. It's okay to ask for help sometimes." Pushing me aside, he hauled Timothy up off the ground and slung him over his shoulder. "Let's go rescue Sleeping Beauty."

I smiled at that image, then immediately hoped she *was*

Sleeping Beauty and not Juliet.

64
DANNY

Jude screamed as the bullet ripped through her stomach, but it fell on deaf ears. Whatever sympathy or remorse I might have felt had been burned to ash in her apartment where she faked her own death.

"D-Danny, I'm s-so s-sorry," she choked out again. Like she *believed* herself.

"I can't even find the words," I told her, my expression neutral and my voice glacial. "You faked your own death. Why? Why the *fuck* was that necessary? It wasn't enough to masquerade as Blanchet and put a bounty on my head? You needed to make me *grieve* for you, too? You really are one sick, sadistic bitch."

The irony of that statement, when I'd chosen to shoot her in the stomach to prolong her death, wasn't lost on me. But she deserved it… and worse.

Jude gave an agonized moan, her hands clutched to the freely bleeding hole in her stomach, like she could somehow stop her life draining away. Tears streamed down her face, and she gave a choked sob.

"I had to," she whimpered. "I'm sorry."

For a long moment, I just stood there, staring down at her as I tried desperately to contain my emotions. But a side effect of all my recent personal growth in opening myself up to love and vulnerability… it was no longer so easy to harden myself to what I was truly feeling.

Jude's eyes held nothing but regret and guilt, and I no longer possessed the strength to turn my back on her. I broke, sinking to my knees at her side and letting my mask fade away.

"How could you do this, Mackenzie?" I pleaded, my gaze quickly assessing her injuries. She would die, there was no questioning that. But how long it took… who knew? Minutes, at most, by my guess. "How could you do this to us? We were closer than family, weren't we? You were the one person I trusted more than *anyone*."

She reached out a bloody hand, and I took it in mine without hesitation. A deep sigh rattled through her, and she sagged against the dais, her fingers linking with mine.

"I did it *for* us," she croaked out, her eyes pleading. "Please, Danny, don't hate me. I did this *because* of you, and Sabby, and *me*. No one should be raised like you were... I wanted to end it..." She trailed off, her breath shuddering as she tried to contain her tears. "I w-wanted to make things better. Not for us, f-for the little girls like us... S-stop them becoming u-us."

Jesus mercenary Christ, she had a noble purpose and a fucking deplorable method. Wasn't that always the way? It didn't matter how many eggs were broken, so long as the omelet turned out in the end.

"You're an arrogant fool, Judith," I whispered, shaking my head. "An arrogant, power-blinded, backstabbing fool. The Circle was already changing. Leon and Carol—"

"Your mother," she sighed, giving a long blink. "I'm so happy for you, Danny. She seems... tough."

Fuck, of all the things, that was what made me start crying. Tears spilled over, and I gave a choking laugh at Jude's apt description of Carol Atwood. "She is tough," I agreed. "She's also a good person. I think. But suddenly, I find myself really questioning my judgment of character..."

Jude's brow creased in pain, and she gave a tiny headshake. "Don't. Your gut keeps you alive, remember? Even now, after everything I did... you're still alive." More tears rolled, and she gave a whimper of pain, her fingers tightening on mine. "I'm so happy you're alive, Danny. S-so fucking happy."

Fuck, now I was really crying. She brought this on herself. She tried to have me killed, she infected Leon with a virus… and yet, I was mourning for her all over again. Her end goal was admirable, and now that I'd separated myself from the Guild, I could see that. Much clearer than I ever could before.

Children *shouldn't* be raised as assassins. In no world was it okay or acceptable to send an eight-year-old girl into a politician's home and have her shoot him in the head. To have her stand there as blood, bone, and brain matter splatter the white wallpaper and *feel nothing*.

No little girls should be taught to exploit their sexuality before ever hitting puberty. No matter which test tube had created them, or the orphanage that was housing them.

But as much as I agreed with Jude's end game, *nothing* could condone her method. Nothing could excuse the amount of blood on her hands in her pursuit of a seat on the Circle.

"The mole," I said softly, looking down at our interlaced fingers. Jude's blood covered both our hands, but I couldn't bring myself to let go. "It was you, wasn't it? You were feeding Kai's team the orphanage locations."

She swallowed heavily, giving the tiniest of nods. "One of their team… he was being paid to ensure the orphanages would be destroyed. Not just closed and reopened under another corrupt, easily paid-off operator, but destroyed."

Horror and disgust rippled through me, and I shook my head. "Jude… all those children…"

She gave me a sad look. "I saved them, and y-you know it."

Fresh tears spilled down my cheeks, thinking of all those innocent lives lost. All because of the Guild and past generations of exploitation. Mo's child had been in one of those orphanages. He'd died because of Jude. How the *fuck* did I explain that to her?

"Jude…" I sighed her name, at a loss for how to express myself. Because she wasn't wrong, in a way. She wasn't *right* by any stretch of the imagination, but maybe it was more merciful than leaving other little girls and boys to be molded into heartless killers, to have their childhoods and innocence obliterated in the name of *training*.

"I'm sorry," she whimpered again, her fingers squeezing mine. "Danny, please d-don't let me die thinking you hate me. P-please say you understand."

My lips parted as I stared back at her, but no words came out. How the fuck could I verbalize how messed up I was inside after all this? Did I understand why she felt *justified* to kill so many people to further her grab for power? Did I understand the need to murder children? Hell no. No *way*.

But I didn't hate her. I couldn't ever hate her.

"Judith, I love you," I told her with utter sincerity. "And I'm sorry, too. You were right, it should never have come to this. I wish…" I trailed off, shaking my head. "I *wish* you'd done things differently, Mackenzie. You have *no idea* how much I wish you'd just come to me... Maybe we could have avoided this."

Jude gave a gurgling laugh. "Doubt it. This was inevitable. Danny DeLuna was always going to save the day... I was an idiot to think I could ever beat you." Pain wracked across her face but faded quickly into calm serenity. It was almost over.

"Who is *he*, Jude?" I asked, holding her bloody hand tighter, like I could tether her to the living world. "Who were you working with? Who's the traitor in Kai's team? How'd you access the Circle files?" I had *so many questions*.

She blinked slowly. So slowly, I worried she wasn't going to open her eyes again, but when she did, her gaze was glassy and unfocused. "Danny?" she asked, sounding small and fragile.

I clutched her hand tighter, holding it to my chest as I stroked her hair out of her face. "Yeah, Jude, it's me."

"I don't want to die. I'm so scared." Her whole body trembled with fear of the unknown, and I couldn't contain my own sobs as I pulled her closer.

Hugging her to my chest, I whispered choked up reassurances in her ear and kissed her cheek just like she'd done to me. I promised her it would all be okay and that she didn't need to be scared anymore.

Then she was gone, her hand dropping limp to the bloody floor, and I fell to pieces all over again.

Time lost all meaning as I cradled my dead friend to my

chest and wept, feeling utterly heartbroken and lost. How could I have been so fooled, for so long? She'd been trying to have me killed. She almost succeeded, too. Fucking hell, Jude had released prisoners from the Castle—she was that determined to kill me.

That thought made me sick. Bile rose in my throat, and I choked it back, disgust, fury, and hatred all mixing with the soul-deep grief to crowd my brain and fill me with despair.

I didn't hear the church doors open, nor did I hear the footsteps approaching. I didn't even register that I was no longer alone until Kai's warm hand touched my shoulder, and I startled.

"Siren, it's me," he rumbled, crouching beside me. Beside *us*. I got the feeling he'd said my name a few times and I just hadn't heard. "Is that...?"

His wide eyes took in the dead woman still cradled in my arms, and I nodded. He'd seen her in photos, he knew how much I loved her. Of course, he recognized Jude.

Sniffing back the mess of tears and snot, I wiped my face on my shoulder in a pathetic attempt to pull myself together. Leon was here, too, dumping a body on the floor and checking restraints.

Wait... restraints?

"Who is that?" I croaked, realizing they'd taken a prisoner.

Kai glanced over at the man in question, then sighed. "Timothy."

That shocked me enough that I loosened my grip on Jude and sat up slightly. "What? I thought he was dead."

Kai winced. "As dead as Jude, apparently."

Ouch. True though.

"Holy shit," Leon exclaimed, leaving his bound captive and seeing my dead friend for the first time. He crossed over to where I sat on the dirty floor with blood all over me and Jude's lifeless body in my lap.

For a long moment, he just stared at her with an unreadable expression. Then he shook his head sadly. "Judith," he said on a sigh, "I bet you never even got your hands on the thirty pieces of silver, either. Stupid girl."

"She wanted your seat," I told Leon in a raw voice, looking up at him through fresh tears. "She infected you with that virus to take *your* seat. But she was working with someone else for Erikkson's."

Leon nodded, tipping his head to the captive.

"Timothy," Kai muttered. "An Erikkson heir."

I licked my lips, trying to make it make sense in my grief-addled brain. "She killed her whole family," I said in a small voice. "The Mackenzie line is dead now."

"*Ka mate te kāinga tahi, ka ora te kāinga rua,*" Kai said softly, reaching out to close Jude's eyes. "When one house dies, a second lives. I will always, forever, choose your house, Danny DeLuna. No matter how many others need to die to protect it."

Christ, now I was crying again.

"Come here, *taku aroha*," Kai coaxed, peeling me away from the corpse of my best friend and worst enemy. I released her reluctantly, letting Leon move her body away so Kai could gather me into his lap and hug me tight.

I sank into his embrace for a moment, but I could already sense we'd lingered too long. We needed to leave the scene of the crime and let a cleanup crew do their thing to protect our underworld.

"What do you want to do with her, *mon ange*?" Leon asked, frowning down at Jude's corpse. "Leave her for the cleaners? Or, if you want, we could take her down to the incinerator in the basement. Ashes to ashes and all that poetic shit."

I hesitated. I knew she was dead. I'd been holding her corpse, her blood covered me. But a paranoid corner of my brain told me that I needed to be *sure* this time. So I nodded. "Let's do that," I murmured. "I can't give her a burial, but that has to be better than being cut up and dropped into vats of acid with dozens of other bodies."

Despite the intense, gut-wrenching betrayal… she was still Jude. She still deserved respect in her disposal. And when it was all said and done, words couldn't accurately describe the closure provided by watching the furnace reduce her body to ash. This time, the fire was real.

65
DANNY

Stepping foot back on Kai's private island in the Adriatic Sea gave me the most intense sense of nostalgia. I'd sworn to *never* return to this island, this house… but I'd also never intended to return to Kai himself.

It'd taken some debate to decide on a secure location to interrogate Timothy, but as we'd already been in Europe, Kai had made an excellent point. There was nowhere more secure than his island, and we were no longer hiding from his team.

"This is where he held you captive for a month?" Leon muttered, standing on the end of the jetty with me as I stared out over the water. I could still feel the bite of that ice-cold water, despite how the weather had warmed since my escape. "It's... kinda nice. My house was better, though."

I tilted my head to look up at him. "Was?"

He shrugged. "I demolished it. A compromised location is no longer safe, so I had my guys drop a missile on the whole thing. Caused a fucking avalanche, but there's nothing left."

My jaw dropped. "Bunny, that—"

"Was just a house," he cut me off, his gaze soft. "My *home* is with you, wherever that might be."

Oh man, when had Leon learned to be such a romantic? My pulse was racing so hard I couldn't catch my breath. So instead, I just rose up on my toes and kissed him with *all* my emotion.

"I love you, Leon," I whispered against his lips.

He smiled, kissing me back. "I love you, too," he replied when our kiss ended. "Are you ready to go do what you do best?"

Excitement zapped through me. "You wanna do the DVP thing again?"

He tossed his head back with a laugh. "I meant interrogate our prisoner and extract answers from him like decaying teeth... but fuck, Timothy can *wait*." He scooped me up in his arms, kissing me as he strode back down the jetty toward the house.

Kai was waiting for us at the door, though, his thick arms folded over his chest and a scowl on his face. "I just spoke with Moana," he told us. "They're enroute, should touch down in about six hours."

"Excellent," Leon practically purred, pushing past Kai. "Plenty of time."

"Plenty of time?" Kai repeated, following us into the kitchen. "For what? I thought we were going to interrogate him before Mo gets here?"

"We are," I replied. "Right, Leon?"

He gave me a wicked grin. "Which way to Sasquatch's bedroom, beautiful? I wanna fuck you on his bed."

I laughed but tipped my head in the direction of the bedrooms. "We really do need to go interrogate Timothy, though."

"Where the fuck do you think you're taking my siren?" Kai growled, following. *Good boy, take that bait.*

"Master suite," I told Leon quietly. "Double doors at the end of the hall." Then louder. "Leon, we don't have time for this!"

Leon grinned, pure mischief. "Bullshit. Dickhead said his bitchy sister lands in six hours. You wanna tell me you need six hours to interrogate that guy? Come on, DeLuna, you're better than that."

He was right, and he knew it.

Still carrying me bridal style, he kicked open the doors to Kai's room and tossed me gently onto the bed. "If you want those clothes to survive, you better take them off yourself."

"Hey, what the hell?" Kai protested, whacking Leon in the arm. "Don't ignore me. You're not going to—"

"Fuck DeLuna on your bed and make you sit there in the

corner like a good boy? Hell *yes*, I am." Leon tugged his shirt over his head, then started on his pants, kicking his shoes aside. "Take them off, baby, or I'll cut them off." He produced a dagger from his boot, and suddenly my attempt to strip out of my clothes slowed right down.

Kai's scowling gaze flicked between us. "Fuck that, I'm not—"

"Sit in the chair, Big Man," I snapped, giving him a challenging stare.

His eyes narrowed, but he did as he was told. Sort of. He dragged the big armchair over from the window until it was right at the end of the bed before he sat down.

I bit back a laugh. "Good. Stay there while Leon defiles me in your bed."

Kai gave a magnanimous gesture, like we were putting on a show at his bequest, and Leon snorted a laugh. I was still in my clothing, so Leon made good on his threat—or promise—and used his blade to carefully cut the fabric from my body while I lay *dead* still. My arms remained draped above my head, keeping my casted arm away from the action, and I was still fragile enough that it'd have to stay that way.

Kai cleared his throat as Leon peeled my jeans away, and I crooked my knee up.

"Relax, Malachi," Leon teased, tracing the tip of his deadly sharp knife over the delicate skin of my inner thigh. "We have plenty of time. Or did you just want a better look?" He shifted to the side, nudging my knee to spread my legs. Then he flipped the knife over and gently ran the handle through the wetness of my pussy.

"Bunny…" I groaned, wanting to writhe but not wanting to get stabbed. At least not with a knife that sharp.

He flicked me a dark look, one that told me to *trust* him, and I wet my lips with anticipation.

"Bringing weapons into the bedroom is supposed to be *my* thing, *kohuru rapeti*," Kai growled, swiping a hand over his mouth. His gaze was so hot it was practically scorching my skin, so I rocked my hips ever so slightly against the knife handle that Leon was teasing me with. He was just running it up and down my slit, nudging my clit every now and then. Nothing crazy.

Yet.

"I wanted to walk a mile in your shoes," Leon sassed back, holding the blade carefully between his fingers to avoid cutting his hand. "Turns out, they fit surprisingly well." He dipped the handle into my cunt, and I moaned.

"Fuck," Kai breathed, biting his knuckles as he watched Leon push the handle deeper, then start to thrust it slowly. "If you cut yourself, you're bleaching these sheets. Clear?"

Leon gave a soft chuckle leaning in to lick my clit while his knife handle was still deep inside me.

"Dammit, Marx," I groaned, trying really fucking hard not to thrash. "I need something bigger than that."

Leon's brows hitched. "I bet Kai has one of those impractical revolvers around here somewhere."

"Your dick, Leon," I snapped, reaching down with my good hand to grab his short hair, "I want your dick inside me *now*."

His grin was all Cheshire as he let me pull him up the bed. He tossed the knife aside, slipping between my legs with magnetic precision. "So demanding today, DeLuna. But I'm not in the habit of refusing when you ask so nicely." His pierced tip sank into my warmth, and I pushed my hips up in anticipation.

"Keep that wrist on the pillow," he warned me with a serious glare to my cast. "It needs to heal properly so we can skip through the meadow slaughtering fuckers again soon."

I grinned. "Deal. Now fuck—" *Oof.* He slammed into me so hard it knocked the wind clean out of my lungs. Kai stared hard, his hand making its way into his pants as Leon went to work, railing me in Kai's bed.

Leon wasn't in the mood for a quickie, either. He made me come twice, then flipped me over and took a quick pause to make sure my arm was comfortable. Kai generously handed him some lube, and a moment later, he was fucking my ass hard enough to make me howl. That seemed to be the tipping point for Leon, and he unloaded right there inside me while his fingers found my clit, pushing me harder over the edge.

Once he'd eased out of me, I stayed there with my ass in the air for a moment, feeling the wet drip of Leon's cum leaking out as I looked over my shoulder to Kai.

"You just gonna sit there?" I teased, waggling my hips.

Heat flashed across his face, and he surged out of the armchair like I'd just cut his leash. His pants were already open, as he'd been stroking his hard dick the whole time Leon had been working me over. So there was no hesitation before he slammed into my cunt, right up to the hilt with one thrust.

"Fuck," I squeaked, breathless as he fucked me into the bed with so much force that the headboard sounded like it might break as it hit the wall.

Leon had disappeared into the bathroom, presumably rinsing off, but he returned to take his turn watching only a minute or so later. He flopped down on the bed beside us, propping his head up on his hand and seeming totally at ease in the nude.

"Smack her ass, Kai," he suggested. "The way her pussy clenches up is out of this fucking world."

Kai grunted, but his palm cracked over the flesh of my butt, and I jerked, moaning.

"Right?" Leon laughed as Kai hissed a breath between his teeth. "Do it harder. She can take it, can't you, DeLuna?"

I was a whimpering mess, all strung out on sex. "Yes," I gasped as Kai continued fucking my pussy with punishing strokes. "Harder."

"Filthy woman," he growled but delivered on my plea nonetheless.

Within minutes, I'd come again. Both my ass cheeks were scorching and buzzing from his smacks, and my pussy was so wet it was like a damn Slip 'N Slide between us. There was absolutely no need for more lube as Kai eased into my ass.

"You love that, don't you?" Leon asked in a breathy voice, his dick already hard again as he watched. "Being filled up with cock. Being used, ridden hard, and drenched in cum."

It was clearly rhetorical, because, *duh*.

"Turn your face this way, beautiful," Leon coaxed. "Give me your mouth while he fills your ass."

Moaning, I did what he asked. I couldn't put weight on my right arm, but Leon just shuffled up the bed until he could push the head of his cock between my lips without ever lifting my head from the pillow. I ran my tongue over his tip, tasting the salt of his pre-cum and toying with his piercings as Kai finished himself off in my ass.

"Christ," the big guy exclaimed, panting as he pulled out. "Where's your fucking phone, Marx?"

Leon barked a laugh, pointing to it on the floor. Apparently, they were both into role reversal today, because Kai ordered me to keep sucking Leon's dick while he snapped some new shots of my glowing rear for the spank bank.

"I'm going to shower," Kai announced with a groan, kicking his pants off the rest of the way.

I sat up, my head swimming with dizziness from multiple

back-to-back orgasms. "I need one too," I admitted.

Leon barked a laugh. "Not yet, you don't. Come here." He hauled me into his lap, and with one deep thrust, he was back inside me.

Oh yeah. Showering could wait.

Kai must have sensed he was missing out, because he returned from the shower some minutes later and demanded another turn himself. Somehow, they managed to drag it out just long enough each time that when one finished, the other was ready to go again. It was like sorcery... or maybe they had some little blue pills in the bathroom. Not that I was complaining.

By the time we called it quits, I had less than an hour left to interrogate Timothy, and I could barely walk. Whoops.

66
DANNY

Thankfully, even at my worst, I could interrogate a man in under an hour. Particularly when I didn't need to be careful. When it was a foregone conclusion that the subject wouldn't be walking away, the gloves came off. And this time, I had help.

Leon and I took turns on Timothy, bleeding him for information while Kai watched and directed the line of inquiry. All three of us were fucking wrecked from Leon's little game up in Kai's room, so it was nice that we could torture this prick together. Like a team bonding activity.

He held out well initially, but eventually, he cracked. They all did, sooner or later.

When he cracked, it was with the arrogance and ignorance of an entitled piece of shit. A man who'd learned that he stood next in line to inherit a seat on the Circle but had been passed over by his father.

Asking Timothy why he'd thrown so much effort behind hunting *me* had hurt, though. Or his answer had.

"That wasn't me," he admitted with a sick laugh. "Don't get me wrong, I wanted you dead. I needed *all* of you dead... but you... no, that was all Jude. Every time you slipped through the cracks, it drove her mad."

I swallowed back my anger and hurt, shaking it off. It no longer mattered.

"Jude said she was feeding the intel about the Guild-run orphanages to Kai's team," I said, changing the subject. "She said one of his team was paid off to ensure the locations—and occupants—were destroyed instead of freed."

Timothy raised his eyes to Kai at that, his bloody lips twisting in a sneer. "You thought you were *saving* children," he taunted, "when all along, you were murdering them."

This was news to Kai. I hadn't told him what Jude said before now. I should have, but I couldn't find the words. I wanted to hear it from Timothy himself, since Kai's team was already on their way to the island.

Kai drew a deep breath, plucking a pair of brass knuckles

from the table of tools we'd set out. Then he crossed to Timothy and punched him so hard I half expected his head to explode. *Fuck*, that was impressive.

"Who?" Kai snarled as Timothy hung limply from the chains. Somehow, he hadn't died or even been knocked out... or not entirely. His answer was slurred, but it was clear enough to make out the name of the snake in Team Ares's grass.

"S-sam," Timothy groaned. "And Mauricio. They were planning on leaving your business *years* ago, and I convinced them to stay and sabotage your plots against the Guild." He coughed a bloody laugh at that, and Kai punched him again.

This time, it knocked Timothy out, and Kai tossed the brass knuckles back on the table with barely contained rage.

"Hey, don't look so glum, chum!" Leon enthused. "That's good news. Mauricio was that dick I shot back in Shadow Grove, wasn't he? And you killed Sam, so... good news! I seriously had my money on your sister as the traitor, not going to lie."

Kai shot a feral glare at my bunny, and I gently placed my hand on Kai's chest to keep him from pouncing.

"Okay, too soon, Marx," I scolded. "Kai... can you get me a glass of water? I seem to be somewhat dehydrated. No clue why. But... go. Take a minute."

He scowled, his jaw clenching, but stomped back out of the dungeon a moment later. He knew just as well as I did that he was right on the edge of killing Timothy... and we agreed to let Mo have that pleasure.

Shooting Leon a warning glare, I grabbed the bucket of ice water from the side of the room and splashed some over Timothy to wake him up again.

"Let's cut to the chase, because you're probably not going to last much longer, Timmy, old friend." I slapped his badly bruised cheek, bringing him back to consciousness. "How'd you access Blanchet's servers? You had to have his passcodes."

He gave a slightly delirious laugh, which was a good thing. As he lost grip on reality, his tongue would loosen up. "Jude," he mumbled. "That was all Jude."

I hated that I believed him. "How?" I pressed. "Or does Leon need to remove another toe?" He was already down to seven. Not that he would need them where he was heading.

Timothy looked like he might clam up, so Leon picked up the bolt cutters again, whistling a happy tune under his breath.

"Honey trapping," Timothy quickly blurted, his eyes rolling back with all the pain he was already in. "She used her cunt."

I frowned my confusion at Leon, and he cocked his head to the side. "The archivist," he said thoughtfully. "How did that help her?"

"He wasn't just an archivist," Timothy mumbled. "He moonlit for Blanchet. Clement didn't have the stomach to run a Circle seat, so he passed his work off to the outer circle. Franklin had access… Jude stole it."

Jesus fucking Christ, who *was* she?

"How?" I asked again, zapping his ribs with a cattle prod just to alleviate some of the tension stoked up inside me. "How did she steal the access? I met Franklin, and he takes his jobs *very* seriously."

He jerked against the chains, screaming in pain as I zapped him again. "Scopolamine!" he cried out, panting as he dangled from his wrists. "She drugged him during sex, extracted sensitive information while edging him, not letting him come until he told her what she needed. Then he would fall asleep and have no memory of it the next morning."

A sharp memory popped into my head, Franklin mentioning his memory was failing. He thought it was old age, but it was Jude. I should have known that was what she used; it was one of the most basic, entry-level weapons in a honey trap's arsenal. Rumor was that someone on the Circle produced the entire world's supply of scopolamine, because registered Guild honey traps never had *any* supply issues.

Knowing what I now knew of those key players, I'd bet it was Zhou.

I wet my lips, mulling that information over. Clement Blanchet was supposed to be taking over his father's seat but probably didn't want to give up his cushy life of luxury. So he'd committed a *major* break in security and given his access codes to Franklin to ease the workload.

"We need the passcode," I told Timothy. "You can give it to Leon now, or I can start pushing shards of broken glass under your foreskin. Your choice, Tim. Think quick."

Unsurprisingly, he decided to cough up the codes, and Leon verified them by logging into the so-called secure server as Emmanuel Blanchet. Talk about a fuckup in the Circle's systems.

"Broken glass under his foreskin?" Leon murmured to me as we left Timothy hanging and made our way back upstairs with the laptop in hand. "Brutal. Even I shuddered at that one."

I chuckled, leaning up to kiss him. "I often find men quickest to spill info when you start threatening their dick."

Kai was in the kitchen, glaring down at a glass of water like it'd been the one to betray him. He glanced up when we came in, though, his expression questioning.

"I'm in the system," Leon informed him with a smug smile. He sat down at the island, getting to work on removing the kill order from me, first and foremost.

Kai's brows rose in surprise. "Damn, that was… quick. Nice work."

Leon scoffed. "Thank Danny. She was going to—"

"Standard interrogation techniques," I spoke over him before

Kai could take the glass of water he'd just handed me away. "Nothing fancy. Tim was just a little bitch."

An alarm sounded on the touch panel near the hall, and Kai went to check it as I sipped my water. He pressed a code, then gave me a nod. "They're here. Do we need to ask him anything else before Mo gets her claws in?"

I shrugged, but Leon shook his head. "I'm happy if he wants to die now. We got what we needed and..." He typed at top speed for a few more seconds, then looked up with a grin. "Danny DeLuna, you're now free and clear. Kill order is dissolved. The protective order is reinstated. Your Guild access has been restored in entirety."

The relief that those words brought was staggering. I sagged into a chair and scrubbed my hand over my face. "Holy shit," I whispered.

Any further celebration had to wait, though, because Kai's team had arrived home. Mo was in the lead as they entered the house, all smiles when she saw her little brother. She grabbed him in a huge hug, telling him she missed him, while the rest of the team trailed into the house after her.

They were all tired, carrying their bags over their shoulders.

"Boss," Eli greeted Kai when Moana released him. "Is everything okay?" He was more perceptive than Mo, his eyes flicking up to the fresh wound along the side of Kai's skull, then down to his arm where the bandage bulked out his sleeve.

Kai gave his friend a reassuring nod. "Nothing we couldn't handle."

Jae and Cyryl were lurking uncomfortably near the doorway, and Jae blanched when he glanced at me and Leon.

"I'm, uh, I'm gonna... go..." He jerked his thumb over his shoulder. "Just not be here."

"Smart choice," Leon commented as Jae disappeared toward the bedrooms.

Cyryl gave me a small nod of acknowledgement, then picked his bag up from where he'd dropped it. "I will also make myself scarce," he commented in a quiet voice.

I shook my head. "No, you should stay, Cyryl."

His brows shot up in surprise, and his gaze tripped between me and Kai, then back again. "Uh..."

Even Kai was confused, giving me a puzzled look.

"You should come downstairs with us," I elaborated. "You can learn something today. Mo, we picked you up a souvenir on our travels."

"Me?" she asked, her eyes darting around like she was waiting for an ambush. Interesting reaction. "What kind of souvenir?"

Kai shot me a half-smile, then started toward the stairs. "Best if we show you. Come on, it's down here."

Eli was watching all of us closely, and as I moved to follow Kai and Mo, he stopped me with a hand on my arm. "Danny, why do I get the feeling there is someone locked up in our dungeon?"

I grinned. "Because there is. Come on, I don't want to miss this."

Mo reached the dungeon before me, and I heard her confused questions to Kai when she saw our captive hanging from the ceiling, dripping blood. I could understand how she might not recognize him, as Leon and I had really gone to town getting those answers. But Kai helpfully threw more water in Timothy's face, making him wake up with a loud gasp, raising his face back up.

The shriek that escaped Moana was exactly what I'd expect when someone saw a ghost.

"You're *dead!*" she hollered. "I shot you myself, years ago!"

Timothy gave a bloody smile. "No, you killed my body double. Sucker."

I leaned against the dungeon wall, giving some space for Eli and Cyryl to see what we'd been getting up to without them. Cyryl sucked a sharp breath, looking over at me with haunted eyes. Told him he could learn a thing or two. *That* was how to interrogate a person. Not tickle their feet with a razor.

"Vicious woman," he murmured, but it was admiration, not insult, so I just smiled back.

Mo was so worked up she was shaking, and I mentally set a timer for how long Timothy had left to live. Spoiler alert, it wouldn't be long.

"Y-you *bastard*," she snarled, her balled fist cracking him across the face. "You *stole my baby!*" Another brutal punch made Timothy swing from his chains. "You *killed him, you son of a bitch!*"

This time her scream was accompanied with a solid kick between his legs. See, I wasn't the only one who hit where it hurt the most.

Timothy coughed and moaned, then cracked his eyes to glare at Mo. "He's not dead, MoMo, you know that. I told you weeks ago, when you started tipping off Danny's location."

I froze.

"*Pierdolić*," Cyryl breathed in shock. "You didn't."

Kai had frozen just as surely as I had, his wide eyes turning to his sister. "Tell me he's lying, Moana."

She seemed to snap out of her own shocked state a fraction of a second later. Snatching a small axe off our table of tools, she shrieked at Timothy that he was a liar, then swung the axe and lodged it deep in his chest.

"We will be upstairs, when you need us," Eli murmured, taking Cyryl by the arm and dragging him out of the dungeon.

Mo wasn't satisfied with just one strike, though. Over and over, she swung her axe, hacking into Timothy until nothing but a bloody carcass remained, hanging from the chains. Only then did she drop the weapon, sinking to her knees and sobbing.

Leon and I didn't move. We didn't even speak. This was for

Kai to settle… she was his sister. Even if it had been my safety she'd been bartering.

"I'm sorry, Danny," she sobbed, like an eerie echo of Jude. "I didn't have a choice."

That seemed to break Kai's tenuous hold on his temper. He grabbed his sister by the hair, pulling her up from the floor where she wept and slamming her into the wall. *"You always have a choice!"* he roared, his hand wrapping around her throat. "Give me *one reason* why I shouldn't kill you, Moana. One *fucking* reason, after you betrayed *me*. It wasn't just Danny in those ambushes, it was *all of us*."

She didn't even try to defend herself, just wept as she looked up at her brother. "The mole… *Timothy*… he told me my baby was still alive. He sent a photo. I couldn't…" Her eyes closed in utter anguish. "I'm so sorry, Kai. He made me choose."

Kai's jaw clenched so hard I could see it twitch, and I exchanged a look with Leon. Kai had killed Sam for less, but this was his *sister*.

"Kai," I said out loud, trying to diffuse his murderous rage. He didn't even hear me, though, as his hands tightened around Moana's throat. "Hey! Big Man, I'm talking to you!" I snapped, threading steel into my voice and making him jerk back an inch. His hands relaxed enough that Mo could breathe, and I tugged on Kai's arm to release her entirely.

"Siren, she nearly got you killed," he exclaimed, giving me

the most heartbreaking look. "And me. I almost died, because she betrayed us."

I nodded. "I know. And that's something she will need to come to grips with. But she is *still* your sister. You two have had each other's backs your entire lives. If you kill her now, you'll never forgive yourself. Or me."

His brow dipped, like he didn't understand the connection.

"If you kill me," Mo croaked, rubbing her throat, "you'll always resent Danny for pushing you this far."

Kai's eyes blazed in fury, and I gave Mo an irritated glare. "Mo, shut the fuck up."

"Or don't," Leon drawled. "I wouldn't mind seeing Malachi commit sororicide."

"Not helpful, Marx," I snapped. Then I turned my attention back to Kai. Bringing my good hand up, I stroked his cheek, turning his face to mine. "Hey, Big Man. You need to let this one go. I'm not going to let you kill your sister. We've got enough baggage without adding the kitchen sink."

He was hurt. Betrayed. I knew that feeling all too well.

"How can you forgive her for this?" he asked in a husky whisper. "How can she—"

"I never said that," I quickly corrected. "Mo fucked us. Hard. No one is questioning that fact. But I'm *still* not letting you kill her. So, go upstairs, talk to your team. Pour a drink. I will deal with this."

He wanted to accept. I could tell by the way he hesitated and leaned into my hand.

"Malachi, listen to the woman. Fuck off and let her handle your bitch sister." Leon shifted forward, standing clear of the door with a clear message. Leave.

Kai hesitated only another moment before releasing a long breath and nodding. He cast another agonized glance at Mo, then exited the dungeon.

None of us spoke a word after he left, his heavy footsteps echoing through the basement as he made his way back upstairs, carrying the weight of his sister's *fucked* choices with him. Only when the door at the top of the stairs closed did I turn my attention back to Mo.

"Is this when you kill me?" she asked softly, tears dripping from her jaw.

I stared back at her for a long moment. "I should. Did you know Kai had his head bashed in with a baseball bat a couple of nights ago? I assume you sent a tip about our meeting in Shadow Grove and the assassin followed us from there." She flinched but said nothing. "Did you know he got shot that night?" I added, omitting the fact that Leon shot him.

Guilt flooded Moana's eyes, and she dropped her gaze to the floor. "I'm sorry," she whispered, "but I would do it again. I believed him when he said my son was still alive. You don't understand..."

I swallowed deeply. "No. I don't. And I never will. Maybe that's why I'm not going to kill you, though."

Mo's gaze jerked back up to mine, startled and confused. "You're not?"

"Dammit," Leon whispered.

I wet my lips, then raked my fingers through my messy hair. "Not killing you is not the same as forgiving you, Mo. Kai may never forgive you, and that's something you will need to live with." I paused, thinking through what I was about to say and wondering if it was the right thing to do. Probably not, but being with Kai was making me soft. "You need to leave this team, Mo. Leave this island, and for the love of fuck, get help. You've spent a decade chasing *revenge*. Now Timothy is dead. Really, undeniably dead. It's time you moved on. Get a therapist, a fucking *good* one, and work on fixing what's broken inside. Until you do that... don't contact Kai. Am I clear?"

Mo swallowed hard and nodded. "Clear," she whispered, sounding hoarse with emotion. She started to leave the dungeon, sensing that I might change my mind any second. Then she paused and turned back to look at me with a small frown. "Look after him for me, Danny."

I said nothing back, because Kai didn't need looking after. He wasn't a little boy being beaten by his father anymore. He was strong and capable and a better person than I could ever hope to be. Maybe if Mo had seen all that sooner, she would have come to him for help instead of tossing a hand grenade into their relationship.

"I'll be watching you, Moana," Leon called after her as she left the dungeon. "Don't fuck up, or I'll be there to lop off your head."

Aw, my Bunny. He didn't just have my back, he had Kai's too. Big softy.

67
LEON

Kai could hit me for it later if he felt the need, but I wasn't letting anything deter me from questioning what was left of his team. Considering we'd just learned that three of the seven of them were dirty, rotten traitors, it would be fucking moronic to just assume the last of them were faultless.

Danny backed me on it, though she didn't explicitly *say* as much. She also didn't actively disagree, except to warn me not to leave any serious injuries. I *did* note that she didn't say *no injuries*, just no *serious* ones. I loved that we were on the same wavelength.

The Sasquatch wasn't happy about it, but his confidence in his so-called team had taken enough blows that he let me take over.

To my disappointment, the remaining three soldiers on Team Ares appeared solid. My only discovery had been that Eli was suspicious of Moana and had been watching her more closely recently. Oh, and maybe I went a little hard on Jae… but he deserved it.

"It's almost over, huh?" Danny asked quietly as the three of us—Team *Danny*—left the island. Eli, Jae, and Cyryl were left behind to clean up Timothy's remains, but we had a date with Carol Atwood to get to.

Kai shook his head, settling into his seat. Carol had sent her plane back to pick us up, which was useful, to say the least. Especially since her jet had that big old bedroom in the back. I'd need to convince Carlos to upgrade Danny's plane. Could I buy one for her myself? Absolutely. But why spend our money when I could spend someone else's? That was just good economics.

"Over?" Kai repeated. "Nah, this is just the beginning of the rest of our lives, *ātaahua*."

"Aww," I sarcastically cooed. "You're such a romantic, Sasquatch."

His eyes narrowed, and he raised his middle finger in my direction. "Suck my romantic dick, Marx."

I wrinkled my nose and made a gagging sound, about to toss another insult back, but Danny speared me with a sharp glare before I could get it out.

"Cut it out," she scolded. "The only one sucking dick around here is me. Neither one of you is bi-curious enough to follow through. Now, can I trust you two to play nicely while I call Carlos?"

"Probably not," I replied with a lazy grin.

Kai grunted his agreement. "Definitely not. But go on, anyway, Siren."

She hesitated, frowning at the both of us, and I waved her off. "Go, I have some calls I need to make of my own, now that *someone* forced me to destroy my Alaskan hideout." I shot an accusing glare at Kai, and he just smirked back at me. Dick.

For the next few hours, we all just sorted out our own shit. When I had done as much as I could, I looked up to find Kai and Danny nowhere to be seen. Fuck. That slick bastard had probably taken advantage of my distracted state and—

Oh. They were sleeping.

I'd headed down to the bedroom, expecting to catch Kai balls deep in our girl, but instead, I found them both curled up in the bed, fully clothed and dead asleep.

Quietly, I toed off my shoes and crawled in with them. There was a small gap between Danny and the side of the plane, so I wiggled my way in there, and she rolled in her sleep to give me space. Perfect.

All three of us slept almost the whole flight, which was

unusual all around. Then again, after everything we'd been through recently, it was badly needed.

Kai woke first, nudging me to let me know it was almost time to land. He went to get us drinks and snacks from the galley, and I took a few extra minutes to watch Danny sleep. She was so relaxed, I hated having to wake her up.

"We're nearly there," I murmured in her ear as she slowly roused.

She hummed a sleepy sound, then yawned and nodded. "I needed that sleep."

I met her beautiful sapphire eyes and smiled. "We all did. Now, let's prepare for whatever exciting discovery Carol made while we were getting shot at in France."

Carol didn't keep us waiting, either. She was already at the airfield when we landed, climbing out of a subtly armored SUV when we disembarked. A distinguished Asian gentleman with salt-and-pepper hair climbed out of the other side, coming around the car to stand beside Carol as we approached.

I eyed the man with suspicion, but Carol paid me little to no attention whatsoever. Her sole focus was on Danny, pulling her daughter into a hug. The relief on her face as she embraced her younger self was undeniable, and I arched a brow at Kai just to say *I told you so.*

Not that I could blame him for being suspicious. Carol was Circle, and she *had* abducted Danny once already. But... we

Guild legacies just operated differently from normal humans. We showed our love in different ways. That was something Danny had helped me to see.

Carol was whispering to Danny, who squeezed her back before releasing her.

"Who's your friend?" Danny asked, arching a brow at the well-suited man still standing beside the car. His gaze was sharp and calculating, taking in everyone's body language, closeness, and expressions… he was no mere *friend*.

Carol indicated for him to join us. "My new friend," she said with a smile, "Bingwen Zhou."

Surprise rippled through me, but really, nothing Carol did should come as a shock. She was a sly fox, that was for damn sure. She introduced me to Zhou, and he reached out to shake my hand.

Evidently, when Carol didn't like the response from Blanchet about the *massive* breach in security allowing Timothy and Jude to play Circle member, she'd reached out to Zhou. He'd been considerably more amenable to plugging the Circle's leaks and had agreed to meet with her in person.

"Three Circle seats all in one place," Danny commented as she looked between us. "When was the last time *this* happened?"

Zhou gave her a small smile. "It's been several hundred years." His accent was Australian, of all fucking things. The Guild really had spread far and wide. "But it's well overdue, in my opinion.

I'm shocked it took this long for someone to exploit the system flaws."

"I'm inclined to agree," I murmured. "Not to be rude, Zhou, but why are you here? We've dealt with the imposters who hacked Blanchet's server."

His eyes crinkled as he smiled. "Marx. I see you made a full recovery after that nasty virus business. I'm glad. After Carol and I connected, I flew out to offer another piece in your puzzle." He gestured to the SUV. "Shall we? Time is of the essence."

He popped open the back door, and my instinct was to be suspicious. But Carol gave Danny a reassuring nod that convinced *ma moitié* to get into the car. So I had no choice but to follow. Kai muttered something under his breath about spiderwebs but also followed.

The car took us toward the Hamptons, where we already knew Carol lived. But it passed the Atwood mansion and continued for several minutes until stopping in front of a modest beach house. The whole thing would probably fit inside Carol's pool, and there were no flashy cars in the driveway.

"Consider my curiosity piqued," I whispered, stepping out of the car and linking my fingers through Danny's. "Any clues?"

She shook her head. "None."

The front door burst open before we even made it halfway up the front steps, and a scruffy faced, vaguely *familiar* man stepped out looking panicked.

"What the hell are you doing here?" he exclaimed, making shooing motions and looking around us. "You can't be here! This is too dangerous; you need to go!"

"Dangerous for *who*, Marty?" Carol snapped, her voice brittle and cold. "For you? Or for *our daughter* who you deliberately hid from me for twenty-eight years?" She gestured to Danny, and my lips parted in shock.

Oh shit. This was Martin Erikkson. And…

"You live here?" I blurted out, confused as all fuck. "Here? The audacity…" I gave a disbelieving laugh, looking over at Carol as if to ask whether this was a joke.

She grimaced, shaking her head. Nope, she was just as outraged.

Danny's expression was so carefully neutral it made me worried, though. She was closing herself off, hiding what she was feeling. Meaning she didn't trust this prick, and for good fucking reason.

"I think we have a lot to discuss, don't you?" she asked coolly, staring at her biological father blankly. "You should invite us in."

Martin Erikkson scowled, his eyes darting from Danny to Carol, then to Zhou, with whom he seemed more familiar. His eyes narrowed into an accusing glare, then he spun on his heel and stalked back inside, leaving the door open for us to follow.

"Timothy, or Justin Brancott, is dead," Danny announced, barely even waiting until everyone was inside. "If that's what you were so worried about."

Erikkson visibly stiffened in shock, then slowly sank into an armchair near the balcony that faced the ocean. I couldn't help noticing that his view *also* included Carol's mansion. How long had he been living here, watching her? It was creepy.

"Are you sure?" Martin asked. "He's used body doubles before."

"We're sure," I confirmed with a nod.

Kai said nothing, just folded those tree-trunk arms of his across his chest and glared silent threats at the scruffy man. Erikkson wore pajamas, despite it being late afternoon, with a robe over top. He was every bit the recluse, and I wondered if the scarring across his throat had something to do with that.

He nodded a couple of times, then gestured for us to sit. "Tell me everything," he ordered. "Leave nothing out."

Carol gave a scoffing laugh. "You're dreaming, Marty. We have *no* reason to trust you, so we're sure as hell not here for storytime. Zhou and I linked up a few days ago, and imagine my *shock* when I found you were living within *sight* of my home. For *all this time*, you've been right here." Her lips pursed with fury, and I sensed there was a whole lot more history between the two of them than just a test tube baby.

"We came here so Danny could meet the man responsible for so many atrocities committed against her as a child. The man who robbed her of the childhood I have fought tooth and nail to provide for my other children." She was still standing, and her clenched fist was trembling with her pent-up anger. "How *could* you, Marty?"

He gazed up at her with sorrow in his eyes, then shook his head. "I didn't, Carol. I didn't know about her until she was already old enough that it didn't matter." His apologetic look shifted to Danny. "I swear, if I'd known... things would have been different."

"A rather hollow sentiment now," Danny commented, her voice lacking emotion. "We understand you named an heir for your seat to pass along to in three weeks when you're officially removed. Based on the fact that Timothy was literally trying to wipe out every single Remus baby born, I'm guessing he didn't know *who* you'd picked?"

Martin nodded, giving Carol a nervous look. "Yes, that's right. Justin—or Timothy, whatever he was calling himself—discovered he was my biological child some years ago and incorrectly thought he was my only child. He tried to kill me." He winced, indicating his throat. "But stopped when he discovered that should I *die*, my seat passed to the heir I'd already named. Not him. So he kept me alive, and... well, it sounds like you already know."

Danny gave a curt nod. "We do. And Timothy has been eliminated."

Carol cleared her throat, still scowling. "Given that *our daughter* has cleaned up *your* mess, Zhou and I feel it prudent that you abdicate your Circle seat now, rather than waiting for the time to elapse."

Zhou nodded, pulling a folded paper from his inside breast pocket. "I prepared the document for you. It just needs the name of your successor, who I assume you stored with the archivist?"

Martin scoffed. "That loose-lipped old fool? I wouldn't trust him with a house plant, let alone the fate of my family line. No, I simply filed it in my will. That way, it would be revealed in the event of my death."

No one spoke for a moment, then Kai screwed up his face. "Fucking seriously? You just... left that kind of information with your *lawyer*?"

Martin shrugged. "Why not? You didn't think to check there, did you? Well, neither did Justin. Not that it would have made much sense to him, anyway." He paused, but no one was in the mood to play games, so he sighed. "He was determined that the identity of my chosen heir could be found in Project Remus. After all, I'd unknowingly fathered dozens of children out of that program. But my will states that my heir is the one child carried to term by the natural mother."

I frowned, piecing that together. "You mean, the one child you fathered *not* within Project Remus? Following your logic, I'm assuming all of the Remus babies you fathered were carried by surrogates."

Carol had gone deathly pale. She already knew the answer,

and when I glanced over at Danny, I think I guessed it too.

"Marty, you didn't," Carol whispered.

He gave a helpless shrug. "Who else would I leave my legacy to?"

Danny gave her mother a sharp look, then gasped. "No. Absolutely not. Pick someone else, Erikkson, because I will *not* let you drag him into this shit so young."

Kai shot me a confused look, and I mouthed *Koen* back to him. Understanding dawned, and he gave a slow nod. *Yep, my thoughts too, Sasquatch. It all made so much sense now.*

Koen was Carol and Martin's love child.

Martin held Carol's furious gaze for a long, tense moment. Then he gave a slight nod. "Fine."

He held out a hand, and Zhou handed him the document that would abdicate his position on the Circle. Zhou also handed over a Mont Blanc pen, and Erikkson spent barely a minute scribbling on the document before folding it up and handing it back.

Then he gave Danny a tight nod. "Congratulations, Danny Erikkson. You just got appointed to the Circle."

68
DANNY

Meeting Martin Erikkson had been *nothing* like I had expected. To be fair, I hadn't expected anything at all because I had never even entertained the idea of meeting him in person. But when I realized that he would be appointing my sweet, mischievous *ten-year-old* brother as a ruling member of the Mercenary Guild? I was willing to do anything to stop that happening.

Which was how I ended up accepting the transfer of power from my *father*—that word was used loosely at best—to me. Holy shit. I was on the Circle.

After lengthy discussions back at Carol's house with

Bingwen Zhou—or Benny, as he said to call him—we came to an agreed course of action. Benny joining forces with us meant that we now had the majority rule over the Circle. And we unanimously agreed that things needed to change, starting with the security, and part of that meant becoming a whole lot more familiar with the other ruling seats. Personally.

Two weeks later, we had tracked down and paid visits to both Osei and Levitsky in person. We'd laid out our plans for the future of the Circle, and both had agreed. Of course, it'd taken some convincing—and thinly veiled threats—but ultimately, both seats had accepted our progressive new future for the Circle *and* the Guild as a whole.

We had saved Blanchet until last. Benny had to fly home to Sydney because his daughter was in labor, but between Carol, Leon, and me, we could handle Emmanuel Blanchet. Kai was with us the whole time, too, playing the strong, silent, intimidating role flawlessly. Osei had recognized him as Ares—having purchased from him in the past—and it definitely smoothed *that* negotiation.

Emmanuel Blanchet had been dodging our attempts to meet, though, so it was a significantly more hostile mood as we arrived uninvited and unannounced on his doorstep that day.

His security team tried to tell us that we had the wrong house until Leon pulled a gun on one of the maids and threatened to shoot her if they didn't let us in. That didn't convince them, so Leon released the maid and shot the dickhead security agent who'd casually told him to shoot.

The maid in question had been all too happy to show us the way to Blanchet himself—stepping over the dead security guard like she was worried he would jerk back to life as a zombie.

"What in the *hell* is going on?" an old man bellowed as the girl directed us along the oil-painting-lined hallway, which ended in an opulent drawing room.

The five of us—Carol had brought a severely professional man named Grendel with her—strode into the room like we were enacting a coup. It didn't need to be like that, but we weren't leaving without Blanchet's agreement to the changes we were making. The number of visible weapons on both Grendel and Kai served as a visual threat of how serious we were.

"Carol," the old man in a wheelchair sneered, locking his beady eyes on my mother. "I told you not to come back here again. We are a *secret* organization, and that means—"

"Absolutely nothing," Carol snapped, cutting him off. "It's time for a change, Emmanuel. Since your son is training to succeed you, I suggest you call him in for this meeting."

Evidently, Carol hadn't been exaggerating when she called the elder Blanchet a crotchety old bastard. He spat derogatory insults about women being the weaker sex and how it was an insult to have Carol on the Circle. Well, tough shit, because now I was too.

The old fart lifted a gun from under his lap blanket, aiming to shoot Carol. His hand trembled so badly, though, the shot went wide and the recoil made him drop the gun entirely. My mother didn't even flinch, the fucking badass. She just arched a brow, giving Emmanuel a pitying look.

Leon turned to the maid he hadn't shot and bestowed a charming smile on her. "Sweetheart, is the younger Blanchet here in the house?" She bobbed her head yes, her eyes huge as she gazed up at my sexy Bunny. "Be a dear and go get him for us? We need to have a serious talk."

She scurried away to do Leon's bidding, and Grendel professionally patted old man Blanchet down to ensure he wasn't hiding any other weapons in his wheelchair. The old bastard cursed us out the whole time, but no one paid him any attention, considering nothing he said was of any value.

After all, we still had the access codes to his Circle server. He had no bargaining chips here, and if the four of us—Leon, Carol, Benny, and myself—were slightly more corrupt, we'd simply keep it. But as it was, neither Leon nor I particularly *wanted* our own positions, let alone someone else's. So here we were, trying to talk sense into an idiot.

A minute later, the maid came speed walking back into the room with huge eyes and a red-faced, balding man following her, looking irritated as all hell. A beautiful, sad woman accompanied him, but it looked like she was so mentally checked out that she didn't even know where she was.

"What's going on in here?" younger Blanchet asked, his nervous glance taking in our group and then resting on his elderly father. "Who are these people, father? Why have you allowed them access while armed?"

"You remember me, Clement," Carol observed in a terse tone. She was a natural leader, and I was more than happy to let her run point. "I visited with your father recently to discuss the monumental fuckup in security within the Circle. Tell me, have you managed to regain control of the Blanchet seat yet?"

Clement turned a darker shade of red, but we already knew that he had not.

"No, of course you haven't," Carol continued, barely giving him a chance to make excuses. "Because we have it. I bet you're just dying to know how we got it, aren't you?" She arched a brow at Emmanuel, who shot a scathing glare at his son. "Oh, I see you've already worked it out. Good. Then we can keep this quick and to the point. Things need to change within the Circle, Emmanuel. Starting with our security and the gaping hole created by our anonymity pacts."

Emmanuel Blanchet did not agree and had some strongly-worded statements about how vehemently he disagreed. Shocking.

Carol pursed her lips, not reacting to the vile misogyny spewing out of the old fuck's mouth. Instead, she shifted her attention to Clement. "Do you share your father's opinion?"

Before younger Blanchet could respond, two gunshots ripped through the drawing room. One in Clement's head, the other in Emmanuel's.

I automatically turned an accusing scowl at Leon, but he

showed me his empty hands defensively. Kai shrugged, too, then I realized who the shooter had been.

"Well," Carol murmured, wiping blood splatter from her face. "That was unexpected. Eleanor, is it?"

The dead-eyed woman who'd accompanied Clement into the drawing room no longer looked so dead. A fire burned in her eyes, and she lifted her chin to meet Carol's gaze unflinchingly.

"It is. I understand that I'm not a Blanchet blood, but my daughter is. I would like to proxy her position until she is old enough to take over." She curled a lip at her dead husband and father-in-law. "It's about damn time someone made changes in the Guild, and you have my confidence, Carol."

Carol exchanged a glance with me, and I inclined my head in agreement.

"It's been done before but needs a majority vote from the rest of the Circle." Carol pulled her phone from her pocket and placed a call. It was answered after a couple of rings, and in the background, a baby squalled. "Congratulations, Benny. We have a quick item for you to vote on..."

She made quick business of explaining Eleanor's surprising plot twist to our plan, and Benny roared with laughter. Then gave his vote in Eleanor's favor.

Leon gave his, too, and Carol reached out to shake Eleanor's hand. "Welcome to the Circle."

The thin woman sagged in relief, dropping her gun to the

sofa as she released all the bravado she'd been channeling. "Thank you," she whispered. "Is she okay? I know you have been keeping an eye on her for your own reasons."

Carol gathered the other woman into a warm hug, rubbing her back in a comforting way. "She's perfectly safe and just a delightful child. Let's pour some wine and make arrangements for you to see her again." She led Eleanor away from the bloody mess in the drawing room, giving Grendel instructions for a cleanup.

Kai wrapped an arm around my waist, kissing my hair with a sigh. "What did I miss there?"

I smiled up at him. "Eleanor's daughter thinks her parents are dead. And she's Koen's best friend, so… when Carol says *delightful*, she definitely means she's trouble."

"Huh," Kai murmured, nodding.

Leon rolled his eyes. "That's it? No deep and insightful proverbs for this unexpected situation? I feel let down, Malachi."

"Here's some insight for you," Kai said, extending his middle finger at Leon. But then he leaned down to brush his lips over my ear. "*Ka pū te ruha, ka hao te rangatahi.*" His deep voice gave me shivers, and I melted into his muscular frame. "*As an old net withers, another is remade.* When an elder is no longer fit to lead, a healthier one will take his place. Seems pretty apt in this situation, don't you think?"

"Incredibly so," I agreed, walking with my guys through to the kitchen where Carol and Eleanor were already opening a thousand-dollar bottle of wine from the Blanchet cellar. Why not? It was a celebration, after all. New beginnings.

Leon offered to make the calls to Levitsky and Osei to inform them of the change to Blanchet's seat, waving to Carol to relax and enjoy her wine.

Crime scene cleaners—the Guild type—came and went, erasing any trace of the double murder in the drawing room, but we barely paid them any attention. Carol and Eleanor bonded over wine and cheeses, talking about Estelle and Koen and laughing over some of their more precocious moments.

Kai and Grendel got into Emmanuel's forty-year-old Port Ellen scotch, chatting about weapons and military moments. While they talked, Kai pulled my feet into his lap and started rubbing them with his strong thumbs, turning me into a puddle.

Leon was content to sip his sparkling water but remained busy with calls and emails for the rest of the afternoon.

Me, though? I was entirely content to just listen. Just… press pause and breathe. No one was chasing me. No one was hunting me and trying to deliver my head for a reward. But more than that, I was no longer beholden to the Guild. The invisible collar around my neck since birth had been released.

Somewhere into my fourth glass of wine, I wandered out to the patio and sat down on the little stone wall, looking out over the vineyards. My phone was in my hand, but the person I wanted to call was no longer reachable.

"Hey," Carol said softly, brushing a hand over my back. "Can

I join you?"

I nodded, and she sat down on the wall beside me. For a few minutes, neither of us spoke. Then she gave a small nod in the direction of my phone.

"Who are you thinking about?" she asked, reading my mood accurately. "Jude?"

I swallowed hard. "Yeah. She was the first one that I thought of just now. The first person I wanted to talk to and share all this exciting news with." I sniffed, holding back the tears that came all too damn easily these days. "It's not painful enough that she's gone, and I can *never* share those things with her again... but I have to keep remembering that she wasn't who I thought she was. I have to constantly remind myself that she tried to kill me, repeatedly. She tried to kill Leon and nearly succeeded. So it's a double kick to the gut. She's gone... *and* she was a traitor. I can't even cherish my memories of her."

Carol didn't try to talk over me, nor did she offer empty platitudes. She just listened. Then she sighed and draped her arm around me in a hug.

"I'm so sorry, Danny," she whispered, kissing my hair. "I wish I knew how I could make it better for you."

My eyes spilled over, and I leaned into her embrace to hug her back. Maybe I was wrong when I first met her. Maybe I wasn't too old to need my mom.

69
DANNY

The next few months flew past in a blur. We had our work cut out for us in restructuring the Circle, then making changes throughout the entire Mercenary Guild. Not the least of which was surrounding how in the *fuck* we were going to deal with all the remaining escapees from the Castle. The general consensus was to kill them, not attempt another moronic *capture*. But so far, most of them were in the wind.

I didn't blame them, either. If I were in their shoes, I'd have already scrubbed my identity, gotten plastic surgery, and moved to Siberia. Only arrogant shits with an axe to grind, like The Sandman, would stick around to be found.

After lengthy discussions, Kai had ultimately decided *not* to dissolve his business as Ares. The simple fact of the matter was, if he no longer dealt weapons, someone else would. Someone with less of a moral compass.

So it was a strange, stressful few months while we all adjusted to our new positions, with new dynamics and all new responsibilities. I had to fully immerse myself in learning *how* to hold a Circle seat. There was so much more involved than just voting on decisions. The Circle were literally running a multi-billion-dollar, worldwide empire. There were tens of thousands of "employees" involved, and when I'd accepted the Erikkson seat, I'd vowed to be active.

To my relief, I wasn't the only one riding the steepest learning curve in the world. Eleanor was right there with me, though she had a significant head start having silently absorbed all the Blanchet information across the years.

Despite the workload, there were so many incredible moments over those months that I could never forget. Like when Benny invited us to visit his home in Vaucluse, a suburb of Sydney, and introduced us to his first grandbaby. Then showed us his jaw-dropping poison collection.

Or one of my favorites was when Eleanor and Estelle were reunited. The little spitfire slapped her mom across the face and swore at her for pretending to be dead all these years. Then hugged her so tight I worried she would suffocate.

Now, though, I was trying to get through the last of my files—I was trying to select my own outer Circle to ease my workload—before taking a weekend vacation with my guys. It was already after dark, and I yawned heavily as I tossed another file into my shredder.

Without even a whisper of warning, a huge gloved hand clamped over my mouth from behind and an arm banded around my belly, lifting me from the floor. I sucked a sharp inhale, thrashing to free myself, kicking out at my attacker. Somehow, though, a blindfold got secured over my eyes in a matter of seconds, making it ten times harder to fight back.

My outraged curses muffled against the tight hand over my mouth, but my feet found the edge of the desk, giving me enough purchase to shove my entire weight backwards. The man holding me was knocked off-balance, tumbling to the floor with me still tightly confined in his grip... but there was more than one. Someone risked getting kicked and snared my ankles. Within seconds, the secure bonds of rope bit into my ankles, my calves, and all the way up to my knees.

They didn't speak, not even a word, just manhandled me like a netted shark as they bound my wrists and arms in a similar fashion and gagged me. Fuck. Not that I was a screamer even with the best assailants, but I did enjoy the ability to get under their skin with pointed insults.

Still thrashing, I was carried out of the office I'd been using for the last few months and dropped into the trunk of a car. Not for the first time, I thanked my genetics—and Carol—for my small stature. It made these occasional trips in a trunk *so* much more comfortable than most guys must have it.

The lid slammed shut, then the car rocked as people got inside. The engine purred as it started, and I cataloged all the details I could put my finger on. Then I started testing my bonds. Nine times out of ten, kidnappers didn't do their due diligence. They didn't prepare thoroughly for a job, and although they took me by surprise, it was highly unlikely they'd restrained me in a way I *couldn't* escape.

So, imagine my shock when I realized the ropes weren't going to budge. I'd been thrashing so hard in my office that I hadn't even noticed that the ropes not only bound my ankles and wrists but they crisscrossed my torso, too. Making it utterly impossible to free myself.

Motherfuckers had tied me up with shibari.

I mean… smart. I'd give them that. But it kind of left me up shit creek without a paddle when it came to saving myself. Was I seriously going to need *rescuing*? After all I'd been through… had I finally ended up in a bind that I genuinely needed to be saved from?

Fuck. Surely not.

But as I lay there in the moving vehicle, totally unable to move, see, or speak... I had to admit my own failings. I was not superhuman, and this time? I was out of ideas.

The car drove for about a half-hour, then I was retrieved from the trunk and slung over someone's shoulder to be carried into a waiting helicopter. Fuck, this was bad. How would the guys track me?

I would need my strength when we landed. When my abductors eventually slipped up and gave me an opening. So for the hour-long helicopter flight—where I was strapped in securely the whole time—I rested and conserved energy.

On landing, I was hauled out once more and carried from the aircraft and into a building. A house? It sounded like hardwood floors under my captor's boots, and he ascended a flight of stairs before hitting carpet. Someone else was following... or ahead... it was hard to tell based on sound alone, and a door handle gave a small squeak as it was turned.

The one carrying me shifted his grip to lower me to the floor, and I braced myself to fight... but they were too quick. Before my toes even touched the soft floor covering, my wrists had been clipped to a suspended hook and raised above my head. Crap.

Not a *single* word had been uttered since they surprised me in my office, and that in itself told me these were professionals. I was dealing with people who knew *exactly* what I was capable of and had planned accordingly.

For a moment, nothing happened. No one spoke, no one moved. I wasn't stupid enough to think I was alone, though. No one had left the room.

Then the unmistakable touch of a knife blade against my stomach made me stiffen.

Oh, I see how it is.

In swift, confident slices, my clothing was removed without ever loosening the ropes... leaving me naked and bound, blindfolded, and gagged. But the one cutting my clothing had made a mistake, and now I was no longer so concerned.

When their gloves were removed, and a pair of warm hands cupped my breasts, I didn't flinch. I moaned and leaned into that touch. My gag was removed a moment later, and a pair of familiar lips found mine for a long, drugging kiss that left me breathless.

"Naughty Bunny," I breathed as those lips feathered across my throat. "I should have known you two were up to no good." I tilted my head back, my lips parted in request for another kiss.

Kai obliged, kissing me deeply as his fingers dipped between my legs. I moaned against his lips as he pushed two fingers into me, and Leon's teeth teased my hard nipple.

"Where are we?" I asked on a breathless whisper, rocking against Kai's hand and loving the whole scenario they'd set up for me.

One of them tugged my blindfold free, and I blinked at the influx of light. The bedroom we were in had been filled with dozens of candles, casting an obscenely romantic glow across the rose-petal-strewn bed. They'd hooked me up to rigging in front of a floor-to-ceiling glass panel, though, overlooking a luxurious outdoor pool and exquisite gardens, the trees sparkling with fairy lights.

"Welcome home, *ātaahua*," Kai murmured, his thumb finding my clit and teasing me into a mini orgasm.

I moaned, rocking on his hand but otherwise helpless. "Home?"

Leon sank to his knees in front of me, kissing my belly before looking up with a sly smile. "*Our* home," he elaborated. "Just the four of us."

Kai's fingers plunged deeper, and Leon parted my thighs just enough that his tongue could reach my clit, making me tremble all over.

"W-wait," I gasped, despite how fucking incredible it felt to have Kai's fingers *in* me and Leon's tongue *on* me. "Four of us?"

Both of them gave low chuckles, but neither one answered. They just went to work, bringing me to a full orgasm with some seriously excellent teamwork.

Then, without releasing my ropes, they took turns fucking

my pussy. Kai from behind, and Leon from in front. It was pure torture, and eventually, I begged them to quit taking turns because I needed them both... and they obliged.

Sometime later, after they released me from the rigging and helped me clean up, I extracted more information from them. We were in Echo Creek. The two of them had worked together, first *buying* the entire town and then overseeing crews who worked literally day and night for months to construct the perfect home for us. It even had an indoor-outdoor hot tub, just like the one in Leon's Alaska house.

Then I remembered my question that had been ignored.

"You said *four* of us," I reminded Leon as he dried me from the incredible three-person kind of shower. "Who is the fourth person calling this amazing house *home*?"

Leon shot a sly look at Kai, who was pulling on a pair of boxers. "Shall we show her?"

"Yes!" I replied instead. "Fucking show me!"

Rather than getting dressed, I accepted the black silk robe that Leon offered, then followed Kai out of what must be *our* master bedroom. He led the way back down the main staircase, and I tried to look everywhere at once. There would be time for a tour later, though. Right now, I wanted answers.

Kai paused in front of some moss green double doors and arched a smile at me over his shoulder. Then he pushed the doors open, and I gasped. My hands clapped to my mouth, and my knees turned to jelly.

I crashed to the carpet right there in the doorway, sobbing like a little bitch at the sight of my baby. My sweet, innocent baby… looking healed and better than ever.

"Stanley," I croaked through my happy tears. "Is that you?"

He didn't answer. Shocker. But *holy shit, he's here!*

It really was *our* home now. My heart was complete.

EPILOGUE

DANNY

two years later...

The flight was a long one, but I'd gotten plenty of work done and slept well on the way. I'd then needed to take a helicopter transfer to reach my destination, because my jet was too large to land on the local runway. I smiled as I climbed out of the helicopter, seeing a familiar face waiting for me beside a car.

I waited a moment as the pilot retrieved my bag and handed it over, then strolled over to my welcoming party of one.

"Tena koe e te tuahine," I greeted her with a wide grin.

Moana scoffed and rolled her eyes. "Don't be a fucking

show off, Danny. Your pronunciation sucks." She said it with affection though, pulling me into a huge hug. "Thank you for coming."

"Thank you for asking," I replied with sincerity.

She released me, giving me a sad smile with tears in her eyes. "How is he?"

I shook my head. "You know not to ask me about Kai. Not until—"

"I know," she said quickly. "I know, and I respect the rules. I just miss him."

I squeezed her arm, feeling sad for her. Despite the progress Moana had made in therapy, Kai was nowhere near ready to see her again. Even mentioning her name sent him into a dark mood, and I couldn't blame him for that. He would forgive her one day, I had no doubt. But that day wasn't any time soon.

She took my bag and tossed it in the back of her car, and we both climbed in. She'd been pumping the heat, which was a damn good thing because *fuck*, who knew New Zealand in July was so damn cold? I mean, aside from the whole of the Southern Hemisphere. Apparently, I needed to travel more often, as I was starting to forget how diverse the world was.

"So," she said, giving me a pointed look as she drove. "How are *you*? Really."

I knew what she meant. We'd reconnected about six months ago after Carlos confessed he and Moana had been casually hooking up. This was the first time we'd met up in person, though, and just a month ago, I'd had some bad news.

I wet my lips, looking out the window. "I'm okay," I replied truthfully. "I know when we spoke the other week, things were… different. But we've all done a whole lot of *communicating* in the last month, and I think we're more in agreement now than we ever were on this topic."

Mo gave me a shocked look. "Communicate? My little brother? And *Leon*? Surely not."

I laughed. "You'd be surprised."

A year ago, we had started talking about the possibility of children for our triad. The Remus labs had genetic material stored for both me and Leon, and there was nothing wrong with Kai's swimmers. We were all over thirty, our lives were stable—if dangerous—and it had seemed like the next logical step for our future. With all the technology and a *willing* surrogate, we had gone ahead on trying to make a baby.

A month ago, we learned that none of the embryos were viable. Whatever experimentation Project Remus had evolved into before Leon started killing off the doctors involved, it'd drastically altered the structure of all samples stored in that lab.

"We ordered all the remaining samples to be destroyed," I told Mo, giving her a sad smile. "Whatever they did there… it needs to be wiped clean."

She gave me a troubled, pitying frown. "That doesn't need to be the end of it, though. You could—"

"We *could* do a number of other things," I agreed, my voice kind but firm. "But we won't. Because what this whole process has taught us is that *none* of us really wanted to be parents. Not even big Daddy Kai. We had this *awful* realization when we got the news that the embryos weren't viable... because stronger than the sadness, was overwhelming relief."

Mo shook her head. "I don't understand."

That didn't surprise me. Our feelings and priorities on these topics were drastically different, and that was perfectly okay. But she was my sister-in-law, and I wanted to help her understand.

"We all came to realize, since this loss, that we thought we *had* to have children. Like that was the requirement for us to have a happy ending, you know? Sounds so stupid when I say it aloud. Two ruling members of the Mercenary Guild, and one of the world's most powerful arms dealers... and we all subconsciously caved to an outdated expectation from society." I heaved a heavy breath, raking my fingers through my hair. "It's not what everyone would choose, it's not what *you* would choose, but... it feels right for us."

Mo said nothing for a while, then she reached out and squeezed my hand. "Well, then I'm happy for you. And I'm glad you and the guys are on the same page."

I gave a low laugh, thinking of Kai's face when I finally found the courage to tell him I really, honestly didn't want kids. I didn't want to try again with the surrogate. I'd been so sure he would hate me for it… but he'd just relaxed like I'd lifted the weight of the world off his shoulders. Then Leon had come home and found us fucking like rabbits and confessed that he was also relieved not to have another life to care for.

It was some truly sensational sex that night, and the night after, and… well, so on and so forth.

Besides those facts, I wasn't exactly lacking for children in my life now. There was Koen, of course, who had decided I was his favorite person on the whole planet after discovering we were, in fact, full brother and sister. Carol had reluctantly admitted that all three of her children, between Koen and me, were adopted. Including Bram, who was named as her heir.

Carol simply said that her late husband hadn't been fertile, so they went to great lengths to pretend her children were biological when they weren't. To her, it made no difference, which was why Bram was still her heir.

Aside from that, I'd agreed to take on a training role within one of the Guild central boot camps. After we disposed of the abusive and corrupt trainers, they were sorely lacking in staff. So… Professor Danny had stepped in. But not without dragging Leon and Kai into it with me. Part-time, of course.

"So, are you nervous?" I asked Mo, changing the subject.

She nodded, her hands tight on the steering wheel. "Yeah. Big time."

"I don't blame you," I admitted, biting back a grin. "I'd be shitting myself in your shoes right now."

Mo snapped a glare at me, and I chuckled a teasing laugh.

"Thanks, asshole," she muttered. "We're here."

Nerves were starting to get the best of her, so I didn't hesitate before getting out of my seat and marching for the front door. It left her no option but to follow, racing after me as I rapped my knuckles on the door. It was a nice house, big and old, and I bet there were fantastic views from the other side.

The woman who answered the door was somewhere in her early forties, with ink-black hair and big green eyes. Fine stress lines around her eyes said she was just as nervous as Mo.

"Hi," she said softly, opening the door wider. "You're early."

"My fault," I replied with a smile. "I'm Danny, you must be Louise?"

She jerked a nod. "Yes. Yes, I am. Sorry, where are my manners? I'm Louise." She extended a hand for me to shake, then switched her wide eyes to Moana beside me. "Christ, you look so much like him. I didn't realize how hard this would be." Tears pooled in her eyes, and I nudged Mo to hug the poor woman.

Louise pulled herself together, though, inviting us into her beautiful home and leading the way through to the living room. "Sorry, the boys aren't back yet, but um… could I get you a tea or coffee?"

Vodka sounded more appropriate, but I probably shouldn't

suggest it.

Mo glanced around, taking in the vast display of family photos on the wall, and—I assume—feeling how *warm* the whole house seemed. It was a family home. "Could I, sorry… do you think I could see his room?"

Louise stiffened slightly, then gave a jerking nod. "Yes, of course. This way."

She took us up the impressive staircase and opened one of the bedroom doors, standing aside to let us enter. Inside, Mo froze like she'd been struck by lightning. The bedroom contained so much personality. From the posters of famous soccer players on the walls to trophies lined up along the bookshelf. On the wall, amongst photos of friends, was a framed family photo.

Mo crossed the carpet to take a closer look, and a tear rolled down her cheek as she stared at the *happy family* in the picture.

"Moana," Louise whispered, "I'm so sorry…"

Mo shook her head, swiping away the tear on her cheek. "You did nothing to apologize for. Thank you for letting me see this." She indicated the bedroom. To her son's bedroom. The child she never knew was now almost a teenager.

Louise gave a nod. "Of course. Come downstairs. Maybe wine would be better than tea?"

"Shit yeah," I muttered, and Mo jabbed me in the ribs. I was there for moral support, because Mo knew she couldn't do this alone. But he was also my nephew… weird as that was. I was excited to meet him.

With a glass of wine in hand, Louise relaxed somewhat. She showed us around the whole house, including the half basketball court that her husband had apparently built last summer to nurture their son's interest in sports. By the time the front door opened again, things were less tense.

At least until a twelve-year-old version of Kai walked in wearing his soccer uniform.

I knew Louise said he looked like Mo, but I hadn't realized how much he looked like *Kai* too. I hadn't looked all that carefully at the family photos, so I was surprised, to say the least. I choked on my wine, and Mo elbowed me.

"Will, honey," Louise said, "this is—"

"My birth mother, Moana, right?" The kid gave Mo a long look, his dark brown eyes studying her. Then he dropped his school bag and crossed the space to hug her.

Mo froze in shock, then awkwardly patted the kid on the back.

He released her with a huge smile. "Mum told me you were coming. She explained everything already. I need to go shower. We just had soccer practice, but are you going to stay for dinner?"

"Um..." Mo seemed lost for words.

"We sure are," I answered for her, and the boy raised an eyebrow at me.

He went back to grab his school bag from where he dropped

it, then gave me another long look. "Who are *you*? Mum didn't mention Moana having a girlfriend."

Mo snorted a laugh, and I bit my own cheek to keep from grinning. "I'm your aunt, Will. And possibly the coolest aunt on this planet, so *you're welcome*."

Sassy kid just pursed his lips as he shouldered his bag. "I'll be the judge of that."

While Will showered, Louise introduced us to her husband, Kevin. Then the five of us had a surprisingly comfortable dinner together. Louise and Kevin told us all about the school that Will attended, and Will boasted to Moana about his sporting achievements. It was... nice.

At the end of the meal, though, Mo thanked Louise and Kevin but made an excuse for us to leave. Will's smile slipped, but when Mo assured him she could come back the following day to spend more time with him, he hugged her so tight it made me all warm and fuzzy inside.

Louise walked out to the car with us, wringing her hands nervously with a question she was too scared to ask.

Mo must have known, though, because she folded Louise into a hug. "Thank you," she told the other woman with sincerity. "Thank you for loving him. I hope you'll let me stay in touch."

Louise seemed utterly shellshocked. "Y-you're not going to take him away from us?"

"Take him away from his home? From a clearly loving family

and the only parents he's ever known? No way. You're his mother now, Louise. I just wish…" Mo's glassy eyes shifted to the house, where Will was waving from an upstairs window. "It doesn't matter now. The past is the past. I'm just so thankful that he found such amazing parents."

Louise was openly crying now. She'd told us earlier how they had been open with Will his whole life about his adoption. They just never understood the circumstances or that he'd literally been stolen. I didn't blame her for thinking Mo would take him away, but… that wasn't her.

Moana decided she was going to stay in town for a while, to gently get to know her son without threatening Louise and Kevin's parenting. But I had shit to do, so I had her drop me back to my helicopter first thing in the morning. I checked my phone again, like I did every morning, hoping to see a message from Sabine. There never was one, though, and I respected her decision too much to go searching for her.

My jet was fueled up and waiting for me on the tarmac at a private airstrip in Auckland, and I grinned as I stepped through the door to the main cabin.

"Welcome aboard Aroha Airways, ma'am. We will be your flight attendants for your journey across the Pacific Ocean. No request is too small; we are *very* attentive flight attendants." Kai grinned, slouching back in his seat and fixing his rolled shirtsleeves.

Leon reached over and whacked him in the head. "Fuck, you're cheesy. You ever get sick of being so lame?"

Kai and I exchanged a secretive grin, and I laughed. "You just have to *cheese the day,* Leon!"

He groaned and grabbed me around the waist, pulling me into his lap. "I missed you, *mon amour.* Killing people isn't as fun without you."

I moaned into his kisses, letting him maul me thoroughly as the pilot closed up our aircraft and started to taxi. "I missed you too, Bunny." Then I clambered into Kai's lap and kissed him just as deeply. "And you too, Big Man. Take me home."

His grin was pure wickedness. "Oh, *taku aroha,* we'll take you alright."

"Repeatedly," Leon agreed, dragging his thumb over his lower lip seductively. "What's the record, brother?"

"Eight," Kai responded, then claimed my lips again in the most sinful kiss.

I wasn't sleeping again until we got home to Echo Creek, that was almost guaranteed. And I couldn't be happier... *ever after*.

The End.

Want to know what's next from Tate?

FORGERY

Valenshek Legacy #1

Every four years, the criminal underworld engages in a game. *The* Game. The challenges range from the impossible to the deadly to the truly insane. Things that only a crazy person would tackle.

I've won the game 5 times. This time will be no different.

I'm at the top of my field now, the best of the world's thieves. There's nothing I can't steal, and this time, the game is *all* about theft, subterfuge, and sleight of hand. Starting with a legendary painting of poppy flowers.

It's a painting that disappeared into the black market decades ago, but I know where to find it. The only person standing in my way is *her*.

Nothing will stop me winning the game, not even the sultry, quick-witted brunette who lures me into her painting studio with the most irresistible bait.

I have no option to fail at The Game. It's my legacy.

The Valenshek Legacy.

Forgery is book ONE of THREE in the Valenshek Legacy series. This is a contemporary MF romance, set within the Shadow Grove world. Content is suitable for a mature audience.

POISON ROSES
BOYS OF BELLEROSE #1
JAYMIN EVE & TATE JAMES
WSJ AND USAT BESTSELLING AUTHOR
USAT AND INTERNATIONAL BESTSELLING AUTHOR

POISON ROSES
Boys Of Bellerose #1

You know that saying, things can't possibly get worse? They always can.

I thought I'd hit rock bottom when I turned sixteen. The day I broke my first love's heart, ending things before I could ruin his career as a rock star.

But damn, was I wrong.

Things got progressively worse from that moment on, until now. Eight years later, when I find myself homeless, jobless, covered in blood, and running from a ghost of my past.

Angelo Ricci--the second boy I ever loved--knows I saw him shoot a man. He's coming for me, has men out all over the city looking for me, and if they find me I'm as good as dead.

But I'm not giving up so easily. I'll do whatever it takes to escape the Ricci family's wrath, even if it means seeking sanctuary with the most unlikely, and unwilling of allies.

Bellerose is the hottest rock band in the world right now--in popularity and looks--and it's just my luck that I stumble into their laps while running for my life. It's not the best plan to hide out on their tour, but it's the best I've got.

Except, the only person that Bellerose's frontman hates more than Angelo Ricci... might be me. Too damn bad. Jace owes me. After all, I'm Billie Bellerose.

Poison Roses is book ONE of FOUR in the Boys Of Bellerose series. This is a mafia/rockstar reverse harem romance series with dark elements and gripping cliffhangers throughout. Content is intended for a mature audience.

ALSO BY TATE JAMES

Madison Kate

(Dark Contemporary Romance)

#1 HATE

#2 LIAR

#3 FAKE

#4 KATE

#4.5 VAULT (to be read after Hades Series)

Hades

(Dark Contemporary Romance)

#1 7th Circle

#2 Anarchy

#3 Club 22

#4 Timber

The Guild

(Dark Contemporary Romance)

#1 Honey Trap

#2 Dead Drop

#3 Kill Order

The Royal Trials

(Fantasy)

#1 Imposter

#2 Seeker

#3 Heir

Kit Davenport

(Paranormal Romance)

#1 The Vixen's Lead

#2 The Dragon's Wing

#3 The Tiger's Ambush

#4 The Viper's Nest

#5 The Crow's Murder

#6 The Alpha's Pack

Novella: The Hellhound's Legion

Box Set: Kit Davenport: The Complete Series

Dark Legacy

(Dark Contemporary Romance)

#1 Broken Wings

#2 Broken Trust

#3 Broken Legacy

#4 Dylan (standalone)

Royals of Arbon Academy

(Dark contemporary/dystopian college romance)

#1 Princess Ballot

#2 Playboy Princes

#3 Poison Throne

Hijinx Harem

(RomCom Paranormal)

#1 Elements of Mischief

#2 Elements of Ruin

#3 Elements of Desire

The Wild Hunt Motorcycle Club

(Dark PNR/Fantasy)

#1 Dark Glitter

#2 Cruel Glamour (TBC)

#3 Torn Gossamer (TBC)

Foxfire Burning

(UF/PNR)

#1 The Nine

#2 The Tail Game (TBC)

#3 TBC (TBC)

Undercover Sinners

(Dark Contemporary Suspense Romance)

#1 Altered By Fire

#2 Altered by Lead

#3 Altered by Pain (TBC)

WANT TO KEEP UP WITH ALL THINGS TATE, AND CHAT WITH LIKE-MINDED READERS?
BE SURE TO JOIN THE FOX HOLE ON FACEBOOK!

WWW.FACEBOOK.COM/GROUPS/TATEJAMES.THEFOXHOLE